# Raising Aphrodite

A Novel

by

**Kirk Curnutt**

*River City Publishing*
*Montgomery, Alabama*

Published in the United States by River City Publishing
1719 Mulberry Street
Montgomery, AL 36106

First Edition–2015
Printed in the United States
1 3 5 7 9 10 8 6 4 2
ISBN 13: 978-1-57966-104-5


Library of Congress Cataloging-in-Publication Data


Curnutt, Kirk, 1964-
Raising Aphrodite : a novel / Kirk Curnutt. – First edition.
pages cm.
ISBN 1-57966-104-1
I. Title.
PS3603.U76R35 2015
813'.6–dc23
2014048308 <tel:2014048308>

River City publishes fiction, nonfiction, poetry, art, and children's
books by distinguished authors and artists in our region and
nationwide. Visit our web site at www.rivercitypublishing.com


Edited by Fran M. Norris
Layout by Rachel Prosser Graphics
Cover image: William-Adolphe Bouguereau, *The Birth of Venus* (1879)
with additional design by Jack Durham.

"...And with her went Eros, and comely Desire followed her at her birth at the first and as she went into the assembly of the gods. This honor she has from the beginning, and this is the portion allotted to her amongst men and undying gods–the whisperings of maidens and smiles and deceits with sweet delight and love and graciousness."

–Hesiod, describing the birth of Aphrodite
in *Theogony* (c. 850-725 BC)

# I

## Daughter
## Rock 'n' Roller

# 1

My daughter, Chloe, celebrated her sixteenth birthday by having sex with her boyfriend.

I find this out the morning after when I discover a suspicious wrapper in her trash basket. At first I tell myself it's just packaging from an Alka Seltzer tablet, or a Peppermint Pattie or Klondike bar, maybe. But the reality is impossible to deny. As a single man who tries to make his way responsibly in this world, I have a forced familiarity with oily squares of foil like this, right down to the teeth marks in the upper corner and the squiggly tear across the top. Plus, if there's any doubt, both sides of the plastic feature a picture of Madonna in her bustier-and-Boy-Toy-belt days.

The wrapper reads, I SAID *LIKE* A VIRGIN.

This rude awakening is an accident. I'm not the type to ransack my child's bedroom searching for evidence of indiscretion. I'd like to say that's because I believe in trust and that I want Chloe to grow up knowing I consider her a responsible young adult, but the truth is more complicated and a lot less flattering. For close to a year now I've given Chloe as much privacy as conscience permits for the simple reason that nothing terrifies me more than the thought that she's becoming a woman. I'm a single parent, you see, and I've prided myself–too much, as it turns out–on being a secret sharer with the opposite sex. I've always felt more at home around women than men, and despite a failed marriage in my early twenties, I told myself I'd done a decent job of avoiding the gene for jackassery that my friends said was inborn in my breed.

I congratulated myself all the way up until last fall when I fumbled into a beyond-dumb dalliance with a twenty-year-old waitress from a locally owned eatery named (in the great tradition of Southern spelling) Katfish Kountry. The fling ended in about the most embarrassing way imaginable, and ever since I've had to face the mirror knowing I'm not as squeaky clean as I thought. I'm not even forty yet, but lately I wake up feeling old and lecherous, and it worries me that I won't know how to communicate with my daughter once she joins this strange species that I'm suddenly so adept at disappointing. In a vague way, I assumed Chloe intuited this and that we'd struck an unspoken pact. Maybe it never entered her mind that I would tiptoe into her bedroom to sack the dirty plates and cups from her birthday party. Since her sweet sixteen coincided with the last day of the school year, she probably figured that, like her, the rest of the world planned to celebrate summer's arrival by sleeping until noon.

At the very least I'd like to think Chloe would do me the favor of hiding the wrapper, and yet here it is, in my hand, ripped and twisted like shrapnel.

"Are you sure it's not yours?" my best friend asks. Campbell lives three doors down, so it's nothing for her to jump out of bed to come calm me.

"How would a wrapper of mine end up in her bedroom?" I fix coffee in return for this consolation, but my shaky hands scatter grounds and sugar across the countertop. "Even thinking about that–Jesus, God–you're sick."

"What were you doing in her room? I figured you found it in the hall bathroom."

"Even if I had, I would've known it wasn't mine because a) it's not my brand and b) when I pitch one of these things, I make sure nobody will ever find it. This wrapper was sitting there, right out in the open, like it had nothing to be ashamed of."

"There isn't anything to be ashamed of."

I have to remind myself to avoid that word around Campbell. She's a lesbian, so she's had a lifetime of people telling her their ideas of what's shameful.

"Sex is perfectly natural, Vance. I can see how sixteen might seem premature to you, but it's not in the eyes of the law. I mean, Chloe is legal now, and she's using protection. That seems mature. Credit her with that."

I muster all the disbelief I can, but I'm no match for Campbell. She sports these stiff bangs that whisk her eyebrows when she's in a disapproving mood.

"Don't give me that look," she says. "How old were you your first time?"

I start to say I was also sixteen before realizing this is a trap. Campbell and I have had the first-time conversation before, many times, so she's testing me to see whether I'll lie. I won't give her the satisfaction. Instead of spouting a number, I tell her that no matter how old I was, I wasn't old enough, and it messed me up for a long time. Campbell takes a chair at the breakfast table and gathers the lapels of her bathrobe tight to her throat, as if she can't risk exposure to my foolishness. Then she hits me with her diagnosis. "Your problem," she decides, "is that you're never not a teenager when you sleep with someone."

I give her a sarcastic smile. "Well now, if anybody would know...."

It's true. Campbell and I have messed around. Every once in a while she falls off the wagon and onto me. I try to take it as a compliment when she thanks me for convincing her that she really is gay.

"I'm not being mean," she assures me, "but you've never had a mature attitude about sex. It's no crime. It's, you know, your circumstance. You were a kid when you had your kid. I bet you've never talked to Chloe about sex, have you?"

"No, and I'm not going to. I don't want to mess it up for her. I hate men too much; I hate what they do to women. I'd only sour her on them. If she would've come to me first, I'd have gladly talked to her about it, but now, finding this wrapper, any conversation we have is going to make her feel she's been busted. It may even stigmatize her. Right now Chloe needs somebody who can listen without getting parental, a confidante. Somebody who's like, you know, *a big sister.*"

I flash Campbell an appreciative smile.

"Oh, no—no sir. You don't want to give me that responsibility. You won't like it when I tell her what she's doing is okay as long as she's careful."

"As long as who's careful?"

Chloe glides into the kitchen on the contrails of Campbell's agitation. I stammer something about an acquaintance and stuff the wrapper in my pocket as she shuffles to my Krups Aroma Control coffeemaker. The machine's patented drip-brew technology is supposed to enrich my sipping pleasure, but the thing chugs along at an arthritic pace. As Chloe discovers, the coffee isn't ready. "Where's Lleyton?" she asks, referring to the eleven-year-old from the only man besides me Campbell's ever been with.

"He's asleep," says Campbell. "Like you ought to be. Why are you up so early?"

"Not because I want to, that's for sure. Daddy's been clanging around since before sunrise. Every time I start back to sleep I hear him knock the walls."

Her back is to the breakfast table as she pours a sloppy glass of juice and drops bread slices into the toaster. She's a slim girl with athletic shoulders, no longer a tomboy, but certainly nothing approaching a sexpot; just your average teenage girl whose slouchy gait, good-natured silliness, and reverence for the iconic women of rock 'n' roll deluded her father into believing she had better things to think about than boys. How naïve of me to assume that she would practice abstinence just because she's happy-go-lucky and hates melodrama.

"Maybe you should put some shorts on. We've got company, you know."

Chloe stops mid-slurp, lips ringed with pulp, and snaps the thick waistband doubled around her hips. "Um, these are shorts—boxer shorts. It's just Campbell, anyway. What's the big deal? She's seen me in a lot less."

"I've seen your friends in a lot less," admits Campbell, "and I hardly know them. I'm curious. Is this the first time your dad's ever told you what to wear? Because he's being a total control freak this morning. You're not the only one he's ordering around."

I let them know how much more controlling I could

be. Chloe's best friend, Nina Laughlin, has a dad who measures her skirt length. I know this because Nina's mom, Marci, ranted about it to me the other day while we were at the music store buying strings and drumsticks for the girls' band. Marci is divorcing her husband, Luke, who's a Baptist choir director in town. Luke's not handling the situation very well. You'd think he could take his grief out on the soprano section, but instead, whenever Nina's around, he whips out the tape measure and wham, more than four inches above the knee and the kid's not allowed out of the sad one-bedroom apartment Luke now rents. And it's not just the girl's skirts, either. It's also her low-rise jeans. According to Marci, Luke measures the distance from Nina's bellybutton to her waistband so she doesn't expose any—

"Gooch," Chloe finishes for me. Neither Campbell nor I have ever heard this word before. "Mr. Laughlin doesn't want Nina showing off any tummy gooch. And you know how she gets around the tape measure? She stashes clothes at her friends' houses. Her dad thinks she's out looking like a Junior Leaguer when really she's ho'ing it up. You should've seen the cami Nina had on last night. Oh my God, it was tight enough to crush the ribs of a third-grader. There's a mini-skirt of hers in my closet as we speak." She interrupts her story to toss me a sheepish face. "You won't nark her out, will you?"

Before I can ask why my daughter would suspect me of narking, she's off to another thought.

"Ooh, Dad, can you run me to the thrift store? Nina got me a gift card. Just think, this'll be the last time you have to take me. Because come Monday, I get my driver's license. I'm sixteen!"

She raises her arms above her head and does a victory dance.

"Trust me, I know how old you are. And, no, sorry, no vintage clothes shopping today. I've got to meet Mike Willoughby at Rivervesper for eighteen holes. It's going to kill my entire Saturday."

Chloe's face hardens into a squint. She wants to know how many millions we're turning down this week. Since last winter, the son of my former boss has been trying to buy out my majority stake in the fifty-acre estate I inherited from his old man. Chloe would love for me to sell, imagining the decadent fun we could have drinking our sweet tea out of brandy snifters. If I were smart I'd take the money and run, but for reasons I can't quite articulate, I can't let go. With its nearly two hundred reproductions of famous Greek statues, Macon Place has for decades been the anchor of the local arts scene in our little town of Willoughby, Alabama. There's nothing I'd rather do than convert the mansion and gardens into a full-fledged center sponsoring exhibitions, plays, and concerts. The only problem is that Macon Place hasn't provided for much of a living since my boss died.

"You're off by a few decimal points, sweetie. Whatever Mike might offer, it probably wouldn't cover one of your sprees. I have some work I need done, anyway. We've got a luncheon coming Monday, and the baseboards need bleaching. Since you're my chief bleacher, you're booked."

Chloe spins around, mischievously blinding me with her Cyclops' eye of a bellybutton. "You're making me bleach baseboards on my birthday?"

I remind her that her birthday was yesterday.

"But it's my birthday *week*," she pleads. "You don't want me at Macon Place by myself, anyway. Think of the friends I might let inside to do God knows what in the portulaca."

I thank her for that image and tell her I'll remember it the next time she wants to stay out past eleven on a weekend. Then I turn to Campbell and inform her I'm taking her dad to the golf course with me. Mike's not happy that I'm letting kids in Willoughby use Macon Place for a battle of the bands in three weeks, and I need Luther to run interference.

A new excuse pops into Chloe's mind. "Ooh, I forgot! That's another reason I can't work! I've got band practice at four. We need it, too. You said yourself that Stu and Nina and I don't have our chops yet. We have less than a month not to suck."

The band is news to Campbell. "I didn't know you were in a real group, Chloe. I thought you and Stu just jammed together."

"Oh, we're for real now. We just don't have a name. When I ask Daddy's help all he comes up with are sucky ones. I mean, G*rrrl*vana, G*rrrl* Jam, G*rrrl*L7. I wouldn't be surprised if he came up with SoundG*rrrl*don. That's the level of clever I'm dealing with."

I'm too busy frowning at Chloe's uninhibited use of *suck* to explain why Grrrl Jam is funny to me—funnier, anyway, than I Said *Like* A Virgin. Campbell has a solution.

"I bet Stu would do the baseboards. He asked last week if he could keep my yard this summer. He needs cash for time in the recording studio. I can go shopping with

Chloe. It'll give us single ladies time to catch up. The only hitch is that you'll have to take Lleyton with you to the golf course."

"That's cool by me," announces Chloe. Before I can shoot down the idea, she's out the door, flinging crumbs in her regal wake. "Only that's *two* hitches, Dad. The other is you'll have to pay Stu. Just because he dates your daughter doesn't mean he works cheap."

The coffeemaker lets out a gurgle, which I mistake for my nausea.

"All right, but don't fight me about this luncheon Monday. It's the women's book club from the public library, so lay off the raccoon eyeliner and Ramones T-shirts for a day, hear? And hey, what time did your party break up? I conked out, despite the racket."

"Sorry about that. Nina stayed until 12:30. She would've gone earlier, but she had this idea of getting Zak back for dumping her. Did you know Zak dumped Nina? Well, he did, so she came up with this idea to email him a picture of herself in nothing but boyshorts and a sign over her chest saying *Free of Z*, just so he knows what he's let go. If we ever cut an album, that's what we're going to call it: *Free of Z.*"

I'm dumb enough to ask in a concerned voice if they actually took that picture. As Campbell rolls her eyes, Chloe busts out with a mad-scientist laugh. "Whatever you do, don't Google it!" she calls from the other room. "The FBI will break down our door and arrest you for being a perv!" In my mind I scramble to plot last night's timeline, hoping to pinpoint the exact moment that wrapper was ripped open. I can't decide which makes me the worse parent, if the deed was done while I was upstairs surfing the Internet when I should've been patrolling the party, or if they made sure I was sawing logs before they got down to business. Almost as a challenge to Chloe, I wonder aloud what time Stu, her boyfriend, went home.

"Oh, God, you're such a goof." Chloe returns to the doorsill to flick a curl off her face. As her birthday present to herself, she bobbed her hair, Louise Brooks-style, but she's not sure she likes it. The flapper look makes her jaw too square, she complains. That and wisps keep crawling up her cheek. I have my own reasons for not liking it. The hairdo makes her look far too sophisticated for sixteen.

"Stu had to be home by eleven. He's retaking his ACTs this morning. He only got a twenty-eight on his science test and his mom wants him to have straight thirties across the board."

She betrays no hint that I might be on to her.

"Thirties in three out of four subjects," Chloe informs me, "means Stu is smart."

She leaves for good, so I fix just two coffees, whitening Campbell's with hazelnut creamer.

"'Maybe you should put some shorts on?' Smooth, Vance. Very smooth."

I tell my best friend not to get judgmental. She's not the one who has to pay a kid who's dropping condom wrappers in her daughter's bedroom. Campbell's not amused. She tells me I need to understand how self-conscious girls get over their bodies.

"Right now I'm worried she's not self-conscious enough," I sigh.

"Funny. Would you like an honest opinion, though? From where I sit, there's only one reason you want Chloe conscious of her body."

Campbell trains her laser-beam glare on my frontal lobe.

"It's so you won't have to be," she says.

# 2

I wasn't always this inept. Before Chloe turned teenager I was a best friend, not a father, and no topic of conversation between us was taboo. Back then I could explain how easily a finger will break if a free hand comes near a softball glove before a ball is safely caught. I could demonstrate how to foxtrot so the clop-footed boys at cotillion didn't mash her toes. I could even defend Jo's decision to marry Mr. Bhaer at the end of *Little Women*. When I floundered for what I didn't know, I did what good parents always do: I faked the answers.

Of course, Chloe and I never would've grown as close as we were until recently had her mother stayed in the picture. Seventeen years ago I was the assistant director on a sophomore production of Chekhov's *The Seagull* at the University of Georgia when our Irina Arkadina informed me that she was pregnant. The bomb dropped in Act IV during a lotto game that drives the play to its devastating climax. Irina Arkadina is an aging actress, full of herself and obsessed with maintaining her fame. Even as her despondent son, Constantine, pines for her affection, all she can do is brag about past ovations. I remember this scene unfolding from the cramped wings of UGA's Cellar Theater, the velour skirt of the masking curtain gripped in my fist as I tried to process the news that I was going to be a father. (Coincidence of coincidences: for reasons I've never known, this curtain is called a "tormentor.") My head pounded so hard I thought I was the victim of that old vaudeville gag where a guy gets clocked by a sandbag dropped from the rafters. The second the play ended with the deafening gunshot that signals Constantine's offstage suicide, I yanked Deb into the greenroom where I proceeded to incinerate my lungs screaming. If I remember correctly, my exact words were, "What are you trying to do to me?"

Once the shock settled, Deb and I talked over our "options" and agreed to handle things like adults. We married two weeks later in the non-denominational campus chapel and honeymooned at an Embassy Suites, where for three mornings in a row we pigged out on the breakfast buffet. For a wedding present my father sent two jumbo bags of diapers. Her parents gave us a lecture. I spent the next nine months feeling clammier and queasier than morning sickness ever made Deb, but the minute Chloe was born, I felt surprisingly confident and settled. I'd discovered who I wanted to be—a dad, simple enough. At first I reveled in that identity for all the wrong reasons. Being a father made me feel like a man for the first time in my life. Nobody my age that I knew had a kid yet. And that made me special. Chloe was barely a month old when I started strapping her to my chest in a kangaroo carrier and showing her off on the quad, where ten paces was all it took for me to go from being a nonentity to being Big Daddy Badass. I swear I strutted around like I was Tony Manero in *Saturday Night Fever*, only swinging Pampers in each hand instead of paint cans. I might as well have lugged a sign that said BABY ON BOARD = BIG SWINGIN' DICK because that's how cocky I'm sure I looked. Still, I loved having those pudgy legs dangle at my waist and that soft crown right there to sniff. The smell of baby dome got me higher than ten toots of cocaine ever could. As I grew up, parenting became less about me than about watching Chloe's personality take shape. The one thing that didn't change was my commitment to raising my daughter. I never doubted I was made to be her dad.

Deb was a different story. She was single-minded about making it as an actress. Our fellow theater nerds used to say that ambition was her anvil and that she would pulp the world into complying. I doubt she ever thought something as insubstantial as my spermatozoa could interfere with her aspirations. I never resented her for being so driven. She came from hardcore Church of Christ stock that regarded actors as only marginally more reputable than cardsharps and saloon floozies. I had it much easier. My dad (my mom passed when I was eleven) was hands-off when it came to parenting, and I wasn't burdened by ambition. Back then I entertained vague notions of working in regional theater, or, at worst, teaching high-school drama. As it turned out, the worst was a private *junior* high, the only job I could find after earning a Ph.D. from the University of Florida at twenty-six. For two years I taught eighth graders how not to mispronounce Aeschylus and Euripides before an improbable friendship with the patriarch of Willoughby, Alabama, led to an equally improbable stint as his majordomo. Deb had no way of foreseeing the unusual path my life would take, but she probably guessed my indirection. Behind my back she applied for a fellowship with the National Actors Conservatory. Who was I to stand in the way of stardom?

The night Chloe and I drove her to Hartsfield to catch

her flight she cried. In the time I'd known Deb she'd never shed a tear, not even when she was newly pregnant and we were terrified. I didn't believe her capable of that vulnerability, but I understood why she was suddenly so upset. Leaving her child went against the whole bullying thrust of evolution, which is a tough burden for a twenty-two year-old. You can imagine what the Church of Christ thought. I tried to soothe Deb by telling her she'd never be happy if she didn't pursue her dream. I let her carry Chloe through the security check-points–you could still do that back then–and I waited from a respectful distance at the jetway as she held the baby to her cheek. In my infinite generosity I even offered to let her change one last diaper.

"I can't believe you didn't leave first," she whispered during our parting hug. "I was waiting for you to."

What could I tell her in return? I said the first thing that came to mind: "If at any time you should have need of my life, come and take it."

It's a line recited by a naïve young woman in Act III of *The Seagull* as she reminds a novelist, a sellout named Boris Trigorin, that he once wrote it in a book. Trigorin has no recollection of saying it.

Those were our last words for eight years.

Last fall a therapist told me the reason I never remarried after Deb left was because of my primal scene.

"You know what that is, don't you?" he asked from the cozy comfort of his overstuffed settee. "It's that pivotal event in the formation of the self that you return to so compulsively that it determines all your future actions.

Kirk Curnutt

Your whole life becomes a variation on that moment, and all those nice engines that we like to believe propel our lives forward—choice, decision, free will—why, they're just dreamy self-deceptions."

Because my Ph.D. was in theater, I admitted to being intrigued by the idea of primal scenes. Because I was a paying customer, however, I told the guy his theory was horseshit.

"You don't think your history bears the scars of repetitive behavior?" he asked. "All these relationships you're in and out of—"

"Hey now, hold on just a minute. What do you mean, 'all these'? I've had five relationships in sixteen years. That's only one every three years. They were all friendships, too. I'm still friends with every single one of those women.... Well, except for one."

I'll admit I was touchy. I made myself see a therapist after getting busted *in flagrante delicto* with a young woman named Ardita Farnam—she of Katfish Kountry fame. We were caught by her parents, in her parents' Alabama room, no less. Even before the scene set a new standard for embarrassing, it was awkward, thanks mainly to Bear Bryant, whose disapproving face glared upon our locked legs from several glossy photographs mounted to the walls.

"You told me in our first session that you walked in on your parents as a child," the therapist said, explaining his theory. "That's the classic definition of a primal scene. You saw your father and your mother in a vulnerable moment, and shortly after that your mother was gone. Don't you see the link between those two things?"

I really didn't. I was probably too busy regretting sharing the memory with this guy. I'd never told anybody about it before. When I was ten I caught my folks in a moment of passion. It was no big deal, nothing more embarrassing than a kiss, except that my mom was shirtless and my dad's left hand was working her chest so hard I thought he was doing CPR. That's not a joke. Mom was dying of cancer at the time, and I was sure her heart had stopped and Dad was frantic to revive her. Instead of reassuring me she hadn't kicked the mortal coil, all my father could say was, "Get the hell out of here." Later they both came to my room, where I'd drenched my pillow crying, and they instructed me on how to knock on a door before entering. I took a swat to the fanny for suggesting God made locks and bolts for a reason. As I said, to me it was just a memory, but to this therapist it was the entire key to my personality.

"See, Vance, these past five women with whom you've—um—hung out, as you like to phrase it, the ones you say you loved but didn't want to marry, that you only 'wanted to be friends with,' including the one you *did* marry because you didn't want anybody getting mad at you for getting her pregnant.... Don't you see how you encouraged them to leave you so you could reenact the feeling of abandonment you suffered when your mother died? You're so attached to that feeling it's become your way of avoiding problems. It's allowed you to stay single for fifteen years so you can be free of complication, the kind of complications we associate with a healthy, durable relationship."

I wanted to tell him I hadn't realized being single was such a crime. I could've sworn it was a choice.

"Well," I said instead, "even if I'm no good at relationships, I'm good at other stuff. Doesn't that count? I'm a good dad."

The therapist smiled, grimly. "Of course you are. But what I invite you to consider is what your actions teach your daughter. This instability, this going from one person to another, might you not be establishing a pattern that Chloe will think is the norm, only because she's known nothing else?"

He rested his back against the settee and yanked his tie straight.

"Just something to think about," he added—quite gratuitously, I thought.

When you're a single parent you put up with a lot of that talk. People assume that if you're not married, then you're not settled and you still have lots of growing up left to do. Living in a small Southern town has taught me how much marriage is like martial law. If you don't do it, you're obstructing other people's peace. I thought I did an okay job when it came to being a responsible dad. For four out of five of those relationships, I was discreet, and I was also honest with Chloe. If my daughter asked why I didn't want to jump the broom again, I said it was because my heart belonged to one woman—her. After that Chloe was usually too busy sticking fingers down her throat pretending to puke to press the issue.

Only now there's an unidentified condom wrapper in my house.

I can't look at this thing without hearing it talk to me. *This is all your fault*, it says.

In the voice of that therapist.

# 3

"It's a travesty," complains Campbell's dad, Luther Culpepper. "An injustice. These girls are *artists*. They were doing what artists are supposed to do: they were fighting oppression, challenging the patriarchy, speaking for the human condition...."

Four of us are teeing up for the third hole at Rivervesper Golf Course–Luther, me, Lleyton, and Mike Willoughby–and all Luther can talk about is the breaking news that had him up all night. Somewhere in a distant country called Herzoslovakia, five members of a feminist punk-art collective have been arrested for protesting a dictator named Bronislavis Stylptitch. Campbell's dad has been an insomniac since he underwent a prostatectomy last December, but this particular event was guaranteed to keep him from sleeping when CNN went wall-to-wall with it shortly before midnight. Luther is the closest thing we have in Alabama to a godfather of punk. From the seventies through the early two-thousands, he owned a label that released records by several cult bands in the South. He still operates the studio where many of his artists' "hits" were recorded, although it's on the brink of insolvency. He's never doubted that the best way to fight oppression is with three grating chords and an anarchic beat, so Stylptitch's repressive response to this insurgency has him wanting to hop a plane and rock the casbah. I have my own concerns about the group's arrest, but for different reasons. Chloe first got into music back when Vladimir Putin sent two members of Pussy Riot to the Russian Gulag. Luther was all about fighting that injustice, too, and he started teaching my daughter drums so she could feel she was part of his grassroots battle for worldwide artistic freedom. I liked that Chloe was into punk activism, but I didn't appreciate having to explain to a fourteen-year-old why wearing her homemade FREE PUSSY RIOT T-shirt to school was inappropriate, especially when it landed her a two-day suspension. If Luther had his druthers, we'd have fought the punishment all the way to the school's Board of Trustees—which, coincidentally, Mike Willoughby chairs. The last thing I need right now is to have to explain to people in Willoughby that some new punk group's name is only offensive if you choose to ignore the sexism that it challenges. That argument set the eyes of the principal at Willoughby Academy rolling when I made it in my daughter's defense. However, when Luther reveals what this Herzoslovakian band calls itself, I'm pleasantly surprised.

"The group is named 'Lifting Belly'? Really? That's interesting. That's a Gertrude Stein poem."

I did a whole chapter on Gertrude Stein in my dissertation, so I know a lot about her. It's not knowledge I often get to call upon.

"'Lifting Belly' is a stupid name," grumbles Luther. "It has no punch. You know why? Because it's a gerund, the worst thing to ever happen to band names. Your generation was all about gerunds, Vance. I used to tell kids in the nineties not to call themselves Picking Blueberries or Tickling Rosemary. A name needs to be short, precise, and memorable, like The Clash, The Jam, or The Buzzcocks."

From the teebox Mike Willoughby asks what Lifting

Belly even means. I'm tempted to lie and say it has nothing to do with a human gut, that it's a pun on the French city Belley where Gertrude Stein vacationed and that the "lifting" part doesn't mean physically lifting at all but "uplifting." I could ladle out some hooey about how the poem is about picking up the spirits of the people of Belley during World War I, but I'm not sure I'm swift enough to sell it. I certainly can't tell Mike the truth. "Lifting Belly" is a lesbian love poem, and what's happening to make that belly lift is the exact image his pornographic mind probably conjured up in the first place.

"Lifting Belly is a yoga position," I say after Mike takes his shot. "Like 'downward facing dog' or 'inverted tortoise.' Ashanti yoga, I think. Gertrude Stein was big into it."

The thumbs up Mike gives us isn't because he approves of my answer. It's because his ball lands in easy range of the green. Mike's a tall guy, impeccably athletic, rich, and still good-looking in his forties. He's never had a setback in his life, so he has no reason not to give himself thumbs ups all day long. Parring on this hole will cost him about as much sweat as checking his mail. It just may take forty-five minutes given how many strokes Luther and I need to finish a fairway.

"So I guess 'Lifting Belly' will be a thing around town now?"

"Absolutely not," I promise.

"People still complain to me about the graffiti from last time," he says. "Little old ladies remind me about having to pass the words Pussy and Riot spray painted on the way to the Piggly Wiggly. Of course, little old ladies don't say either of those words. I'd really rather not have to hear those complaints again, even if this new name isn't as offensive."

Mike owns a company that designs and manages golf courses throughout Alabama. He also happens to be the mayor of Willoughby, which is appropriate since his daddy's money has floated the town for seventy years. I tell Mike, in the same breath that I remind him nobody ever caught the kids who briefly blanketed our alleys with support for Vladimir Putin's victims, that he doesn't have to worry about graffiti. I also remind him that Willoughby has plenty of non-political graffiti he could worry about. I don't remind him of the patch that says F– Mike Willoughby. I'm afraid he'd accuse me of writing it.

It's Lleyton's turn to tee off. His dad used to be a golf pro, so he's grown up with the game, and he's good. Lleyton's a short kid, a bit on the pudgy side, but what he lacks in physical grace he makes up for in competitiveness. We no sooner hit the first hole this morning than it became clear that he and Mike would be locked in something just short of mortal battle. The kid takes his swing and launches his ball into the horizon. It lands about two inches past Mike's. To celebrate, Lleyton spins, sticks out his tongue, and gives us a double-barrel shot of devil horns with his beefy boy fingers.

"Your grandson's cutthroat," Mike tells Luther. Despite the smile on his face, I can tell he's more annoyed than amused. "Don't take this the wrong way, but does his mom know how hyper he is? If he were my kid he'd be medicated."

Luther explains that Lleyton's had it rough growing up. His dad lives in Nashville and sees the kid almost as infrequently as he pays child support. "The dad's a shit," Luther complains, despite the fact Lleyton can hear his every word. "He's not like Vance here. Lleyton's dad doesn't do squat for his kid. He's got a grudge because Campbell came out after she dumped him. He can't stand having a lesbian for an ex-wife. Campbell manages the best she can on what she makes, but single moms, especially single gay moms, don't have it easy when it comes to raising boys. There aren't many strong male role models left in the world. The few that are around still tend to have ulterior motives."

This last sentence is directed at me. Mike chuckles, his artificially tanned cheeks wrinkling like jerky. He knows that Campbell's dad has never understood how his daughter and I ended up messing around. Luther is convinced I waylaid Campbell with hetero hoodoo.

"I rooted for Vance and Campbell," Mike says, taunting Luther. "It's not her fault the relationship didn't work out. Seahorse here drove her to defect to the other team. When it comes to women, he's the Fidel Castro of sex."

"Seahorse" is Mike's nickname for me. My last name is Seagrove, and to him "Seahorse" is both clever and appropriate. "Because seahorses," he likes to say, "are the only species in which the males birth and raise the babies." I cut Mike a glare, but riling Luther is one of his favorite pastimes.

"Campbell was the best option Seahorse ever had," he continues. "Not that he's ever had that many. But Campbell was definitely way better than

Kirk Curnutt

this new one of his, this Sadie McGregor girl—"

Luther is standing over his tee, finding his form. With his shrubby hair and untrimmed mustache, he looks unsettlingly like Samuel Clemens, which only reinforces the impression that he has no business playing golf. He suddenly lets his arms go slack and turns to face me.

"Wait, you're dating Sadie now? When did this start? I'm in the studio with Sadie all the time and she's never mentioned you once."

"Take your shot," I beg him. "I need to get home to Chloe. I can't be stuck here all day while you interrogate me."

As Mike and Luther are well aware, Sadie is the latest recipient of the Willoughby Family Foundation Fellowship, a prestigious award that gives an Alabama artist enough money to pursue her craft for a year. It's an award that I helped Storm set up when I first became his majordomo.

"Sadie and I are keeping the news on the down-low," I explain. "There's too much gossip in Willoughby as it is."

"Especially about you," Mike kindly points out.

"Does Chloe know?" Luther asks. "She never talks about the two of you at youth group."

"Sure Chloe knows. She loves Sadie. She wants Sadie to teach her how to write songs. Maybe Chloe has more important things on her mind at church—like Jesus. Or Buddha." I turn to Mike. "Luther's got the kids in his youth group studying Buddhism. Now Chloe collects these votive sculptures called tsa tsas. Thanks to Luther, my daughter jokes about her 'bodacious tsa-tsas.'"

Nostrils flared, Luther won't let me change the subject.

"Don't you think Sadie's a bit—"

"Young?" Mike generously offers without blinking an eye.

"Sadie's twenty-three," I concede. "But she's an old soul. She was playing coffeehouses at sixteen and she's cut two homemade CDs already. She was an emancipated teenager, too, because her parents had legal issues. As in, they went to prison. They're still locked up. Her dad's in for identity theft and her mom for selling meth. So Sadie's not a kid—she's never been a kid."

Luther finally takes his shot. It falls about sixty yards shy of Mike's and Lleyton's. That means it's my turn, and I do even worse.

"What about your rule, Vance?" Luther still can't get over the news about Sadie and me. "You said you'd never date anybody closer to Chloe's age than yours. It was your '10½ Commandment,' you said, because you were twenty-one when Chloe was born, and any difference more than half of that seemed perv—"

"I know what I said." I'm huffy because I imposed that rule while trying to piece my life back together in my AA period—i.e. the Aftermath of Ardita, the Katfish Kountry waitress. "You've heard Sadie's songs. Do you seriously think she's closer to sixteen than thirty-seven? And why do you even care, Luther? Do you have a crush on Sadie yourself or something? If she's too young for me, then she's way too young for you."

Everyone is so busy prying into my private life that nobody notices Lleyton. The kid has slunk to the cart he shares with his grandfather. He's in the rear seat, his cheeks sullenly resting on his fists, eyes on the floorboard.

Kirk Curnutt

He only looks up to see if we're talking about him yet.

"Maybe his medicine finally kicked in," shrugs Mike.

Luther goes over to the boy and leans down like a faith healer laying on hands. We can't hear what he says to Lleyton, but we have no trouble making out the kid's response.

"Shut up about my dad!" he screams in a voice sharp enough to carve the sod. "He's not a shit!"

Distressed, Luther tells Mike and me to play on through; he and Lleyton will catch up. Wonderful. Being stuck alone with Mike is exactly what I've dreaded since we arrived at Rivervesper. Back when I taught junior high at Willoughby Academy, Mike suggested students might better appreciate the Greek tragedies I assigned if they visited the sculpture garden his father devoted his life to building. Storm Willoughby founded Macon Place in the 1940s while making his fortune in construction. It was actually his second fortune, the first one coming from bootlegging, though nobody talks about Storm's hooch days. I'm sure that when Mike introduced me to his dad it never crossed his mind that I might strike up a friendship with the old man that would lead to my becoming his personal Jeeves, a role I served faithfully until Storm died back in February, four months short of his one-hundredth birthday. I also doubt Mike ever imagined Storm would bequeath me any portion of Macon Place, much less fifty-one percent to Mike's forty-nine. Long before his daddy passed away, Mike made plans to sell Storm's prime piece of real estate to developers, who intend to turn the fifty acres into a high-end gated community. At the moment land is at a premium in

Willoughby, the demand for housing bigger than ever. That makes me the one thing standing between a lot of people and a lot of profit. Ever since Storm's will surprised our entire community, Mike has been summoning me to the links and putting the strong arm on me to sell. His last offer—$750,000—took me four holes to decline. I feel obligated to turn it down, both for Storm and for Willoughby. Before he died, my boss told me several times that he wanted me to maintain his statuary and to keep the grounds from being broken into lots. Whenever Mike dangles money in front of my eyes, I try to talk him into partnering with me in turning Macon Place into an arts mecca. I'm convinced we could make the town a big-time tourist destination. I'd rather live in a place that's known for the arts than for its gated communities.

"How about we just skip to the offer," I say to Mike as we rumble down the cart path. I grip the roll bar in case he has any ideas about hitting a bump and launching me headfirst into a loblolly pine. "Make it more than last time so I can brag to Chloe."

Mike's eyes are fixed firmly on the path. "Chloe's the real reason I want to talk to you," he says in a concerned voice. "Our kids have been friends for a long time, right, Seahorse?"

He is correct. Mike and his wife, Terri, have two teenagers who've attended Willoughby Academy with Chloe since we moved here ten years ago. Their boys' names are Travis and Zak, but they're better known throughout Willoughby as the "Gold Dust Twins" because they're spoiled as hell and have no qualms flaunting their wealth. Zak is the same kid who dumped Nina in the middle of Chloe's party last night. I don't share this news with Mike, mainly because I don't want him telling me I have more pressing concerns than worrying about whose teenagers are dating whom.

"I–I'm not sure how to let you in on this, Seahorse, but if Chloe were my daughter, I'd want to know."

He stops the conversation abruptly to take his next shot. Of course, his ball lands on the green.

"I have it from a reliable source that Stu got kicked out of Walmart Thursday. For trying to buy condoms. The clerk refused to ring them up, he pitched a fit, and security tossed him. Apparently, he screamed up a scene. The F-word and everything else you can imagine. By the way, it's your shot."

I'm so frazzled that I drive my ball square into a pine bough only twenty yards away. Mike tells me we'll walk the fairway.

"Raising teenagers sucks," he consoles me as we cross the grass. "You want some advice? Get a lock on your bedroom door. Boys these days, I don't know why, but they turn into bulldogs the minute they start getting some. They feel like they've got to mark their territory. Nothing makes a teenage boy feel like a big dog more than having sex in his father's bed. It's an Oedipal thing. Trust me, I speak from experience."

I stop in my tracks. "You think Zak and Nina got it on in your bed?"

"I know they have. A few weeks back I found a long brown hair on Terri's pillow. I find Terri's hair there all the time, but hers are short and the peroxide leaves them glowing like plutonium. Nina's the only brunette who's in and out of my house. The only good thing is that I found it, not Terri. If that had happened, I wouldn't be here. I'd be in a courtroom trying to convince a judge I wasn't screwing the cleaning lady. I'm telling you, Seahorse, I can only imagine one thing worse than discovering that your son laid his girlfriend in your own bed. You know what that is?"

I feel a sympathetic palm slide up my arm and across my damp back to my shoulder, which is squeezed and then patted. It's a rich man's way of saying he cares about you: it's both fraternal and patronizing.

"The worst would be finding out your daughter's been laid in your bed. You better Katy-bar your door, friend."

Nearly four hours later, in the parking lot finally, we trade soaked polos for dry Ts.

"Don't take it so hard," Mike keeps telling Lleyton. The kid is couched Indian style on the back of my Scion, crabby because after locking horns with Mike for eighteen holes he lost by a single stroke.

"It's what happens," Mike keeps taunting him. "Some days are diamonds, others are dung."

The kid turns away, staring toward the ornate porch of the clubhouse that, twenty yards past the last of the speed bumps, shimmers like a mirage in the heat. This is the wettest Alabama summer in my decade here. The chalk of the gravel drive, which usually floats freely about in powdery drifts, is stained red from the soggy ground, and there's not a vehicle in the lot whose tires and side panels aren't streaked in muddy scallops.

"How about we grab a drink?" offers Mike. "Beer's on me."

Kirk Curnutt

I beg off, too numbed by the story of Stu in the Walmart. Luther declines as well. Mike's offended, although he won't complain. Why should he? He's got dirt on us. He knows who everybody's sleeping with in our families.

Not two miles out of Rivervesper, I decide I've had it with Lleyton's whimpering.

"It's just a game. How do you think I feel? Your grandpa beat me, and I'm not jumping off a roof. Who cares who won?"

The kid detonates: "Mike didn't win! He cheated! I saw him."

"What are you talking about?" I wait for him to swim through a lot of slobbery agitation before he can answer.

"That last hole! Mike kicked his ball onto the green. He couldn't beat me otherwise. He had to sink the putt in one stroke to win and he wasn't sure he could do it from that angle on the apron. So he just scooted the ball closer to the cup, right out in the open."

"Are you sure? It's been a long morning. You were hot and upset. Maybe you just—"

"I saw him do it, and he saw me see him. 'Some days are diamonds, others are dung,' he told me. Then he looked me right in the eye, and he said, *'Little buddy, you are dung for.'*"

# 4

It's late afternoon before Chloe comes home. I bribe Lleyton into forgetting about Mike's cheating by ordering a pizza. As we wait to burn the roofs of our mouths together, we catch up on the news from Herzoslovakia. At first there's not much information. We're treated to a lot of B-roll of Bronislavis Stylptitch, who resembles a matinee idol more than an Eastern European dictator, along with still pictures of Lifting Belly members. "They look like fashion models," notes Lleyton, and it's true. The women in this punk-art collective are lithe and dewy enough to appear on the cover of *Vogue* or *Cosmopolitan.* This bothers the talking head that CNN brings on to comment on Lifting Belly's tactics. The pundit is an expert in feminist protest movements, and she finds it troubling that the group performs topless when it stages an event, even if members' chests are smeared with slogans about revolution and liberation. The expert is particularly hard on Lifting Belly's leader, Oksana Dybek, for denouncing American women as too spoiled and lazy to rise up against their oppressors. "There've been rumors," says the pundit, "that Lifting Belly isn't even a real movement, but a counterinsurgency, a sort of fifth column, meant to ridicule women by making anger over rape and sexual violence look like Barbie-doll theater. There are stories on the Internet claiming that Lifting Belly is really a Stylptitch prank on the West, and that Oksana Dybek is on his payroll. It's not as far-fetched as it sounds. When he was in his twenties, Bronislavis Stylptitch played bass guitar in a neo-Nazi skinhead band. He knows how easily music can be manipulated as a form of social control."

If Lifting Belly is a hoax, it's a pretty elaborate one. After the pizza arrives I'm on my third slice, picking sausage from between my teeth with a wedge of crust, when CNN's Breaking News chyron explodes on the screen. Cell-phone video of Lifting Belly's arrest is beginning to show up online. "Just a head's up," the anchor says. "The footage is graphic." We pan across a crowd of rowdy protestors, mostly women with fists in the air, alongside journalists and photographers. The camera settles on what looks like any all-female band you might see on a Saturday night at the armory or at the bowling alley, if only all-female bands weren't a rare sight and these women weren't shirtless. The group bashes away ferociously at its instruments, the music harsh and atonal, like sheet metal going through a wood chipper. "Not exactly the Beatles," the news anchor can't help but slip in. The camera zooms in on the lead singer, whom I recognize as Oksana Dybek. Her chestnut hair whips across her face and phlegm flings off her lips as she spits words as if she's unloading an AK-47 clip. "The name of this song," says the anchor, "translates into 'Get Out, Bronislavis Stylptitch, Before the Furies Rain Matriarchy Down Upon Your Head.' According to our producers, the Furies were a band of women warriors in fifteenth-century Herzoslovakia who deposed the ruling king, Nicholas IV, and instituted one hundred years of women's rule. Peaceful rule, I might add."

Almost before the anchor can finish his final sentence a melee erupts, and the camera angle goes sideways. The picture struggles to right itself to capture a squad of military police rushing the band. The goons whack at the women with batons and billy clubs, stopping only to stomp on amplifiers and kick in drumheads. Some of the soldiers invade the audience and shove random women, hoping to scatter the crowd. One of Stylptitch's bruisers clocks Oksana upside the head. She staggers but doesn't crumple, her guitar slipping off her shoulder. Male hands reach out and grab her from every available angle, lifting her off her feet as if she's crowd surfing against her will. She kicks her combat boots and tries to throw elbows, but several thugs wrestle her wrists behind her back. One jackboot steps into the frame and punches her square in the face. The crowd lets out a collective scream as Oksana's body goes limp. The camera wobbles once more and flops downward, almost as if the person filming the spectacle has been smacked on the head from behind. The lens catches a pool of blood gathering under the feet of Stylptitch's enforcers. "No word yet about the condition of Lifting Belly," concludes the newscaster as the footage goes black.

"Was that for real?" asks a mesmerized Lleyton.

It looked real enough to me. I flip the channel to cartoons. I can't get the violence out of my head, though. The shape of the dribbles of pizza sauce on my plate reminds me of that blood pool. More than even the knockout blow, the image I can't erase is the sight of male hands sliding awkwardly over Oksana's bare torso, brushing her breasts as they clutch for her throat. I need a while to realize what the image reminds me of. Without warning I flash back to the memory of that afternoon when I was ten and walked in on my father kissing my shirtless mother, his hand doing some sort of violence to her chest. I want to turn back to the news to know for sure that Lifting Belly survived the beating and that a comatose Oksana Dybek isn't hemorrhaging in a dank Herzoslovakian cell, but I know I'll just be condemned to witness endless replays and feel more and more powerless each time they loop around.

When I can't shake off the juxtaposition of Oksana and my dead mother, I go to the kitchen and scrub the dishes, mopping the kitchen floor for good measure. Glutted with cheese and pepperoni, Lleyton falls asleep on the couch. I spend the afternoon dusting and vacuuming to avoid the temptation of TV. At some point I decide I should worry more about my finances than some faraway punk band, so I balance my checkbook. Before Storm Willoughby died I had roughly $70,000 in savings. With an inexpensive mortgage ($525), a cheap car payment ($230), and tight budgeting, Chloe and I should've been able to live this past year for around $2,000 a month. What I didn't factor in when I first decided to open Macon Place to the public was the cost of health insurance ($830 a month for a family plan). That and how little principal $300 a month pays off on a Visa within a hair's inch of its $12,000 max. Or how much capital I would actually have to invest in Macon Place when Mike refused to partner with me. So far I've gone through $15,000 for a kitchen renovation, $2,500 for paint, $5,000 for a new septic system, etc. By my count I have four months to generate a cash flow. After that, it's back to teaching, the only work anybody thinks I'm qualified for. Needless to say, when Storm passed, he took the market for majordomos with him.

When the girls finally return I learn the source of their delay is Stu. Chloe's boyfriend is his own time zone. I used to think I should make a better effort to get to know him, to empathize with him even. Like Chloe and Lleyton and as Nina will soon be, he's a child of divorce, and his mom struggles working for a caterer and cleaning houses around town to make ends meet. For the three months that Chloe and Stu have dated, I've heard nothing from my daughter except how sweet and sensitive this kid is. How he has the soul of a poet and only feels comfortable around people when he's got a guitar or paintbrush in his hand. The way she sells him you'd think he weeps when flower petals fade. The sad thing is that right up to the minute I discovered that wrapper in Chloe's trash basket I fell for his act. Even now, our first encounter after he left his litter for me to find, Stu comes off as so shy and withdrawn it's hard to imagine that any lust bubbles through his bony frame.

"You should see my stuff," Chloe says excitedly. She dumps her purchases on the couch near Lleyton's tucked legs. The boy bolts upright, gleeful at the prospect of being buried alive in a raggedy mountain of women's Ts and tanks and halters, some piqué, some cap-sleeve and some crewneck, some cotton and some spandex, along with twill chinos, a red sundress, and one matte tricot underwire bra—with matching thong.

"I thought you were hitting the thrift shop. This stuff's all new."

"I changed my mind. I'm tired of wearing other people's things. Ooh, Daddy, check this out."

She drapes a jersey across her chest, pulling it taut until she seems disconcertingly busty. I'm unsettled by how many edges and angles her body has now, how her form has become ribbed in sinew and grooved with tendon, veins, tear channels, and laugh lines. When she was a baby, she was shaped so simply, like an empty sack topped by a ball of a head that flopped indiscriminately from side to side. Then, as a child, she was such a popsicle stick that I nicknamed her "Stackabones." Now she's dimensioned, intricate, bulging with something I can only regard as adulthood.

Or maybe not. The T-shirt features the cartoon mascot of a popular brand of women's accessories defaced to look like Satan. HELLHOLE KITTY, the lettering reads.

"Funny, huh?" grins Chloe. "It was marked down to four bucks."

"Down from what, five? Don't wear that to school, all right? We don't need you getting suspended again like you did over You-Know-What Riot."

"How about this?" Chloe snaps at my arm with a studded red leather belt. "But I'll have to put my name on it, or else Nina the Gooch will borrow it and I'll never see it again."

She runs to the kitchen for a Sharpie, then shows off her handwriting: PROPERTY OF CHLOE S: FAILURE TO RETURN MAY RESULT IN DEATH.

"Good thing it's a long belt," I point out.

Stu suggests Chloe give us a fashion show. I tell him I didn't know he was into fashion. I've never seen Stu in anything but size twenty-nine jeans and extra-large T-shirts that hang off his shoulders as stylishly as hospital smocks. His arms are usually dotted with paint driblets that resemble measles.

"No time for a show," decides Chloe before I can make another sarcastic comment. "We've got to practice. And we have a name now, Daddy. Campbell gave it to us: *Pink Melon Joy.* Awesomesauce, huh?"

The kids whisk off to Chloe's room. I tell my daughter to leave the door open.

"Pink Melon Joy?" I say to Campbell. "That's a Gertrude Stein poem. That's twice in one day I've heard of a band borrowing one of her titles for a name. The odds of that being a coincidence must be astronomical."

Campbell agrees. "The Lifting Belly story was all over NPR while we were shopping. We stopped at the coffee-house and watched some of the reports, including the footage. Have you seen it? It's horrific. Dad's fit to be tied over it. Anyway, when the reporter on the radio mentioned Gertrude Stein, Chloe asked if I knew any other Stein titles. She wants to show solidarity. That was her actual word: *solidarity,* like she's Lech Walesa or somebody. I guess she remembers you giving me a couple of Stein books in the past. 'Pink Melon Joy' was the only title I could think of. Chloe immediately snapped her fingers and said, 'That's it. That's what I'm calling my band.'"

Like "Lifting Belly," "Pink Melon Joy" is a lesbian love poem. The title is also a double entendre. I'm almost certain that Campbell remembers this. I have a vague recollection of telling her that all Gertrude Stein poems are about the love that dare not speak its name, women's division. Campbell's mind is elsewhere, though.

"We stopped by Dad's studio while we waited for Stu to finish bleaching the baseboards. That's where we saw the video of Lifting Belly getting beaten up. I don't want to get in the middle of you and Dad, but he said to mention to you that he's still waiting for your RSVP for the banquet Thursday."

In addition to being the godfather of Southern punk and the youth-group leader at our Unitarian Church, Luther is the founder of Willoughby's P-FLAG chapter. Every year he hosts a fundraiser at Macon Place. Back when I had Storm Willoughby's money to throw around, I thought nothing of buying a table for a thousand bucks. This year if I want to go I may have to wait tables.

"I was with your dad all morning. He didn't mention the banquet once to me. Are you sure Luther even wants me around that P-FLAG crowd, anyway? He made a few choice remarks this morning about both me and your ex-husband, about how there are no good male role models anymore. Sometimes when I'm around your dad I feel like I'm a walking reminder that you've dipped your wick in a couple of Y chromosomes. Maybe it's better if I don't do these banquets anymore."

Campbell shakes her head, then shrugs. "Bisexuality is confusing to people, although I'm not sure if I've only been with two guys I really count as bisexual. Why name our sexuality at all? Dad doesn't understand you and me because he's invested in my being gay. It's one thing to support your daughter by starting a P-FLAG chapter; explaining that she likes women *and* men is a whole other pickle. People are really rude to him about me. Last week Mike Willoughby's wife said somebody downtown saw Dad kiss me on the cheek. She was concerned about how that might confuse Lleyton 'given my history and all.'"

Before I can say anything the house explodes in tom-tom fills and power chords. Chloe is actually an impressive drummer for only taking up the skins two summers ago. At first she wanted to play bass, but I told her that was a cliché. When I was a teenager every band I liked had one female member, and she was always the bassist. "Let Nina play bass," I told her. "I want you to be the female Keith Moon."

To escape the squawks and squeals of Stu's guitar, I motion Campbell to the twin wicker rockers on my porch. "All right," I tell her. "Enough chitter chatter. Give me the skinny. What did you find out from Chloe about that wrapper?"

As it turns out, Campbell didn't find out anything. "With all the Lifting Belly stuff going on," she says, "sex was the last thing she wanted to talk about. When we weren't shopping we spent the day trying to figure out exactly where Herzoslovakia is. Before we knew it, Stu was back from his ACTs and done cleaning already."

"So the day was a total waste?"

"No, it wasn't. Chloe bought clothes, which made her happy. Plus, she's really interested in learning about this Oksana What's-her-name and about protest movements. Are you hearing me? *Your daughter is thinking more about politics than she's thinking about her boyfriend.* Most parents would do backflips hearing that."

We stare out to the horizon, noticing how the sky has darkened.

"There is something about Stu that threw me," Campbell admits. From the tone of her voice, I know she's not convinced she should tell it to me. "I caught him twice trying to take my picture on his phone. That makes me very nervous."

"What kind of picture? Like an upskirt? *Great.* I'm really questioning this kid's judgment. Mike told me this morning that Stu pulled something the other day at Walmart that was just plain dumb."

"You mean about getting kicked out for trying to buy condoms?"

I can't believe Campbell knew about this and didn't tell me. As it happens, Mike had called Luther when he heard the story, asking if he should tell me about it. Luther told him no, then called Campbell, asking if he should be the one to break the news. Campbell told Luther what he'd told Mike. Apparently all this happened during Chloe's birthday party. That means if somebody had bothered to pass along this intel I could've done a better job of policing the kids and spared myself finding that wrapper.

"Honestly, Vance," Campbell says when I make this point, "between you and Dad, I'm wiped out being everybody's favorite mole and messenger. You know that your daughter is sexually active. What else exactly do you need to hear about it? And if you did hear it, do you think you'd feel relieved, or will it just upset you more?"

The rain that's been coming since late morning finally arrives. It's the kind of summer shower I like, the kind that you hear before you see or feel it. It's the sort that scuds along the vaulted sadness of the sky, invisible as wind, exciting a shiver from the blackgums and willow oaks as it pelts their upper leaves before breaking hard and plunging to the asphalt. Soon the porch is drenched in the music of the downpour, from the humming drumroll beaten on the skin of the shingles to the operatic gargle of the eaves struggling to swallow the runoff. I could spend an hour just listening, but Campbell looks stricken. Either she's stuck here with me or she'll get drenched by the dash home.

"All I want to know," I say, "is why Chloe couldn't talk to me about it first. I wouldn't have freaked out or preached at her. I wouldn't have pried. I'd have been all ears. I would've listened to her, just listened, swear to God."

# 5

By dusk I'm in a mood to escape into music when I discover gaps in the CDs I shelve in my upstairs study. For years now Chloe's been in the habit of ransacking my collection. It would probably irritate me if I hadn't outgrown the singers and bands I once cared about. Never one of those guys who made mixtapes or compiled playlists for every woman he fell in love with or got dumped by, I had musical interests in my teens and twenties, but not passions. I kept up with certain artists out of a sense of loyalty, the same way I did old classmates. Once I started working for Storm Willoughby, there wasn't time for immersing myself in whole CDs, and as music evaporated into digital downloads and taps on a touchpad, it just wasn't enough of a physical object to hold my attention. Every so often at the gas station, I'll pick up a cheap $3.99 cutout to listen to in my car, but it's been years since I knew what the latest release by So-and-So was, or when Such-and-Such was touring. On the rare occasion I tune into music these days, I tend toward glam and bubblegum from the seventies, the sillier the better. I think it's because those songs remind me of how carefree my mother was in that last full decade of her short life. In less than a month, I'll turn the age she was when she died. That milestone makes me want to preserve her before she got sick, back when she was young and stylish, outfitted in chenille and scarves with a full head of hair and a baby nestled at her cheek. I don't know why exactly, but a few bars of Starbuck's "Moonlight Feels Right" or "Cherry Baby" by Starz, and

I feel I'm tucked safely in her arms. For the duration of those songs, I feel as if she never left me.

"Sweet's *Greatest Hits.*" I navigate the cozy disarray of magazines, drinking glasses, purses, book bags, and dromedary humps of laundry cluttering Chloe's bedroom floor. "I need some 'Fox on the Run' and 'Love is Like Oxygen.' I don't suppose you could point me to them."

Chloe is perched on her drum stool, her back to her TV, which is tuned to CNN but with the sound down. As her right hand beats imaginary eighth notes an inch above her hi-hat, she pulls a headphone from an ear, and a black dash of hair spills across her eyes.

"Check the desk. And don't get footprints on my notebooks, okay?"

I suggest that if she kept her notebooks off of the floor footprints wouldn't be a worry. Chloe ignores me. On her desk uncased CDs lie stacked like coasters.

"I wish you'd put these back when you're done with them. You nick my CDs leaving them out."

"It's not like you ever listen to them, Dad. But hey, we started a song for the battle of the bands today. Our own song, our first original."

"Oh, yeah? What's it called? I should preview it." I glance at the full-length mirror on her west wall, making sure she's not looking. Then I sneak a peek into her trashcan, but it's empty.

"We don't have a title yet. Stu has to finish the lyrics. Then we'll demo it at the studio if we can get some money together. Campbell said Luther would produce it for us."

"Stu's writing the lyrics? Why don't you do that? Your lyrics would be better than Stu's."

"You're evil."

"I meant that as a compliment—to you, anyway. Hey, look here, L7's *Bricks Are Heavy*. I haven't listened to this CD in forever. I saw L7 in concert once. 1992. Their most famous song is 'Pretend We're Dead' and it still shows up on movie soundtracks. My girlfriend and I drove from Georgia to a place called the Visage in Orlando without telling our parents—but don't you ever do that. L7 was the one and only time I ever stage dove. I was too old for it even then. I would love it if they got back together and you could see them in concert."

The footage of the Lifting Belly beating plays again on the TV. I nod to the violent images and mention to Chloe that Campbell told me the story had hooked her.

"That's why I dug out *Bricks Are Heavy*," Chloe says. "L7 is a big influence on Lifting Belly according to websites about them. Amnesty International has gotten involved already with the case. I signed the online petition demanding to know Oksana Dybek is okay. They're holding her in this dingy prison called The Chimneys. It's where they decapitated people in medieval times and stuff. Do you think you could sign the petition, too? Campbell and Luther already have. I was thinking I might also, like, do a website for Lifting Belly, too, my own newsfeed about the situation."

"Wow, you're really into this story. Maybe we could go to Herzoslovakia and bust Oksana out of jail ourselves, a little daddy/daughter espionage. We could call ourselves the New Furies, after those women warriors who deposed their king back in the day. We could bring Oksana back to Alabama, and Lifting Belly could play the battle of the bands."

Chloe thinks I'm making fun of her, but I'm not. When she was a child we always invented silly little scenarios like this, usually as bedtime stories. Inevitably, the superhero adventures we starred in ended with me captured by a villain just like Bronislavis Stylptitch, and Chloe had to rescue me.

"You know who else is a big influence on Lifting Belly?" Chloe slips from behind her kit and dips into the inlets of her wadded duvet, fishing for a CD. "I recognized the name from your collection right away. Liz Phair, *Exile in Guyville*."

"Whoa. Now that's a blast from the past."

The summer I graduated high school I only had ears for Liz Phair. I think it had to do with going to college. Although tuneful and limber, *Exile in Guyville* is an aggressive collection of songs about lust, rage, and regret. Those emotions hung in the air thicker than humidity in my small Southern hometown, but none of the women that I knew could express them—not verbally, anyway. Same for men. Big ideas where I grew up were about as unpopular as Democrats and the IRS. Somehow I got it into my head that the University of Georgia would be chock-full of women as intelligently assertive as Liz Phair and that I could learn from them. Maybe the women would even be as profane as Liz was. I'd be lying if I didn't admit the thought of that excited me. I remember a representative lyric from *Guyville*: *I'll fuck you and your minions, too.* Those were words my prom date definitely didn't say as we cruised through the Dog 'N' Suds ordering cheese fries. Believe it or not, in context, the line

Kirk Curnutt

is rather sweet and reassuring, not crude at all. I played *Exile in Guyville* so often that summer that Liz Phair pretty much served as my surrogate id.

"What made you grab this?" I ask as Chloe hands me the jewel case. On the cover, Liz Phair, dressed as an exuberant gypsy in a dark bonnet, swoops toward the camera, her mouth open and head cocked back so her neck is a long plunge of pale skin leading to a nipple, barely visible along the bottom right edge.

"I don't know. What made you grab it way back when?"

"She was smart. Smart-tough. I respect smart-tough."

"She's not ugly, either."

"No, she's not. I remember liking her philtrum."

"Her what?"

"Her philtrum. It's the space between your nose and lip. Hers is shaped like a raindrop. It's cute."

As I scan *Exile's* back jacket, I spot a title I'd forgotten: "Fuck and Run." It's a great song about a woman who grows tired of presumptive sex. *Whatever happened to a boyfriend?* the narrator wants to know. *The kind of guy who tries to win you over?* The man takes intimacy for granted and looks at the gestures of affection women expect ("letters and sodas") as burdensome demands. In this way, the song's a plea for romance. And it's got a sweet lilt of a tune, right up to the chorus when the rhythm tightens and a tambourine claps on each downbeat and the narrator rebukes herself for having needs she knows won't be satisfied. *I can feel it in my bones / I'm gonna spend another year alone / It's fuck and run, fuck and run / Even when I was seventeen.* It's serious emotional stuff, not crude for crudity's sake, and yet the sight of that word in my daughter's bedroom, a room in which not twenty-four hours ago her boyfriend ran after he fu–

I can't even think the word, much less say it.

"Chloe, you know I've never had a problem with you borrowing my CDs. I've always wanted you to because music was something we could share. There are words and ideas, though, that I'm not sure you're ready for. Before you grab a CD, next time ask me first, okay?"

She gives me that look of bafflement that the human face only forms between the ages of twelve and twenty, the look of supreme indignity that says, "You can't be serious."

"You can't be serious," Chloe says.

"I am. Hold on, I have an idea." I dash up to my study to grab a different CD. Chloe isn't impressed with my selection. "Who's Maria McKee?" she wants to know.

"Maria McKee is awesome, that's who she is. She was in a band called Lone Justice when I was a kid. One of my stepsisters played the hell out of her. There's one real torcher on here, 'Dixie Storms,' that I absolutely loved because it made me think of your grandmother. Don't try covering it, though."

"Why? You don't think I can sing?"

I tell her not to be so sensitive. Maria McKee has a heck of a voice, and Chloe hasn't had much experience singing. She's been too busy learning to lay down a beat. I assure her that she's as great a drummer as I've ever heard, male or female, and that Maria McKee is as awesome as Liz Phair, just in a different way.

"Different how?" asks Chloe. "As in, Maria McKee

doesn't talk about sex and stuff?"

She gives my offering an indifferent once-over before tossing the CD to her duvet.

"You know, sweetie, if there's anything we need to talk about—*anything*—you can come to me. You know that, right?"

"Anything but Liz Phair, huh?" Chloe slides back on her mattress, sulkily devoting her attention to an open notebook. I'd ask her what she's reading, but I get the distinct impression I'm not wanted, so I leave.

Just to prove who's in charge around here, I take *Exile in Guyville* with me.

Upstairs, in my study, I call my best friend and ask if it's a bad thing that my recently deflowered sixteen-year-old listens to Liz Phair. Campbell doesn't have time for my angst, however. This afternoon she ran home in the rain to discover a letter waiting for her from a lawyer. Her ex-husband, Steve, is petitioning to reduce his child support. He claims he took a salary cut with his new job and that he can't afford to pay $550-per-month for Lleyton. I reassure Campbell that no judge reduces a woman's child support, even though I suspect it happens all the time. Then I realize Campbell is worried less about money than about getting dragged into court.

"I shouldn't have called Steve," she says, "but I was so fucking pissed I couldn't help myself. The call proved exactly what I knew. This is him playing hardball. He told me so. If I fight this petition and we go in front of a judge the first thing Steve intends to do is testify that I've been gay. I could lose Lleyton. Courts in Alabama aren't friendly to lesbian moms. Imagine how they'll treat a bisexual one. He's going to put my whole history on trial."

"What do you mean by 'been gay'?" I ask. "Did I miss something? Have you flipped the switch again? And who's the guy? Because I will have to strangle this interloper in a jealous rage."

Campbell laughs, but not in a relieved way. More in a "you-may-wish-my-switch-had-been-flipped-when-you-hear-what-I-told-Steve" sort of way. A deep, hesitant breath swallows our phone connection.

"I sort of said we'd gotten back together," she blurts.

"We who?"

"You-and-me we."

I let out an inadvertent *wow*. I'm flattered. "I've never gotten to be someone's—wait, what's the male version of a beard called? A 'merkin,' right? But did you think about how Luther will react to the news that we're back together? Never mind the guy I was going to kill. *I'm* the dead man."

Campbell admits she wasn't thinking about anything when she lied to Steve. "It slipped out of my mouth in a panic. I don't know what I'm going to do, Vance. If I tell him I was bullshitting him he'll claim I must be lying about everything else concerning Lleyton. There won't be a single part of my life his lawyer won't stick under a microscope."

I offer to run out for wine and Chinese food so we can talk in person, but Campbell doesn't want company right now. Hearing the anxiety in her voice, I realize how much I've imposed on her today with Chloe, and I feel bad. Campbell gets off the line hastily, saying she needs to call her dad for advice. Those words set off a pang in my heart. As nosy and overbearing as Luther is when it comes to his daughter's personal life, Campbell still consults him about everything: relationships, money, work. The only topic off the table is me. As I ease back in my chair, I listen to Chloe practice a funky, syncopated pattern on her kit. If it weren't for the buzzing rattle her snare flams ignite in my lampshades, I would think she's a million miles away. My eyes fall on my old copy of *Exile in Guyville*, and I wish suddenly I'd said something smarter when Chloe asked what I liked about Liz Phair. Who listens to a singer's music because her philtrum is cute? Why did I take the CD away from her? It's only words and music, only ideas.

Rummaging my desk drawers, I pull out a Walkman I haven't touched in a decade. I find some AA batteries in the kitchen and then, back in my study, I slip the CD onto the spindle and hit play. In many ways the music seems more complex, more elusive even, than I remember it being when I was eighteen. That's because I'm not really listening to the songs. I'm pretending I'm eavesdropping on Chloe as she loses herself in them for the first time. I imagine overhearing Liz Phair through my daughter's ears, hoping it'll help me know what she thinks, feels, fears.

This is research, and it's hard work.

# II

**FaTHER Figuring**

# 6

On Monday I have to mow the grounds at Macon Place before the book club from the library arrives. Before Storm died, mowing wasn't in my job description; my job was to hire the guys who mowed. Immediately after his father's will was read, Mike froze the estate's maintenance account, hoping to pressure me into selling, and I quickly discovered that I'm a better Jeeves than a gardener. Before I rev up the blades I walk the grass perimeter inventorying the overgrown lantana and yarrow, the shriveling roses and browning petunias. I'll have to dig deeper into my savings and hope a landscaper can teach me how to keep this stuff alive until I can open Macon Place—*if* I can ever open it.

Within minutes, the morning humidity soaks my shirt, so I peel it off and hang it from the grass catcher. Because I'm not used to the zero-degree turn radius, I do a couple of practice 360°s before trimming around the first of Storm's two hundred alabaster sculptures. Every so often I stop to gather beer bottles and hamburger wrappers from the mosaics of caladium and phlox. At times like this I think Mike is right to say my dreams for Macon Place are pie-in-the-sky. In ancient Greece an idyllic garden like this was a place to praise gods and beg divine mercies. In Willoughby it's where teenagers come to party and pet. Storm was barely interred under the giant magnolia that shades his mansion before kids started sneaking onto the property. Some days as I water or weed, I find that Hermes, the gods' messenger, now cradles a decapitated Barbie doll;

that the armless Venus of Melos sports mannequin hands; that the wings of the Nike of Samothrace are draped with discarded panties; that Lord Byron's famous tribute to the Dying Gaul–HE CONSENTS TO DEATH, YET CONQUERS AGONY–has been crossed out in ketchup and replaced with HE'S QUEER; that busts of Zeus and Hera have been wrapped in toilet paper; or that the genitals of various Athenas, Homers, Socrates, satyrs, piping Pans, diadem wearers, and maidens playing knuckle bones have either been fitted with prophylactics or painted metallic red with fingernail polish.

This morning I discover the vandals are up to their favorite mischief. They've egged the statuary's center-piece, the Aphrodite of Knidos.

I idle the mower to flick away a pair of shells fashioned into makeshift pasties, glad that my former boss isn't here to witness this blasphemy. Aphrodite was his favorite item in his collection. He commissioned her in 1933 with money he made from bootlegging when he was barely twenty. Storm spent nearly eight decades telling visitors to his garden the story of how Aphrodite became the first nude in Western art. His passion for her could be unsettling, pervy even. He would squat to gaze into her eyes, roll a hand across her breasts, then scramble around her flanks to tap at her tailbone. I often overheard him tell guests about the hand that she holds at her genitals. The *pudica gesture*, scholars call it. For later artists like Botticelli, it became a sign of shame. That was the exact opposite of how the original artist who first sculpted the figure c. 360 B.C. regarded it. For Praxiteles that hand was an assertion of divine power. Other times Storm would grouse that whenever historians want to condemn Aphrodite's nudity, they dredge up the rumor that she was modeled on Praxiteles's mistress, a whore named Phryne.

On my first official day as his Jeeves, Storm kicked off my new career by narrating a disturbing legend about the statue. It involved a young Roman tourist who killed himself upon damaging the Aphrodite of Knidos in the little seaport of what is now Tekir in southwest Turkey. Or maybe it wasn't the story that struck me as weird but the comment Storm made afterward. "You should've named her that," he told me. He was looking at Chloe, whom I'd brought with me that first day because our babysitter called in sick.

"Named her what?" I asked.

"Aphrodite, of course. You'll understand someday."

Because I was paid to entertain such eccentricity, I couldn't admit that to my ears Aphrodite sounded like a good stage name for a stripper, or a porn star. I was really glad I kept my mouth shut when I learned that Storm had christened his own daughters Clytemnestra, Hestia, and Demeter.

After I finish scraping dried yolk from Aphrodite's nipples, I phone Chloe, thinking she's probably still asleep. She has more initiative than I give her credit for. She's at Luther's studio already, recording a drum track for one of my girlfriend Sadie's songs. I remind my daughter that she's scheduled to serve as hostess for today's book-club meeting and that she needs to get to Macon Place sooner rather than later.

"You never said anything about me working today," she complains.

"I most certainly did–I told you Saturday. That was our deal, remember? If I paid Stu to bleach the baseboards so you could run around with Campbell, then you would help me out today. Now come open the front gate and wait for me downstairs. I don't think I can clean up before the catering gets here, so you need to be on the lookout for the food truck."

Hanging up, I ride the mower up the hill to Storm's Greek Revival mansion and park it next to the John Deere Gator in the garage. In the master bedroom where my former boss died peacefully in his sleep, I shower and shave, then splash on enough aftershave that if I sweat too profusely in what's supposed to be a one-hundred-degree day I won't stink. To look professional I dress in a crisp pair of white chinos, tasseled loafers, and a periwinkle polo with a nametag I ordered for the occasion. HI, I'M VANCE, it says. I'M YOUR HOST AT MACON PLACE AND I WANT TO MAKE YOU HAPPY.

"That's way creepy," Sadie told me when I showed the badge to her. "It sounds like a come-on."

When I go downstairs I find that Chloe isn't quite as concerned about customer service as I am.

"What are you wearing? I thought I told you to lose the raccoon eyes and the slogans today." I tug the sleeve of her T-shirt. GERM-FREE ADOLESCENCE, it says, the name of an old punk album by X-Ray Spex. "The ladies coming today are all retirement age, sweetie. They want to relax to cocktail piano tunes. You'll have them thinking Lydia Lunch is their noontime entertainment."

"Poly Styrene was in X-Ray Spex, not Lydia Lunch, Daddy. And I have to dress like this to play well—it gets me in character. Maybe you could remind me about these things you're relying on me for before they happen? Saturday was two days ago. I've got a lot going on. Did you even hear what I told you on the phone? *Sadie asked me to play drums on this cool song she just wrote.* You should be proud of me."

I tell her I'm indeed proud but that I'm also frazzled. I also blurt out how surprised I am that Luther is letting her record. These days he usually programs electronic drum tracks because they're faster and cheaper than hiring a human beatkeeper. I remind Chloe that she and Campbell's dad are supposed to start voice lessons after the book club leaves. This was the deal I struck with Luther yesterday when he called to guilt trip me into buying a table for his P-FLAG banquet. If I have to cough up a grand for his fundraiser, he has to donate an equal number of hours in vocal tutorials. Chloe asks if she can't start her lessons tomorrow since today is her first time in the studio "as a professional." I remind her that her band is playing in front of an audience for the first time in only three weeks. Right now she has trouble keeping pitch at the end of her lines. Luther can teach her some breath-control tricks to keep her from going flat.

"All right already, I get your point. You've told me I can't sing like Maria McKee."

She frowns in a way that seems too girly for a girl drummer. I'm almost afraid of what I'm going to tell her next because it's something that's really going to make her pout. Upstairs in one of Storm's guestrooms is the outfit I brought for her to wear for the party. Knowing my daughter, I had a feeling she would ignore my instructions and show up looking like she'd crawled out of a skate park.

"You didn't," Chloe says, stunned.

"I did. Don't worry. I brought that Ellie print sundress you like, the sage green one with the bell sleeves that's off the shoulder. Go put it on and take off that eyeliner, seriously. Three hours is all of your life I'm asking for."

She stomps off upstairs. I walk the living room and foyer spot-checking for dust bunnies until a car horn honks. I realize that I sent Chloe off to change before she had a chance to open the gate, so I rush outside and hit the button on Macon Place's stately wrought-iron fence. A train of Volvos and Priuses and Volkswagens fills the circular drive, each festooned with bumper stickers about eating organic and gun control and reproductive rights. I'm under no illusions. This gathering I'm hosting is a mercy rental. For a certain constituency in Willoughby, it's important that my plans for Macon Place succeed. If I tank and lose the estate the whole character of our little city could change. Most members of this book club moved here in the late sixties, shortly after Luther convinced Storm to rent him a plot of land where he could build a recording studio that would rival the famous Muscle Shoals facilities in the northeast corner of our state. That brought in an influx of musicians, which in turn drew writers, puppeteers, and theater people, and after them all manner of artisans. Almost to a one, the women filing into this creaky old house are either painters, weavers or macramé handicrafters, potters, graphic designers, jewelers, or glass blowers. For many years they had Willoughby all to themselves, creating a community of acceptance that nurtured everybody who considered himself an outcast, from gays, feminists, hippies, and eco-hipsters to politically progressive punks and interracial couples. Around the time Chloe and I moved here, a funny thing started to happen. Folks from bigger cities within commuting distance discovered how cheap the housing was and how little crime occurs here. They started a land rush and with them came chain stores and fast-food franchises and now golf courses. We've been two cities ever since. There's a sense among old timers that if Mike Willoughby has his way anybody who doesn't swing a nine iron or own a Land Rover will get driven out of here like a snake out of Ireland.

The ladies wander between the main parlor and the sunroom admiring Storm's antiques and paintings, all of which are predictably Greek and Roman in theme. I make small talk with them, even though I'm flustered that our caterer has yet to arrive. When I can excuse myself to the kitchen I fill an ice bucket and break open several bottles from the wine cellar to keep the guests occupied. I text the guy I'm paying eight hundred dollars to wow these women with lobster roll sliders and Thai beef wraps, telling him to shake a leg. He assures me his server for the occasion, a woman named Iris, is on her way. I guess I shouldn't be surprised. Iris is Stu's mom, and like her son, she's her own time zone.

When I go back to the sunroom, I nearly drop the tray with the wine and ice. Chloe has come downstairs, and she's changed, all right. She's put on the sundress I picked out for her, but instead of taking off her eyeliner she's ringed her sockets with enough of it that she might as well be wearing shoe polish. Two spiky pigtails poke off the top of her head like antennae. Her liquid red lipstick is puckered up in a Cupid's bow and there's a circle of dabbed rouge on each cheek with homemade freckles dotting their center. It looks as if the illegitimate daughter of Pippi Longstocking and Betty Boop straggled into my party after getting mugged.

"I can't believe you let her cut her hair off," sighs a guest helping herself to a glass of 1978 Chateau Margaux. I could use a drink myself. "That child used to have the prettiest long hair."

"She read Louise Brooks' autobiography and got infatuated with Lulu. Maybe a little too infatuated, obviously."

The woman is the book club's president, Miss Kathy. She's also our local taxidermist. There's probably not a deer head in a fifteen-mile radius that she didn't skin, stuff, and mount. As Miss Kathy sips, she slides an envelope of cash in my pocket.

"It's not much, Vance, but it's the best we could do. A little less than $2,300. I hope you can put it to good use in the garden."

I thank her and admit that I feel like a charity accepting the donation. I don't tell her today's catering bill will eat up a third of what her friends collected. I certainly don't mention that if Mike finds out I've tapped Storm's wine collection I'll end up owing more than the club's rental brought in. Meanwhile, I watch the women do their best not to gape at Chloe's deranged Kewpie-doll look. She manages to stay a few paces ahead of me as she works the crowd. It's amazing how charming she is even in full Alice Cooper mode. Not until we circle into the sunroom can I corner her next to the wide window that overlooks Storm's garden.

"How would you like for me to react to this?" I ask.

"There's nothing to react to. You said you wanted me to look pretty. This is what I think of when a man tells a woman she should look pretty. I think of a new-wave hooker."

"I never said anything about pretty, and let's leave prostitution out of the conversation while we have company. I said I want you to look 'nice.' Is that asking too much?"

Chloe stretches a leg, showing off the cracked leather of the combat boot only half-laced around her ankle.

"You grabbed an outfit from my closet, but you didn't bring shoes to go with it."

"I'm sorry. I'm even sorrier I remembered to bring your makeup bag."

We have to stop and plaster on polite smiles. Miss Kathy is headed straight for us once again. She breaks into the conversation, wondering how soon before the food is served. If the ladies keep downing wine at the rate they are, the entire membership will be drunk before the meeting is called to order.

"Ms. Iris just texted me," reports Chloe. "There was a wreck on the highway that backed up traffic, but she's pulling through the gate now. Daddy's going to help her unload while I set up the buffet. I've got to head out after that, though. I have to finish helping a friend record a song. Then my boyfriend's taking me to get my license before our band practices. Because I'm sixteen now."

"Don't you need a parent at the public-safety office, dear? For the paperwork at least?" Miss Kathy looks at me, not Chloe. I have no clue and can only blink like an idiot. I completely forgot Chloe was scheduled to get her license today.

"Ms. Iris says all I do is drive around the block and parallel park. What would they need a parent for? I'm already on the insurance. That's the main thing the license bureau wants to know. It's not inconveniencing Stu to drive me there. We're practicing after I finish recording, anyway."

I can't help myself. "Are you keeping the makeup on in your license picture?" I ask.

Our guest chuckles, and immediately I regret being a smartass. It feels as if we're ganging up on Chloe.

"Miss Kathy," Chloe says, her lips so tight her Cupid's bow is a fist, "do you notice I'm not wearing a bra? That's because Dad brought me an off-the-shoulder sundress to wear but didn't bring a strapless bra. I won't ask you to guess about my underwear. I'll just say that this morning when I got up I put on boxers. Maybe you can explain to Dad how well a pair of those go with a sundress."

"I think I'll have some more wine," Miss Kathy decides, making a hasty exit.

Chloe and I study each other, trying to decide who'll attack next and who'll parry. A light sweat glazes my forehead. I need to ask where Chloe and Stu plan to practice, but I already know the answer. My house. Without me there. Which probably means there won't be much practicing going on, at least not of the musical variety. I'm going to have to tell her there's no way Stu is allowed over if I'm not there. I'm almost scared of how Chloe will react, though. A ping on her phone breaks our deadlock.

"Miss Iris is waiting for you," she says, reading a text.

"Okay, but listen, don't go ballistic over what I'm about to say, not in front of these women. We'll talk about this tonight after dinner. I'll run you to get your license after the party, but if you and Stu plan to rehearse this afternoon, you'll need to haul your drums up here so I can keep an eye on you. I'm letting you go back to the studio even though I need your help this afternoon, but I'm not letting boys in my house unsupervised. I think we both know why."

Chloe looks at me with great disgust. "*Your* house," she says, and walks away.

I'd like to tell her that if Macon Place flops it'll be the bank's house, but I doubt that would make a difference to her right now.

As Chloe sullenly begins arranging chafing dishes and sterno sets on Storm's massive mahogany dining table, I slip through the kitchen and down the back steps. The caterer's Nissan is parked so close to the house I can barely swing the screen door open. I have to suck my gut in and squeeze sideways, the door handle practically giving me an appendectomy. Iris is on the driver's side of the tricked-out food truck, stacking cartons of hors d'oeuvres on a rolling cart. I've tried to be friendly with Stu's mom, and not simply because our kids date. Thirty years ago she played bass for what was probably the most famous band Luther ever signed to his record label. From what Luther has told me, they were darlings of the underground press for most of the Reagan era, hailed as worthy successors to the Runaways after Joan Jett busted that outfit up. Iris is also a dead ringer for Ani DiFranco, on whom I had a huge crush in her *Not a Pretty Girl* days. Like Ani, Stu's mom is dreadlocked and defiantly punky in the butch way that says she has zero interest in living up to a guy's sense of what's attractive. I suppose someday I ought to ask myself why I'm so intrigued by women who are too strong to need men. For now I'll simply wonder why Iris has never seemed to like me.

"Sorry about that wreck," I greet her, "but I'm glad you made it. Something's come up with the kids I think we need to talk about."

"You mean the band name? I'm fine with it. Pink Melon Joy is dumber than most I've heard, but at least it's not a double entendre. I told Stu in no uncertain terms could they name their group anything I can look up on urbandictionary.com."

"That's not it. What we need to talk about is a pretty big deal. I'm a little distracted keeping this book club happy. Is there a good time we could get together? His dad should be there."

Iris freezes with three thick dome-lid platters between her forearms. Her triceps are flexed and the arteries in her arms ripple. "Is that supposed to be funny?" she says.

"Sorry?"

"That crack about his dad. Is that supposed to be funny?"

I confess I don't know what she's talking about. Iris

wishes me good luck getting Stu's dad to sit down with us. Stu hasn't seen his dad since he was seven. I really have to scratch my head over that. Just last weekend the kid told me his father bought a Wellcraft boat for his place at the lake. His *weekend* place, Stu made a point of saying. Iris rolls her eyes.

"Oh, sure, Clem used to have a lake place. It was a 1982 camper van he parked by Ferry Oaks before it was platted. It's what he got me pregnant in. The only boat he ever had was a canoe, though, and he rode it straight up Shit Creek by screwing around on me. Don't call me racist, but last I heard he was fond of making black babies." Her glare hardens. "You understand why Stu didn't tell you this, don't you? He's afraid you wouldn't let him around Chloe if you knew he didn't have a daddy. I told him you were a better man than that. I said you wouldn't punish a kid for his old man's mistakes. After all, nobody gives Chloe any grief because of you."

This is the type of snarky aside that makes me wonder what I did to earn Iris's dislike. I point out that the last time I checked, Chloe's *mom* was the one who cut out on her, not me.

"True," agrees Iris, "but from the way Chloe talks about her mom, I can't see her running around with the wait staff at Katfish Kountry. I don't normally rub folks' noses in gossip, but remember, I'm a woman whose ex-would rather make new babies than pay for the old ones. I don't have a lot of tolerance for the old fuck-and-duck-out routine you boys like to pull."

She realizes she can't carry her rolling cart up the steps with the Nissan parked so close to the back door.

Before I can defend myself she's in the food truck, swearing as she guns the accelerator and jerks back three feet without bothering to look in her rearview for anybody behind her. We're in the kitchen before I get a chance to respond.

"Hey, I don't know what you heard about me, but that Katfish Kountry thing? That was *a* waitress, not the entire 'wait staff.' We're not talking about me, anyway. This is about your son and my daughter. Stu tried to buy condoms at Walmart last week. We both know what that means."

Iris is genuinely surprised. Her forehead knots tighter than her dreadlocks. "I don't know why he would buy condoms," she says. "I've always bought them for him."

Now my forehead wrinkles.

"Don't act so shocked, Dr. Seagrove. How old were you when you had Chloe?"

I ignore the fact that Iris pronounces "Dr." as if it gives her menstrual cramps and admit that I was twenty-one when I became a father. She cuts me off to explain that she was *nineteen* when she had Stu's stepbrother, as if we're competing. She was thirty-five when she had Stu. Both kids were accidents, sixteen years and two men apart. Iris has handled all the accidents she intends to in life. She's not raising grandbabies. "I put condoms in my kids' hands the minute they got girl crazy. When Stu started mooncalfing over that Chelsea Bruccoli I–"

"Whoa, whoa, whoa," I interrupt her. "*Chelsea Bruccoli?* Little-Debbie-Cakes-looking Chelsea?" I just bought a Boston butt from a kid named Chelsea Bruccoli for a Baptist church fundraiser not three weeks ago. It's the same Baptist church where Nina's dad, Luke Laughlin, is the choir director. "Are you telling me Chloe's not the first girl Stu's been with? Does Chloe know this?"

Iris lays out the platters on the kitchen table and begins popping off the dome lids. By the time she peels back the plastic wrap, the air is thick with the smell of lobster roll sliders and Thai beef wraps, cheese, relish, deviled eggs, and horse radish. I suddenly feel heavy with responsibility and choices, as if I've crammed every morsel of this spread in my fat mouth. Meanwhile, Iris talks about our kids' sex lives as nonchalantly as reciting a recipe.

"Stu is eighteen," she shrugs. "Show me a boy who waits that long to lose his virginity and I'll show you the chip on his shoulder. He and Chelsea broke up a year ago. You don't have to worry about him screwing around on Chloe. Or about giving her a STD. Didn't I just tell you I raised my sons to respect women?"

I pop a cheese straw down my gullet hoping to choke before I say what I need to.

"Look, I don't want to piss you off, Iris, but there's a legal concern we need to talk about. Chloe is sixteen *as of Friday.* That means if they were active before that day, then—well, you know—we've got a statutory issue on our hands. As you just admitted, Stu is eighteen. According to the law, he's an adult. That means the consequences for him could be serious."

Iris rolls her tongue inside her cheek. "Are you going to the police?" she asks after a hard stare.

"No, of course not. Not unless I have to. Unless I have a reason, I mean."

Kirk Curnutt

What I want to say is that if I were Bronislavis Stylptitch and I ruled a whole country her little shithead would go to the gallows for leaving a condom wrapper in his girlfriend's father's house.

"Since you've brought this up," Iris decides, taking the offensive, "we should talk about Chloe's responsibility in this situation. I'm not saying she's this way, but some girls look at babies as a way of keeping boys. Ask my ex-husband's girlfriends. It's naïve. Babies don't oblige men to anything, do they? Stu shouldn't have to shoulder the burden of making sure Chloe doesn't get pregnant. It's unfair to him. He's been through enough in life."

I try to be polite. "I'm not sure I understand what you're asking of me."

"I'm not asking anything." Iris chomps a deviled egg in two, barely bothering to chew before swallowing. "I'm saying. I'm *saying* that if you're a responsible parent, Vance Seagrove, you'll get your daughter on birth control. Otherwise, the next time you and I have an argument, it'll be over which of us is gonna babysit our grandkid."

# 7

Iris's words keep me rattled throughout the entire party. When the book club adjourns, Stu's mom senses my agitation and tells me to go ahead and get my head on straight. She promises to wash the dishes and straighten up while she waits for Mike to swing by. He owes her a check for cleaning his house, something Iris has been doing since doctors ordered Mike's wife, Terri, to avoid physical exertion in her last trimester. I ride the estate's golf cart down the road behind Macon Place to Luther's studio. It's not an easy place to miss, despite the thick copse of blackjack oaks in which it sits. Next to the gravel lane bisecting the trees is a huge sign listing the famous acts that have recorded here, headed no less than by the Rolling Stones. What the sign doesn't say is that the one track they cut on their way to Muscle Shoals to do "Brown Sugar" and "Wild Horses" in 1969 was so bad that it's never been released.

"Where are the kids?" I ask when I find Luther hustling between a drum kit and the control booth. "I'm taking Chloe to get her license this afternoon."

Unaccustomed to recording live drums, Luther is testing microphone levels on his digital soundboard. By the looks of things he's been doing this for several hours now. Maybe he'd have an easier time if his new albino Chihuahua weren't yapping at his every move.

"I haven't seen Chloe since you told her to hightail it up to the house," Luther tells me. "I'm missing a songwriter, too. Sadie ran off to come up with a new bridge for this piece we're trying to get down, but I would bet that she's getting high. You need to talk to her about her smoking, Vance. She's toking up way too often. Quiet, Edgar!"

The Chihuahua's name is Edgar Winter.

"Chloe wasn't at Storm's place more than a half hour." I pull out my phone and dial her, but she doesn't answer. "Dammit, she said she was coming right back here. Now I'm going to have to head to my house and make sure she and Stu didn't go straight there knowing I'd be held up most of the day."

"You can't go busting in on them," scoffs Luther. "If those kids went there thinking you were out of their hair you don't know what you're liable to walk in on. You'll humiliate the poor girl, shame her. Just stay here until you hear from her, and then you can talk to her."

I can't believe I'm exiled from my own house. I don't know what other options I have, though, besides filling up Chloe's voicemail. Against my will, I picture kicking open a bedroom door and catching her and Stu in the white heat of teenage passion. The thought makes me want to Clorox my brain. As Edgar nips at my toes, I distract myself by admiring the photos decorating Luther's studio. His Wall of Fame features pictures of him with every celebrity he's come within ten feet of meeting during his fifty-plus years in the music business. Here he is hugging Donna Fargo during her "Happiest Girl in the Whole U.S.A." heyday; here squeezing between a tolerant Captain and Tennille when the latter (a Montgomery native) was inducted into the Alabama Music Hall of Fame; even him with Jim "Dandy" Mangrum of Black Oak Arkansas after B.O.A. headlined our local Elmore

County Fair last summer. In his younger pictures Luther sports kinky hair and a Fu-Manchu mustache and looks more like a Molly Hatchet roadie than Samuel Clemens. Sadly, the images remind me of how much weight he's lost since his prostatectomy. Smack dab in the center of his wall is his prized possession, a gold record for a 1964 Joan Baez album called *Riding Freedom's Wheels.* Luther wrote the title track during a brief career as a folksinger in the early sixties.

"Do me a favor," he nods. "Go hit that floor tom. And you, Edgar, you shut up!"

I tell Luther he should've gotten himself a new woman instead of a new dog to celebrate the success of his surgery. He's not in the mood for teasing. He reminds me how few single women there are in Willoughby. "Few that are my age, anyway," he adds. Now that he knows Sadie and I are dating, he'll never miss an opportunity to remind me of our age difference. To get him back I station myself behind the drum kit and do my best Gene Krupa, which sounds more like Animal from *The Muppet Show.* Edgar buries his head under a blanket. Luther yanks off his headphones and angrily rubs his ears.

"Let's talk about *your* daughter for a change," I say. "I know you talked to Campbell about her ex-husband. I hope you've convinced her to take Steve back to court. I can't believe that toad's trying to weasel a reduction in his child support. In some ways it's even harder to believe Campbell is afraid of him. The courts won't let Steve drag her through the mud just because she's a lesbian."

"Oh, I can believe it. The environment in this state is hostile to gay parents."

"But this whole business of Campbell lying to Steve saying she's not gay anymore–or again, I guess–and then telling him she and I are back together, that's gonna backfi–"

From the pained expression crossing Luther's face I know right away that Campbell didn't tell him this part of the story. For as much crap as I've taken from the man over my friendship with his daughter, there's a part of me that would like to gloat over this fact. I can't because I know Campbell will be mad that I told her dad about the ruse. Luther hobbles into the main room and sinks into a chair, muttering profanities and wondering aloud what his daughter is thinking. When he can gather his senses he wonders what Sadie thinks about this lie. The question puts me in a corner. I have to admit to Luther that I've never exactly told my girlfriend that my best friend and I know each other in the Biblical sense. My confession brightens Luther's mood. Now he has dirt on me. He shakes his head and says he can't believe I've lied to Sadie. "No wonder you can't make it past six months with a woman," he makes sure to add.

"I never *lied* about it," I clarify, "not blatantly, anyway. I don't know why I've never been straight up with Sadie. It's easier not to, I suppose. How do you tell your girlfriend you've dated a gay woman? It's hard to explain. But you're my main point, Luther. We need to nip this lie of Campbell's in the bud."

I go back to banging the floor tom. Edgar yaps. Luther shuffles to the upright piano pushed against his east wall and flips down the console, deciding he needs a drink. Inside the piano isn't a wrest plank of strings and tuning pins, but a fully stocked bar. Luther may be Willoughby's most prominent rock 'n' roller, but he's also a genteel Southerner, and that means he hides his liquor from public view.

After two glasses he brightens up even more and decides the time is right to remind me again about his P-FLAG fundraiser. I groan and start counting out bills from the donation that the book club gave me. Between Iris and now Luther, the envelope is down to $200.

"You don't want to let somebody buy your table out from under you," Luther assures me with tipsy grin. "You'll miss Chloe's debut. She and Sadie are doing a duet."

This is news to me. The banquet is only four days away and Chloe hasn't even had her first voice lesson yet. I tell Luther the banquet is too soon and that she'll embarrass herself. I'm not sure if his sour pucker is because of me or his port.

"Jesus, you're not this encouraging to Chloe's face, are you? It might give her a big head, make her conceited. Who knows? She might go so far as to feel good about herself."

I tell him I'm not discouraging Chloe; I'm protecting her. I don't tell him that between the wrapper in her trash and the story of Stu at the Walmart I don't feel as if I've done a good job of that lately. Luther decides I need a primer on my daughter. He tells me what a good head Chloe has on her shoulders, how creative and intelligent she is, how very adult. How she's the sparkplug of his youth group.

"Her maturity is refreshing, too," he says. "Most of

Kirk Curnutt

those other church kids want to talk about sex when I try to talk Buddhism. I guess I shouldn't expect more from teenagers."

"Chloe talks about sex at church?"

"No, no, no. Not often anyway. Haven't I already said this? Chloe's a good kid. You have nothing to worry about. Now if you were Nina's father…"

I ask how long Sadie and Chloe have been planning a duet at the banquet. After some hemming and hawing, Luther admits it's been in the works for a couple of weeks. I wonder aloud why Chloe didn't tell me about it. I want to believe she planned it to surprise me. Luther quickly disabuses me of that notion.

"She's afraid you'll say just what you told me. *You're not ready; you'll embarrass yourself.* Don't you think she's worried enough about flopping that she doesn't need to hear it from you? When Chloe looks at you, Vance, she doesn't just see her father. She sees her fear of disappointing herself standing right in front of her. The voice of doubt in her head speaks in the dulcet tones of Dr. Big Daddy Seagrove."

In case I don't get his point, Luther decides I need to hear a story. He asks if he's ever told me about the time he sang for Martin Luther King, Jr. He has, many times, but I play dumb and let him narrate his tale. It was during the Selma-to-Montgomery March way back in 1965. *Riding Freedom's Wheels* was on the *Billboard* charts that spring, and because its composer was from Alabama, Luther was invited to perform at one of the rallies Dr. King was headlining. Only when Luther stepped up to the microphone, he *stank.* His voice cracked, he went off-key, he forgot a line of the chorus. But none of that mattered. After the rally, Dr. King came up, shook his hand, and thanked him for joining the Civil Rights Movement. The Rev. Martin Luther King, Jr. thanked *Luther*.

"What does this have to do with Chloe?" I ask him.

"My point is that Chloe can sound like Alvin and the Chipmunks on Thursday night and nobody will give a damn. It's the gesture that's important. The people who're coming to this banquet want to know that kids her age aren't homophobic. Parents and families of the LGBT community around here need to know it. They feel like Willoughby's not theirs anymore. Chloe wants to sing with Sadie to show solidarity with these people, not to show off in front of them. Solidarity is what you should be proud of, not her breath control."

Before I can respond, we're serenaded by a ringtone version of the old Walter Murphy hit, "A Fifth of Beethoven." It's Chloe's latest prank. Once or twice a week she spirits off my phone to program in the golden oldies she's convinced are the soundtracks of my life.

"Hey, Daddy. Where are you at?"

"I'm in the studio where you're supposed to be. What's this business about you singing for P-FLAG? Why am I hearing this from Luther?"

Chloe doesn't answer. I have to fill in the silence myself.

"You didn't want me knowing, did you?"

She takes a desperate breath. "I just thought it'd be easier not to have you...that I could do it without you... that it'd be cool to surprise you?"

"Nice try. Newsflash: I don't like not knowing what's

Kirk Curnutt

going on. You're keeping a few too many secrets from me lately. Now, where are you right now so I can come get you? We need to get your license."

"That's why I'm calling. Don't get mad, but I'm already at the testing center. Stu told me that no matter what time you go, forty people are in line ahead of you, and it takes hours to get anything done, so I went ahead and had him bring me here. I'll be home by dinner. Later, Daddy."

She hangs up, leaving me gazing blankly at Luther.

"If I let Chloe sing at your banquet," I tell him, "you have to do me a favor."

Luther shrugs and says sure, anything I need. I boot Edgar away from the heel of my loafer, which he's sunk his teeth into.

"I want to know everything she's ever said at youth group when those kids talk about sex."

# 8

Luther gives up nothing. He claims being a youth-group leader is no different than being a priest and that he has to respect his kids' confidentiality. Flustered, I leave the studio and rumble up and down Willoughby's back streets in my golf cart looking for Sadie. When I can't find my girlfriend, I retrieve my Scion and go home. Pacing the living room, I decide I've had it with being kept in the dark. If nobody's going to tell me what I need to know, I'll do my own detective work. I march to Chloe's room and go *CSI* on it.

These are the things I find

—one paperback called *Cinderella's Big Score: Women of the Punk and Indie Underground.* The title page has a scribbled inscription that reads, "To Chloe, from one tough bitch to another, Rock on, you ho! Hearts, Iris. PS: Check out p. 291." When page 291 is checked out, I discover a reference to an "Iris Pottle (b. 1962), bassist for the Wussy Pimps (1979-1992)," who "left the band briefly in 1981 to have a son," the baby "raised by Iris's stern Rome, Georgia, parents until the Pimps broke up for good, and Iris left music to settle down in suburban Alabama." The word "suburban" is underlined with an "har-har!" in the margin

—newspaper stories about the attack on Lifting Belly, with pertinent facts about Oksana Dybek, Bronislavis Stylptitch, and Herzoslovakia highlighted in yellow, pink, and blue pen

—a dozen highlighters, including yellow, pink,

and blue ones that have dried out because the caps weren't put back on

—a set of empty glasses, which explains why my cupboard's bare every time I go to grab a drink

—sticky rings under those glasses

—dust, everywhere

—one computer, which when scoured proves to contain nothing more incriminating than a Word-Press.com website devoted to Lifting Belly. I know Chloe is the creator of this feed aggregator for social-media mentions of the world's most famous incarcerated feminist art collective. That's because the headline says KEEPING EYES ON THE STORY WILL EFFECT EVENTS and no matter how many times her English teacher dinged her writing last year, Chloe can't keep the difference between *affect* and *effect* straight.


I've never rooted around in my daughter's belongings before. I feel funny doing it. Not that I don't think it's my right. As many shattering revelations as I've had to shoulder the past two days, I'm not fretting about a six-teen-year-old's privacy. No, what's disconcerting is the stiffening sense that this is my introduction to Chloe.

Why would a punk-rock drummer tab a layout in *Marie Claire* advertising "Two Weeks to a Better Butt"?

Why would a young woman who just bobbed her hair Louise Brooks-style have a coupon on her desk for extensions?

Who gave her this new poster hanging above her nightstand, the one on which the seemingly naked blonde covered only by a guitar sits above the legend Lɪᴢ Pʜᴀɪʀ?

I must answer these questions, so I shovel through the snowdrifts of paper strewn throughout the room.

Among them I find

—a list of potential band names that are uniformly terrible (Kittyfeather, The Pretty Accidents, Heavy Duty Water Damage, The Old 1998s)

—a rough draft of verse, presumably the lyrics to Chloe and Stu's song for the battle of the bands.

They read, in part

*Darkness in this pen*
*Darkness is my friend*
*Through the darkness send*
*Darkness in the end.*

But that's not all.

There's also

—a note addressed to Stu, folded with origamic precision and written in swirling, calligraphic loops that bring to mind Catherine and Heathcliff romping across some foggy moor.

It goes

*Dearestcoolestlovingestfunnesthottest,*
*I hope you're not mad at me because I'm not mad*
*at you. I'm sorry we fought last night but I'm tired*
*and algebra is killing me. I have to make an 88 on*

*this test or I'll end up with a C and that's never*
*happened to me before. You don't know how hard it*
*is at the Academy. I wish we were together at*
*Willoughby High. I know you don't worry about this*
*kind of stuff bc you are a natural-born genius, but I*
*do so please stand with me and help me because*
*that's what I would do for you. I love you!*
  *Chloe...*

—and Stu's response, which is noticeably less effusive.
It begins

*Hey*

and continues, in its entirety,

*No problem.*

I move to the closet. It's supposed to be a walk-in, but
it's packed so tight I can barely squeeze a shoulder inside.
What I discover

—an avalanche of dirty clothes piled beside the empty
hamper I bought so Chloe would stop throwing laundry
on the floor
—hangers, pork rinds, and a jar of peanut butter,
inexplicably sitting side-by-side
—pictures from a spring pool party: Chloe and Nina,
their apparent nicknames scribbled next to their
shoulders (Rockjaw and Fat Ass, respectively); Stu in a
swimsuit, showing off a chest that's so white that I

wonder if I squint I can spot a polar bear or baby seal stranded somewhere in the middle of it; Stu bookended by Chloe and Nina, one hand clasped to each girl's hip, his face torn in two by the biggest shit-eating grin I've ever seen–

But that's okay, I decide, because there's not a beer bottle or bong anywhere in sight.

And nobody's making out.

I sit on the edge of Chloe's bed. I should be happy. I haven't come across another wrapper or any other sign that she's sexually active. Yet all I see reflected in her full-length mirror is sadness, a crushing, annihilating sadness. The only thing of me in the room is a single framed image, the worst photograph I've ever taken. Lips stretched wide, tongue stuck to one side, eyes rolled upwards as if trying to curl them over my lids–this was supposed to be a goofy face made to entertain a five-year-old marveling at the magic of a Polaroid camera, but my expression now seems evidence of something more incriminating–frivolousness, irrelevance, wolfish-ness even....

Because the frame sits on Chloe's nightstand directly under her new poster, I appear to be gaping lasciviously up Liz Phair's thighs.

I turn the picture to the wall.

I don't need much acknowledgment. I certainly don't expect to find the little drawings and construction-paper cards she colored for me before she turned ten. Years ago I stored those mementos in a closet knowing that the time would come when expressing unreserved affection for her father would make Chloe uncomfortable. Every so often I pull those cards out and reread them. They're humbling. In them my hair may be green and my lips purple, but I'm always taller and handsomer than I am in real life. I like that image because the exaggeration allows me to feel I've lived up to the words that Chloe invariably signed her artwork with back then: *I love you.*

I don't expect that sentiment from a sixteen-year-old, unless it's Christmas, Father's Day, the occasional birthday that Chloe bothers to remember, or those Saturday nights when she asks for twenty dollars and I give her thirty. What's the more likely emotion from a teenager? Resentment? I could handle that. I flip through one of the many notebooks chucked to the carpet, imagining myself the subject of an angry journal entry or poem. I can see Chloe scribbling a pseudo-Sylvia Plath diatribe, one of those disturbingly off-kilter rants that roils with nursery-rhyme invective: *Gibbeldy, gobbeldy, gabbeldy goo. Screw you, Daddy—no, seriously, Screw you!* At least then I'd know I was on her mind. Yet to be so completely absent.... It's as if when she shuts her bedroom door, I don't exist.

I drop the notebook to my feet, noticing a shoebox sticking out from under the bed. It's full of old cassettes, mostly late eighties/early nineties stuff I'm embarrassed I ever owned. Chloe must've dug the box from the hall closest without asking. But why? We don't even have a cassette player in the house anymore.

Turnabout is fair play, I decide. I drop to all fours and squint between her bed legs. Only vague outlines are visible: shoes and slippers, a book bag, an umbrella, more clothes. I would reach in to sort this treasure, but I don't like to touch anything I can't see, so instead I hop up and squeeze my fingers under her box springs. I can flip it and the mattress up with just a grunt. Only I no sooner get them at a diagonal than I step on a notebook–the same notebook I just dropped–and my footing slides out from under me. Before I know it I fall through the bed frame. The box springs tip back down, crashing onto my hindquarters. I'm face down in a corduroy wad. Not a half-inch from my nose is what appears to be a dirty paper plate. I try to leverage my weight to pop the bed off of me, but a metal edge is slicing my thigh, and I can't get my right foot to the ground to get traction. Either I wait to be rescued by the jaws of life, or I'm reduced to wiggling ass-backwards out of this embarrassment.

With a few thrusts and jerks I manage to free myself. Only from the bed–not the humiliation.

Because standing in the doorway, horrified looks on their faces, are Chloe and Nina.

# 9

The sign says HELP US REDUCE THE SIN OF ABORTION.

It's the mission of the Willoughby Pregnancy Center, which sticks out like a sore thumb next to Chub and Joe's, a diner that's served this town since 1901, long before Storm came down from the Tennessee mountains with a trunkful of stump juice to hawk on the sly, and even longer before our humble burg was so grateful that his money brought it back from the brink of bankruptcy that the city fathers renamed it in his honor. For a minute I consider entering the center to inquire about the pros and cons of pills, rings, patches, and IUDs. Too many potential rubberneckers lurk here along Company Street. Thanks to my misadventure with a certain Katfish Kountry waitress, I've given locals enough to gossip about for one lifetime. Besides, the townspeople I'm friendly with are none too happy about an anti-abortion group setting up shop smack dab in the middle of our historic district, and I can't afford to be seen as a Benedict Arnold. The center appeared without warning after a rumor circulated that a Birmingham doctor planned to build a reproductive health clinic right outside the city limits. More conspiratorial folks claim the story was planted to give the Family Pregnancy Center an excuse for moving into our midst. They say the center is part of Mike Willoughby's plot to take over our little Utopia and make it as right-wing as the rest of our red state. I doubt Mike is behind this group, though. Conspiracies require subtlety, and that's not something he's known for. What I can say for certain is that staring at the word "pregnancy" after gobbling down a $2.99 plate of biscuits and gravy from Chub and Joe's is not good for one's digestion. I know that if I'd simply addressed the wrapper issue with Chloe on Saturday, I could've avoided making things ten times harder as they are now. It's not easy to reassure yourself that your daughter is discovering her sexuality wisely and safely when she refuses to speak to you.

I cross Company Street and head toward the realty company where my best friend works as an office manager. Along the way, I pass the former home of the Christ the Redeemer Church, which recently reopened as a teen cantina called the Tabernacle. The name caused a minor stir because nobody could decide whether it was blasphemous or not. Maybe it is. I spy a flier taped to the window:

COMING SOON—WORLD DEBUT—PINK MELON JOY
WE KNOW YOUR WAITING

Jesus Christ. Is it too much to expect my daughter to lose her virginity to a boy who knows the difference between *you're* and *your*?

"I'm guessing she's still mad," I say to Campbell after I tap at the stenciled letters on her plate-glass window and we stand together under the awning. "Usually by this time of the morning she's called me twice to run errands for her."

Chloe was so angry last night that she stayed at Campbell's.

"She brought Lleyton up here an hour ago," Campbell reports. "She was fuming because you hadn't called this morning."

Kirk Curnutt

"I called her last night–four times. She wouldn't answer her phone."

"That doesn't mean she wanted you to stop calling. You really don't get women, do you, Vance? I can't say I blame her. What were you doing in her bed?"

I explain that I wasn't in Chloe's bed, just under it, but that distinction is meaningless to Campbell. She says I'm screwing the situation up, just as she predicted I would. She asks if my parents ever rifled my room this brazenly when I was a teenager. I remind her that my mom passed away before I was old enough to have anything worth hiding. My dad hardly knew I lived in his house. I did have a stepmother who could've stepped straight out of the pages of *1984*, but she had daughters older than I was to go totalitarian on. I wasn't much of a menace to society until I got Chloe's mom pregnant. I think what shocked my old man most was that I was even capable of that.

"What are you looking at?" I ask.

"I think it's Minnesota." Campbell points at my cheek. I've suffered from cold sores since I was a child. They pop up when I'm stressed. They only last a few days, but they're big enough that Campbell and Chloe compare them to states. If one looks like Rhode Island, it's no big deal, but if it's shaped like California, things can't get any worse. Minnesota isn't Texas, but it's no Delaware, either.

"We have Listerine in the employee lounge," says Campbell. "Hold on a sec."

She disappears inside and returns with a small bottle and a cotton ball. A second later my cheek burns like a meteor entering the atmosphere.

"Chloe has something to tell you that's very

important," Campbell says. "Don't ask me what it is because it's her news to break. When she shares it, do me a favor and don't react. Just listen. *Listen*."

She's gone again before I can quiz her. My mind goes straight to the worst case scenario. I don't have to imagine it because I've lived it. Only this time I'm not me; I'm my father reeling from the embarrassment of an unplanned pregnancy. At least I waited until he was past forty to make him a grandfather. To rid my head of these ridiculous thoughts, I play with the automated listing display mounted to the storefront. For sale not far from Luther's house is a $135,000 three-bedroom with its own guesthouse in back. *Perfect for renters, in-laws, or rambunctious teenagers*, the description reads. I'm so busy daydreaming of installing Chloe in separate quarters that I'm unaware she's barreling out the door until the Victorian knob smacks my elbow.

"How about we head home and talk?" I say, massaging my funny bone.

"How about I spot you a five-minute lead? That will give you time to dig around."

I point to a bench in front of Chub and Joe's where we can sit to talk, but I decide against it when my eyes drift to the pregnancy center next door. This is not a conversation to have with the words SIN and ABORTION at one's back. Instead we go to the picnic table under the overhang at the Chicken Shack, Willoughby's drive-up home-cooking stand.

"What were you hoping to find, Dad?" she wants to know.

"I guess I was looking for what you think I'd look for."

"Drugs? I keep my kilos in my pillowcase."

I have to resist the temptation to rake my cold sore. It's not that it itches or that it's still burning. It's just that I can feel it at the corner crease of my lip, clinging to me like dread. I slip into a riff about how all parents scope out their kids' bedrooms, how it's part of the job, how being a parent is tenuous authority. I yammer about the power I have over my daughter, how I can tell her what to do, how to act, what to wear, how I have to be very leery of not abusing the control I've been given over somebody else's life until she's an adult because in the end boundaries and barriers and what's appropriate and what's not are all so arbitrary. Although I prefer to listen to other people, I have to admit that I'm a pretty good talker. Vance Seagrove can fill some dead air when he needs to. It's why I originally went into teaching. Talking for me is just a matter of turning on the manure spreader and seeing what sticks when I let fly. As I tell Chloe, there are certain things parents are obligated to do and say so their kids know how to avoid getting in trouble. In all honesty, we wish our children knew those things from birth so we wouldn't have to get involved, but that's not how responsibility works. Parents who don't make rules are bad parents. It's inevitable, I add, that raising Chloe by myself I'll impose rules I don't follow. I'll insist certain things are wrong, and I may not really believe they are, but I have to tell her they are so she doesn't get hur–

"God, Dad, come on. What are you even talking about?"

"I'm talking about Stu, baby. I'm telling you why Stu can't come over when I'm not there."

"Stu's never been in the house when you weren't! Newsflash: Stu doesn't like to come to our house period because you're always so mean to him."

I explain to her my vision for the summer. I was up all night grappling with it, struggling to decide whether it was draconian or not. I don't think it is. I think my idea only makes sense and that in the end it'll be good for our relationship. I tell Chloe I want her to come with me to Macon Place for the rest of summer. No staying home by herself. She doesn't have to think of it as punishment. We can hang out together, all day, just like we did in the old days.

"The old days?" she says, astonished. "Like when I was *eight*?"

"That wasn't such an awful period in our lives. Listen, Chloe, it's time we have a serious talk. About you and...."

*Sex* no sooner leaves my lips than she jumps to her feet and speeds off. "No way, dude!" she squeals. I follow, insisting we should've done this already, that I need to make sure she knows what she's doing—well, not *literally* what she's doing, just that she's being safe. Chloe fires an agonized glare over her shoulder. She tells me I don't have anything to worry about and that's all I need to know. There is something else I need to worry about, however. We're bustling down the middle of Company Street and people are looking. I catch up to Chloe and try to settle her down so we don't create a spectacle.

"Listen." I talk from the side of my mouth as I smile and nod to folks watching us from the sidewalks. "Your grandfather called last night. He's coming to town this weekend. I thought we'd have a party Saturday night–me, you, Sadie, Campbell, and Lleyton. I'll let you invite Stu if we can have this talk right now. I won't make fun of him, either. Let's get this conversation over with, and we can have a good time Saturday."

Her embarrassment hardens into a taunt. "A party? That's way great. Because Mom'll be in town this weekend, too. How about I talk to her, and *she* can tell you there's nothing to worry about? You might actually believe it coming from her. Then again, probably not."

I stop in the dead middle of the blacktop. "Mom? Whose mom?"

For a second I think she means my mom, but my mom was dead ten years before Chloe was born.

"You remember her," she says. "Your ex-wife."

I do indeed remember, and I'm beyond shocked. Deb's never visited Chloe in Willoughby. For the first eight years of her daughter's life, she didn't visit at all. They didn't see each other until Chloe was in elementary school, when, out of the blue, Deb called wanting visitation. Since then she's flown Chloe to New York for a week at spring break and two in the summer. Her schedule doesn't allow for much more. She's on the road nine months at a stretch with various touring companies.

"Why is your mom coming here? She can't just show up without asking me!"

"She's not coming to see you!" We startle an innocent man stepping out of Chub and Joe's. "She's coming to see me!"

Chloe rounds the block and heads toward the

Tabernacle. The Saturn I drove before I bought my new Scion is parked there. As much of a junker as it is, I have a nostalgic attachment to it, mainly because I've owned it since Chloe was a month old. I'm put off to see the back bumper has been festooned with stickers. FREE LIFTING BELLY, one homemade one reads. Another features an illustration of Oksana Dybek smashing a guitar to smithereens. THIS IS WHAT A FEMINIST LOOKS LIKE, it says. The one that really catches my attention hits a little closer to home. DON'T DEFACE MACON PLACE, it reads. It's decorated with a picture of a golf club with a red slash through it.

"Where did this come from?" I say, tapping at the sticker with my toe.

"Stu and I made them. We've given away a lot more Macon Place ones than Lifting Belly ones. Probably fifty or sixty."

"What are you thinking, baby? Mike Willoughby will go ballistic when he sees those around town! He'll probably sic his lawyer on me with a cease and desist."

Chloe starts to say something about free speech, but too many things I can't control are pounding in my head. I can feel my throat tighten and my skin radiate heat. At this rate I'll be covered in cold sores by the end of the day, a walking, talking vat of Herpes Simplex II. I order Chloe to peel the sticker off the bumper. She stares me down, forcing me to repeat myself. This has become a contest I'm not sure I can win. The look in her glare is almost feral. I've never seen so much hostility before. Who is this person? My Chloe used to shrink and whimper when I got parental on her. Without warning she drops to a squat and rips the sticker into a wad.

"I made those for you," she says, tossing the paper peels at my feet. I don't endear myself by telling her not to litter.

Chloe hops in the Saturn and nearly mows me down as she backs out. As she shifts into first gear her disdain hardens into malevolence. Unlike her feral face, this expression strikes me as oddly familiar, even if new to her. Not until she's driving away do I realize where it comes from.

It's a look her mother used to give me.

# 10

I know how to win her back. I head out to the meat specialty store on the highway that was voted the Best Butcher Shop in Alabama last year. I blow nearly sixty bucks on a pair of high-end filets, along with double-stuffed baked potatoes, baby spinach, roasted parsnips, and the country bread croutes that Chloe loves. One of the first things I learned as a single parent was the importance of knowing how to cook. I'm pretty swift in a kitchen if I do say so myself. When Storm was alive I thought nothing of spending upwards of a thousand a month on exquisite cuisine. Chloe and I have had to cut back at the grocery since my income evaporated, but my grad-school days weren't so long ago that I haven't forgotten how to make a lowly asparagus sprig taste like the nectar of the gods. I give Chloe a couple of hours to cool down and then as I season the filets I text her to come home for a surprise dinner. While waiting for her to respond I break into a six pack of Sweetwater 420 I've been saving for a special occasion. I manage to down three of the beers before remembering to toss the potatoes in the oven. Meanwhile, nothing from Chloe. I whip up a balsamic marinade for the parsnips and then pan sear the meat so it has a nice crunch. After that I rack the skillet and just stand a while, basking in the aromas.

It's a good thing I don't set the table because when my daughter does finally message me I don't think my heart could stand the sight of her empty chair.

*Just had pizza,* she writes. *Not hungry.*

For a short while I sit on the porch watching

rainclouds drift by without breaking into a summer shower. My cold sore feels as if it's swollen to the size of Antarctica. I realize I've finished the entire pack of beer and that I'm tipsy enough to eat both filets out of pure spite. Instead, I box the food in a picnic basket and drive to my girlfriend's apartment. As generous as Sadie's fellowship from the Willoughby Family Foundation is, she still lives on a tight budget, so I know she won't turn up her nose at eight crunchy ounces. Sure enough, she's delighted by the surprise and tears into the meat as if she'd killed it herself. About halfway through dinner as we talk about the statuary at Macon Place, she reminds me that the word "aphrodisiac" comes from Aphrodite. Picking up on her signals, I start to get the idea that cooking this meal will pay dividends after all. Most people who gobble down a steak this rich would probably need to nap afterward, but not my girlfriend. She's the most sensuous person I've ever met. I don't just mean that she's very sexual, although she's certainly that. She radiates an energy I wish I could dose on, all enthusiasm and ambition. I doubt she sleeps four hours a night and I don't think she's had a down day since she left her druggie parents and rotten childhood behind. Before I met Sadie I thought "passionate" was a polite synonym for "pushy," but she's made me see that some people really are driven by an appetite to learn, experience, and to grow. Sometimes when I'm with her I could just sit and bat my eyes while she talks at me. Tonight, as she recites for me all the erotic properties the ancient Greeks associated with beets and artichokes, I want to drink butter sauce off of her lips. The dirty dishes don't even make it to the sink before our clothes hit the floor and we kiss with filet still stuck between our teeth. I'm grateful she has no qualms kissing a man blighted by cold sores. After a round of heavy-duty petting against the counter, we stumble with our legs interlocked to her bedroom.

There's just one problem.

"What's the matter?" she asks, giving me a flummoxed tug.

"Nothing's wrong. It's not automatic, you know. Sometimes you've got to work it."

"Dude, I've been working it for ten minutes. At this point I'm past work and into overtime."

"Maybe don't pull so hard then. It feels like you're trying to start a lawnmower."

She makes a valiant effort but loses patience and releases me. As she turns away and sits up, she rolls her wrist and stretches her hand as if I've given her a bad case of carpal tunnel syndrome. She ignores the conciliatory finger I run across the tattoo on her lower back. Sadie has twenty-one more of them on her body, including an Eye of Horus around her bellybutton. These oddly shaped letters at her tailbone, she's taught me, spell out *Give*, *Cooperate*, and *Control* in Sanskrit.

I explain that I drank two too many beers, but she doesn't buy the excuse. Or the one about how stressed I am lately. The truth is I don't believe either of those reasons, either. I've been far drunker on occasions when I could still deliver the goods. Maybe I've never had financial worries like the ones that Macon Place is giving me, but even out of work I still have more money in the bank than I did in graduate school, and I could rumble

Kirk Curnutt

back then like a bonobo, a species of monkey known as the horniest animal on the planet. As Sadie nabs a kimono from her closet, I want to confess the real reason that I'm swinging a pecan between my legs. I'm cursed when it comes to sex. There's no other way to say it. Thirty-seven and suddenly impotent is just the inverse of twenty and discovering you've gotten someone pregnant. In either case, the universe is laughing at your expense.

Sadie slips from the bedroom, leaving me little choice but to gird up in a bed sheet and follow. I catch up to her in the kitchen, where she squats at the refrigerator, digging for a bottle of water.

"I can explain," I promise. "This is going to sound crazy, but you have to hear me out and trust me on it. I have a theory."

"I know what you're going to say. You're going to blame Chloe for not being able to get it up. You're going to tell me you're freaked out because your daughter lost her virginity. It's an original excuse, Vance, I'll give you that."

I deflate against the sink. I can't believe everybody in this town knows Chloe's business. I ask where Sadie heard the news. I'm thinking Chloe may have confided in her about Stu, but that's not the case. Luther told her the story about Stu getting kicked out of Walmart for attempting to buy condoms. Sadie tells me not to get mad at him for spilling the beans. He wasn't gossiping; he was genuinely worried and didn't realize I hadn't told her about the incident yet. I decide I'll deal with Luther later and admit to Sadie that the Walmart isn't the most awkward part of this whole sorry business. I describe finding the wrapper in Chloe's trash basket on Saturday. Only in telling her what an upsetting experience that was, I let slip a crucial detail.

"Wait a minute," Sadie says, interrupting me. "You called *Campbell* to come over and hold your hand? Hmmm, I guess I know where I stand. Here you have a crisis, and you call your gay friend, not your girlfriend."

She doesn't believe me when I tell her I didn't think it was polite to wake her up early on a Saturday morning. Sadie asks what advice Campbell gave me, "if that doesn't violate the sanctity of your friendship," she adds sarcastically. I assure her that Campbell said exactly what she herself would have: I need to make sure that Chloe's being responsible; I can't confront her in a way that will be shaming; I need to be sex-positive. Then I make an even worse slip.

"You shouldn't be jealous of Campbell," I tell Sadie.

"Oh, honey, don't even go there. I don't get green-eyed over anybody."

I could note that she cuts me a withering glance while she says this, but considering how withered I already am, that feels redundant. Sadie sets her water bottle on the peninsula counter and steps into her living room, which is visible through the wall's pass-through. I start to follow until I spot a familiar object.

"Hey, what's my old Walkman doing here?"

Sadie informs me that Chloe came by for a song-writing tutorial that afternoon. Apparently Luther and Campbell have been working in cahoots to make this happen, because the first one suggested it to Sadie and the second to Chloe. I should be grateful that my extended family in Willoughby is so eager to nurture my daughter's talents, but I can't help but get a little pissed when I flip the lid on the CD player and discover what music was the subject of Professor Sadie's first lecture: *Exile in Guyville.*

"Dammit, I told Chloe I didn't want her listening to Liz Phair. I specifically took it back from her after she grabbed it from my office, and now she's stolen it back. The language on this record is way too graphic for a sixteen-year-old. There's a song on here about blowjobs, for God's sake."

Sadie's never heard me get this parental. It amuses her.

"One whole song, huh? Out of, what, eighteen on that CD? Chloe was playing me lines she likes on *Exile*, nothing more. There are feelings in those lyrics she wants the confidence to know how to articulate. Don't worry, not a single one of the passages we talked about involved sex. There are a lot of different emotions in those songs. There's anger, vulnerability, sadness, desire, and even attitude. Girls don't always get the full gamut when they're looking for music to identify with. Usually in music we're wispy and weepy or else we're smacking our asses singing about the boom-boom. Relationships are what Chloe is interested in, not in upsetting and offending adults with purple prose. You know her favorite song on *Guyville*? It's this one."

Sadie grabs her Ovation six-string from a stand next to the couch and sits on the coffee table beside several notebooks of lyrics. I try not to focus on the inviting slice of leg the guitar is balanced on. Once Sadie starts playing that's not a problem. Whenever I watch her perform, her hands put me in a trance. She has a unique style that's part Flamenco and part classical, which means she never uses a pick but instead plucks the strings, really quickly too, so her playing fingers seem to ripple across them like streamers in the wind. She's into unconventional chord voicings, too, so her fret hand is always stretched wide across the neck. Swear to God, with the span she's got she could keep a thumb in Paris and a pinkie in New York. She also has a great voice with just an edge of huskiness that's one big reason I find it hard to believe she's only twenty-three. Listening to Sadie sing Liz Phair, I find myself batting my eyes all over again. I recognize the melody and some of the words, which are about the vicious things a couple will say while bickering during a long car ride. I can't place the title until Sadie stops in the final refrain to remind me of it: "Divorce Song."

I drop into Sadie's recliner, making sure the bed sheet doesn't slide off my hip and ruin the moment by reminding us both that I'm hung like a cashew.

"That's really Chloe's favorite? 'Divorce Song'? I didn't know she could tap into feelings that...I don't know... adult, I guess. She's never told me what she thinks about her mom and me divorcing. She wasn't even a year old when we split up. Our divorce never seemed an issue for her because she couldn't remember a time when Deb and I were together. Maybe I should talk to Chloe more about why her mom and I dated in the first place, what we saw in each other. Maybe I need to accentuate the positive. I should reassure her that Deb and I have never fought like the people in this song."

"Vance," Sadie says, exasperated. "Chloe's not thinking about *you* when she listens to these lyrics. She's thinking about Stu. You don't get it, do you? You should be happy. This is a *breakup* song. It's about a woman who's realizing she can't be herself with a certain man because he's trying to change her. He's telling her everything between them could be fine if she just weren't so emotional, if she didn't have so many feelings and didn't need to talk so much. And it's hitting her that if he really loved her–if he were capable of love–he'd accept these things, because they're who she is."

I ask if Chloe specifically told Sadie that she intended to break up with Stu. Not in so many words, Sadie says, but there was a definite sense of dissatisfaction there. Every single song Chloe played was about a woman learning that her happiness isn't dependent on a man. I want to hop out of the chair, yell "Hot damn!" and pop some champagne.

"You know," Sadie says, "Liz Phair is touring this summer. She's playing all of *Exile in Guyville*, too. It's a twentieth-anniversary celebration. She's in Atlanta next week. Tix are still available. I think you should take Chloe. It'd be a great way for her dad to say, 'I understand why this album speaks to you.'"

As much as I'd love to see Liz Phair live (I haven't been to a concert in years), the thought of pumping my fist to "Fuck and Run" while standing next to a teenage girl makes me feel uneasy. I don't say yea, I don't say nay. Sadie doesn't seem too invested in the suggestion, anyway. She sets her Ovation aside and pulls out the bong she stores behind her couch. If there's one drawback to dating a twenty-three-year-old, it's that she still smokes pot. *A lot of pot.* As in, if a doctor examined her blood cells under a microscope he would probably discover they contained more smiley faces than platelets. Sadie packs the bowl of the translucent red-glass gizmo, which is shaped intimidatingly enough like a phallus to remind me once more of how shriveled I am. Cupping her lips to the mouthpiece, Sadie covers the rush hole as she lights the mossy looking clump and inhales. After she swallows she offers me a hit, a ritual we go through the two or three mornings a week I catch her "relaxing" at the back gate of Macon Place before she heads into Luther's studio to record. When we first started going out I would caution Sadie that getting stoned in her Volkswagen in a spot that Mike Willoughby could easily roll up on isn't the wisest choice she could make. I stopped when I tired of her curt comeback: *You're not my dad.*

"You know I can't smoke," I say, waving off the offer. "I have a teenager. What if I did and then Chloe asked if I'd done dope? I'd feel like a hypocrite looking her in the eye and fibbing."

"What if she asks if your girlfriend smokes?"

I shrug. "What choice will I have? I'll look her in the eye and fib. Is your Febreze still in here? I'm going to have to spray my clothes if you're going to toke up. I can't go home smelling like pot."

"Nobody calls it 'pot' anymore, dude. It's weed."

I look around the apartment for odorizer. Sadie usually has a can of Summer & Splash rolling around her floor-boards, which is why sitting in her car makes me feel like

Kirk Curnutt

I'm trapped inside a sealed can of fruit. The only thing in the apartment is a spray bottle of Poo-Pourri on the toilet tank. I take a pass on it. On my way back to the living room, I spot yet another notebook on the accent table in the hall. It's one of those spiral, pocket-sized memo pads that reporters stuff in their shirt pockets. Sadie probably spends as much money on journals as she does pot; she's always writing down snatches of lyrics and chord progressions in them. I flip this one open and five pages in discover a work in progress.

"Hey, are you writing a song about me?"

I recite a scribbled verse from "That Careful Man with Complicated Veins."

*Smoky cloves and tangled hair, cold waterfall commitment to spare*
*Sip of port, his lucky star, last night he traded his soul for a cigar*

"What's that supposed to mean? I don't smoke. I don't drink port, either."

"Then that would probably mean it's not about you—although it could be. It's about an older man."

"What older man?" I want to know.

"It's about my father, all right?" Sadie snatches back the memo pad. "I don't like people seeing my work before it's finished."

I don't know why, but I feel the need to defend myself. Just because I'm older, I say, doesn't mean I'm an "older" man. I point out that Sadie was almost a kindergartener when I graduated high school. In my book that's not a generation gap. It's not as if I'm old enough to be her dad. I remind Sadie I'm not even forty yet.

She tucks the notebook in the coffee-table cubby where she stores her tin of pot and then lobs a bomb at me. She asks how much older than Ardita Farnam I was. Yowza, that one hurts. I've never talked about my Katfish Kountry debacle with Sadie. I thought I'd put that disaster behind me several months before we met. I ask who told Sadie about Ardita. Her answer isn't encouraging.

"Who didn't tell me about it?" she shrugs. "When I first came to Willoughby, Ardita Farnam was all I heard about. You probably think you're known for being the guy who quit teaching to work for the richest old dude around, maybe even for inheriting half of the old dude's house, but nobody cares about any of that except Mike. I hate to break it to you, but if the city put up a plaque honoring you, you'd be the guy who committed the Most Infamous Act of Fornication in Elmore County, Alabama. Of course, nobody mentions Ardita to me since we started going out. The Bud Light story, that really happened?"

Ardita didn't take it well when I told her I couldn't see her any longer. She cracked a beer bottle on my head. Fortunately, thanks to my spongy hair, I wasn't hurt. Unfortunately, it happened in the parking lot of Katfish Kountry as her dinner shift was ending. I may not have been cut, but I was humiliated. "And it was a Coors Light, not a Bud Light; but basically, *yes*, it really happened."

"And the Alabama room? That's not an urban legend, is it? Her parents really caught you two in the act? That must make for awkward conversation when you and Ardita run into each other."

"You have to understand Southeastern Conference football," I explain. "It's a religion around here. Sex in an Alabama room is like desecrating a temple. And, no, I haven't seen Ardita since I was picking glass out of my hair. Last I heard she'd moved to Birmingham. I see her father occasionally downtown. I can't say as I blame him for not saying hello."

The confession leaves me feeling woozily depressed. I excuse myself to the bedroom, where I stretch out on Sadie's lumpy duvet and blink into the dusk tinging the Venetian blinds with a sepia glow. Maybe I was in denial, but until Iris brought up Ardita Farnam yesterday, I had no idea the sordid tale was such gossip fodder. I never told anybody about it, and I doubt Mr. and Mrs. Farnam did either. That leaves only Ardita as the one person who could have. How the story made the rounds is less important than how far it's circulated, though. When I even consider the possibility that Chloe has heard about what happened in that Alabama room, my stomach knots, and I can feel all that beer and steak in me back up into my throat.

I'm in the bedroom a good fifteen minutes, thinking and regretting, before Sadie joins me.

"Sorry to bum you out," she says, "but to get into a situation at your age with a twenty-year-old who still lives with her parents—man, that's Self-Destruction 101. How did you think a relationship like that would end? Did you think you and Ardita would just go your separate ways and still be friends?"

Actually, I did. That's how every other relationship I've had worked.

Sadie lies next to me, her chin on my shoulder. I slip the kimono over her hip so I can feel skin instead of silk. I'm not sure I can admit to myself why I got involved with Ardita, much less cop to it to somebody else. Not yet; it's still too soon. So instead I tell Sadie a different story. I don't leap into it straightaway. I come at it from the side by asking if Sadie's repertoire includes any Shelby Lynne. The question catches her off-guard. A few seconds pass before she admits she knows the name but not any specific music. I tell her that when she was talking about the kinds of songs Chloe is into I wished Sadie had had a copy of *I Am Shelby Lynne* handy for them to discuss. That was always one of my favorite CDs. On it is a song, "Dream Some," that reminds me of a time in graduate school when I saw Shelby Lynne live. I was so broke back in those days my date had to pay for my ticket. For better or worse, my date at the time was my dissertation director. Sadie laughs out loud at this revelation. "Man or woman?" she asks. Somehow it's even funnier to her when I clarify that, yes, my dissertation director was a woman, a top scholar in her field. I guess the dynamic is more comical when the man is the younger, more impressionable one in the relationship. Sadie really chortles when I tell her I had a hard time not calling my dissertation director "Dr. Hunemorder" even after we were sleeping together. I admit to her that a dozen years later I'm still not sure how that fling began. One minute you're in an office nervously lobbing out interpretations of Gertrude Stein's *The Mother of Us All*, and the next you're drunk off three margaritas fumbling to unlatch a forty-seven-year-old's bra. What Dr. H saw in me was a mystery at first. "I'm surrounded by dickheads and booger eaters," she used to complain. I didn't ask what category I fit in. Probably both. I had no money, no car, not even any original ideas when it came to a dissertation proposal. Only one thing distinguished me from the endless parade of grammatically illiterate undergraduates and career-ladder-climbing Ph.D. candidates she'd grown disillusioned teaching as she confronted the midpoint of her career. I had a four-year-old daughter. I was so poor that I had to carry Chloe to my babysitter's in a Radio Flyer wagon–poor enough that the babysitter gave us her government cheese–but that little girl was mine, and I took care of her. As Dr. H told me the night of that Shelby Lynne concert, the only reason she was "susceptible" to me was because I was an anomaly. I was a single father, and for that reason alone I would always be her favorite mistake.

"Why a mistake?" Sadie wants to know. "What did you do that was so wrong?"

Honestly, I didn't do anything wrong. The time and place just weren't right. I ended up in Dr. H's bed only a few months after she and her husband divorced, and he was having a hard time coping. He did creepy things like drive by her house at all hours of the night. I'm not sure exactly how he discovered his ex-wife was sleeping with one of her graduate students. It's not as if I parked my Radio Flyer in her driveway at night. However he figured it out, though, he made a stink. He was also an employee at the U of Florida, and he lodged a formal complaint against Dr. H that triggered an investigation. I had to sit down with Human Resources for an interview that was only a rubber hose short of an interrogation. Dr. H was in the running to become chair of the theater department, but the fiasco tanked any chance she had for a promotion to administration, which she desperately wanted so she could get out of the classroom. She never did manage that, but she's not bitter, at least not to me. We're still cordial online and trade emails all the time. Last year she sent a Christmas card saying she couldn't believe how grown-up Chloe looked.

"What does Shelby Lynne have to do with you and your Dr. Mrs. Robinson?" asks Sadie.

Maybe not much at all. It's just the most vivid memory I have of that relationship. Dr. H and I went to that concert right after we'd been informed about the investigation. Considering what a stalker her ex- had become, we might have been wise to resell the tickets on eBay and keep our distance from each other. Dr. H was adamant that we still go, however, and not just because I'd converted her into a Shelby Lynne fan. Going was her F-You to the man she'd divorced and to her colleagues, many of whom had been banging their students since Jimmy Carter was president but were suddenly outraged that a female prof would dip her oars in the grad-student pool.

"You know what I remember most about that concert?" I say as my fingertips stroke Sadie's thigh. "Dr. H dancing. I'd never seen her do it before. She wasn't an outgoing woman, but this one number of Shelby Lynne's, 'Dream Some,' got to her. You should learn that number; you'd sing it so well I'd probably start crying. It's one of those songs that's so creamily sad—you know, swirling flute and tiptoeing piano figures—that you forget it's about

Kirk Curnutt

squandered love. It makes a breakup seem about as upsetting as a lick of meringue. When the band slinked into it, Dr. H went straight up to the stage, wafting and lilting until she became the show. I remember other women rushing up to surround her, hoping her spontaneity would rub off on them, but that wasn't her scene, so she spun off into her own world. She closed her eyes, cupped her hands behind her neck, and sang the chorus. *Did you miss me?* it goes. *Did you miss me?*"

"I take it you missed her."

"I didn't enjoy getting dumped the minute the encore was over, but I knew it was inevitable. That night really had nothing to do with me, though. Dr. H was dancing for herself, to molt the pain. She was telling herself that if sadness could be experienced in as uplifting a form as 'Dream Some,' then no mistake she ever made could break her spirit. She could shake off whatever consequences came from landing in the sack with me as easily as she shook off those other dancers. And meanwhile I'm sitting there, saddled with something heavier and harder to rise above. I mean, here I was partly responsible for this woman's career hitting the skids, but in a weird way I understood that what I needed from the beginning from Dr. H wasn't sex or love but regret. I needed the guilt to scare me out of ever getting into an inappropriate relationship again."

"Looks like that guilt didn't come with a lifetime guarantee. Where was that Shelby Lynne song when you decided to hit on your waitress?"

"I didn't hit on Ardita. I've never 'hit on' anybody in my life. But that's what scares me about that situation. I don't know why I let myself get involved with 'my waitress,' as you're having so much fun calling her. Look, there were very real consequences for me for the Dr. H thing. Not only was I the joke of a whole department, but it's the reason I could never get a job teaching at a university. Stories like that make the rounds; rumors follow your name. I reconciled myself to those consequences because I was young and dumb. That excuse doesn't work with Ardita. I'm back to being a joke, and unlike twelve years ago or like Ardita herself last fall, I can't leave town to get away from the story and pretend it never happened. That's what scares me the most about Chloe having sex this early in life. I don't want her being humiliated because a man didn't think he needed to care about the consequences."

I can sense Sadie rolling her eyes in the dark.

"Ah, guilt, the last refuge to which a scoundrel clings," she says, paraphrasing Samuel Johnson. "You're acting so chivalric wishing you'd had better judgment, as if you wish you could've protected all of womankind from the scourge of men. Give me a fucking break, Vance. Dr. H and Ardita made their own choices. It's condescending for you to regret on their behalf. Honestly, do you realize how old-fashioned you sound sometimes? You're the only guy I've met under forty–make that fifty–who thinks self-reproach is part of sex. Why is that?"

She doesn't wait for an answer. She asks how old I was when I lost my virginity.

"Maybe it scarred you," she says. "My old man once told me he was twelve–with a babysitter, no less. It was one of many inappropriate things my daddy said to me."

I don't have much interest in mingling my sex life and her father in the same conversation, but Sadie won't drop it. When I don't answer her question she asks again how old I was, so I toss out a number. She clicks on her bed lamp and stares into my eyes. Say it again, she orders me. You first, I go. Big mistake: she waited until she was twenty-one, largely because of all those inappropriate things her father used to say to her. It doesn't make me feel any better to realize that twenty-one for Sadie was all of two years ago.

"Quit needling, okay? I said I was fifteen, sixteen, somewhere in there. It was twenty years ago."

"Bullshit," Sadie smiles. "Your voice quavers when you lie. Your pupils jitter, too. Come on, buster, cough it up."

"What does it matter? I didn't come here to trade stories. I came for action and satisfaction."

To prove it, I roll onto her. Sadie slaps a palm to my lips so I can't change the subject by sticking my tongue in her mouth.

"Guys are only embarrassed when they're late bloomers. That means it wasn't until college. Ooh, better yet–you were still a virgin when you were with Chloe's mom! Haha! I bet she was your first, wasn't she?"

I abruptly back off the bed. As I tell her to change the subject, my voice is sterner than I've ever heard it. My seriousness startles her.

"Chill out, dude. I'm only trying to get to know you better. Why are you so insulted? It's not like I said your first time was when you knocked her up."

This time I'm too worried about my voice quavering and my pupils jittering even to try to lie.

"Oh my God!" Sadie says with gleeful surprise. "That's it, isn't it? No wonder you're screwed up! Your first time at bat and you made a baby!"

I've had enough of the past. I need a shot of guilt-free fun for the present. I look to Sadie's bookshelves for a sexy novel or some poetry, but flipping through several I can't find anything guaranteed to put some step in my stick. Then I spot Sadie's closet and begin searching through her clothes. A battered pair of Doc Martens tops her shoe pile. Bingo. I toss the boots to Sadie and then rummage the closet until I find a black mini, a tight sleeveless T, and the pièce de résistance: a studded red leather belt.

"Nothing's hotter to me than a punkette," I tell her, "so here's the deal. It's 1992. Your name is Siouxsie, you're on tour, and I'm an errant Banshee who needs to be put in his place. No matter what, the boots stay on."

The outfit is just what the doctored ordered. Sadie no sooner knots her laces than I'm wiggling the skirt up her thighs. A few soul kisses and I can feel redemption taking shape. We tumble onto the bed, and she yanks the sheet away to discover that I won't be putty in her hand. Soon I've forgotten all about my impotence, her incarcerated father's inappropriate comments, losing my virginity and impregnating Deb in one fell swoop, my daughter's boyfriend shopping for condoms at the Walmart, Dr. H dancing to Shelby Lynne to escape the fact that we'd damaged both of our careers, Ardita Farnam and the Alabama room where her dad walked in on us, Liz Phair and the CD I told Chloe she was too young to listen to—a whole head's worth of heavy thoughts. I wrap Sadie's French braid in my fist while my other hand peels the T

Kirk Curnutt

over her shoulders and my lips nibble her neck. My tongue traces the hermetic symbols dotting her entire body until neither of us can wait any longer. I kick the mini from between our tangled legs, leaving the belt on until the studs bruise my hipbones and I finally snap it off, too. Giddy with control, I swing behind Sadie and plant my feet among our shorn clothes, my knees nearly knocking the mattress off her box springs. In my delirium I grip her ankles, squeezing until the boots' leather sweats in my palms. As a gust of relief rushes through my center of gravity, I let my head fall forward, eager to be emptied and freed....

I could've probably enjoyed the relief, too, if at the exact second I give myself over to the surge, my eyes didn't happen upon that belt. It's dropped face down on a pillow, snake-like, stretched just straight enough for me to make out the Sharpie letters scribbled across its back:

PROPERTY OF CHLOE S: FAILURE TO RETURN MAY RESULT IN DEATH.

# 11

"That's the new rule," decides Campbell when I share the story. "Repeat it in weaker moments. 'I promise not to date anyone young enough to borrow my daughter's clothes.'"

Things shouldn't be this complicated. There's a seven-year difference between Chloe and Sadie. One's a woman, one's a girl. It's not Sadie's fault that Chloe listened to Liz Phair's *Exile in Guyville* and wanted to model some tough rocker-chick fashions from her dad's girlfriend's closet. Nor is Chloe to blame for lending the belt she bought last weekend to her new musical guru. The fault is mine. I haven't been good about keeping Chloe her age. Now I'm wondering if I shouldn't comb through her clothes and get rid of any outfit that looks too adult. Campbell blanches at the suggestion. Doing that would put me in league with Nina's dad, Luke Laughlin. The only good thing that could come from going Gestapo over my daughter's wardrobe is that I'd have a room to rent to Luke after Chloe ran away from home.

"Don't rile things up with the child's mom coming to town," Campbell scolds me. "You'll ruin the weekend. I don't even want to know what schemes you're cooking up. In case you haven't noticed, I'm not in a good mood tonight. I don't like these events. I feel like a performing seal."

She's talking about Luther's P-FLAG banquet, which we only arrived at thirty minutes ago. I can't say I blame her for feeling awkward. Like the intense red and blue gels that spread an almost Day-Glo brume throughout

Macon Place's ballroom, this fundraiser is burnished with the strain of parents showing their support for their gay and lesbian children. Most of the event's honorees are squirming in the spotlight of their ennoblement, aware that this spectacle is really less for them than for their families, who need each other's comfort and community. Campbell and her friends would rather be loved and accepted without all this pomp, but they recognize that the pageantry is necessary comfort for parents who're trying to convince themselves that they're cool with their kids having "gone" gay.

"At least we're not at the head table," I say, trying to cheer Campbell up. My thousand-dollar contribution has bought me an anonymous spot at the back of the room. "Remind me to thank Chloe for switching our place cards. Maybe if she sings again next year she can set up my table in the garden at the amphitheater."

Campbell has no patience for my self-pity. She reminds me that Chloe is so nervous about staying on pitch that my sitting right under her nose could spark a panic attack. I point across the hall, remarking on how poised and in control my daughter appears. Chloe and Nina are crouched along the stage risers, intently studying Sadie and an ad-hoc backing band of Luther's friends as they winnow through a silky rendition of "Stormy Weather." Chloe and I have managed a quiet détente the past two days, our peace treaty struck mainly so we can get the house cleaned for our guests' arrival this weekend. I didn't realize how important her mother's visit was to her until I caught her scrubbing the guest-shower grout with an old toothbrush, her way of distracting herself from her jitters. Glammed to the gills for this party, she hardly looks like the same person who only hours ago was on all fours dumping a fat can of Ajax onto our soap-scummy tiles. For her debut Luther bought Chloe a new cocktail dress, a strapless red number with a ruched bodice. I'm not sure I like it. The dress makes her look way too much like a siren, as if she ought to be singing for Lucky Luciano and Meyer Lansky at the Tropicana Club. I'd give anything if Chloe had shown up for this event looking as punk as she did at the book-club meeting the other day. She would never embarrass Luther that way, however—only me.

A friend of Campbell's named Tish leans into my face, giving me a hot blast of champagne breath. "This new girl of yours," she says with a slur, "this Sadie McGregor. *Rawr.* I approve. She's hot and talented. I'm not sure about all those tattoos, though. That's a lot of graffiti covering up those goods."

Every year that I've bought a table for Luther's banquet, I've invited Campbell's circle to join me. They're a tolerant crowd, very forgiving of me for being a man. Willoughby actually has a diverse lesbian subculture, and this crew is only one facet of it. Mostly, Campbell's friends are country women who moved here because they can hold hands and nuzzle in the city without anybody gawking or promising to pray for their souls. They're not as political as the gay women I knew in grad school. Get them drunk and a couple will even admit they vote Republican. I like to hang with them to hear their coming-out stories and how they struggle with deciding how comfortable they are announcing their sexuality to

**116**

the world. I'd be lying if I didn't admit I get a weird sort of pleasure from the relentless razzing they give me, too. I tell Tish that I like tats, but only on women, not men. They're brave to me because they're unfeminine. That comment wins me more than a few funny looks.

"Vance isn't big on femme," Campbell explains when the rest of the table turns to her for a translation. "Femme is too emotional."

"That's not true," I protest. "My preferences just run more punk than girly-girl. Although girly-girl gets a bad rap these days. I think we're too hard on femininity. Nothing wrong with softness. The world is hard enough. I think men should be more like women than women should be like men. Honestly, I think I'm confused about what I like. Maybe I should rethink my preferences."

"Like I said," Campbell assures her friends. "Femme is too emotional."

This isn't the teasing I'm used to. It's edgier and angrier, but I try not to take it personally, knowing how ill-at-ease my best friend feels at this shindig. Before I can object again, Brody Dale—one of two female deputies in the Elmore County sheriff's department—pipes up.

"I bet if your daughter came home tattooed stem to stern like your girlfriend you'd feel some emotion."

"Better yet," smirks another friend, Jill Nesmith. "Let your daughter come home with a femme. We all remember what that's like."

I smile and take a slug of wine, aware that I'm being tested. I tell the women I'd have no problem if Chloe decided she was a lesbian. In fact, I'd prefer it. I give the table my permission to convince my daughter of the benefits of being gay. Once she is, I say, I won't have to lie awake worrying about boys. "See, I know about boys," I tell them. "I am one. Or I was, rather."

Tish purses her lips, doubtfully. She's a fiftyish nurse, fair-skinned and still saddened by a recent breakup that's forcing her to sell her house. She tells me that's easy for me to say right now, but the reality of coming out is much harder. "Parents here talk about being accepting, which is their way of saying they've had to work to come to grips with it. Sure, they love us, but you don't think a single one of them doesn't wish we were straight? It'd make life easier, for us as well as them."

"Girls aren't any kinder to girls than boys anyway," adds Jill. "A woman'll screw you over as bad as a man. The only difference is that a woman's willing to tell you why afterward."

Brody is watching Chloe and Nina. "As close as those two seem to be, I wouldn't be surprised if there was some...*experimenting* going on. You might get your wish more than you know, Doctor. I bet when that Laughlin girl sleeps over, they stay in the same bed, don't they? You ever walked into your daughter's room and caught them spooning?"

I admit that I do everything humanly possible these days to avoid walking into Chloe's room.

"It happens to the straightest of straight girls," Jill shrugs. "Not intentionally. Girls are just more affectionate. They curl up together to sleep, and the closeness of their skin, their smell, it'll lead to a touch here, a kiss there. It's a sweet thing, hardly sexual at all–at least until a straight girl wakes up worrying if a touch and a kiss makes her queer."

"Or bi," smiles Brody. Campbell, who's been watching Sadie sing, turns and gives our deputy friend a scowl.

I try to ignore the uncomfortable undercurrent by focusing on Nina. I used to see a lot of myself in Chloe's best friend. Until lately Nina was our comic relief. She had this daffy persona she played up, as if she were our Lucille Ball. She'd say off-the-cuff things like, "What if somebody invented boyshorts for men? What would you call them?" At first her punch lines made you think Nina was air-headed, but the more you thought about her jokes, the cleverer they struck you. You could tell she put a lot of time into crafting her wit. Since her parents' separation, though, Nina's reinvented herself as a hot toddy, all bust, midriff, and short-shorts. I don't judge it, but instead of self-deprecating she comes off as more self-absorbed. I'm curious about why Nina's decided to serve herself up like a Denny's Grand-Slam platter all of a sudden, but that's not a conversation an adult man needs to have with a seventeen-year-old. Usually when Nina's at our house I put on mental blinders and act oblivious. Tonight, though, I can't look at her without thinking of the story Mike Willoughby told me about her and Zak having sex in Mike's bed. I'm so used to the silly Nina that it's hard to picture her in the throes of any passion. It makes me wonder how passively both girls are giving into pressure from their boyfriends. Then I realize how creepy it is of me to wonder at all about their sexuality.

"See," Tish is saying, "that's where men and women are different. A woman'll caress you while you sleep. A man'll just poke you in the back. When I was married I told my husband I didn't like that. I worked at KCWU then, and I had this Uncle Bonsai record, 'Boys Want Sex in the Morning.'

*Before my eyes are open, I don't want to have to hide / From a simpleton still poking / With a thimbleful of pride.*

You'd think he'd get the message, but Kurt was dense. One morning I woke up before he did, so I grabbed my douche and jabbed him in the spine with the nozzle. 'How do you like it?' I kept saying. "How do you like it?' That was when I knew it was time to get out of that relationship."

Everybody laughs, except Campbell, who's visibly wincing as she pretends to watch couples take to the dance floor at Sadie's invitation. I wince as well when I spot Chloe and an uncharacteristically suited-up Stu bobbing gently among the sea of shoulders.

"Since we're on this subject," I say, "I've got a question for you guys. What do you get out of sex, anyway? I mean, as women. What do you like about it?"

I'm met by another tableful of funny looks.

"That right there," announces Jill with a snicker, "is why I Like Dyke. If you've got to ask, honey, you don't deserve to know."

"Come on, I'm being serious. If I were a woman, I'd be turned off of sex—seriously. So much of the way it gets talked about is so male. I'd feel targeted all the time. Ever since Sadie and I hooked up, Mike Willoughby keeps asking if I'm 'getting any.' He doesn't say, 'Hey, Seahorse, you sharing any?' All this pursuit and conquer stuff makes me wonder what real intimacy is, if it's even possible between men and women."

I tell them about one of the classes in feminism I took when I was in grad school. We read Andrea Dworkin, who argued that the whole physiology of sex encourages the domination of women because they're the ones who are penetrated. The very word sets Campbell's friends giggling, but I don't stop. Men screw but women get screwed, I say. Isn't that how we talk about sex? The mechanics of the deed make me curious what pleasure it has for women. Is that such a stupid question?

Tish shakes her head. "Right off the bat, I'm disqualifying Brody from this conversation. She's never seen a pecker, much less been on the receiving end of one. Better not ask me either–I haven't been married in seventeen years. You know who here to ask."

Campbell continues to ignore us.

"So this Andrea lady says any sex is rape, huh?" Jill isn't really interested; she's just covering up the awkward silence.

"That's what her enemies would have you believe. Dworkin herself was never that extreme. Mainly she looked at how men talk about it–how to us it's about invading and occupying a woman's body–and she was challenging women not to be taken. How, I'm not exactly sure. I didn't really understand it. She used the word 'violate' a lot. As you'd expect, some guys couldn't take the heat and dropped the class. The surprise was how freaked women were when I asked them what I'm asking you. I was only curious about why they enjoyed sex, but they thought I was hitting on them."

"I've got a curious uncle," reveals Jill. "He's why most women wouldn't want to talk to you. It's hard enough for women to figure out what we're sexually into on our own. Having a man push us to explain makes it worse. You know why? No offense, but most of those questions reveal a guy's ignorance. Take my uncle. When I came out he'd talk to me about why I was 'going' gay, and the first thing he'd ask is if I'm into 'phony pickles.' You know what a phony pickle is, right? They sell them at the X-Mart out on the Birmingham Highway, ones both with and without batteries. And you can guess what Uncle Rex was getting at. In his mind if I owned one I couldn't really be lesbian, because lesbians, in case you haven't heard—" Her voice drops into an icy, ironic whisper—"We ain't keen on cock."

"Really?" Tish gushes in mock amazement. "I didn't realize it was that simple. If I could learn to love cock, my problems would be solved?"

Brody has an idea. "We could send you to one of those programs that get gay men off the cock and gay women back on it: Exodus International. Better yet, let's start our own. As many Lezbyterians as there are in Willoughby, Alabama, we could make some money."

"We need a good brand name, though. Too bad Betty Ford wasn't a dyke. We could use her name for our center."

This leads to a whole discussion about Betty Ford's sexual orientation. I regret what I've started. The women start throwing out other possible names for the conversion program: *Scared Straight, Snapperholics Anonymous,* and a nice dirty acronym: *Caring Lesbian Inversion Therapy.* Then come the mock slogans: *Fight the Global War on Cooter! Down with Cameltotalitarianism!* Campbell shifts even deeper in her seat, her back nearly to us now.

"Sorry," I apologize to the table. "I'll shut up. I don't know why I'm even thinking about all this. It's been thirteen, fourteen years since I read Andrea Dworkin."

"I know why," Brody says. She points to the dance floor where Chloe and Stu are still swaying. As we watch, Chloe slides her palm up his back to cup his neck, gently stroking it with a single wisp of a finger.

"Hate to break it to you," Tish says, "that child ain't no lesbian."

Out of sympathy, Brody empties the last of the community merlot in my glass. "You don't have to apologize for asking questions, either. We know you're not like most men, Doc—you're cool."

Without warning, Campbell twists our direction, her bangs as stiff as a horsehair switch.

"Vance isn't different from other men," she says coldly. "He just wishes he were."

That crack kills the conversation, so as the table goes silent we turn our attention to the beef medallions and asparagus Iris's catering company serves. Although she's working the banquet, Stu's mom doesn't come anywhere near our table. I do catch her hugging and encouraging Chloe as she prepares for her big debut—something I've been explicitly forbidden from doing. Nursing my rejection, I slouch low in my seat and try to enjoy Willoughby's one and only female impersonator, a portly performer who bills herself as Eartha Quake. She's doing a mock burlesque routine, lip synching ABBA's "Does Your Mother Know" in Luther's ear. The crowd erupts in subversive giggles when she refers to Willoughby's godfather of punk as "a chick like you." I keep wiping my forehead on my suit sleeve. I'm sweating like a donkey.

"What's the matter?" a concerned Tish leans over to ask. "You look whiter than the cream sauce. You've got no worries. Eartha won't hurt ya."

"It's not him," I moan. "Or her, I mean. Is this beef fresh? I think I may be sick. My stomach's all kinked up."

Campbell's sour frown curdles my midsection even more. "Chloe's singing one song," she chastises me. "It's one song in front of friends, not her Broadway debut. She'll be okay."

I have to down a glass of Evian to settle my queasiness. After stripping to a fringe G-string and a fluffy pair of Sally Rand fans, Eartha purrs into the microphone.

"Ladies and gentlemen, under no circumstances are you allowed to hoot or holler for our next guest. She may come on like a dream, all peaches and cream, but she only just turned sixteen, and her father's here tonight and wants her kept pristine. Now don't clap too loud because you won't like me when I'm jealous, but here she is–the one and only–the chanteuse you're not allowed to goose.... *Miss–Chloe–Seagrove!*"

Chloe steps onto the risers, followed by Sadie, who nods reassuringly. She plucks Eartha's shimmy belt off Luther's shoulder and spreads it across the velvet accent on her dress's empire waist, wiggling her hips in a silly approximation of the dancer's campy choreography. It's supposed to be an icebreaker, but the move is fidgety and self-conscious–definitely not punk–and it makes both Chloe and the crowd aware of just how nervous she is. As if to make matters worse, Luther cuts her off at the mic and nearly fries the PA promising that she's going to be spectacular. Now it's Chloe's turn to go white as cream sauce.

"Before I do this," she nervously says into the mic, "I just want to say that I know tonight's about gay rights, but I want to remind everybody what's going on in the rest of the world. There's a country called Herzoslovakia where people don't get to have parties like this. It's been five days since Lifting Belly was attacked. Five days without any word about Oksana Dybek. I just want to say I consider her my hero because she's a feminist, and she's not afraid to speak out, and those are both what I aspire to be."

There's a smattering of applause, but more heads turn than hands clap. Some of these parents have clearly never heard of the evil that is Bronislavis Stylptitch. I smack my palms together to make up for the lukewarm reaction. "Woop! Woop! Feminism!" I yell until Campbell grabs my tie and orders me to shut up. Onstage, Luther takes to the piano, and he and Sadie trade a slow series of notes. I close my eyes and knot my napkin around my fingers. The first line of the lyric is about a woman receiving a letter from her mother. The mom asks how life in the city's going. The letter then slips into small talk full of cozy details about home, like how much the narrator's sister has grown, and how much rain the family farm's received lately. The narrator's lucky, her mom says, she doesn't have to deal with terrible Dixie storms.

"Holy smokes," I blurt. "Chloe's singing Maria McKee! That's my favorite Maria McKee song!"

I have no way of knowing if Chloe hears this, but Campbell and her friends do. The whole table shushes me; Campbell actually smacks my hand. It's supposed to be a soft, discreet smack, but I'm so wound up I jerk away and knock over my Evian bottle. Judging by how many surrounding tables crane their necks, the clank must be audible throughout the ballroom. By the time our chairs stop scraping the floor as we avoid the gushing water, Chloe's voice is trembling. She's off-time, her phrasing weakening as she struggles to find the staccato melody through the clustered swarm of Luther's chords. By the time we sop up the water with our napkins, she's off-key.

Sadie takes over the second verse. After only a few words I see her look to Chloe, encouraging her to jump back in, but Chloe is staring at her feet, scared. I know why: the second verse is sung higher than the first and she's afraid of missing the notes. Luther doesn't help. He mouths "You can do it!" so blatantly that he might as well bark his support into the mic. Chloe only rejoins the song on the upward climb of its bridge, but her harmony is too soft to be heard. Finally, she gives up completely and lets the mic dangle at her throat. Sadie finishes the final verse on her own, abandoning it a few words from the end to pull Chloe into an embrace and lend a sisterly kiss to the cheek. Luther jumps up from the bench to browbeat the audience into applauding, but Chloe is nowhere to be found. She's hopped off the riser, disappearing through the kitchen door.

"Fuck," I say, still dabbing my pants. "This is exactly what I was afraid of. I told Chloe she wasn't ready for Maria McKee yet. There are a bazillion easier songs she could have debuted with. I better make sure she's okay."

As I weave through the tables, I know there's only one reason Chloe would attempt "Dixie Storms," and that's to impress her father. Part of me wants to click my heels in triumph. The other part knows she needs to hear her debut wasn't as big a bomb as it felt from the stage. In the kitchen I discover Nina and Stu trying to coax her out of the bathroom. Nina does all the talking, leaving Stu to stand along the wall, looking put upon, as if all this unexpected emotion has stacked bricks on his shoulders.

"Come on out, baby," I say, rapping on the door. "It's a party. There's no reason to spend it locked up with nothing but a toilet to talk to. You did great–I promise. Didn't you hear all that applause? Maria McKee would've been proud."

I hear a whimper, then the faucet, a towel snapping off the rack. As the lock unbolts I prepare a comforting embrace, but the arms Chloe rushes into aren't mine. They're Stu's. And he doesn't even get that he's supposed to hug her. For several seconds Chloe hangs at his chest, her face buried in his shirt, until he realizes something is expected of him. As Stu finally wraps his hands around her back, I'm left looking to Nina for comfort.

"She'd have come out eventually," I nod. "Sometimes you just need to hear your dad say everything's okay. You know, reassurance."

"Uh-huh," Nina blinks dimly at me.

Slipping back into the banquet, I find Campbell waiting for me along the wall behind the risers. "Let's dance," she says, not even bothering to ask whether Chloe's okay. Sadie is playing "Joyful Girl," one of my favorite Ani DiFranco songs.

"You sure that's cool?" I ask. "I wonder if we even need to sit at the same table after that Vance-only-*wishes*-he-were-different-from-other-men crack. If I make you uncomfortable around your gay friends, let me know, and next year I'll send your dad my contribution, supposing I have a thousand dollars next year."

Campbell doesn't answer. She takes my hand and leads me into the swirl of dancers, both gay and straight. She asks if I remember the time we slept together after attending a Rotary Club ball as each other's date. I smell her perfume, and I'm reminded of waking up to it on my pillow. I remember the Rotary Ball well, I admit. Somewhere in my garage I still have the pink Fedora the band gave out when it kicked into Morris Day and the Time. *O-wee-o-wee-o*, I sing in Campbell's ear.

"I'm talking about the jungle love that went on after the ball," she tells me. "I'm talking about how when we came home I couldn't even get my key into the lock before you had your head up my dress. How you rushed me up against the bookcase and bent me over into my Harry Potters. How I thought you must really be into the beast with two backs until you revealed the real surprise you had to slip me. What do men in the South call that move? A 'Southern trespass'? Oh wait, I keep forgetting: *Vance Seagrove isn't that kind of man.* Still, that doesn't get you out of admitting what you felt by doing it, lover. You felt power, didn't you? Chest thumping primal power, and what turned you on was that you had somebody to wield that power over. Trust me, I know. The way you were grunting and growling I thought the Abominable Snowman was humping me."

The aggression shocks me. I don't how to respond.

"The roles seemed to have changed," I stammer. "Because all night you've been up my ass. What's the beef?"

Campbell smiles. "I want you to be honest, Vance. I don't want you to go all faux-naif and gee willikers pretending you haven't gotten off on the power of 'getting some' just so lesbians will like you. Or because you think it makes you nobler than Stu. Unless you can grow your own vagina, you're not going to change the physiology of sex, so stop being a pussy about it."

Boy, if that's not a mixed message. Again I don't know how to respond.

Campbell stops in the middle of the dance floor. "You want to know what pleasure women get out of sex?" Apparently the couple behind us does, because their heads snap in our direction. Campbell ignores them. "It's the pleasure of feeling safe and secure with the person you're with. Of knowing that they respect the vulnerability that comes with you letting them in, no matter what part of you they're trying to get into."

"You know," I tell her, "if you didn't want me going that—um—route, all you had to do was say no. I—I was just trying to be spontaneous. I mean, we'd talked about it before. You told me it was something you'd never tried."

"If I hadn't felt secure with you, we wouldn't have, either. A woman intuitively knows when she's respected. She may deny it when she's not, but that's a different issue. I was guilty of that with my ex-husband. I could sense when I was no longer me to Steve, when I was just a woman. And maybe not even a woman but a receptacle. Now, are your testicles going to retract if I tell you that these are the realities your daughter needs to learn as she grows up?"

I'm pouring sweat all over again. "I tried to talk to her, but she shut me down. The other day, outside your office, Chole told me she'd rather talk to Deb. She threatened me with that."

"You're only threatened if you allow yourself to be. Same for getting shut down. Try again. I'm worried about Stu and his phone. He snapped a picture of Nina while Chloe was onstage."

The dance floor grows more crowded as couples break apart to applaud the final notes of "Joyful Girl." Sadie stops only long enough for a special dedication.

"This next song is for the person who introduced me to it," she says. "I thought I knew every good song there is, but this one slipped by me. Thanks for teaching me what it's about. You know who you are."

The bass player slides a note down several frets, leading to a tiptoeing piano figure from Luther that makes the somber beat about as sad as a lick of meringue.

"Holy crap," I blurt. "That's 'Dream Some.' It's my favorite Shelby Lynne song."

Campbell backs away. "We definitely don't need to dance to this one. Not after that dedication."

"Why? Sadie's not the jealous type."

"It's not about jealousy. It's about feeling safe and secure, remember? It's about knowing a man is with you because you're you, and not just any woman. I'm not sure even the most un-jealous woman could have that security if her boyfriend danced with another woman and she spotted this—"

She gives me a discreet fillip to the zipper. Only then do I realize I'm rock hard.

"Go walk it off," Campbell orders me.

Embarrassed, I ball my hands in my pockets and do my best to waddle away without my arousal arousing suspicion. Slipping into the kitchen, I wander through the scrape and clatter of Iris and the other servers cleaning the dirty plates. The kids have disappeared—at least, Chloe and Stu have. Nina stands at a table of leftovers nibbling on a slice of key lime pie. I would probably interrogate her on Chloe's whereabouts if I weren't bearing this awkward cross, so instead I aim straight for the steps of the landing, thinking a brisk walk through Storm's statuary will take the starch out of me. A hundred yards along the walkway, I hear a rustle that sends me sneaking into the shadows of the lawn, which under the gray moon looks blue and sad. I drop into a hunch and scamper behind the nearest cover, which just happens to be Storm's beloved Aphrodite of Knidos.

With my hands on the statue's cold alabaster hips, I peek over her shoulder toward the amphitheater where Pink Melon Joy will debut at the battle of the bands, the same spot where, someday, with a little luck, Willough-beans will congregate for a dose of culture from a play or recital or a poetry reading. There, in a swirl of starlight, Chloe sits on a white diamond rail. As her fingers weave through Stu's hair, he pushes his pale face at hers, but she stops him with a soft thumb to the chin.

"Lose the bubblegum, champ."

Stu obediently spits a pink wad into one of my carefully coffered rudbeckia beds, and suddenly I'm watching two heads bob to the greedy suck of a liplock that nothing short of a tectonic plate shift could break apart. Before I can think to turn away, I've clutched Aphrodite so hard it's a wonder her pelvis doesn't crack.

"Did you get rid of that stinger?" Campbell asks when I wander back inside.

"Oh, yeah–definitely–forever, I have a feeling."

# III

# Gardening at Night

"Aphrodite is obviously not virginal, but this 'obviousness' actually masks a number of less obvious issues about which we know very little. No myth, for example, deals with her virginity or its loss, nor is she ever abducted or raped or the subject of an attempt of this sort; presumably she is so powerful sexually that to rape her would be implicitly contradictory."

–Paul Friedrich, *The Meaning of Aphrodite*

# 12

It doesn't hit me until the weekend that my ex-wife is coming to Willoughby for the first time ever. I have no reason to feel uneasy about Deb's visit. This is my turf, and the guest list for our Saturday night cookout is my tribe— *my* girlfriend, *my* best friend, *my* best friend's dad, *my* dad.

The porch is thick with the aroma of charcoal and marinade from the shish kebabs *I* grill. I've set out Roquefort cheese for my family and friends to spread on waterwheel crackers, and I've stocked the fridge and a couple of coolers with wines and beer that fit *my* tastes. Maybe I can't take credit for the gentle rain that's stoking a pine-scented breeze through the balusters, but the music pouring from the outdoor speakers is definitely mine. For the first time in ages, I've gone through my CD collection and made a playlist of *my* favorite songs.

Still, even though I control the environment, I can't relax. As the party kicks off I find myself staring to the street. The steam sizzling off the rainy asphalt seems an appropriately eerie curtain waiting to rise on Deb's arrival. I feel as if we're waiting for a movie star to bless us with an appearance on a red carpet. I shouldn't care whether someone who ditched me and her child fifteen years ago will approve of the home I've made in her absence, but I can't help it. I have an ominous feeling that Deb will take one look at Chloe and Stu sitting side by side in my twin wicker rockers and know exactly what the two of them have been up to.

"You've let our daughter say, 'Lose the bubblegum, champ,' haven't you?" Deb will demand.

Fortunately, my father, sensing my anxious mood, takes up my hosting slack. Miles Seagrove is a young seventy-eight and in such strong health that the two-hundred-and-fifty-mile drive from my hometown doesn't even tucker him. Dad's always been a charismatic guy, a born salesman. Chloe was just a baby when he sold off the chain of flooring outlets he founded, but where I grew up he's still known as the Carpet King of Dalton, Georgia, thanks to corny TV commercials he filmed in the seventies and eighties. From what Chloe tells me, his entire oeuvre is available on YouTube. Physically, Dad's always reminded me of Burt Lancaster, rugged and imposing, maybe a tad thicker in the middle. He has one of those wine-cask torsos. Whenever he sits or stands I expect to hear vintage Bordeaux slosh from behind his belt.

"Oh, no, no, no—it's not a fan club," he corrects me after I ply that unfortunate label to the hobby that keeps him busy in retirement. He edits the official journal of the International Dick Haymes Society, which is mailed out twice a year to a surprisingly large number of subscribers—almost three-thousand at last count, Dad reports. He so enjoys researching and writing articles on the crooner that he's been passionate about since he was a teenager that he's decided he may run for president of the organization. "We don't tape pictures to our walls," he informs us. "We're a historical society. Next year's conference is in Los Angeles. If I'm elected, it'll mean a lot of organizing. I hope I'm young enough to pull it off."

"This is quality stuff," Campbell says, skimming the latest issue Dad has brought to show off. "Four-color and on glossy paper even–very snazzy! Do you have a website? If not, you should get Chloe to design you one. Chloe, you should show your grandpa what you did for Lifting Belly. She's singlehandedly going to topple Bronislavis Stylptitch, Mr. Seagrove."

Dad has never heard of Oksana Dybek or Herzoslovakia. I'm not sure he's ever heard of punk rock. If it's not performed in a big-band style, he's not interested. This edition of *Dick Haymes: For You, For Me, Forever More* features his five-thousand-word investigative report into the singer's television career in the seventies. Like many faded swing-era stars, Haymes spent his middle age scrambling for guest roles on network shows.

"You wouldn't believe the digging I had to do," insists Dad. "Now, *McCloud* and *McMillan and Wife,* I remembered those shows, but *Alias Smith and Jones? Hec Ramsey?* I guess I didn't watch enough TV back then. I couldn't–I was always working. I never had any fun until I retired. The cop shows are harmless compared to how the movies demeaned Dick, though. His last appearance was a cameo in one that came out when Vance here was still in diapers. *Won Ton Ton: The Dog that Saved Hollywood,* it was called. Thirty years earlier, Dick had shared the screen with Betty Grable and Deanna Durbin, and now he was supposed to pet a drooling German shepherd. He was smart to return to the recording studio. There were two fine albums before the cancer came. That's what got him, the cancer: 28 March 1980."

I'm tempted to remind Dad of somebody a little closer to home that cancer "got," but I stick to sipping my

Sweetwater 420. Except for a passing reference now and then, my father and I don't talk about Mom.

"You know the hardest thing about being our age and alone, don't you?" Dad asks Luther. It's a question that fires up the aggrieved sense of mortality that Luther's prostatectomy has given him. He takes up the invitation not realizing it was meant as a rhetorical one. Luther starts telling about how hard it is to meet women in Willoughby, making sure to work it in that he won't date anyone ten years his junior, just to needle me about Sadie.

"Not only are single women in this area as rare as leprechauns, but the few widows and divorcees we do have are scared to date a man in his seventies who's survived a cancer scare." Luther has brought his port from his studio, so he's already a little drunk, and as he confesses his loneliness, I can sense Dad trying to find a polite spot to break in so the mood doesn't turn too downbeat. I take advantage of the lull to flip the kebabs. On my way to my Weber Summit Grill at the far end of the porch, I spot an odd logo on the jersey Chloe has on: *WHS*.

"Where did you get a Willoughby High T-shirt?"

"It's mine," Stu blithely informs me.

Chloe shrugs as I ask why she's wearing Stu's shirt. She'd rather tell me how lame the private school is that she and Nina attend. Nina, who's a year ahead of Chloe at Willoughby Academy, agrees. She'll be a senior in a few months and can't wait to graduate. I nearly shoot beer out of my nose when Nina announces she's getting a part-time job so she doesn't go stir crazy waiting for college. Come Monday she'll start waitressing at Katfish Kountry.

"The thing is, Dad," Chloe says, "WHS is starting a creative arts program in the fall. It's an awesome curriculum. The theater track is offering college-level classes–performance studies, theater crafts and design, even one where you study the creative process."

"Those are pretty specialized classes. Who's going to teach them?"

"They haven't hired anybody yet, but they've got all summer. The school's inviting the artsier kids from the Academy to apply for the program. I was sort of thinking that I might like to try it out."

I frown at Stu. I suspect he's behind this sudden push. He's too busy scarfing potato chips to notice my irritation. Chloe's never really felt comfortable at the Academy. She says it's full of rich kids and snobs, which isn't necessarily untrue: Mike Willoughby's kids, Travis and Zak, aka the Gold Dust Twins, go there. I've kept Chloe in private school, though, because our county's public system is dodgy, its SAT and ACT averages far below the national standard. Parents who can afford to send their kids somewhere else do, even if it's a Catholic or Baptist school. Up until Storm died, I was one of the ones who could afford it. Now I think of the tuition payment that will come due in a month–$7,000–and my innards cramp. If I went back to teaching at the Academy, Chloe could attend for free, but it would be a Mephistophelian bargain, costing me something more than money: Macon Place.

"We've got all summer to talk about it," I say. I don't want to tell her no in front of guests.

Meanwhile, at the other end of the porch, Dad is

trying to convince Luther that online dating will solve his woes. This is news to me, but apparently Miles Seagrove is the author of one of the most popular profiles on SeniorPeopleMeet.com.

"A lot of great women email me," Dad assures us. He doesn't sound like a braggart claiming this. He has a touch of melancholy in his voice, as if he wishes sincerely he could befriend everybody who shows up in his inbox. "I feel bad that I'm not what's best for them. This friend of mine from Rotary–his wife died, and two months later he married her best friend. I can't imagine doing that. The website advertises itself as 'Where to Meet a Mate if You're More than Forty-Eight.' A mate is more than I'm looking for, though. I just want to talk to women. If it were in my power to cure their loneliness I would, but I'd have to make a commitment, and at seventy-eight, who needs that complication? Don't get me wrong. I'm not out to seduce them–I'm a gentleman. I think of my companionship as a gift. Oh, I ran with a wonderful woman last summer. I took her to Grayton Beach for Memorial Day. But I finally had to say to her, I've already had two wives, and I've been widowed by one and divorced by the other, and I can't risk it again."

This might be touching if Dad stopped here, but he doesn't.

"You met Patsy Anne, Vance. She's the one who had the flat tire that night you and Campbell came up to visit and we all went to dinner. Remember? Patsy couldn't get back home. You and Campbell had to sleep on the foldout couch so she could have the guest room–"

The music can't begin to drown out the silence that

greets this revelation. Luther's eyes shoot straight to Sadie as Campbell goes stiff in her seat. Stu looks like he wants to high-five me. I gaze into my beer bottle, where a lime slice struggles to stay afloat in spume.

"Oops," Dad says, sheepishly patting Sadie's hand. "That's rude of me, bringing up the past. I'm talking out of school."

"More than you realize," agrees my girlfriend, scowling.

I excuse myself to the kitchen, Dad following a few minutes on. "How was I supposed to know?" he asks when I admit that I've never told Sadie that Campbell and I have been lovers. I'm chopping cucumbers and slicing tomatoes so I don't have to return to the porch. "You never tell me anything, son," Dad complains over the staccato whack of the blade on the cutting board. "You don't talk to me."

He's right. Ever since Chloe was born I've had a bad habit of stiff-arming my father. I think it's because he's never once asked me what I remember about Mom, if I even still think about her after nearly thirty years. I'd love it if Dad realized I'll soon be older than she was when she died, but that's not his style. Miles Seagrove has always been an unerringly optimistic man, a forward-looker. No time for tears, there's always a better day around the bend, that sort of relentless good cheer. He was so committed to not letting the past drag him down that a mere four months after we buried my mother he married his secretary, Janice. I bawled like a broken pipe at their wedding. When I asked how he could even consider moving on, Dad offered a doozy of an explanation. "Other than your mother, there's no woman who understands me any better," he said.

"All right," I tell Dad, resenting that memory. "Let's talk. Have you noticed your granddaughter has a boyfriend? Two nights ago I walked up on them making out. They didn't see me, but I sure saw them. It happened not five minutes after Chloe broke down because her singing debut didn't go as planned. Her tears weren't even dry, and suddenly she's snogging in my statue garden."

Dad shrugs, which isn't quite the response I expected. He reminds me that teenagers are all about extremes. A prime example: me. He recalls the horrible yelling matches Janice and I used to have. There was a good decade of those, for sure, all the way up until I left for college. Maybe even one or two after that when Janice decided she wasn't happy and divorced Dad. Conveniently, that realization happened right after the last of her three daughters, my stepsisters, had their degrees. One of those daughters still lives with her mother in my childhood home, which Janice won in the property settlement. I could live without thinking of my stepmother ever again, but unless I've repressed a lot of trauma, I draw a total blank on what Dad brings up next.

"However tough Jan was on you, you always managed to pay her back, didn't you? You and that girl of yours. What was her name? Oh, yes, Beth Tulbert. You would run off and have sex in Janice's Grand Prix. Janice couldn't believe you were that ungrateful. 'My car's not even paid for!' she used to complain."

I have to set my knife down so I don't slice off a finger. "Where did you get that idea from, Dad? I never had sex with Beth Tulbert. Not in Janice's car, not anywhere."

He wraps his arms around me and pats my back. "No need to lie about it! What am I going to do, ground you? That was twenty years ago."

I point out that men don't lie about not sleeping with their high-school girlfriends. Besides, Beth Tulbert wasn't the type to crawl into a backseat. She wasn't the type to crawl anywhere. She wanted to be a youth minister. She became one, and I think she still is, but I could be wrong. We haven't talked since she broke up with me for playing Liz Phair's *Exile in Guyville* in her presence. Beth had an aversion to bad words.

My admission so surprises Dad that he has to pull up a chair and sit. "Are you sure? Janice used to take that Grand Prix to breakfast on a Saturday morning and she'd swear she could smell the sex. She wouldn't let her shitzu ride in that car because she thought it'd get riled up. Lord, you should've heard the 'I told you so's' from Jan when you called to tell us that Deb was pregnant."

This pisses me off. I grab another beer from the fridge and pop the top loudly, tossing it onto the counter with a *clink*. I tell Dad he ought to take his granddaughter and do what I can't seem to bring myself to—get her on birth control. That would let him assuage his hindsight and spare me all the shame and embarrassment I caused him and Jan by knocking Deb up.

"Good God," he says, startled by my sudden vehemence. "You don't say 'knocking Deb up' in front of Chloe, do you? And what shame and embarrassment are you talking about? I was never ashamed of you. Never."

"Then how about giving me some credit? You don't

need to remind me that Chloe was an accident. I can name a dozen guys who cut out on their kids before their kids were out of diapers. In sixteen years and seven days, I've never once thought about shirking my responsibility."

"Nobody said you had. Why are you so defensive? Chloe's sixteen, and protecting her is part of that responsibility you're bragging about. You know how you can tell if she's lost her virginity? Tampons. If she's started using them instead of pads, chances are she has because most young girls are uncomfortable using tampons before their hymens are broken. It's uncomfortable for them to—you know—*insert* those things. Janice taught me that when your stepsisters were turning sixteen. Be glad she didn't ask Beth Tulbert if she was still using pads. She wanted to."

You know it's time to change the subject when your father broaches your daughter's hymen. I don't tell Dad that the tampon theory is a myth; I doubt he can damage the world too badly with this misinformation. I scrape the cucumbers into the bowl of lettuce I chopped earlier in the afternoon and arrange the tomatoes on a plate, peppering them lavishly. As I check the rice pilaf warming in the oven, Sadie appears in the doorway. "Guess who just rolled up," she says. Dad rushes into the hallway, but I'm cornered at the breakfast table, my fingers still cold and juicy from handling the vegetables. Sadie folds her arms over her chest, her French braid flopped over her shoulder.

"I was going to surprise you," she says, "but now I think I'll just hand you the bill. You owe me $140. I bought four Liz Phair tickets for Atlanta next week. I thought you and I could take Chloe and Nina, but now I wonder if you wouldn't prefer to take a different date. Maybe you and Campbell could crash at your dad's after the show."

I could swear I shot down Sadie's idea of going to that Liz Phair concert, but I'm not stupid enough to remind her of it. Not now.

"It was such a long time ago," I explain. "More than a year ago. Campbell and I are friends, that's it. The se–the, uh, physical stuff...that just sort of happened. No more than ten, twenty times at the most."

"The way you describe it, I'm sure Campbell's flattered. If there's one thing you need to understand, it's that I don't do lying. Not even lies of omission, Vance. If you can't be honest, you're wasting my time."

If I could be honest I'd admit that I'm about to throw up in my socks. I don't know why I'm nervous all of a sudden, but I am. I take Sadie's hand, but halfway to the porch I realize how desperate I'll look clinging to my girlfriend while I greet an ex-wife for only the second time in fifteen years. Sadie tells me to relax and that tonight's about a kid seeing her mom, not about me, but outside in the glow of the idling taxi's taillights, something more–something sinister–is occurring. Chloe is wrapping her arms around her mother's waist, hugging her from behind as Deb pays her driver. When did she last cling that tight to me? I can't remember. The cab pulls off, and the pair giggle and kiss despite the drizzle. I can feel Sadie, Campbell, and Luther stealing glances at me, gauging my reaction. Thank God Dad has better things to do. He's refilling his Solo cup with wine.

"This is quite a welcome," Deb says as Chloe drags

her up the walkway. She hasn't aged. In fact, she seems younger than when I last saw her, five or so years ago when her touring company was in Nashville and I drove Chloe up for an afternoon. The only difference is her hair. She used to keep it trimmed in a pixie cut, but now it's thick and layered, framing her face in raven jets that land at her collar bones. Chloe introduces her mother to everyone—*this is Dad's friend,* she says of Campbell, *and Dad's other friend,* she says of Sadie—and then steps aside for my dad, who throws his arms around Deb as if he's out to tackle her. As she pries herself free, I try to retreat, but Sadie and Chloe are behind me, and there's no weasel room. The greeting is unavoidable. Deb and I force a hug.

"You're going gray!" she says, plucking at my temples.

"He blames me for that," Chloe tells her.

"No, I don't," I grunt.

"I'm kidding, Dad. Chill, will you?"

*Lose the bubblegum, champ....*

"Well, you both look great," Deb politely assures us. She runs a hand along the curve of Chloe's bob, commenting on how adult the cut makes her look. Deb namedrops Louise Brooks, and Chloe twirls the tips along her jawline, playing cute. I'm tempted to tell her that Louise Brooks was sultry, that Clara Bow was the daffy one, but I don't. Instead I note that the idea for this new look came from a book Chloe read. *A book of mine.* The remark convinces me I have nothing intelligent to offer the conversation, so I shut up. In my silence, a strange rapport is struck. As Chloe pumps her mother for news of her life, Sadie and Campbell find ways of weaving themselves into the exchange, cracking jokes, adding their observations, connecting. Deb tells us about the bit part on *Law and Order: SVU* she recently auditioned for. She didn't get the role, but if she had, she would've gotten to whap Detective Benson upside the head with a .38-caliber pistol. Sadie mentions the last time she was in New York she jammed with a drummer who works as a gaffer on the show. He told her all kinds of juicy on-set gossip. Campbell, meanwhile, thinks Mariska Hargitay is hot. "And the letters g, a, and y are in her last name, too," she points out. The filaments of community may be thin, but they're being spun, and soon I'm the only one who can't ignore the peculiarity of this occasion.

Out of the blue, Sadie asks Deb if she's heard Chloe's song.

"What song?" I interrupt. "I haven't heard about any song."

"Me neither," mumbles Stu, rising from the coma of his perpetual slouch.

"I only finished it yesterday," Chloe explains. "After I fudged up at the banquet. I didn't write the music either, only the words. Sadie put the chords and stuff to it. What was that cool chord I liked so much? Cmajor7th?"

Sadie won't tolerate such modesty. She assures Deb that the melody was all Chloe and that she merely threw some accompaniment behind it. I ask Chloe what the song is called, and tell her I hope that it's not the one I found in her room, the one that begins, *Darkness in this pen / Darkness is my friend....* Chloe's face tightens at the sound of me reciting these lines. She'd forgotten about me rifling her room, and here I go, not only reminding her of

Kirk Curnutt

it, but insulting her boyfriend's lyrical skills in the same swoop. Her voice turns curt as she tells me this is a different song. Deb is more generous.

"You'll like it, Vance. It's called 'Daddy's Girl.'"

But the song's not about me. Chloe makes that point very quickly. As she explains, "Daddy's Girl" is about how she can't stand girly girls, especially ones who act so spoiled and frilly that they come off stupid and nobody takes them seriously. "That sounds like me!" Nina jokes, but nobody laughs because her self-deprecation seems out of place. We're talking about Chloe, not her. The idea that Chloe is writing songs of her own is a major concern for Stu. From the surprised look on his face, it's clear he never imagined Chloe would take any initiative without him prompting it. He wants to know if "Daddy's Girl" is one of those "'I-Am-Woman-Hear-Me-Roar' things." The reference doesn't amuse Sadie. Chloe's song is much cooler than that old cornball classic, she lets him know. Then she lets him know how tired Helen Reddy references are. Oblivious to the tension, Dad offers Chloe fifty bucks to write a sequel, but only if it's called "Granddaddy's Girl."

"You've heard the song?" I ask Deb.

My ex-wife hesitates, not wanting to embarrass her daughter. "Only one verse, over the phone. Chloe wouldn't sing more for me because she hadn't finished the chorus yet. She was so excited she wanted somebody to hear the idea of it."

*Somebody*, I harrumph to myself. Before I can pout Sadie decides that Pink Melon Joy should debut "Daddy's Girl" at the battle of the bands, which is only two weeks away now. She tells Deb that she could come back to Willoughby for the show and then makes some big claims for Chloe's first-ever composition. It's epic, but it's very punk, too, sort of a "Born to Run" from the girl's point of view, simultaneously hardcore and romantic. Why not throw in "cinematic" while we're being generous with the adjectives? I gulp more beer. Before Deb can accept or decline, Dad cuts in and declares that he's coming back to see Pink Melon Joy, even if nobody has invited him. He has to crash the party, he says, because if he waits for an invitation from me he'll still be waiting when the undertaker powders his cheeks. So many people are talking so quickly I feel a migraine coming. I try to clear my head by focusing on the slow-rising steam on our street, but Dad distracts me by leaning over and taking Deb's hand. He doesn't seem capable of talking to a woman anymore without taking her hand.

"Do you know that Vance never even invited me to the plays he directed when he taught junior high?" he asks his former daughter-in-law. "The only one of his I ever saw was his first one, and he was an undergraduate then. It was the one you were in. What was it again? *The Seahorse?*"

"*The Seagull*," Deb confesses. We trade embarrassed glances.

"We should eat," I tell everyone.

I polish off two kebabs, a lump of rice pilaf, and a buttery roll, not to mention the beer that makes it all gurgle in my stomach like vinegar on baking soda. After the entrée Sadie rolls out her chocolate cheesecake. I'd only anger her further if I didn't accept a slice, so I pack

Kirk Curnutt

it down, each swallow so thick it gums my esophagus.

"Your friends are fun," Deb whispers, leaning over my shoulder as we clear the serving table on the porch. "Your dad, I don't remember him being this big a hoot. And it's great to see Chloe."

"She's your daughter. She wants to see you—she needs to." Without thinking, I add, "Once in a while."

The intro to "Fox on the Run" by Sweet cranks through the speakers. With its gurgling synthesizer and macho vocal, the song is so simultaneously dumb and fun the whole porch starts to laugh. I don't admit the reason that I like it is because it makes me think of being a baby in my mother's arms. My old man must be a mind reader. He can sense the music is important to me. Or maybe he's just crossed the border from tipsy to sloshed. Whatever the reason, Dad is suddenly on his feet, doing his best impression of the furthest possible thing from rock 'n' roll, throwing his hands above his head and shaking his hips. As the first chorus kicks in he grabs Deb, clutching her to his chest and whirling her through the clutter of the porch. Luther takes an opportunity to throw a fatherly arm of his own over my shoulder and share a thought that's been on his mind since my ex-wife arrived. "Don't take this the wrong way," he whispers, "but now I know where Chloe gets her good looks." By the end of the chorus, Dad isn't content to dance with one partner. He grabs Sadie. Less inhibited than Deb, she happily slinks hipbone to hipbone with him. Before I know it, Dad has inched a hand into her back pocket. Where did he learn that move? Chloe has to lean forward and grab her knees she's laughing so hard. Not to be left out, Campbell jumps into the action, and suddenly my father is navigating between the two of them in a stride I call the deckwalker: elbows locked into Ls, he inches five steps forward and then back as if trying to make his way across the poop of a rolling ship.

By the song's goofy synth solo, Chloe and Nina join in, drawing a timid Deb back into the action. That leaves me in an unholy fraternity with Luther and Stu as the only wet blankets refusing to budge. At least Stu has a good excuse: he's recording the scene on his phone camera. He ignores me when I ask what he plans to do with the video.

The song ends far too soon. Dad sinks into his chair, huffing. I ask if he needs me to find a defibrillator. He has his own question.

"Why aren't you dancing, Vance? If I were your age I'd never sit down."

I doubt at my age the Carpet King of Dalton, Georgia, thought of breaking into dance any more than he did bending spoons or farming minks. He didn't even meet my mom until he was in his late thirties.

I only hope she got to see him being this silly, at least once.

# 13

The next morning, beer-headed and kebab-bloated, I rise early and creep downstairs to make coffee. On the breakfast table I find a copy of Marge Piercy's *Woman on the Edge of Time*. It's a first-edition hardback of Mom's. One of the first things I did when Storm Willoughby put me on the payroll was to take a carton of her books and have them bound in leather. I'd carried the box with me through college and grad school after liberating it from the attic where Dad had tossed it at Janice's request. Out of sight, out of mind. I display mom's modest library on the living-room shelf directly across from our front door because the only place where she seems to exist nowadays is between my ears. You can't walk into my humble Queen Anne without the embossed spines staring you in the eye. Like the songs I find myself turning to these days, most of Mom's titles date back to my birth era: John Updike's *A Month of Sundays*, Joanna Russ's *The Female Man*, Bharati Mukherjee's *Wife*, this one. The only explanation for Piercy lying here is Dad. He must've recognized the title, pulled it off the shelf, and left it here after flipping through it. I go to my guestroom and peek in on him, but he's snoring like a blender set to liquefy. I tuck the novel back into its rightful cranny and coat my insides with sips of chicory blend, wondering whether he still thinks of Mom.

My mood warms until I step outside to discover we're in our fourth straight day of a drizzle. At least the rising sun colors the subdivision with something other than the sky's cheerless gray—an orange glow bleeds under the cloudbanks, throwing marmalade shafts over the blue roofs. I wrap my thoughts in the lambency until I notice Chloe's phone abandoned on my sorbet table. After taking a quick look around for eyewitnesses, I pull up her texts, emails, and social-media posts. Nothing incriminating. Nothing interesting, in fact, except for a two a.m. Facebook blast declaring, *my mom is cooler than yours.* My finger hovers over the delete key until I realize what an irredeemable dick move removing the status update would be. Rather than stare at the post, I switch over to Chloe's music-streaming app and scroll through her recent playlists. She's been listening to Liz Phair almost nonstop, it seems. Most of the titles are unfamiliar to me. Although I have a vague awareness that Liz has released a handful of albums since *Exile in Guyville,* I've never paid attention. I slip in the earphones dangling from the phone jack and hit play. The more recent tracks sound nothing like *Exile in Guyville.* They're loud and upbeat, with crunchy guitars and drums pushed so far forward in the mix that each crack of the snare fires off pleasant waves of euphoria. Maybe Liz Phair is exactly what I need to launch me from my mid-seventies' rut.

Because the porch is still littered with beer bottles, paper plates, and meat-sticky skewers, I grab a trash bag from the kitchen and begin cleaning up. The party didn't end until after midnight when Luke Laughlin called angry that Nina wasn't home yet. (Home for last night being Luke's sad one-bedroom apartment, not her mother's house.) Stu volunteered to run Nina to Luke's, giving Campbell and Luther an opportunity to make their exit. After tucking Dad in, I waddled upstairs to Sadie, who'd already crashed. I guess I spooned a little too

Kirk Curnutt

snugly because around three-thirty she threw an elbow that could've snapped a ninja's neck. "Stop smothering me," she moaned in her sleep, and I rolled back, embarrassed at how desperate a man must look clinging to his girlfriend just because his ex-wife is in his house for the first time in fifteen years.

As I straighten the porch, I discover Chloe has showed her mom the stories about Lifting Belly she printed off the Internet. A stack of updates sits under a chair leg, pinned to the floor so the wind won't blow them into neighbors' yards. As I gather the loose pages, I catch the headline of the top report and start reading.

Topless Punk Rock Jihadists or
Elaborate Performance Art
by a Puppet Master?
Rumors Swirl That Lifting Belly is Just Another
Great Rock 'n' Roll Swindle

Exactly one week after video of an attack on a self-described "feminist punk-art collective" in the tiny Eastern European state of Herzoslovakia ignited an international political outcry, significant questions about the identity of the group's fiery leader are raising the possibility that the bloody beating was staged.

Singer and songwriter Oksana Dybek, 26, founder and guitarist for Lifting Belly, has not been seen in public since graphic footage of state police beating her unconscious circulated online. Rumors claim that she and her bandmates are incarcerated at The Chimneys, a notorious prison that dates back to the medieval age. Yet political supporters of

Dybek may now have to grapple with questions about the authenticity of the rabble-rousing punk provocateur known for performing topless with slogans such as "My Body, My Rules" and "Obscene Because of You" decorating her chest.

According to an online report by the Eastern European gossip magazine *Pupok* (*Bellybutton* in English), a twelve-year-old member of the Youth Scouts, the Herzoslovakian version of the Cub Scouts, was touring the palace of President Bronislavis Stylptitch last week when he captured an image of a woman on his phone. The woman was spotted sunbathing on a chaise longue thanks to an open window that, according to palace sources, is usually bolted shut. The grainy photograph, which resembles Ms. Dybek, has been widely reproduced in the Herzoslovakian press, inspiring commentators to draw comparisons between the woman's height, hairstyle, and posture and those of the missing singer. According to a forensic scientist *Pupok* hired to evaluate the photograph, there is a seventy-five percent likelihood that the mysterious figure is indeed the leader of Lifting Belly.

"If true, this report confirms long-running gossip linking the band to President Stylptitch," said Professor Anne Siddeoms-Wenzel, chair of the women's studies program at Belvedere College in Belvedere, Georgia. An expert in feminist protest movements, Prof. Siddeoms-Wenzel was widely criticized during CNN's coverage of the purported attack on Ms. Dybek for suggesting that Lifting Belly is a prank concocted by the mercurial Stylptitch to mock Western feminism.

"In the past, Internet commentators have posted paperwork purporting to show connections between the dictator and Oksana," Prof. Siddeoms-Wenzel said. "Some of these documents are admittedly a stretch. I don't believe the fact that a distant cousin of Mr. Stylptitch's works at the same studio where Lifting Belly recorded their revolutionary anthem, 'Get Out, Bronislavis Stylptitch, Before the Furies Rain Matriarchy Down Upon Your Head,' is all that relevant. But paperwork that suggests that Ms. Dybek's own mother worked as a housekeeper for the Stylptitch family thirty years ago when the president was a teenager? That hardly seems coincidental."

For every commentator like Siddeoms-Wenzel accusing Lifting Belly of being a fraud, an equally assertive supporter of Ms. Dybek's can be found defending the volatile performer. A website started by one anonymous fan in the unlikely American state of Alabama even includes a page called "Let's Refute the Lies" that argues President Stylptitch himself is behind the rumors of Ms. Dybek's collusion with the regime.

One thing is for sure: regardless of whether Lifting Belly is a legitimate art-punk protest against the Herzoslovakian government, the controversy is doing wonders for the group's popularity. "Get Out, Bronislavis Stylptitch, Before the Furies Rain Matriarchy Down Upon Your Head" is currently No. 44 on the UK record charts, and in the Top 10 in France, Spain, and Italy.

The song is expected to be released next week in the United States.

I'm so absorbed by the story that I don't feel the tap. Not until Deb takes hold of my wrist do I realize she's snuck beside my rocker.

"I didn't mean to startle you," she says tentatively, as if we're meeting for the first time. Her eyes are puffy, her left cheek creased from sleeping on a twisted pillowcase. I make up a story about how I have to listen to music on Chloe's phone because mine freezes up from downloading too much junk. I don't think Deb buys the explanation; she changes the subject quickly, telling me how grateful she is that Chloe self-identifies as a feminist. Before they went to bed last night Chloe showed her one of the bumper stickers she designed of Oksana Dybek smashing her guitar next to the legend THIS IS WHAT A FEMINIST LOOKS LIKE. Fortunately, Chloe didn't tell her mom that I made her peel the sticker off the back bumper of our Saturn, along with the DON'T DEFACE MACON PLACE one. I place my hand to my heart and with faux modesty accept credit for my daughter's progressive politics. The whole back and forth leaves me wondering how much awkward bullshit small talk Deb and I are going to put ourselves through.

"I want you to know how I admire what you're trying to do with Macon Place," Deb says. "I'm more than admiring–I'm envious. It's such a great opportunity."

"You might want to see my bank account before you say that. But I appreciate it. You're the first person who hasn't tried to talk me out of it. Everybody thinks I'm nuts for not selling my half to Mike Willoughby."

"Anything that puts more art into people's lives is good. I'd love to see the statue garden sometime. Chloe's told me all about it. Getting Macon Place in order can't be easy when you're raising a daughter at the same time. Do you ever wish you had help?"

Kirk Curnutt

"Sure. I've tried to get financial backing, but nobody thinks there's any reason to have a public statuary in this town. Folks are even more doubtful about an arts center and artists' colony."

"I meant help with Chloe, Vance. Help parenting her."

For several seconds all that passes between us is the wind. I ask what kind of help Deb is talking about. She takes to my second rocker, fingers spread wide over the handgrip.

"I don't know how to say this—or ask it. Part of me doesn't feel that I should have to ask, because Chloe's mine, too. She'll always be part of me. I'd like to see Chloe more often. Will you let me?"

"How often is more often?"

"I was thinking…joint custody more often."

My back lifts off my chair. I'd be out of my seat if I had somewhere to march my surprise.

"Don't get mad, please," Deb says before I can even speak. "I should be grateful Chloe even talks to me, but I think about her all the time. I think about what I have to give her. At her age she needs a mother. The truth is I don't want to tour anymore. I'm too old for it, and the roles aren't there for me. I thought I'd find an apartment… close by."

"How close by?"

"In Willoughby close by."

I stomp to the porch edge. My indignation would probably be more impressive if I weren't wearing bath slippers. I take a deep breath as I stoop over the rail, my fingernails gouging the wood. I have to dig them in; there's not enough scab left on my cold sore to rake.

Minnesota has eroded into New Hampshire. I spin around. "How would you get by?"

"Vance," Deb says, eyes dropping to my feet. "Your robe."

The damn thing has come undone. Thank God I'm wearing boxer briefs. I grab the belt ends and cinch them Heimlich tight so the knot sits upon the sudden knot in my stomach. I ask when this move is happening. Deb hesitates, then admits that her furniture will arrive on Monday. Chloe has rented her a ten-by-ten shed at Uncle Bob's Self-Storage until she can find a job and an apartment. Just in case I was wondering, Deb isn't asking to stay with me until those things happen.

"Campbell is lending me her guest room until I get on my feet."

"Campbell? *My* Campbell?"

I sink back into my rocker. My head is reeling. All I can think is how unfair this is. After all these years of Deb doing her own thing, suddenly she's concerned about Chloe having a mom? I've been her mom, her dad and her mom both. Where was Deb on her daughter's thirteenth birthday? Where's she been these past Christmases? Now that I think about it, where the fuck is my child support? Deb's never paid a penny. She probably owes me close to $100,000.

Deb cries when I bark these questions at her. The tears flow so fast she has nowhere to put them. She keeps wiping her eyes with her thumbs because no tissue is handy.

"Do you want to know what made me decide to come back?" she asks. "I've reached the age where there's only one real role for me anymore. I'm always cast as the mother. I've played it for years, of course, way back when I was a teenager even, but suddenly I'm almost forty, and I can only get work in that part. And not the good mothers, either. I'm always the bad mother because there are no good ones. Clarissa in *Seven Lears*, Essie in *Ah, Wilderness!*, and Agave in *The Bacchantes*–she kills her kid. But you know what the kicker was? This winter I did *The Seagull*. I'm Irina Arkadina for the first time in more than sixteen years. It brought back so many memories, Vance. I could barely come offstage without crying. I kept thinking of the last thing you said to me: 'If at any time you should have need of my life, come and take it.' You thought you were so clever quoting Boris Trigorin."

Was I supposed to beg her to stay with me and Chloe? I remind Deb how miserable she was in the year we tried to make a go of our family. She fires back with her own memories.

"Playing that part again made me realize that Irina Arkadina is really a man's fantasy of a woman," she says. "Cold, uncaring, self-absorbed. You wouldn't think it, but it's true. Men want to believe women are incapable of love because it excuses them from the complications we bring. And at some point, trading all these emails with Chloe while doing that part, I realized that I was living that fantasy. Not for me, either, but for you."

I can make neither hide nor hair of what she's saying. She's spitting out so many I's and you's I get hamstrung in her sentences.

"You've needed me to be the deserter so you could forgive yourself. You've probably blocked it out of your memory, Vance, but it happened. What you said when I first told you I was pregnant. Those first few weeks, you said it several times, before we told our parents. You said I needed to get an abor–"

Suddenly everything is clear. *Way too clear.* She went there. Deb just went there.

"You're going to throw that in my face?" I say in disbelief. "Now? After all this time and all I've done? Damn! I was twenty then–I was scared!"

"But you can't deny that *all you've done*–how many times are you going to say that?–all your congratulating yourself, it's your way of settling your guilt, of pretending you never thought about not having her."

I'm speechless. I don't have a defense. I feel as if my tongue has been ripped out of mouth. But Deb's not done with me.

"I have need of my daughter's life," she tells me, "and I've come to take it."

Why she still sobs after finally getting me back for going Boris Trigorin on her is beyond me. It's bad enough to be stuck beside a crying woman, but when that woman is your ex-wife, it's unbearable. And when your daughter walks into the middle of all that crying, any hope for a decent day is shot.

"I guess she told you," Chloe mumbles. She sidles toward her mother, as if Deb were the one here needing comfort. "Are you mad, Daddy?"

She's in the same cami and boxers as the morning I found the condom wrapper in her bedroom. Could she put on some clothes once in a while?

"'Daddy,' huh? Four straight days of calling me 'Dad'

and now we're back to 'Daddy.' *Daddy waddy piddy paddy.* Aren't you a little old for that? Or is that your way of tricking me into thinking you're still *my little girlie curly whirly?* You know what I say to 'Daddy'?"

I yammer faster than I can think. So much so I'm not even aware of what I've said until Chloe recoils in confusion.

"Baby gum?" she says. "What's that supposed to mean?"

"I meant *talk*, dammit, *talk*. Lose the baby talk, champ."

# 14

When I think back to the first years after Deb left, it hits me how little I knew about parenting, and I'm amazed that Chloe ever made it to six, much less sixteen. Tucked in her carrier like a plump porcelain doll, she seemed so vulnerable that I often left her in it, fearing my touch might crack her. Then when she was mobile I wouldn't let her crawl or toddle from my sight, convinced she would swallow a pen cap or jab a finger in an electrical socket. For a long time I could only see my failures reflected in her. Dirty palms and knees reminded me to mop the floor more regularly; coughs and sniffles left me wondering what nutrients and vitamins I'd left out of her diet. Plenty of women assured me I was doing the right things, Dr. H among them, but I rarely asked for help. Needing it only sharpened my anxiety that I wasn't the right man for the job–that I wasn't right for the job, that is, because I was a man.

The scariest times were at night, when I suffered bad dreams about suffocation that were full of purple faces, goggling eyes, and swollen tongues. I'd click on the table lamp on the rattan nightstand, having to reach *up* for the switch rather than *over* because I didn't even own a bed back then, just a futon mattress I unrolled across the floor, and I'd check to make sure Chloe was breathing. Even then, I couldn't relax. I didn't feel as if I should. I'd lean against the wall and watch her chest rise and fall until the rhythm hypnotized me to sleep.

Years have passed since I've worried about losing my daughter, but that fear is now back, so fresh and intense

I can't believe I didn't appreciate its absence. I spend the morning aimlessly driving, circling the outskirts of Willoughby, speeding ten miles south to Montgomery only to speed straight back, wanting to run away but afraid of what might be looted from me while I'm gone. Every so often my phone blasts Chloe's latest prank ringtone. Appropriately enough, it's "King of Pain" by the Police. It's neither Chloe nor Deb calling, however, but Campbell. *My* Campbell, recruited, no doubt, to lecture me on how my daughter will benefit from having her mother back. Because I'd rather plummet off the corniche-like curves of Highway 231 than hear that, I ignore Sting's alluring melody and disappear to the one oasis where I'm sure I won't be bothered.

At Macon Place I pace Storm Willoughby's garden, desperate to carve a lull from the chaos. I can't get over the feeling that everything I touch turns to failure. The pond is covered in a slick of algae, brown patches mar the grass tapestry, the petals of the moon flowers are clenched tight as fists. Several statues are still crusty from their egging. If the grounds had looked this bad when Storm was alive I'd have been back teaching at Willoughby Academy before the yolk dried. The neglect reminds me of the myth of the Fisher King, whose land falls into infertility when he's wounded in the groin. I wonder whether that injury might've been inflicted by an ex-wife who came to plunder his territory. Like the Fisher King, I, too, must restore my kingdom to order—even if only fifty-one percent of this kingdom is mine. I hike to the main house and root through the cellar for borax. Soon I'm shirtless and up to my elbows in rubber gloves, scrubbing yellow smears off Aphrodite. The whole time, I can't help but wonder what a pervert I'd appear were a stranger to wander by and spot me scouring a pair of alabaster breasts.

However neurotic, that worry keeps me from dwelling on how many changes I've suffered through this past year. Deb's return not only reminds me that those changes are far from over but of how little control I have over them. For the eight years I worked for Storm, there was a soothing permanence to this garden that I naïvely mistook for the rhythm of my own life. Statues never moved, fountains never quit bubbling, the flow of the landscape was inexorable. So, for that matter, was my boss, whose dying gave birth to the upheaval foiling me. I want to believe that if only Storm had lived to see his centenary there'd be none of this loss. No lost job, no loss of a daughter's virginity, no loss of a daughter to her mother. It's crazy to say, but I doubt Storm would disagree. The first time he told me he wanted to live to see a hundred years his ambition seemed arrogant, as if he didn't think time would dare drop a man with his cash. I soon recognized that the milestone was meaningful to him for the same reason he revered Greek art, for the same reason he created this garden. He wanted to believe that he could stake a claim on immortality with Macon Place–not for fame or vanity's sake, but for the sake of something broader and deeper, something that Storm was convinced is essential to being human even though he was canny enough to know it has become unfashionable in the hustle and bustle of the nowadays. He believed in the idea that what's best about us is larger than ourselves, in the something that goes beyond the immediacy of desire and want, the something that is imperishable, immutable, irreducible.

I know because for eight years what it means to be human was all we talked about. "People think I'm a nut to spend a million dollars on statues," Storm would say. "They wouldn't blink if I poured my money into a minor league baseball team or a gaudy Cadillac fleet or a rib shack serving slobbery heaps of Boston butt. Don't get me wrong—I like a good Boston butt, but it doesn't mean a damn thing to my soul. It has nothing to do with my divinity, whereas the attention to detail in these statues, the perfection of their form, even the contrapossto stance, which was a new innovation for Praxiteles's generation— these are all devices for inspiring me to transcend the brokenness of being human, of encouraging me to believe in what is most vital in me. And I don't mean *just* me, Dr. Seagrove. I mean all of us. What is that part? It's the sacred, the eternal, the spiritual. What do I get out of a Boston butt? A burp, maybe a fart, a long turd if I'm lucky. Those things pass, thank Christ, and the sooner the better. But this art, it lasts because the Greeks are reminding us of what's godly in ourselves, how we can always aspire to more even though deep down we know we're mostly made of clay and crap."

A major part of a majordomo's job is to serve as his employer's devil's advocate. That was the one duty I was really good at, in all honesty. I've always had this weird Hawthornean infatuation with fallenness and guilt, which explains why I feel so guilty about having fallen so often in my life. I was well-armed and more than willing to shoot down Storm's airy ideas about human nobility.

"What the Greeks really wanted," I would say, "was to humanize godliness, not the other way around. How otherwise do you explain all the hanky-panky in their mythology? Their stories are full of rape, adultery, and incest. It's all well and good to say that the *pudica gesture* is Praxiteles's way of celebrating the divinity of female sexuality, but you're ignoring all the unseemliness that Aphrodite inspired. Remember Ares? He was so consumed with possessing the Goddess of Love that he turned into a wild pig and gored her lover Adonis in a jealous rage. What about Zeus? Aphrodite's own dad lusted after her—what's divine about that? He wanted his daughter so badly he masturbated over her image, and when he didn't bother to swab up his spillage, his seed gave rise to a race of rowdy centaurs. Ooh, and then there's the story of what happened when Zeus actually had his way with Aphrodite. She ended up bearing her own half-brother, a crooked bastard called Priapus. What's he the god of? The phallus. Don't you see? Male genitalia go hand in hand—no pun intended—with the illicit and misbegotten, with defilement even."

"You're talking stories," Storm would snap back. "Obscure stories to boot. But they could be the famous myths and it wouldn't matter because I'm talking about statues. There's a reason sculpture is the greatest art form. It frees a gesture from the downfall of time. Only gesture's not the word I want. What's better? Something that doesn't sound like posing, like something contrived."

Without fail, I supplied the word he was looking for: *stance.*

"That's it! Yes! Sculpture frees a stance from the downfall of time. It captures a heroic moment in all its complexity, without any before or any after, a sliver of action holding still against space. Look at my garden. What do you see? There are no stories being told here, only stances we strive to emulate. You want equilibrium in your life? Look at Polycitus's *Diadumenos*. You want courage? Study Lysippos's *Eros Stringing the Bow*. You want to know what true beauty is? She's right there for you: Aphrodite. Take your time. She's not going anywhere."

"Maybe a sculpture freezes a moment in time, but that moment still needs an audience to make sense of it. How do we make sense of Aphrodite? We project plots onto her. We have a pool of stories about what it means to be beautiful, and we drape her in them, dressing her to accommodate our understanding. Aren't you doing that if you say the *pudica gesture* is a sign that Aphrodite's not embarrassed to be seen naked? Aren't I doing it if I say that pose to me reeks of shame? Because plots are human inventions, and because all humans are fallen, then all of our plots convey our fallenness. That's called a syllogism, sir. Invented by your friends, the Greeks. You don't believe what I say?"

At this point I always stood behind Aphrodite, tapping at the alabaster purity of her tailbone.

"The story you told me about the guy who killed himself because he thought he ruined this statue, that story is my proof. He was convinced he'd defiled Aphrodite by leaving a mark. What mark? It was the story he projected onto her. Inevitably, you and I defile her as well. We all have our own stories, don't we? We vandalize her with them as badly as if we spray-painted obscenities across her chest. If you really wanted an authentic reproduction of Aphrodite, you'd have commissioned your sculptor to include a spot right here to memorialize the mark left by that man. Then you'd be commemorating what art's really about–the stain of humanness."

My argument was usually greeted with a silence that left me wondering if I hadn't just lost my cushy job. Where else could I ever blow such smoke and still get paid so handsomely? Certainly not in teaching. Fortunately for me, Storm didn't ruffle that easily. He'd simply point to his mansion and let me know our debate was done.

"See those pigeons on my roof? I've got them to shit on my statues, Dr. Seagrove. I don't need you doing it, too."


A golf cart rips over the hill. I think it's either my dad or Luther out to broker a reconciliation with Chloe and her mother, but it's not. It's Mike Willoughby, and from the way his moussed hair wilts in the humidity, I can tell he's agitated.

"My, my, Seahorse at work. I never thought I'd see such a sight." He hops out of the cart to lean against our amphitheater stage. "Tell me what I'm to think when I look at Aphrodite. Because all I see is tits and twat."

I ask what has him in such a pleasant mood this morning. I bet my bad day can top his.

"I'm being serious," he insists. "You and Daddy could spend whole days out here gabbing about goddesses and gods and satyrs. I'm just trying to figure out what's so great about them. I've looked Aphrodite up and down all my whole life, and I don't get it."

It must be nearly one-hundred degrees out here. I wipe my sweaty eyelids and do the only thing I can. I play along, reciting his father verbatim.

"You're supposed to appreciate the symmetry, the intricacy of the construction, the balance, the fact that she's complete. That was the Greek ideal. Form embodies content, giving us the satisfaction of harmony and wholeness. Because the art contains itself, no interpretation is necessary. She is what she is because she doesn't need any more. She's a perfect image of a body."

My explanation assures Mike he was right. Aphrodite *is* just tits and twat. I tell him I'm glad he's getting his kicks saying those words but I'm really not in the mood. I start to explain that my ex-wife is invading my turf, but he cuts me off.

"Did Daddy ever tell you the freaky story about the guy who killed himself over Aphrodite? I'm sure he must have. Personally, I never bought it. Nice mythology, but who offs himself for a statue's sake? Storm wouldn't have. He was married three times. The last time was to my mother, who was his cleaning lady. He was sixty when I was born. Do you think a woman's beauty ever sent Daddy off a cliff? No, it was just something else for him to consume.... But now that you've explained how the meaning is self-contained, maybe the story's not so farfetched. After all, a lot of men do insane things in the name of tits and twat. You included."

Man, I want to punch Mike in the face. The one time

I've ever been in a physical confrontation, though, taught me I'm not a brawler. One afternoon in grad school, Dr. H's ex-husband confronted me as I walked from the library to the babysitter's to pick up Chloe. He cussed me out, told me what a loser I was, then spit on me. I took a lame lunge, he bopped a shoulder into my chest, and then slapped my face. *Slapped, not slugged.* I couldn't have felt more emasculated than if he'd yanked down my shorts and told me I was hung like a Jujyfruit.

"Speaking of work," I say, "don't you have any to do this morning? Or is insulting me your new job? I haven't done anything crazy over a woman since—well, since you know who. Please don't say her name."

Mike says her name. "Ardita Farnam is old news. So old I can't keep your women straight. Let's see, there's the guitar-playing tattooed girlfriend, the bisexual best friend you get to bang, and now the black-headed babe who's been on your porch all morning."

"That black-headed babe would be my daughter's mother."

"I don't disapprove. You want disapproval you should hear what my wife says about the example you set for your daughter. Personally, I don't judge, but I do like to live vicariously. Is it too much to ask that you save a seat at the table for your partner? Last night I started thinking about why you and I ended up owning this jalopy of an estate together. I thought maybe I'd swing by to hash things out, once and for all, and in your favor, I might add. Maybe I should've told you this earlier on, but your ideas for this place, they're very noble. It'd be wonderful to open these grounds to the public, *if the public wanted it.* Does it? Have you done a feasibility study? Do you have a business plan?

"Get a proposal together, Seahorse. That's what I was going to tell you last night. Let's study it. But then I pull onto your street, and what do I see? Three gorgeous women dancing on your porch. I would say five gorgeous women, but I realized two of them were Chloe and Nina, and calling them gorgeous is weird to me. So I'm sitting there in my car by myself watching the fun, and it hits me. Seahorse is having a party, and *I'm not invited.* A guy that my family floated for almost a decade. A guy who wants me to back a crazy idea that he can't even explain. It makes me think I'm not only not appreciated but that I'm not liked. I've got to tell you, I'm hurt."

"You're kidding, right? Last night was a *family* thing."

Mike reaches into his pocket, pulling out something long and rectangular. I don't see what it is until he unfolds it. Don't Deface Macon Place, the bumper sticker reads, with a red slash through a golf club.

"I've counted seven of these on bumpers so far this morning. I guess we're escalating, huh? Making this disagreement of ours a public-relations battle? All right, motherfucker, I'm down. But have you ever stopped to ask yourself why Daddy left you half of Macon Place? You think it's because he wanted the statuary preserved, and he knew I saw no reason for that. But here's the real question that you've never considered. If maintaining this garden was so important to Daddy, why didn't he make sure you had the money to do it? Why no bequest for you? He gave you *two percent* more of this place than he gave me but no cash for upkeep. Meanwhile, I inherit ten million. If I were you, I'd take that as a slap. It would make me wonder whether I was really such a trusted confidant, or whether I was simply a means to an end."

When I ask what means to what end he's talking about, Mike's eyes go tight.

"Daddy giving you this place had nothing to do with Aphrodite and these other statues," he insists. "It was about him putting me in my place. About finagling me into this Cain-and-Abel game he's rigged between us. It was Daddy's way of leaving me a lasting memory of the only thing he was ever good at giving me: his disapproval."

I tell him he's got it all wrong, that Storm was proud of him. Storm was Mike's dad, for Christ's sake. Dads don't use other people to get back at their kids.

"If you believe that," Mike snorts, "then you don't know the stories behind these statues. Remember Agamemnon? He was happy to sacrifice his daughter for a swift wind to Troy. Tantalus killed his son Pelops and served him cooked to the gods. Zeus was the biggest son of a bitch of all. You know that one story actually has him *donking* Aphrodite, right? Gets her pregnant even. Those were my bedtime stories growing up. Can you imagine that? A dad putting his kid to sleep with stories of a father screwing his daughter."

I'm stunned. Anytime I told Storm about Zeus impregnating Aphrodite, he acted as if I made that legend up.

Mike isn't done. "You trusted the wrong Willoughby," he snarls. "*I* was the one protecting you, not him. All you had to do was cash out. $750,000, more than fair. You had a chance, but you didn't leave me a choice."

He punches at a number on his cell and orders somebody down the hill. A second later another golf cart rips over the horizon. Not until she's out of the shadows do I recognize the driver. Her deputy's uniform blends like camouflage into the backdrop of our thuja greens.

"Hey, Doctor."

Brody Dale, Campbell's friend from the P-FLAG fundraiser, nods as she hands me a folded passel of paper. She apologizes for being the bearer of bad news and then asks if Chloe recovered from the banquet.

"Tell her I thought she sang real pretty," Brody says. "I hated that she ran offstage."

I rip open the seal, even though I can guess what the papers say.

"It's called a sale for division," Mike says, in case I can't read the lawsuit myself. "And so you don't think I'm a killjoy, you can have your battle of the bands. That's me being generous."

He jumps into his cart and rides off on the red carpet of a smirk. As he rumbles past Aphrodite, he can't resist reaching out and proving a universal axiom: wherever a woman's breast is exposed and a man's hand is free, a nipple shall be tweaked.

After Brody excuses herself, I curl up like a baby in Aphrodite's shadow. I don't know how long I lie in the sweet-smelling grass, but I don't stir until "King of Pain" begins bleating from my phone. I let the ringer go until I realize how badly I want to take out my frustrations on my ex-wife's new landlord.

"Et tu, Brute?" I ask Campbell.

"This is no time to pout about Deb. I need to see you, pronto. I need help."

I agree to meet her at Gold Star, Willoughby's riverside park. It's not as attractive as Storm's garden, but, as Mike told me when I first suggested we open Macon Place to the public, it'll always be more popular because its idea of fun involves a boat launch and barbeque pits instead of Greek statuary. The park turnoff sits on the same corner of Company Street as the Willoughby City Museum, whose main attraction is a life-sized bronze of my dead boss reading *The Iliad* to his classically christened daughters. (Mike wasn't born yet when the statue was cast.) The turnoff ends in a parking lot and a helpful sign ten yards short of the eastern bank of the Coosa that reads CAUTION—RIVER AHEAD. I find Campbell huddled under the farthest pavilion, hiding behind a dark pair of sunglasses. I don't know what paparazzo she's hiding from. Thanks to the drizzle, we have the park to ourselves.

"Steve's coming to town," she informs me.

"Jesus! This is turning into bad science fiction: *Attack of the Ex-s.* What the fuck does he want?"

"He wants to see for himself that we're a couple. What are we going to do?"

I'd forgotten Campbell tried to con Steve into believing we're a family. Now she's freaking out because she's agreed to let Deb stay with her for a few days, and her ex-husband will never believe she's not gay if another woman is living in her house.

"This is why you should've told Deb to find her own house," I say. "It's also why you need to be straight with your ex-, no pun intended. Nothing could be worse than getting caught in all these lies."

"It's too late for that. You don't know Steve. He's vindictive. He's got a chip on his shoulder. He never got over getting dumped for a woman. There's only one thing I know to do." Campbell whips off her sunglasses. "All you have to do is stay with me this week, Vance. Five days at most. I've already explained it to Deb, and she's game. Chloe wasn't sure you'd let Deb stay at your house, but I told her you'd do it for me."

It takes me a second to process what she's asking. I point out that a real friend needing a favor would have told me my ex- was moving in on my turf. Besides, there's a complicating factor to this ruse Campbell has cooked up—namely, Sadie. I note how none too happy my girlfriend was to discover from my own father that my best friend and I have knocked boots.

"You think that explaining things to Steve is compli-cated," I tell Campbell, "how am I supposed to convince Sadie that I'm only staying at your house so your ex-husbo won't think you're gay? Now that Sadie knows we've been more than pals, I doubt she even believes you're a lesbian."

"That's your fault for not being honest with her. You could have been. Sadie would've been cool with us. She's by far the coolest woman you've dated—besides me."

I pull Mike's lawsuit out of my back pocket and tell Campbell that Sadie is the least of my worries. Only she isn't as outraged as I would expect a woman asking me to pretend I'm her life partner would be. She tells me I should've taken Mike's $750,000 offer when I had the chance. I'm shocked. I never whispered a word about that money to her. I want to know where she heard it from.

"I heard it from Deb and your dad both," Campbell tells me. "Chloe told them, separately."

This pisses me off. Chloe has no business talking to anybody about my finances. That's one more thing I've got to straighten my daughter out on. No wonder Deb is moving back. She smells money. I wouldn't be surprised if the first thing Monday she hires a lawyer and sues me for child support.

Campbell slips her glasses back on when I say this.

"Please don't talk like a man," she begs me. "I can't love you if you do."

She tells me I have no business being mad at Chloe for wanting to know why her father is willing to wipe out his savings over a tinderbox he can't afford to fix up. There's a simple reason Chloe has a vested interest in my finances: she's afraid of ending up on the street. That's one reason Chloe asked Deb to move to Willoughby. She's insecure about money and doesn't understand why I won't teach again if I need a paycheck. Campbell lets me know that she doesn't understand either. Nor does anyone else, and the reason is that I won't explain why Macon Place is more important to me than $750,000.

"You're assuming I can explain it to myself," I admit. "All I can say is that selling out feels disloyal to Storm. As for Chloe, the day I can't put food on the table is the day she's allowed to worry about money. What she needs to understand is how much worry she's caused *me* lately. I've been weighing the pros and cons of something all week, and today has made my decision for me. I'm not

Kirk Curnutt

willing to cede control of situations to other people. Not to my ex-, not to yours. If you help me with it, I'll do whatever I can to convince Steve that you're one-hundred percent hetero."

Campbell perks up. "Anything. Name it."

"I want you to take Chloe to the gynecologist and get her on the pill. Before Deb can do it."

# 15

It's after six before I can bear to go home. I make the mistake of assuming the house is empty until I walk in on Luther and Deb watching *Law and Order: SVU* in my living room. I start to ask whether it's the episode Deb auditioned for, but my snarky tone offends even me, so I head upstairs. On my way I spot a blank spot on my shelf of leather-bound books. Since they're arranged in alphabetical order, I know right away somebody has pilfered Lisa Alther's *Kinflicks*. I'm tempted to hunt down my father and tell him to keep his paws off my library, but I'd rather be alone. Unfortunately, that's not going to happen. I don't even make it to the landing before Luther is dogging my heels. He drew the short straw when it came to deciding who would reprimand me for going AWOL all day.

I ignore him until I'm in my bedroom, hugging the pillow Sadie slept on last night. I know it's hers because it smells of talent, beauty, and weed. I ask where Chloe is. Luther passes me a note she left. It's hardly an apology: *Daddy, Had to run an errand. Can't we talk? Don't be mad. C.* I crumple it, angry that I've become anger to avoid. Luther recaps how the day was spent going to church, to brunch, and then to his studio where a tentative demo of "Daddy's Girl" was recorded. Chloe wanted her mother and grandfather to watch her and Sadie record her first-ever composition. Luther assures me she wanted me there, too, but I don't feel wanted.

"What's the song sound like?" I ask.

Luther shoves his hands in his pockets and bops his

head back and forth, noncommittally. "It reminds me of a lot of the bands that passed through Willoughby in the nineties. Interesting ideas, some catchy hooks, but not many surprises. The last minute and a half gets repetitive. But that's okay. Chloe's sixteen; we shouldn't expect 'River Deep, Mountain High,' not yet. Poor thing–she was so excited to lay down the track she couldn't keep a steady beat. We ended up using a drum machine. Sadie put guitars on it, then Deb and Sadie sang backup. Your dad was a little upset Chloe wouldn't let him near the microphone."

I'm not surprised. Thanks to Dick Haymes, Dad doesn't sing–he croons. There's no crooning in punk rock. Luther ignores my witty repartee and lets me know that Dad was upset I wasn't around to say goodbye before he drove back to Dalton. Boo friggin' hoo, I reply. As I wonder whether Dad took *Kinflicks* home with him, Luther's mustache twitches. I interpret that as him being embarrassed for me until I realize something else is crawling up his leg.

"I know about your plan to pull the wool on Steve," he says. "Campbell didn't tell me. Deb did. She says she's staying here in your house now and *you're* moving into Campbell's to fake being a couple. Is that true?"

"I'm not doing it for Deb. I'm doing it for Campbell."

Luther begs me not to. He's worried pretending Campbell is straight will only make things worse for Lleyton. Enough people talk about his mom already, and that's not good for him, Campbell, or for Willoughby's gay community. Campbell's own friends say that she needs to get off the fence. Acting like she can choose her sexuality makes it harder for the others to argue that they were born with theirs, Luther lectures me. His righteousness salts my irritation.

"Have you ever asked Campbell what she thinks of your politicking?" I ask. "Have you ever once thought that maybe she's not cool with you peacocking around as the great white hetero hope of gays and lesbians? Maybe figuring out who she is would be easier if you weren't bragging about being the world's most accepting father, Luther. From where I sit it looks more like your activism is your way of making *you* feel better about Campbell. She's bisexual. Go accept that."

Luther doesn't wilt quite as I expect him to. He merely pivots on his heel and marches out of my bedroom, waiting until he's out the door to get the last word in.

"You're an asshole," he says over his shoulder.

I sink onto my back and read the Sunday *Times*. Dominating the front page is another report on the rumor that Oksana Dybek and Lifting Belly are pawns of Bronislavis Stylptitch. The article repeats many of the details I already know, including the story of the hazy photo of the woman in Stylptitch's palace that's supposedly Oksana. At this point I'm disillusioned enough to believe Lifting Belly is a con. I find my laptop and go online, pulling up pictures of Oksana and telling myself I can see the wicked smile of deceit behind her militant poses. What kind of feminist takes off her shirt to make a point about oppression, anyway? I land on the website Chloe set up for Lifting Belly and scour the comments her guests have posted. There's one from Stu

Kirk Curnutt

("This is cool"), from Nina ("I like their message but not their music"), and, of course, Deb ("So proud of my daughter. Fight the power, Chloe!"). The humbug in me wants to let them know how naïve they are. Even if Oksana Dybek isn't a tyrant's puppet, she isn't her own person. I look up a quote I remember vaguely from grad school and cut and paste it into the reply box.

*Woman is not born: she is made. In the making, her humanity is destroyed. She becomes symbol of this, symbol of that: mother of the earth, slut of the universe; but she never becomes herself because it is forbidden for her to do so.*

The quote is from Andrea Dworkin. I don't post it, however, because on reflection I don't want it misinterpreted. I don't want anybody thinking I'm aiming that "slut" reference at Chloe.

I'm still scrolling through pictures of Oksana and her band when Chloe finally comes home. Sheepishly she peeks through my door, asking where I've been all day. As if I haven't been flat on my ass tonight wondering where she's been all day.

"I have a favor to ask," she says. "Stu wants to do a painting of me. There's an art competition in Birmingham he wants to enter, but he doesn't have space at home to set up a big easel and canvas. I thought about asking if you would let him work at Macon Place, but I know you'd reject that idea outright. So I told Stu we could do the sittings in our garage. Is that okay? He'll be painting, I'll be posing, and when he's done I'll be an *objet d'art.*"

I wonder where she learned that phrase. Being

somebody's object hardly sounds like her brand of ambition. Maybe I know my daughter better than I think. Chloe tells me she's only modeling for Stu because he asked. It makes me wonder what else the little bastard is asking from her that she doesn't want to do. I don't pose that question because I don't want to interrupt her. Chloe goes into this long explanation of why modeling's not her bag. She and Stu tried some preliminary poses and sketches the other night, and she found it brain-deadening. She has too much energy to stand still and be bored. We could be on the cusp of an actual conversation if I weren't broiling with resentment. I have to open my fat face and ruin the mood. I tell Chloe this painting of Stu's better not be a nude.

Chloe lets out a guttural *oomph*, the kind you make when you've been slapped.

"It's not, okay? But can I ask you about something you said this morning, Dad? You said—"

"I know what I said, and you know why I said it. Let's not bullshit. 'Lose the bubblegum, champ'? What sort of line is that coming from a sixteen-year-old girl?"

She's horrified. "You were spying on me?"

"I didn't have to spy. You weren't making any effort to be discreet. You couldn't have called more attention to yourself than if you'd jumped onto Luther's stage and started twiddling that kid's uvula in front of the entire banquet."

Chloe rears back. "God, you're disgusting! Can't we ever talk without you making fun of me?"

"How about I stop making fun of you when you start showing some respect for me? Show some for yourself while you're at it. Seeing you two make out was like watching that movie *Species.* I kept waiting for your tongue to explode out the back of Stu's skull."

Chloe lets out a shriek that could bow my hardwood. I hop off the bed, my voice as stiff as my stride. I tell her that if she wants to indulge in adult behaviors she better understand the adult responsibilities that come with them. Otherwise she'll be saddled with some very real adult consequences, just like I was sixteen years ago. I try to back her into a corner, but that's not the direction Chloe is going. Fists balled, she leans forward so that the ends of her bob meet under her nose.

"Like you're anybody to talk about responsibility and consequences! You're a hypocrite!"

"I've met my responsibility for sixteen years–unlike a certain somebody else you're related to. Care for me to name names?"

"Here's a name for you: Ardita Farnam! Let's go down to Katfish Kountry and ask her how great you are at handling consequences!"

I can't move. I think I've been shanked. Chloe remains only long enough to make sure she's delivered a death blow. When she stomps off I fold face first onto my bedspread and feel something trickling from the wound.

Moral authority, I think it's called.

A short time later, after a hot shower that won't scald away my embarrassment, I sneak downstairs. Stealing past Deb and Luther, who're still glued to the TV, I slip out the kitchen door and tiptoe barefoot to my detached garage. The carriage-style doors are vibrating to the beat of a blaring hip-hop rhythm whose bass thumps hard enough to bruise a spleen. From the viburnum bordering my house, I fish out a decorative wrought-iron bench my landscaper installed a few years ago, back when I could afford a landscaper. Using it as a ladder, I peek through a window at Stu, who's squirting multi-colored acrylics onto a palette. A few feet away, Chloe pores over a coffee-table book spread open on the concrete floor. She flips the pages so casually it takes me a second to register that she's naked. It takes another second to realize that she's not. She's wearing a flesh-colored leotard left over from her ballet days. When she finds the right image to imitate, she hops up and dangles her left hand at her waist while cocking her hip slightly to one side. The angle is just subtle enough to emphasize the diagonal glide of her right arm, which slices across her thigh. I recognize the pose right away. Praxiteles invented it. He didn't name it the *pudica gesture*, but he was the first to stage it with his most famous statue, the Aphrodite of Knidos.

I watch for several minutes—why, I'm not sure. Nothing happens. Chloe and Stu hardly trade a word. If only their entire relationship revolved around him gazing at a blank canvas while she shielded her mons pubis, I might live to see forty.

Kirk Curnutt

# 16

As midnight turns into one a.m. and then two, I lie in the dark, gripped by a sensation I'm not all that familiar with. It's loneliness. I'm remembering a time when I shared this bed, and not with a woman, either, but with Chloe, who used to wander into my room at night to curl at my chest. I'm not sure what brought her creeping to me. Nightmares, probably. I'd prefer to think it was need, the need for the warmth and security of father flesh. I want to believe she slept more soundly with me, even though her skin against mine made relaxing impossible. Chloe was always turning, twisting, tossing–*rotating*, even, in a clockwise direction and with clocklike precision so I could almost predict when and where our bodies made contact: a kick to the shin at midnight, elbow in the ribs at three, foot in the face at six, punch to the groin at nine. I had nowhere to go. It was inevitable; the only way I could hope to rest was to throw my arms around her and pin her down.

I blame those embraces for my insomnia. The possibility that someone might happen upon our tangled bodies and misconstrue that intimacy was both terrifying and infuriating. Deb's leaving had made an androgyne of me–I was father and mother, but because of my chromosomes and the curse of sex, I was doomed to never be seen as anything more than a man–predatory and opportunistic, a creature of impulse rather than reason or love. I'd known women who joked openly about sons grabbing their breasts and licking their faces when kissed, but those stories weren't freighted with sinister overtones.

Nobody would accuse their narrators of inappropriate behavior, not even when the bolder among those women (they all seemed to have read Sue Miller's *The Good Mother*) admitted that the thin line between the sensuous and sensual disappeared when a tooth bit lightly into a nipple or a curious finger poked its way into a belly-button. Those women had given body to their children. Distinctions of identity, the lines separating who from whom, were blurred. That wasn't the case with us.

How could I not fear being misunderstood? I couldn't even come up with words innocent enough to convey what was going on. *We lie together. We bed together. We sleep together.* All I needed was an adult to overhear Chloe say something suggestive along those lines, and I'd be buried alive in innuendo and law. It was a risk I couldn't bear; it couldn't go on. The day Chloe started elementary school, I put my foot down and confined her to sleeping in her own room.

Around two I rise, pace from ottoman to armoire and back, listening for signs that my house is stable. Only there is no noise. Again I'm struck by clammy memories of Chloe's babyhood, when silence intoned the crash of disaster. In the dark I pat the walls, seeking the door, driven by an impulse that's as crazy as it was years ago: I need to see my daughter breathe.

I slink downstairs until the cold zinc of her doorknob is in my hand. I turn it, but only slightly so the latch and spindle won't give me away. Hinges groan; a creak in the hardwood rings like a scream. I keep to baby steps to avoid tripping over the obstacle course on her floor. At the edge of Chloe's bed, I tip an ear and swallow my breath to listen to—nothing. The room is deathly quiet. I stoop closer, convinced something is wrong. I reach back to flick the light switch, my mind racing with images of blue faces, goggling eyes, swollen tongues—

Only I shouldn't have worried. Chloe is still alive.

Or, at least, I assume she is, *wherever* she is, because she's not here.

My first thought is that she's gone to Campbell's to stay with her mom. Then I spy Chloe's window, and I realize I've been suckered. There's a small, almost imperceptible space between the rail and sill that's just wide enough to fit two fingers to raise the sash. I'll be damned, I think. And I deserve to be if I let Chloe believe she can get the better of me. In a fit of pique I close the window and throw the cam, locking my daughter out of the house.

If I learned one thing from earning an otherwise useless Ph.D. in theater, it's that scenes rarely unfold the way a director plans. They can't because chaos has its own choreography. Hoping to catch Chloe in the act of sneaking back inside, I lie in wait on my porch, but forty minutes later what sweeps up the street isn't our old Saturn or even Stu's Hyundai Accent.

It's a sheriff's cruiser.

"Hey, Doctor." Amid the soupy haze of the streetlights, I barely recognize Brody Dale. Her uniform blends like camouflage into the backdrop of my zoysia grass. "Twice in a day—Holy smokes, people are going to talk about us. Glad you're up, though. Usually this time of night I have to bang on folks' doors." Brody pulls her flat cap low to her eyes as she swings open the rear driver's door, pulling a sheepish Chloe out of the backseat. "I believe you know this girl."

"I used to think I knew her. What's happening here?"

Chloe stares into the grass, arms clasped behind her back as if mounting the gallows. When she doesn't fess up, Brody provides the details.

"I was driving by Mr. Luther's studio when I saw a car parked out back of Macon Place. Your friend, Mike Willoughby, has been complaining about kids vandalizing your garden, so I figured I better check it out. Lo and behold I find your daughter here and the Laughlin girl stretched out on a blanket."

I look at Chloe, confused. "You and Nina were stretched out *together?*"

Brody tucks her thumbs behind her gun belt, lips puckered. I can read her mind: *And here you thought you wouldn't have a problem with her being with another girl.*

"Don't worry, Doctor. It wasn't like they were spooning. More like stargazing. I won't say they lied when I asked what they were up to, but they weren't forthcoming. That's not the way to not come off suspicious, I told them. When I asked if anybody else was on the property, the Laughlin girl says 'no' just as a boy waltzes out of your thuja greens."

Why am I not surprised?

Brody tells me that she assumes the young man was Chloe's boyfriend, though she didn't see his face. "That boy saw my uniform and dropped everything but his drawers as he ran off," she says. Brody chased him up the hill toward Storm's house, but she's not used to sprinting even short distances. By the time she returned to the

Kirk Curnutt

pond, the Laughlin girl had taken off, too. Chloe, on the other hand, sat on the blanket frozen stiffer than one of Storm's statues.

"You didn't find any eggs on them, did you?" I ask. "As many problems as she's given me lately I wouldn't put it past her to be the one egging the statuary."

Chloe lifts her chin. "I wouldn't do that," she says with a soft pleading gulp.

"You're the first parent to ask me about eggs," the deputy admits. "Usually they want to know about dope. No eggs, no dope, no toilet paper, either, in case you think they planned to roll you. Just these."

I hold my breath, hoping to God what she pulls out of her backseat isn't a shiny roll of foil packets with the words I SAID *LIKE* A VIRGIN on them. It's not. It's a six pack, along with a coffee-table book.

"I'll assume the beer belongs to the boy. No girl I ever knew brought Natty Lights to a party. The book must be hers, though. I never knew a boy to bring one of them to the festivities."

"How long have you been reading?" I demand of Chloe. "I mean *drinking*, dammit–How long have you been drinking?"

Chloe claims the beer was Nina's. Nina drank two, but Chloe didn't drink any so she could drive home. Brody reaches into the backseat and shows me the final bit of contraband she confiscated from the kids: a shoebox full of bumper stickers, half saying THIS IS WHAT A FEMINIST LOOKS LIKE and the other half, DON'T DEFACE MACON PLACE. What Chloe says next makes me madder than if Brody had caught her slurping a Jell-O shot out of Nina's bellybutton.

"Can I go to Mom's?"

"Hell, no, you can't go to your mom's! You're grounded!"

"You can't ground me from Mom."

I point out that the police have busted her not even twenty-four hours after her mother announced she was moving to Willoughby. Some things can't be written off as a coincidence. Before Chloe can defend Deb again, I order her into the house. She bursts into tears and obeys. I look to Brody for reassurance, only the deputy doesn't offer any.

"Don't let her sweet talk you in the morning," Brody says instead. "That's Trick No. 1 in the Girl's Book of How to Get Her Way. She'll cry up a storm making you feel bad for disciplining her, but you can't give in. Once she knows a little blubbering is all she needs to manipulate you, she'll turn them ducts on and off like they're faucets. Take it from a lesbian: a girl will say anything to get away with something. Personally, I don't trust them."

I ask Brody what she thinks the kids were doing in the garden. I can barely get the words out of my mouth. I keep thinking *three of them*. The three of them were together.

"You're lucky, Doctor. I showed up before whatever was going to happen could happen. Don't put anything past kids these days. That's my second bit of advice. Last week we caught three of them under the Bibbs-Grave Bridge, not a foot from the river. Two boys and a girl. Caught them in the act—though what act exactly I don't think you want to know. All I'll say is that I doubt d'Artagnan ever crossed swords with another musketeer that way."

I assure Deputy Dale that Chloe's not like that. She

Kirk Curnutt

only lost her virginity a week ago, I want to say. Surely she's not into threesomes already. Plus, she snuck out of the house *with a book.* Who takes a book to a threesome? None of this makes it out of my mouth, of course. The only thing that does is a neutered whimper. Brody tries to smile but ends up grimacing.

"You're not the first parent to tell me his kid's not 'like that,'" she says with great sympathy. "That girl under the bridge? Her mother swore the same thing. Everybody's kid is always a good one, especially after the kid gets caught."

# 17

For the second straight morning, I wake up disoriented, only not in my bed this time. I'm splayed in my porch rocker, where I drifted off after hours of torture from the pornographic images that, thanks to Brody, bubble through the cracks of my unconscious. Some of these images were set in gardens and some under bridges, some featured a duo and others a trio, some starred more women than men and others more men than women. All had at least one character named d'Artagnan, though none had faces, thank Jesus, just twisting combinations of huffing abdomens and heaving muscles and gyrating hips, all climaxing with an alabaster hand slung across a pelvis and an almost-centenarian rasping the words *pudica gesture* as if they were a clue to the world's most perplexing riddle.

The only thing missing from my nightmares was my ex-wife. Apparently she had better places to be–like right next to my rocker, where she's shaking me awake.

"I'm handling this," Deb insists, her tone as dark roasted as the coffee she carries in a cup that reads BETTER GAY THAN GRUMPY. I know the cup belongs to Campbell because I bought it for her as a gag gift. In my disoriented state I have to ask what Deb thinks she's handling besides other people's drinkware. She tells me that Chloe called her crying in the middle of the night, claiming I wouldn't let her go to Campbell's to see her mom. To Deb that means I'm not punishing her for sneaking out of the house; I'm punishing her for wanting her mother in her life. I shoo Deb away with a derisive snort, letting her know the only reason Chloe wanted to rush off to her was because she figured Deb would go easier on her out of guilt. To my surprise, Deb doesn't shoot that idea down, although she does insist she's perfectly capable of disciplining our daughter, guilt or no guilt.

"I want to ensure the punishment is administered fairly," she says, as if it's fallen on her to be the judicial watchdog. "Right now, Vance, you can't be fair because you're too angry at both of us."

"What's your idea of fair? Oh, wait, let me guess—you're going to punish her by making her live with you."

My sarcasm doesn't faze Deb. She promises that she's committed to splitting Chloe's time straight down the middle, four nights a week for one of us, four nights the next for the other. That's her way of proving she isn't "stealing" our daughter. Then Deb outlines Chloe's punishment. Our daughter will help me at Macon Place, eight to five, for one whole month, no pay. How very clever of Deb to redefine time with me as a punitive measure. She's not done, however. Chloe's only contact with Stu will be during rehearsals for the battle of the bands. And either she or I will supervise those meetings.

"Pink Melon Joy is practicing this afternoon," Deb says. "I can be there if you can't."

"No way. I'm breaking up the band *and* this relationship. Stu is history. That's final."

Deb takes a slow, ruminative sip and then sets her coffee on my railing. "I won't say from what I've seen of him that he's right for Chloe, but she needs to come to that realization on her own. She won't if we try to break them up. I'm telling you from experience: a girl isn't going to listen to her parents, no matter how right they are."

Chloe will listen, I insist. A parent just has to learn to talk loud. The first step to establishing the authority to make a child listen is to have been in her life for more than a weekend. Deb ignores this jab and comes back with a better one all her own.

"Do you know that we might never have married if my folks hadn't been on me to dump you?" she asks. "They were so cruel when I got pregnant–my dad especially– that marrying you was…. Well, don't take this the wrong way, Vance, but it was my way of showing them up."

I wonder what the right way to take that is.

"I never told you this," Deb continues, "but they wanted me to put Chloe up for adoption. They were embarrassed and didn't want their church friends knowing. Honestly, if I'd gotten pregnant twenty years earlier, I think they would've shipped me to a home for unwed mothers. My father threatened to cut me off if I didn't agree to give her up, so I called his bluff and married you instead. It wasn't until I left you and Chloe that Dad actually pulled that trigger. We didn't talk for years, and even now when we do, there's resentment on both sides. I don't blame anybody for my mistakes, but I would've liked some support instead of being berated. I don't want Chloe to go through that, certainly not because of a boy. No boy is worth it."

The story makes me realize how much harder Deb had it when we were in our early twenties than I did. I can't imagine the Carpet King of Dalton, Georgia, barking ultimatums at me.

"I didn't know any of that," I admit. "I knew your

parents didn't like me, but adoption? Jesus. Didn't it ever enter their minds that *I* wanted Chloe, once I got used to the idea of her?"

"Does it ever enter your mind that Chloe will want Stu no matter what we think of him?"

I rub my temples, hoping to massage away the confused clot of options and consequences. I tell Deb that letting Chloe and Stu see each other at all, even if it's only at band rehearsals, sends the wrong message. Why not throw conjugal visits into the deal while she's at it? What does Deb think the kids snuck out of the house to do, anyway?

"Chloe's not sleeping with Stu," Deb scoffs. "She would've told me if they're having sex."

I laugh and then nod with enough exaggeration to put a crick in my neck. "Sure she would tell you. Of course she would! Just like I'm sure she called you beforehand to tell you she was sneaking out of the house last night. You're so naïve about this stuff! I know you want to believe you and Chloe have a sister vibe going on, but a few emails and one night in the same town don't make you your daughter's confidante. Being a good parent requires having a good bullshit detector."

I'm tempted to tell her about the wrapper in Chloe's bedroom, but I don't want to come off like a snoop. At this point Deb would never believe I discovered it by accident. Part of me–all of me–wishes I'd never found that damn thing. Meanwhile, Deb has her own solution to what she thinks is a mystery. "I'll ask Chloe if she's having sex," she decides. This brings me to my feet.

"No, no, no. You can't do that because then Chloe will want to know why you think she is, and when you say I told you she was, she'll go ballistic and accuse me of spying on her. I've already had that pleasure once. Don't say anything. You want to punish her for sneaking out, then fine—you can be the bad guy for once in sixteen years. Leave the sex to me, though. I've got it under control. How long is three weeks? Twenty-one days? Let's make it twenty-eight and get Chloe through a cycle, just to be safe.... What are you looking at?"

Deb is peering over my shoulder into the house. "I hear the pitter-patter of little feet," she says. She steps to the screen door and summons Chloe outside. As her mother metes out the terms of her grounding, Chloe accepts her punishment heroically. Her chin quivers but, thankfully, there are no tears.

"Can I talk to Mom alone a minute, please?" she asks me when Deb finishes.

I shake my head, irritated but in no mood for another fight. I tell my daughter she'll have to deal with me sometime and head inside. On my way to start some coffee I spot Chloe's phone sitting on the hall credenza. I sweep it into my palm and call up her text messages, where I discover several fresh ones from Nina.

*Sorry I ran off last night but my dad's not like yours.*

*I know you think yours is Bronto-sore-ass Stippletick or whatever that dude's name is*

*But yur dad's a doormat compared to Luke*

*I'd much rather be stuck with Prancin' Vance than Luke the Puke*

*Is yur dad going to call my parents?*

So I'm Bronislavis Stylptitch to my daughter? And "Prancin' Vance"? Did Chloe come up with that, too? What does that even mean?

I go to the kitchen wondering if I prance when I walk. By the time I can pour myself the freshly brewed coffee and make it back to the porch, my best approximation of a swagger feels more like a constipated shuffle. Deb informs me that Chloe has something to say to me. Chloe's in my rocker, gripping the armrests tight, as if she's strapped into Old Sparky and two-thousand volts are about to sizzle her insides.

"I need to know that you believe me when I say nothing happened in the garden," she begins. "We only went there because Stu wanted to look at the Aphrodite of Knidos. He wants to paint me like the statue, but he was modeling it on this picture book we ordered off Amazon.com, and he couldn't get the shape down, so he said we needed to study it. Only when he picked me up, there's Nina already in the car, and she's drinking and when we get to Macon Place, Stu's got this blanket and he says he wants everybody to lie down by the pond so we can talk. We *did* talk, too, for a little bit, but then he started trying, you know, *stuff.*"

"Stuff? You mean sex? You had sex with Stu with Nina right there with you on that blanket?"

Chloe slaps her palms to her knees: "God, no!" She looks to Deb, nodding in disbelief. "I told you he wouldn't listen! He always thinks the worst!"

Deb tries to calm us down. "Stu *tried* to have sex, that's what your daughter is telling you. He tried, *and she wouldn't let him.*"

"And you still don't think we need to cut her off completely from Stu?" I ask my ex-.

"Stu's not bad," Chloe insists, welling up. "He just doesn't know any better. I mean, he's a guy–that's what guys do. They try to have sex with you."

I have to grip my porch rail again. "Don't you think you deserve better than that? Don't you think you deserve *respect*, maybe? You were already talking about breaking up with Stu; I don't understand why you would stay with him if he's pressuring you like this. I mean–Jesus!–he's trying to have sex with you in front of your own best friend in *my* garden!"

Chloe stops wiping her eyes. "Who told you I was thinking of breaking up with Stu?"

"You did," I fib. I'm not a very convincing fibber, however. I can feel my eyes quaver.

"I *didn't* tell you that," Chloe says. "I specifically didn't because I knew you'd fall to your knees singing hallelujah. There's only one person I said that to. It wasn't Nina; Nina can't keep a secret to save her life. Apparently Sadie can't either. I should've known she was narking to you."

I assure Chloe that it doesn't matter who told me. What matters is that she's willing to put up with a boyfriend she has to make excuses for. I let Chloe know I didn't raise her to be weak or clingy. That's why I pushed her to play drums, so she'd be strong and self-assertive and aggressive even–but most of all so she'd be independent.

"And now you want me to give up on somebody because he's not necessarily where he needs to be," Chloe sniffles. "I don't call giving up being independent, Dad. I call that running away. Don't you understand? I've put three months into this relationship."

"Three months is nothing, honey. I have bills that have been past due for longer than that."

But Chloe isn't swayed. She says that if she gives up on Stu now those three months have been wasted, that they're meaningless. "I could get another boyfriend in five seconds and then what?" she asks. "You'd want me to give up on him, too, just because he's a guy. I'm not going to cut and run because a relationship gets hard. I won't do that. I won't be like—"

She stops, catching herself.

I tell her to go ahead and finish that sentence. *I won't be like you, Daddy.* That's what she was going to say. Chloe's eyes drop to the porch. So do Deb's. I squat in front of my daughter and lift her chin with my palm.

"I want you to tell me straight up that you haven't had sex."

From the way her head snaps back, you'd think I'd smacked her. She's both embarrassed and offended, but she doesn't break eye contact. I can tell she's working furiously not to blink.

"I haven't, I promise."

I have to take my hand back or I'm afraid I will indeed slap her. I want so badly to tell her about finding that wrapper in her room, to throw that proof in her face, but what good would it do? Chloe would say it wasn't hers and that she doesn't know how it ended up in her trash basket. She could deny it until we both turned blue.

"You believe me, don't you?" Chloe asks.

Now I'm the one staring at the floor.
"Sure, I believe you."
It makes two of us lying through our teeth.

# 18

I don't force Chloe to go to Macon Place with me this morning. I'd rather not deal with her right now. Or deal with anyone, honestly. I ride down Highway 231 to our local equipment rental shop and pay fifty bucks to take home a tiller for the day. Then I go to the landscaping outlet next door and fork out another $200 for sod to re-carpet the dead rectangles blighting Macon Place's back acres. I should be out hiring a lawyer to defend me against Mike's lawsuit, but I'd rather lose myself in the blissful self-extermination of physical labor, even if I'm not very good at it. My first attempt at laying the grass looks like someone tossed a lumpy down vest to the ground. As I begin clearing a second patch of turf, a vague knocking makes me worry the tiller is locking up. When I cut the gas, I discover the knock is more like a hammer and that it's coming from up the hill. I hike past the algae-covered pond and several yellow statues to our amphitheater. There, on stage, Chloe pummels her drums as Stu, Nina, and their "roadies"–Mike's kids, Zak and Travis–set up equipment. I'd forgotten about Pink Melon Joy rehearsing today. True to her promise, Deb is here to supervise, along with Luther, Sadie, and Edgar Winter, Luther's albino Chihuahua. The three of them sit on a blanket with a chiller of Luther's port and a platter of cold cuts, looking like the picnickers in Manet's *The Lunch on the Grass*, only nobody's naked.

"Nice afternoon for a party. Am I the only one working today?"

Deb offers me a glass, which I decline. "I thought the

mood could use some lightening," she informs me. "Chloe couldn't stop crying after you left. That makes two straight mornings. She and I are both tired of tears. This has to stop, Vance. You can't just stalk off when there's a problem."

As much as I'd like to point out the irony of her saying that, I don't. Along with tears, there's been too much sarcasm lately. I note how little Chloe seems to be crying now. Her eyes are squeezed tight as her arms whirl as fast as helicopter blades over her skins and cymbals. She looks like a Greek fury. Or like one of the Herzoslovakian Furies that Lifting Belly mentions in their hit song, the women warriors who in medieval times overthrew a king and instituted a century of women's rule.

"Chloe has every right to be angry," Luther decides. He has to tug Edgar's leash so the dog doesn't bite my boot toes. "I'm going to talk to Stu. He's bought two hours at the studio this afternoon. He doesn't know I'm throwing in a free lecture on why a real man doesn't abandon a woman to the police."

I'm not thrilled that Luther knows about Chloe getting busted in the garden last night. As much as he likes to act as if he's her surrogate grandfather, he's technically not family. I sit next to Sadie, who seems about as annoyed with me as I am with Luther. She doesn't respond when I stroke her shoulder. When I give her a playful poke in the hip she lets out a hiss. For the first time in our relationship, I'm wishing she was stoned. At least then she'd be mellow.

"Sadie told me she bought you and Chloe tickets for a concert later this week," Deb says. "I don't know anything about Liz Phair, except that Chloe talks about her music all the time. We need to decide whether you're still taking her. We shouldn't let her go after last night, but we'll waste $140 if we don't. We could try to resell the tickets on eBay, but I don't think there's time. The concert's only two days away. Oh, and Vance, Sadie needs you to write her a check for the tickets. Her Visa is maxed out."

I want to remind them that I never approved going to this concert, much less agreed to pick up the tab for it, but I can feel the anger pouring out of Sadie. It's much more pungent than the cloud of Febreze that usually surrounds her. I ask her what's wrong.

"You told Chloe I told you she was thinking of breaking up with Stu, didn't you?" she snaps. "Don't bother straining for an excuse. Just know that some advanced warning would've been appreciated. Then I could've stayed out of her way. As it was I come to watch the band rehearse and I get the ass-chewing of my life—in front of Deb and Luther, no less. She called me a nark, dude. That's the first time anybody's accused me of that."

I assure Sadie that Chloe's just taking her agitation out on her, that the whole misunderstanding will blow over. Chloe can't seriously expect my girlfriend to keep news like a possible breakup from me—I'm her father.

"Yeah, well," Sadie grunts, "I have a feeling my days in her entourage are done. Chloe said she didn't want to have anything to do with me if everything she said was going straight from my ears to yours."

I ask Deb how she could let our daughter speak so rudely to someone.

"Don't pass the buck," Sadie huffs. "This is your fault.

If you'd listen rather than tell her what to do, she might talk to you, and you wouldn't have to recruit stoolies. I hope you didn't set anybody else up to be ambushed. Does Chloe know you're always after Campbell for dirt?"

Luther tells them about me grilling him over what Chloe said at their church youth group. The way he describes resisting my interrogation and not spilling a single bean you'd think he was tortured in a gulag. I wonder aloud how this conversation became about me. I'm just doing my job, protecting Chloe. Luther refills his port. He's so giddy I wonder if he's not buzzed.

"We may have good news in our future," he reveals, "but it can't go beyond this blanket. Chloe absolutely can't know, Vance. I don't care if she's got you in a choke hold, you can't tell her. Stu and I had a long talk about music when he reserved that studio time. He's decided that rock 'n' roll is dead."

What a newsflash. Next Stu will declare that it's better to burn out than fade away. When I don't ask what the kid means by this portentous announcement, Luther explains. Stu has apparently decided that punk rock peaked around the time his mom was pumping the bass for the Wussy Pimps and that hip-hop is where the real creativity is these days. This might be an insightful observation if this were 1995 or so. Nevertheless, Stu plans to use his studio time to try his hand at rapping instead of laying down his contributions to Pink Melon Joy.

I wonder if this is his way of getting back at Chloe for writing "Daddy's Girl" without his input. I admit to the others I'm leery of this career turn. I have nothing against hip-hop–like every other white kid in America, I owned a Run-DMC cassette in my day—but I don't trust Stu to handle the misogyny that rap can indulge in. Luther pooh-poohs my concern. I don't know what I'm talking about, he insists. Hip-hop has just as many strong women in it as rock 'n' roll does. To prove it he reels off a list of names, a handful of which I actually recognize. He comes close to suggesting that if I'm not cool with hip-hop I may have racial issues I need to think through. I'm so busy convincing myself that not liking the music doesn't mean I'm racist that I nearly miss what Luther says next. Stu has invited Travis and Zak to rap with him, but their Beastie Boys-styled trio has no room for chicks. Chloe and Nina are being shut out and shunted aside.

"They're going to call themselves the 'Gold Dust Twinz,'" Luther informs us.

"How can they be twins if there are three of them?"

"You're not listening, Vance. Stu and Chloe have different tastes in music, and that means Pink Melon Joy isn't long for this world. And without the band keeping them together, maybe the kids will drift apart and split up. Your prayers will be answered."

Before I can hop to my feet and do a victory dance, the band rips into its first song, and suddenly we're entombed in a common rock 'n' roll moment. It's not the cathartic one that comes when a pumping beat whips a crowd into a frenzy, nor the liberating one that happens when face-melting energy explodes into anarchy. It's the moment nobody much likes to talk about, the one in which musicians are so infatuated by their ability to make noise that they're oblivious to how terrible they sound. Looking around the picnic blanket, the four of us all agree. There's only one way to describe Pink Melon Joy: they suck.

"Why is Chloe so off-count?" I ask Sadie. "It's as if she's adding extra beats."

"That is the beat. It's a weird time signature; two time signatures, actually. She's alternating between 5/4 and 6/4 time. That's what makes the rhythm feel jittery. Watch her and count. She's actually dead on. The tricky part is not to shift into 4/4 time when you sing to that beat, because 4/4 feels more natural. You recognize the song, right? You should. It's from a CD of yours."

I strain to hear the lyrics over Stu's prickly guitar, which feels as piercing as acupuncture. It takes me a few verses, but eventually I can name that tune. Pink Melon Joy is butchering an old Pretenders' song from the early eighties called "Tattooed Love Boys." I recognize it because the same stepsister who was a fan of Maria McKee and Lone Justice owned this record, too. Or at least she did until my stepmother confiscated it from her. That didn't stop my stepsister from listening to it, though. When her vinyl version was snatched from her she went out and bought a copy on CD, which was easier to hide from Janice. "Tattooed Love Boys" was the reason my dad's second wife outlawed that particular Pretenders' album in our house. The song makes rather impolite use of a common noun it's otherwise hard to avoid in everyday conversation. The word is "hole," and no, it's not preceded by "ass." We're talking a different hole. The exact line that Janice went ballistic over comes to me only seconds before Chloe spits it into her mic. At the time of the kerfuffle I had no clue what it meant.

"Did our daughter just say, 'I shot my mouth off and

you showed me what that hole is for?'" Deb asks.

"She found that song on one of Vance's CDs," Sadie reminds everyone.

I lie back in the grass. I haven't felt this ridiculous since I had to have a conversation with a school principal about a Pussy Riot T-shirt. What does Chloe think she's getting away with singing "Tattooed Love Boys"? Does she think I won't recognize it? That I won't remember that line? What's her encore going to be? "Fuck and Run"? I sit up and tell my three picnickers that one of them needs to talk to Chloe about her language. No way is Pink Melon Joy playing this song at the battle of the bands. Mike Willoughby himself would throw the circuit breakers if he heard it.

"Don't look at me," Sadie says of the job. "Chloe's not talking to me."

"I'll do it," sighs Deb. "Although I never expected I'd have to have two talks with her in the same day."

Luther points to the stage and suggests none of us may have to censor Chloe. He's the only one who's noticed that Pink Melon Joy has clattered to a stop. Chloe is leaning over her toms, shaking a drumstick at her boyfriend. She tells Stu she'd appreciate it if he hit the right fret when he decides to peal out a guitar solo. He's taken aback and defends himself saying it was an accident, something he knows Chloe's never been guilty of. She tells him accidents wouldn't happen if he paid attention and didn't try to show off by going Rock God whenever it's his turn to step into the spotlight. Stu decides he'd just as soon not play "Tattooed Love Boys," anyway. The song's too hard and too obscure for the effort it'll take to learn it. This irritates Chloe even more. For her the effort is the point; playing more complicated songs will make them better musicians.

"What are you so mad about?" Stu says, flustered.

"Uh-oh," Sadie warns us. "He's going to tell her not to get emotional. I can feel it coming."

Stu's voice rumbles through the sound system. "This is practice, that's all! Don't get so emotional!"

Chloe lets out a scream that seems to detonate her drum kit. Her toms and bass fly forward before toppling over, sending an amplified thump through the PA as the shrapnel yanks down a live mic. Zak and Travis go about two feet in the air. It takes me a second to realize Chloe has kicked her kit over. Stu is as shocked as the rest of us, only he has to dodge the spinning cymbal threatening to saw off his leg. He's so busy avoiding it he doesn't see Chloe hurl her sticks at him. One bounces off his guitar. The other catches him on the wrist. "Rehearsal's over! Try not to get emotional packing this crap by yourself!" Chloe shouts. She hops off the stage and runs to Storm's house.

Luther is the first to speak. He points to Chloe's bass pedal, which lies broken in at least three separate pieces. Not to worry, he says. A good one only runs $250.

I'm so shocked by Chloe's anger the price means nothing. I'm so shocked I don't realize my own reaction.

"Dial down the glee," Sadie says in my ear. "You're grinning like a jackal."

# 19

It's late afternoon before I finish laying the sod. I wrestle the tiller into the back of our John Deere Gator and drive up to Storm's house. As I step onto the rear porch I'm nearly knocked backward, twice—first by the door, which flies open and cracks me in the knuckles as I reach for the knob, and then by Chloe, who barrels at my chest. My first thought is that she's attacking me. Not until I hear her squealing, "Thank you! Thank you! Thank you!" do I realize she wants a hug.

"I can't wait—it's going to be sooo awesome...." She flings her arms around my neck, smothering me in the intimacy of her perfume and scalding my neck with the heat of her cheek. She must be as embarrassed as I am that our bodies are this close together; she no sooner pulls me tight than she backs away. "I can't believe you bought Liz Phair tickets. That's cool of you! I'm going to Nina's to see if her mom will let her go. That's okay, isn't it? I mean, I know I'm grounded, but you have to let me and Nina ask Mrs. Laughlin in person. It's tricky because Nina's dad would never let her go. Mr. Luke would, like, investigate Liz Phair and then *forbid* Nina from her."

Learning I'm now cool leaves me too discombobulated to object. Chloe leans in just near enough to plant an appreciative kiss on my cheek before she's off the porch and racing around the house to the driveway. I touch my face, trying to remember the last time her lips came anywhere near me. Honestly, I can't.

Inside, voices draw me to the front parlor. I find Sadie, Deb, and Campbell spread out among Storm's antique rococo settee and Victorian borne. I'm reminded of the Greek graces who were Aphrodite's maidservants, anointing the goddess with olive oil and clothing her in finery as she set off on her adventures. Each of the three women here is too talented and too complicated to be reduced to anybody's attendant, however. I almost feel bad for them that the only thing they have in common is me.

"I've been learning about your new living arrangement," Sadie says, cocking an eyebrow. "Sometimes I amaze myself at what a modern chick I am. Here my boyfriend is scheming to move his ex-wife into his house so he and his best friend can pretend they're a couple, and I don't object, not in principle, anyway."

Campbell insists they won't go forward with the plan if Sadie's not okay with it. There's an urgency in her voice that's begging Sadie to be one-hundred-percent cool with it, though. Something in Sadie's voice lets us know she's not.

"I understand what you're up against with your ex-," she tells Campbell. "I'm just wondering when Vance was planning to let me in on the plot—*if* he was. Knowing him, he probably wouldn't, and when I confronted him, he'd try to lie his way out."

I explain that things have been so hectic that I forgot about Steve coming to town. Deb does me a favor by stepping in. She says this new sisterhood must fix up my house if we're ever going to trick Steve into believing a woman lives in it. I let them know I can't afford a bunch of doilies and dust ruffles right now. Between the sod, the Liz Phair tickets, and Chloe's drum pedal this is shaping up to be a $500 day.

"There's something else we need to figure out," Deb bustles on. She's become quite the organizer after only two days in Willoughby. "I told Chloe not to even bother asking if Stu can go to the concert with her. She was fine with that; she said she'd rather he didn't anyway because he's doesn't 'get' Liz Phair. She wants Nina to go, but I think we need to let Nina's parents know she was in the garden last night drinking."

She's right, of course, but I still feel that kiss from Chloe on my cheek, and I think I'm honestly drunk from it. I want to preserve it as long as possible. Narking on Nina's only going to give me another cold sore the size of Indiana. I explain to Deb all the melodrama going on in the Laughlin house over Luke and Marci's divorce. Maybe it's better if we sit Nina down and give her a good talking to instead of turning her over to her folks. Maybe then I can get to the bottom of that Prancin' Vance remark.

To my surprise, Deb agrees. "That leaves an extra ticket, though. One of us will have to go with Vance."

That "have to" makes me sound as appealing as Thanksgiving with the in-laws. Deb turns to Sadie and says she should go to the concert because she's the Liz Phair fan. Sadie throws up her palms and says Deb should since she's *the mom* of a Liz Phair fan. Both of them look to Campbell, deciding she ought to go if we're pretending to live together. Otherwise, Steve might get suspicious. The prospect of going doesn't thrill Campbell any more than it did the other two.

"I've got to be honest," she says. "I'm sort of with Stu when it comes to Liz Phair. I'm not sure I get her either. Nothing against her personally. I just wonder if her approach to women's issues isn't as limiting as it is liberating."

Sadie doesn't like the sound of that. She asks what Campbell means by it.

"Sometimes I think there's a downside to a woman talking so explicitly about love and sex," my best friend explains. "I don't mean we shouldn't talk about them. It's just that when a woman becomes famous for speaking explicitly like she does, it reinforces the idea that love and sex are the *only* topics a woman can legitimately discuss. There are plenty of other things for us to talk about—like politics. Why aren't we encouraging Chloe to listen to someone more political?"

"Liz Phair is political," Sadie insists. "Never mind that love and sex are politics; not all of her songs are about those things. She has a great song called 'Jeremy Engle' that's every bit as political as Dylan's 'Ballad of a Thin Man' or Paul Simon's 'Richard Cory.' It's not her fault that song doesn't get any attention. Her own record company took that one off her CD years ago because they didn't think it was what fans would want from her. Liz Phair could write 'Give Peace a Chance' and people would only want to talk about 'Fuck and Run.'"

Campbell makes it clear she's not criticizing the songstress, but that's not how Sadie takes it. She thinks Campbell ought to go to the concert to see how important it is for young women to have a role model like Liz Phair who's willing to say what's on her mind about any subject. This makes Campbell square her shoulders. She tells Sadie she's not so old that she doesn't remember how badly young women need role models. "I've been one of those role models since before you got your first tattoo," Campbell adds.

I tell them they don't have to fight over me; there's plenty to go around. From their reaction you'd think I cracked a dead-baby joke. Deb has to play peacekeeper. She sends me to the kitchen for coffee swizzlers. When I return with them she plucks three from the box left over from last week's book-club gathering, biting the end off of one and lining up all three in her fist so they look the same height. My three graces will decide this dispute the democratic way. Whoever gets the short stick goes to the concert with me. I don't point out that "short stick" isn't exactly a compliment.

One by one they draw and compare swizzler lengths.

"Congratulations," I tell my best friend. "You lose."

# 20

After dark, having spent the evening watching Campbell, Deb, and Sadie feminize my house with plum-scented candles and Gustav Klimt prints and green things I think are called plants, I wander to my garage for a book I've wanted to reread lately. Only I can't get inside to fish through the musty boxes stored since grad school because my carriage doors are locked. I can't even peek inside because the windows have been papered over in black. About the only clue to what's going on is the hip-hop beat whose bass thumps loud enough to bruise a spleen.

"Oh, hi, Dr. Sea-G," Stu says when he consents to open a side door, something he only does after I nearly pound it off its hinges. "What's up?"

I tell him to get Chloe out here right now. He reacts to the name as if it were a nonsense syllable he's never heard before.

"Maybe you should talk to Mrs. Sea-G," he suggests. "She's grounded–Chloe, that is, not Mrs. Sea-G. Chloe and me aren't allowed to hang out right now."

I feel my lips draw tight. "I know Chloe's grounded, Stu. And I don't need to talk to her mom, who, by the way, hasn't been 'Mrs. Sea-G' in fifteen years. I was the one who decided you two aren't allowed to hang out, which is why I'm more than a little disturbed to find you at my house hanging out with her."

It takes him a second to unwind that sentence. From the look on his face it's the second most nonsensical thing he's ever heard.

"Oh, I get it.… but, um, Chloe's not in here, I promise. I can't say where she is 'cause, you know, I'm not allowed to talk to her. That'd be pretty–uh–nervy, I guess, if we were, like, hangin' out right in front of you when she's gone and gotten herself busted."

Stu has a simple explanation for why he's in my garage: he's painting. I have to press my tongue to my teeth as I explain how I assumed that when I said he and Chloe weren't to see each other that meant that by extension I wouldn't be seeing him either. Stu gets visibly anxious as it dawns on him I'm about to boot him off my property. He blubbers about how he needs my garage to work on his Aphrodite painting for the competition he wants to enter. I lean in close enough to smell his aftershave.

"You need to know that Chloe told me what happened in the garden last night. Not just about the trespassing, but about what you were trying to pull on that blanket. With Nina right there no less. Do you really expect with me knowing that you're capable of that I'd let you–"

"I wasn't at Macon Place last night, Dr. Sea-G."

I have to swallow my breath and make sure I understand what he said. Even then I have to ask him to repeat it. Which Stu gladly does. He wasn't there, he says. Honest.

"But Chloe said–"

"It wasn't me."

I ask Stu if he realizes he's calling his own girlfriend a liar. Why would Chloe make up a story about her boyfriend trying to have sex with her? Stu's eyebrows shoot up at the sound of the S word.

"Whoa–Chloe told you that? That's beyond weird. She must really be mad at me. If I could talk to her, I'd straighten all this out, but, you know, I'm not allowed around her right now."

I point out that Brody Dale saw him in the garden, too.

"Deputy Dale said she saw *me*? Maybe she saw somebody, but it wasn't me. Like I said, I wasn't there. Maybe it was Zak. He's having second thoughts about dumping Nina. Maybe Nina brought Chloe for backup. I've stayed away from that whole Nina-and-Zak situation. Too much drama for me."

I ask if Stu honestly expects me to believe him over my daughter. He shrugs again. I can't decide if he's incapable of any other reaction or if he doesn't think I deserve a different one. Stu tells me I can believe anybody I want. I can't figure out if he's flipping me a sarcastic middle finger when he adds a "sir" to the end of that. The blood in my head feels as if it may shoot out my ears.

"Really?" I growl, incredulous at this point. "How about I believe your dad has a new Wellcraft at his weekend place up on Lake Jordan? Better yet, how about I believe you actually have a dad? How about you and I go see your dad, right now, Stu?"

The kid looks through me as if I were as transparent as my garage windows, before they were papered over.

"I'd be surprised if you didn't side with Chloe," Stu says with a forgiving, condescending nod. "Like I said, I'm not big on drama, Dr. Sea-G. It's okay if you believe everything's my fault. You have to, you're Chloe's dad. Even when dads and their daughters don't get along–no offense, but I don't get the sense that you and Chloe get along that well—dads are supposed to believe their daughters, right? I don't take it personally, just like I don't take it personally that Chloe's making up stories. She's a good girl; everybody knows that. Just not everybody knows that even a good girl will lie once in a while. Especially to her dad."

I spend the next few hours trying to sort this out. It's so confusing I almost need paper and pen to chart the possibilities. Is Stu really audacious enough to deny sneaking into Macon Place? Or is Chloe trying to pull the wool? If the latter, what's her endgame? What could she hope to achieve lying about Stu trying to have sex with her in front of Nina? Surely she must know that story would prompt her mom and dad to pull the plug on her relationship. Is that what she wanted? Was this lie a cry for help? Did she make up the story about the blanket so Deb and I would step in and do what she herself can't find the strength to?

Around ten o'clock I retreat to the den in Campbell's house I've been consigned to for the duration of our sham shacking up. Chloe is on the computer here, why I don't know, other than Deb is snoozing peacefully on the nearby couch. It's bad enough I've had to cede my house to my ex-wife; now she's taken my surrogate bed. I stand behind Chloe as her fingertips crack at the keyboard so loudly that I'm surprised she doesn't wake her mom. I try to read Chloe's mind, wondering how she genuinely feels about Stu. I keep going back to what she said this morning: *If I give him up now, what did those three months mean? Nothing. I wasted them.... I'm not going to cut and run because a relationship gets hard. I won't do that. I won't be like–*

"Hey Dad, the cheapest bass pedal I can find is fifty bucks. Only I don't think the quality's much to brag about. As hard as I like to pump the downbeat, I don't think the spring could take the strain."

I hand her my debit card, telling her to order the kick pedal that will make her drumming sound the best. My bank account isn't so depleted that we have to go cheap. I compliment Chloe on Pink Melon Joy's choice of a Pretenders' cover, ignoring the issue of inappropriate language, and then I lie and say her band sounds good. As I stand behind her, I do something goofy I haven't done since she was maybe twelve. I slip a finger behind Chloe's ear and pretend to saw it off. Chloe used to think that was funny, but now she whips her head over her shoulder and gives me a look that lets me know I'm not to touch her.

"I had this idea for the garden," she says, out the blue. "They've got day camp next week at church for middle schoolers, and they're looking for activities for Lleyton's class. I thought maybe we could bring them to Macon Place for a picnic and let them tour the statues. You know, sort of like a dry run for when you open the garden. I'll be your tour guide this first time out if you want."

I tell her that middle schoolers aren't into Greek mythology. I know because their indifference was what led me to quit teaching at Willoughby Academy and become Storm's majordomo. Then my suspicions are aroused, and I ask what's behind the generous offer to show kids around our statuary. Chloe feigns a shrug.

"I don't know." Her words are languid and drawn-out.

Kirk Curnutt

"It just seems like we need a jump start if we're going to get Macon Place off the ground."

Her "we" feels like an unexpected gift. I remember my conversation with Campbell at Gold Star Park, about how Chloe doesn't understand why I'm so invested in Macon Place, and I ask my daughter if she's worried about money. Only I'm not really asking. I'm telling her she doesn't need to worry. As gently as I can, I let her know it's embarrassing to me for her to go behind my back and talk to her grandfather and to Campbell about our cash flow and credit cards.

"You make me sound like a deadbeat when you talk to them," I say. "Trust me, we had a lot less money when I was in grad school and I managed to meet my obligations. Do you get on your mom about this? Because last time I checked, she was unemployed, too. Not that I'm unemployed—I'm just not making money yet. Besides, if we were truly broke, I wouldn't spend $140 on Liz Phair tickets."

I see Chloe's shoulders tighten as she steels herself against my admonishing. I wish we could have a conversation that didn't involve me setting her straight over something. Chloe asks if I've paid Sadie back for the tickets. Unbeknownst to me, my girlfriend has a car payment coming due and needs her reimbursement. Then Chloe assures me her mom has job prospects in Willoughby and that Deb won't be out of work for long. I wish we could have a conversation that didn't involve her setting me straight over something.

I sit on the edge of Campbell's couch, Deb's feet at my hip, and ask Chloe a question that has nothing to do with discipline or responsibility: who's her best guy friend? She starts to say Stu but I tell her boyfriends don't count. She thinks for a minute before admitting she really doesn't have guy friends. She knows plenty of dudes, but not in a deep, bare-your-soul way. I ask if she can imagine ever having platonic intimacy with a guy. She ponders the question, then shrugs. What for? she wonders. I start to explain to her why it's good for men and women to have friends of the opposite sex. Finding the words to make my case isn't easy. I don't want to come off like I'm selling some ten-step guide to self-improvement. But I do tell her one of the biggest lies that it's important for her not to fall for in life is the idea that men and women can't be friends. The best friendships I've ever had have been with women. Some of those friendships turned romantic, but most didn't. Even in the ones that did and then fizzled, like mine and Dr. H's or mine and Campbell's, the fondness remained. I learned a lot from those friendships, I tell Chloe. They taught me how to see across the barriers of gender, to respect and empathize with other people's experience, maybe most of all how to listen. I feel a little clammy going into this because I know at any point Chloe could bring up a name that will kick out the Jenga block on this shaky tower of amity I'm trying to build. Chloe is generous enough not to mention Katfish Kountry, though. I tell her how much I value learning from friends like Brody, Jill, and Tish—people whose challenges in life are vastly different from mine—and how if it wouldn't come off creepy I'd even enjoy opening my ears up to Nina. Learning what Nina's going through with her parents' divorce might make me a better dad. Just so Chloe doesn't think I'm claiming I'm better than other men, I tell her to look at her grandfather. Suddenly at seventy-eight the Carpet King of Dalton, Georgia, is going online to meet women, not to pursue and conquer, but to make contact, to give warmth, and to be kind when those things are needed. We should all be as large-hearted as Miles Seagrove, I tell Chloe.

"Then there's us," I say. "You and me. We can't be friends right now because as long as you're a teenager I have to be a hard-ass. But you won't always be sixteen. When you're an adult, I'd love to be your friend. That's more fun than being the disciplinarian laying down the law."

Chloe doesn't unwrap this Valentine I'm offering her. "You and mom aren't friends," she says.

I look at Deb, who's still tucked on her side, her arms curled to her chest under a blanket. If our lives were a feel-good book or movie this would be the point of rapprochement. I would say, "Yes, we are friends," or at the very least, "We will be, soon," and Chloe would turn on the spigots and flood the final paragraphs or closing credits with sentimental tears of joy. Deb would spring to her knees revealing she's been playing possum all along, waiting for me to come to my senses and lose my jealousy and possessiveness. She and Chloe would smother me in hugs and thankful pecks on the jaw. I would earn my way into heaven by being the most selfless of divorced dads, and I could take a bow for rising up to become that thing that way too many stories always seem to be rooting for, a redeemed man. Somewhere amid the fireworks of warm fuzzies there might even be a foreshadowing hint of how down the line Deb and I fell back in love, our broken family was reunited, and all was forgiven. Nicholas Sparks could cash the royalty check and count the box office in the same swoop.

Only I'm not there. As I watch Deb sleep she rustles her shoulders. The blanket covering her slips back to reveal she cradles something in her arms. It's a book. *A leather-bound book*. I gently lower the blanket to her elbow so I can read the spine. Marilyn French's *The Women's Room*. Pulled straight from my mother's bookshelf.

"You two blindsided me with this," I remind Chloe. "You chose to do that. You had to know it wouldn't be easy for me. This situation's going to take time to get used to."

Chloe frowns and nods before swiveling back to face the computer. After a few clicks she picks up my debit card and enters the numbers, paying for her pedal. For the moment, my Visa is all that she needs from me.

# 21

Two nights later, the whole way to Atlanta, the girls razz me. *Hey Dad, are you going to get down front on the barricade and wave at Liz Phair? Hey Mr. Vance, are you going to try to get your picture taken with her? Are you going to stand outside the stage door for an autograph?* I don't mind being the comic relief as long as nobody calls me Prancin' Vance.

"Hey dad, did you know L7's getting back together to protest Lifting Belly's being in prison? Why don't you tell the story of your stage dive at their concert back in the day?"

Wow, I think. If I'm thirty-seven, L7 must be...older. As in Iris's age. I know Chloe and Nina just want more fodder to taunt me with, and I'm still wrapping my brain around the fact that L7's gotten back together, but I think it's a good story. L7 is an all-female punk band and it was at their concert that I did my one and only stage dive. I was all of seventeen and a very reluctant Beth Tulbert rode with me from Dalton to Orlando for the concert. As I tell my dates for tonight, I've never forgotten the feel of the lead singer's boot in my coccyx when I scrambled onstage and then promptly froze up, afraid to jump.

I describe what going to concerts back then felt like, how exhilarating it was to plant yourself among the crush of bodies pressed up against a stage, to feel the shoulders and knees of strangers pressing into you, how you some-times had to fight for breath or even strain to wrestle an arm loose so you could deflect the Doc Martens and Chuck Taylors that flew at your head as kids bowled themselves into the audience after climbing onstage.

There was something intoxicatingly dangerous about that crush, but it was a thrill that I outgrew quickly, mostly because the vibe was way too male. I knew female friends who were groped mercilessly in crowds like that. The Lifting Belly beating reminds me of the undercurrent of violence that rumbled through several shows I attended at Chloe's age. Without much provocation at all, normal, everyday boys became Bronislavis Stylptitch's cretins. I think one reason I've never forgotten the feel of that boot heel in my butt is that I took it as penance, my way of atoning for the malevolent dickishness of men in general.

Campbell's response to this confession: "Jesus said the same exact thing when that Roman soldier pierced his side with the spear."

I remind Chloe of a time that she and I experienced the positive power of a rock crowd, its ability to create community. When she was seven or eight I took her to an outdoor show featuring the Southern mainstays Cowboy Mouth. Their drummer/lead singer, Fred LeBlanc, kicked off their first number by instructing audience members to turn to the nearest person they didn't know and give them a hug. Then, just for kicks, he asked them to do the same thing with a second stranger. Chloe lapped up that gesture. The two guys who hugged her may have looked like Rasputin and smelled worse than Sadie's bong, but they treated Chloe like fine China. As I tell my entourage, if it wouldn't get me arrested, I'd walk down the street every day of my life hugging strangers.

Chloe shakes me from my nostalgia. "It's probably a good thing you're too old for autographs, Dad. You wouldn't have a shot with Liz Phair. Remember, she's into Marines."

That's today's other running gag. Chloe found an article online from way back in 2003 in which Liz Phair talks about getting kicked out of a bar for making out with a soldier. Now, on an hourly basis, I must be reminded of how un-Marine-like I am. Well, razzing is better than resentment. As far as the girls are concerned, I'm good for exactly two things tonight. I'm a reliable punch line, and I'm getting them to the barricade on time.

One hundred miles into Georgia, we arrive at a sweaty former theater in the bohemian enclave of Little Five Points, and I wonder if I haven't stumbled into a frat house. The venue is packed with dudes. Out of a crowd of five hundred, maybe one-fifth are women. I have to check my ticket stub and make sure I didn't misread the date and bring us to a speed-metal thrash-a-thon by mistake. The Liz Phair posters and T-shirts for sale at the merchandise table convince me we're in the right place at the right time. I'm not the only one who's confused. As Chloe and Nina disappear into the loitering swirl, making their way to the stage front, Campbell and I hang back on the periphery. Next to us are two women that would fit the bill if I had to describe the quintessential Liz Phair fan: late-thirties/early forties, intellectual, strong, feminist, slightly older versions of Sadie.

"What the fuck?" one of the women says, pushing her Kate Spade frames off the nub of her nose. "This is a total sausagefest."

As she says it she catches me eavesdropping. I smile,

shyly and with embarrassment, but to her it's still a violation. I fight the temptation to offer my tailbone to her boot toes.

The situation is worse still, though. It's not just that the Variety Playhouse overflows with Y chromosomes; it's that the men here are variations of *me*. Scanning the crowd, I feel as if I look into a maze of funhouse mirrors, seeing nothing but distortions of myself. There's Ph.D. Me in a blue sportcoat and Old Navy denims, a fraying pair of black Converse All-Stars on my feet, reading the latest Haruki Murakami on my iPhone as I wait for the lights to go down. There's Failed Novelist Me, sporting a sweat-stained Pixies T-shirt that's been in my closet since 1987, the year the coming-of-age novel that I lost eons ago to corrupt floppy disks got a revise-and-resubmit request from an agent whom I never heard from again after I revised and resubmitted it. There's My-Wife-Just-Left-Me Me, balding and schlumpy, here because I need Liz Phair to tell me what it is that women really want. There's I'm-A-Nice-Guy, Just-Sort-of-Dull Me. My hands stuffed in my high-waisted jeans because I don't know what else to do with them. My shirttail hanging out because if I tuck it in I'll be reminded that age has given me a gut.

Then there's the worst of the batch, the Overgrown Adolescent Me. Two of these types stand right in front of me and Campbell in Georgia Bulldog hoodies and backwards caps. Swear to God, they look like the love children I would bear if Mike Willoughby got me pregnant. We listen to Overgrown Adolescent Me I and his soul mate, OAM II, do what men without women do best. They talk bumptiously about Things That Aren't

LIKELY TO HAPPEN, like Liz Phair picking them out of the crowd and taking them home.

"What a piece," the handsomer one says. He might pass for under thirty except for the flecks of gray in his hair. He's staring at a commemorative poster the Variety is handing out. It's the same picture that hangs on Chloe's wall, Liz Phair, splayed and seemingly naked, covered only by her guitar. "I wish I was that guitar," slobbers his sidekick. Post-collegiate life hasn't been so kind to OVERGROWN ADOLESCENT ME II. He looks blown-out. The women beside us frown.

"Idiots," decides the one with the Kate Spades.

"Morons," her friend concurs.

"They probably can't even name a Liz Phair song besides 'Fuck and Run.'"

This comes from me. The women shoot me a look that lets me know I'm not welcome in their conversation. "Keep wooing them like that," Campbell whispers, "and you'll have them reaching for their pepper spray."

*I am not one of them*, I want to assure the women. *I brought two teenage girls and a lesbian to this concert.*

But I'd be lying if I actually begged for the women's approval by boasting that I'm different. I'm none of the men here tonight. I'm every single one of them, rolled into one. Lest I delude myself into thinking otherwise, six words pulse through my brain more insistently than the drumbeat of the pre-show music putting us in the mood to rock out:

*Ardita Farnam in the Alabama room.*

It's after eleven by the time Liz Phair takes the stage,

and, boy oh boy, do we need her. The crowd's energy is flagging. I'M-A-NICE-GUY, JUST-SORT-OF-DULL and I keep trading glances, aware that we're twenty minutes past our bedtime. We've watched the roadies test the mics and amps, and we've sat through a tedious opening act. But then lights go out, and the Variety explodes in cheers as the silhouettes of tonight's main attraction and her band strut into view. I surprise Campbell by slipping behind her and wrapping my arms around her waist.

"Just don't mistake me for her up there," Campbell says when I ask if she minds. "Or for Sadie. Speaking of which, is it me or does Sadie seem a little possessive lately?"

I don't answer because I'm distracted. Liz Phair is blonder and more ebullient than I remember from the cover of *Exile in Guyville*. She wears a red romper and funky velvet boots, her Fender guitar the same tan color as her skin. "Before we start," she says after testing a couple of bar chords, "we want you to remember some ladies we're worried about. You've probably seen them on TV. We're dedicating this show to Oksana Dybek and her band. We hope they're okay. It'd sure be nice to hear some real news about them. Tonight is for Lifting Belly!"

I hear a *whoo!* from the front of the stage that's unmistakable. It's Chloe.

The band slices into "6'1"," the opening cut on *Exile in Guyville*. Suddenly, the women next to me don't feel so stranded. They hunch forward, expectantly, demanding from the performance the balm the song has given them for twenty years. I stand on my tiptoes and look for the girls. All I can see are the backs of ball caps, bald heads, and bad dye jobs. When I was Chloe's age the more feminist bands would yell, "Girls to the front!" to clear space for their female fans. I guess that tradition has gone by the wayside. As I look around I see a wall of outnumbered women forming on the periphery, finding their safety in numbers. I'm not sure why I thought I'd be in the minority tonight. I'm not sure what I expected would happen if I had been. Did I think the Liz Phair Amazon Army would invite me into its temple, sit me down, and tell me its stories? Did I believe they would open up about why they're so invested in *Exile in Guyville*? That they would describe to me how these songs come to them in the sadness of dark bedrooms or parked cars or whatever isolated place they retreat to when nursing the disappointments of love? Did I think they would describe for me the transfusion of confidence they draw from the record's blood, the graft of the steeliness that rejuvenates them when they hear these lyrics?

"I love you, Liz!" a voice screams. It's the first OVERGROWN ADOLESCENT ME, the handsomer of the duo. "Love you back," answers the singer warily. "I love your boots, Liz!" the sidekick piles on. A mild chuckle rolls through the crowd, until OVERGROWN ADOLESCENT ME II fires off his punch line: "Put them behind your ears!" The audience groans. In case nobody knows who deserves credit for this charming display of wit, the dipshit screams, "I love you!" for the duration of the next number–and then again three songs later.

"Idiot," decides the Kate Spade-wearer next to us.

"Moron," agrees her friend.

The bastards won't stop. Soon enough, other guys

down front start shouting, "I love you!" between songs. The singer blushes at first, then grows irritated. "Enough already," she snaps, but the audience is laughing, as if the ability to catcall makes them feel brash, daring, alive. "I love your romper, Liz!" somebody yells. "Where'd you get that necklace? I love it!" Some other idiot makes the obligatory reference to pearl necklaces. I rise to my tiptoes again. My fratty doppelgangers have elbowed their way to the barricade, turning to the crowd and egging them on. They ruin my favorite song, "Little Digger," about a single mother explaining the new man in her life to her young son. For two days I've studied Liz Phair's whole catalog, preparing for tonight more intently than I did my Ph.D. comps, and instead I get two Brotherslavis Shtickylptitches making their comedy debut. The dudes won't shut up. "'Fuck and Run,' Liz!" they start yelling. "'Fuck and Run'!"

The crowd joins in, chanting for Liz Phair's greatest hit. The singer is pissed. The stage lights dim and the band retreats offstage. It's not clear if we'll even get an encore. The ceremonial clapping rises to a crescendo. Even I'm-a-Nice-Guy, Just-Sort-of-Dull Me whoops and hollers, shouting the star's name as if he just discovered his voice can drown out a vacuum cleaner. Craning again, I watch Overgrown Adolescent Me I and II jostle along the barricade until they're center stage. Then they do something no real rock fan does at a concert. The men give up their place in the front row. I know why they do it. The pair slither directly behind Chloe and Nina, laughing to each other as they make lusty faces, gaping at the girls' hips, their legs. Time for this show to end.

But it isn't over. The band returns, and to everyone's delight, the first bars of "Fuck and Run" blast from the PA. Live, the song is tougher and meatier than the skeletal CD version. As the crowd bobs up and down, several women throw out their hands as if trying to clutch at whatever wisdom the lyrics hold. The security goons begin backing people off the barricade, including Chloe, who leans over the railing for a pick, a handshake, some memento. Suddenly, Overgrown Adolescent Me II dips to his haunches, disappearing. The next thing I know, my daughter's legs are thrown straight up in the air. Before she's flipped over the barricade, her skirt falls up around her waist, revealing panties every bit as cherry red as Liz Phair's romper.

I lunge forward, knifing between Kate Spade and her friend. Drinks fly, people tumble left and right. As I make it to the stage–it only takes a few seconds, but I feel like I've run an obstacle course–my right arm drips with soda. I crash into OAM I, who bellyflops to the floor. I almost fall myself, but I catch my balance in time to grab the chunkier sidekick by his hoodie. With a tug I jerk him to his knees, dragging him two feet to the pit until his head is swallowed in his collar. Across the barricade I see Chloe bucking in the arms of two security goons. A look of panic flares in her eyes. She doesn't know the men aren't pawing for fun. They are wrestling her off to eject her out a side door, as they do all stage divers these days. "She was pushed!" I scream.

I shout it again because I can't hear myself over the speakers' roar. But then the band stops, the crowd goes silent. When I squint toward the stage, I see Liz Phair hunched over a monitor, gesturing at me like a schoolmarm flustered by a disruptive pupil. "No fighting!" she yells at me. "Not at my show!" I say the first thing that comes to mind.

"This isn't how I thought we'd meet."

The words are hardly out before I'm interrupted by a cymbal crash, though a cymbal would make a buzzing noise, not a buzzing sensation, which is what vibrates through my gums. Then I figure out what's happened. OVERGROWN ADOLESCENT ME II has punched me. He's wiggled to a crouch that gives him enough height to drive a blind uppercut into my jaw. I know it's a solid hit because when I go to gasp, two incisors drop to the Variety Playhouse floor.

"You're lucky," says a paramedic as he hands me my teeth in a cup of cool water. "They came out in one piece. If we can find a dentist this late at night, he can glue them in their sockets. And if not, well, nobody will notice implants. Either way, you'll get your choppers back."

I'd thank him, but there's a cold compress in my mouth. Already the paramedic and his partner have serenaded me with "All I Want for Christmas Is My Two Front Teeth."

"We ready to roll?" A police officer strolls to the ambulance Campbell and I occupy. A few feet away, under the flashing strobes of a squad car, OVERGROWN ADOLESCENT ME I and II look imploringly my way. My teeth no sooner hit the floor than they begged me not to press charges. The tubby one promises to pay for my dental work. I'd like to forget the whole fracas, but the

Kirk Curnutt

paramedics are worried that my jaw's fractured, and my head pounds so hard I can't parse my options.

"The girls," I lisp to Campbell. My words sound like kettle steam. "We need to find them." A paramedic tells the cop about Chloe and Nina. He says we better locate them quick. My teeth won't be any good after thirty minutes. As the policeman disappears beneath the marquee, the paramedics insist that I lie down to stop the bleeding, but I'm embarrassed. A crowd has gathered on the sidewalk, stealing peeks at my swelling face.

"Where were you?" I ask when Chloe and Nina are led to the ambulance. Their arms brim with posters, shirts, and CDs.

"Liz Phair wanted to talk to us. She's cool. Look at the stuff she gave us. It's all autographed, every last thing. She was worried about you."

"I was worried about *you*."

My point is lost as a paramedic returns the compress to my numbed gap. There's a moment's confusion before we can leave. Only Chloe can ride in the ambulance, it turns out. Campbell and Nina will have to follow us to the emergency room in my Scion.

"So what's she like?" I ask once we're moving. The potholes along Peachtree Street set my incisors spinning in the water. Chloe's so close I feel her breath on my neck.

"She said to tell you she's sorry she screamed at you. She didn't know I was your daughter. She didn't even see that guy flip me. She thought I dove the barricade."

"Someday you probably will. Rushing the stage is half the fun. Just don't do it until you're old enough that you don't need me to drive you to the concert. I'm too old for the barricade."

Her hand strokes my hair. Chloe tries to comfort me, but her touch feels alien. It's been so long since I've felt it.

"Liz gave me her manager's email. She wants to know you're okay. She signed a poster for you, too. Now you have your own. She asked how to spell your name. Here, look."

She unrolls the poster. I see my name scrawled across Liz Phair's leg, along with a long message and a signature.

"What's that all about?" I ask, pointing at a line. "Why did she write 'God Bless America' there?"

"That's the funny part," Chloe admits, smiling mischievously. "She was asking about you, and I kind of lied. Not a big lie, just a little one. For you. She wanted to know what you do, and I said something a little farfetched."

"Spill it, will you? My mouth hurts."

Swear to God, with that Louise Brooks bob, Chloe is no longer a teenager. She looks twenty-five.

"Well, Dad, okay, um—I told Liz Phair you're a Marine."

# IV

# The Many Births of Venus

"One night after their love-making, as Aphrodite lay tangled in Botticelli's arms, she wept. For as she predicted, she had fallen in love with the untidy, barrel-bellied painter who she initially found so unattractive. But as she could hear the gods of the west wind calling from the painting and beyond, she knew her mission was complete. It was time to return.

"As if pulling a scab from an unhealed wound Aphrodite pried herself from his grasp. Leaving him undisturbed, her tears splashed onto the floor as she wistfully stepped back into the painting for the last time.

"For days Botticelli waited for Aphrodite to move. Not one brushstroke had touched the painting since that fateful last night. He gently ran his fingers over the contours of her form.

'My beauty, my beauty, come back, come, back,' he pleaded.

'Excuse me, Sir,' said his apprentice Luigi one morning as Botticelli sat transfixed. 'Maybe you should get a real girlfriend.'"

—Nicole Levin, "The Touch of Aphrodite"

# 22

"Lleyton!" yells Chloe. "Get your hand off Aphrodite's ass!"

That last word is enough to turn the heads of twenty hard-to-herd day-camp church kids in my daughter's direction. Leave it to profanity to muster their undivided attention. As I warned Chloe, the rowdy group of sixth graders hasn't shown much enthusiasm for the Greek myths she's been reciting as she escorts them through her dry-run of our garden tour. The kids are too busy whispering, playing with their phones, staring into the sky daydreaming of the summer fun they could be having. None has been squirrelier than Lleyton. Campbell's son defends himself from charges of inappropriately touching Storm Willoughby's prized possession by demonstrating how he's only *pretending* to smack her derriere.

"See, my hand stops before it hits her butt," he explains.

Chloe shoots a pained face my way. I can read her mind: *Can't we medicate him?* I try to smile sympathetically, but my face is puffy after a day in the dentist's chair. Thanks to my new artificial incisors, each of which cost $1,850, I can barely open my mouth. My gums feel as if they're jammed with Pez pellets.

"As I was saying," Chloe continues, returning to the notes I've prepared for her. "Aphrodite–or Venus, as the Romans called her–is best known as the goddess of love. That's how she's usually represented in art. You've probably seen a famous painting called *The Birth of Venus* by Sandro Botticelli. It's the one with the naked girl riding to shore on a seashell. She's on that shell because legend

Kirk Curnutt

says Aphrodite rose out of the ocean in a swirl of foam. Botticelli wasn't the first or the last to paint her that way. He was inspired after reading about another painting by– um"–She loses her place–"Apelles, who was this old Greek guy who pictured her in a similar pose. His work had been lost by the time Renaissance guys like Botticelli and Titan came along, but there were enough imitations floating around that they got the idea. A couple of centuries later, there was another painter named" –She has to consult the pronunciation scribbled in the margin– "*Boo-ger-roo.* Yeah, William-Adolphe Bouguereau. His version of *The Birth of Venus* is the biggest–nine feet tall, seven feet wide. There's an element common to all of those famous paintings except for Bouguereau's that none would have if not for this statue you're looking at. Anybody care to guess it?"

She regrets extending the invitation the second Lleyton yells, "Seashell!"

"Do you see a seashell on this statue, doofus? Guess again. It's right in front of you. The first time it happened was when this Aphrodite was built in the fourth century B.C."

"Built?" one of the boys scoffs. It's Travis, Mike Willoughby's older son. He's not a sixth grader; he only acts like one. He informs Chloe that statues aren't built, they're *sculpted.* Chloe shushes him. A girl points at Aphrodite's pubis, asking why she has her hand "like that." From somewhere in the crowd another boy answers, "She's got cramps." That would be Zak, the younger fruit of Mike's loins, the one who supposedly had sex with his now ex-girlfriend, Nina, in his father's bed.

The Gold Dust Twins have taken a break from the weeding that I've hired them to help do this week to heckle Chloe's efforts to educate the campers.

"Can we just get through this, please?" Chloe twists her notes tight in her fist. "The pose is the influential thing I was telling you about. Nobody really knows what it's supposed to mean, but every Aphrodite since this one has been made to stand this same way except Bouguereau's—and the Venus de Milo, maybe, since she doesn't have arms. Anyway, this pose is called the *pudica gesture*. All the pervs here will immediately start thinking of *pudenda*, but that's only half of where the word comes from. *Pudica* also means shame or modesty. The idea is that as Aphrodite's getting out of the bath she hears some peeper creeping up on her, and she covers herself so he can't get his jollies."

That's not quite how I phrased it in the script. The church kids look at each other, some embarrassed, some giggling, all confused.

"There's a mixed message in what this statue says," Chloe lectures them. "It's in other images of Aphrodite, too. I mean, supposedly, she's the first nude woman in art. Before her, women could only be shown with veils and drapes. And yet here's Aphrodite hiding the parts of her body that are most feminine. You don't see any of the guys in these statues covering themselves, do you? Zeus down there, and Hermes over there—they're letting it all hang out, aren't they?"

Zak agrees with a hearty, "Amen!" He whispers something to his brother, cracking them both up. Chloe ignores the interruption.

Kirk Curnutt

"The mixed message is that this pose says the world likes its women naked, but only if they're shy about it, apologetic even. It says women should be embarrassed by their bodies. That's why I like Bouguereau's picture the best. His Aphrodite isn't ashamed."

"You don't have to be embarrassed or ashamed," Travis insists. "You can take your clothes off right now. We won't stop you."

"Say that a little louder, dumb ass—my dad didn't quite hear you. It's thanks to guys like you that Aphrodite's only known for one thing. What are you doing here, anyway? You're just hired help. You guys really can't be around a girl and think about anything but sex, can you?"

The brothers weren't expecting this attack. One takes an unconscious step back, the other looks to me as if I'm supposed to cork Chloe's aggression. I'd like to explain that she's only hoping to save them from going through life as the type of overgrown adolescents who cost her dad his front teeth, but I think she's just plain angry.

"There was a lot more to Aphrodite. You'd never guess it because all these artists were so scared of her sexuality that they got possessive about it, sort of like y'all get when you're within two feet of a woman. In case Nina didn't tell you, Zak, that's why you were a crap-ass boyfriend. She scared you. There were other sides to Aphrodite's personality that made her the most popular goddess. Nobody cares about those parts of her because, unlike the ones you're staring at, you can't cop a feel off them. They called her 'laughter-loving' because she had a great sense of humor—she was a big prankster. They called her 'peitho' or persuasion because nobody could refuse the advice she gave. Aphrodite was associated with weddings and gardens and fertility, and they called her 'pandemos' which means 'belonging to all people' because she had the power to bring together people in the different places where she was worshipped. She appealed to different classes and political parties, but, hey, let's not talk about any of that stuff when we can talk about sex. Sex sex sex.... I'm so sick of it."

Her tirade is riveting, and not just because by the time she finishes, Zak and Travis's expressions suggest she's made their testicles ascend. I'm struck because there's nothing about "peitho" or "pandemos" in her notes. Chloe's come up with all that on her own. There's no telling what I might learn from her if she weren't suddenly distracted.

"Leyton, swear to God, you touch her again and I will break your wrist! Do you know what'll happen if your wrist is broken? You won't be able to do this—"

Chloe makes a loose fist and jerks it mockingly in front of her crotch. The older boys nearly double over laughing, but Lleyton isn't deterred. He's inspired. He scuttles around the statue and starts tweaking the same left nipple Mike Willoughby did the day he dropped his lawsuit on me.

"I'm sending an SOS! See? Morse code: bee-dee bee-dee beep beep beep.... Mayday! Mayday! The ship's going down!"

Before I can intervene, Chloe grabs the scuff of his neck and whips Lleyton sideways, spilling them both into the grass. She lands on top, one knee pinned in his back.

"No groping! You hear me? You don't touch the tit!"

That last word is enough to again snap the heads of twenty hard-to-herd church kids–this time in my direction. What they see is me cringing, only in agony, not embarrassment. The minute my jaw dropped, my new $3,700 teeth exploded in pain.

After the tour, once the kids leave, I state the obvious.

"Well, that didn't go quite as planned. We may get a call or two from parents complaining that middle school's a little too early to start teaching kids about the *pudica gesture*. That other background on Aphrodite you gave out, though–'peitho' and 'pandemous'–that was fantastic stuff. Where'd you get that?"

Chloe shrugs, unimpressed by her own intelligence. She learned the history of Aphrodite's representation in Western art from the book she and Stu ordered off the Internet. Stu was supposed to study its color plates for inspiration for his own painting, but since he and Chloe have been forbidden from talking to each other outside of band practice, she hasn't been able to get the oversized volume to him. Maybe I'm loopy from the Ibuprofen I'm popping, but I offer to run it to Stu and Iris's house for her. Chloe's still too agitated from this morning's debacle to appreciate the gesture.

"I can't take guys when they act like dilweeds," she insists.

I can't decide if "dilweed" is a bad enough word that I should have the talk with Chloe that Deb's supposed to have about her language. My head hurts too much to do it. I stretch out onto the amphitheater stage, listening as Chloe tells me how many friends she's rounded up to attend our battle of the bands, which is this coming weekend already. I doze off, my head so swimmy she has to say it a second time. "Dad, we have company." I lift my head in time to see a golf cart rip over the horizon.

"You better go up to the house," I tell Chloe.

Mike Willoughby jerks the cart to a stop. He asks what happened to my face. I don't bother telling him that I sacrificed my teeth for a few words from Liz Phair. Instead, I remind him we're supposed to be communicating through lawyers. He agrees but notes that will only happen if I actually go out and hire one. Then Mike informs me he has some favors he needs. Only they're not really favors because he's not really asking. These are things he's telling me I'm to do.

"You're going to let Travis and Zak perform at the battle of the bands. They've got some rap act with Stu, the Gold Dust Twinks or something. They told me that you and Luther put Chloe's band on the bill without making her try out like other kids. If your kid can get in thanks to nepotism, so can my boys."

I read the back of my Ibuprofen bottle, pretending I'm riveted.

"The other thing is I'm letting Stu use the front parlor for a studio. He needs a place to paint since you so ungraciously booted him out of your garage. I don't know why you didn't let him use daddy's house in the first place. Why not give a kid who's worth helping out a break, Seahorse?"

I ask why the sudden concern for Stu. Only a few days ago Mike was telling me to Katy-bar the door against him to protect my daughter. Mike says he didn't realize when

Kirk Curnutt

he made that comment how tough Stu's had it. "Did you know the poor kid lies about his old man having a place on Lake Jordan?" he asks. I pretend this is news to me. I immediately regret lying, though, because Mike takes my response as an opportunity to launch into this long riff about how boys need father figures. They're at risk because they don't have anybody to teach them how to be a man. Without a strong masculine role model they either grow up compensating by trying too hard to be tough, or they end up "limp-wristed" and dependent on their mommies. Ever since Mike heard the story about Stu at the Walmart he's decided the kid needs his guidance. I want so badly to pop another Ibuprofen, but I can't remember how many I've swallowed in the past hour.

"Hey," I finally interrupt Mike, "did Stu tell you he'd tried to have sex with Chloe right here in the garden? He would've done it in front of Nina, too, if Chloe had let him. And you know what he was hoping for, right? A *threesome*. A threesome with a girl who'd dated your son until just a few days earlier. Maybe you could guide the little bastard on how not to be a hornball."

To my amazement, the story doesn't shock Mike. It doesn't even sway his opinion of Stu. Mike's more surprised that I would expect anything different from an eighteen-year-old boy. "Boys want sex," he says, so matter-of-factly he might as well be saying water is wet. "If you don't understand that, you don't understand biology." I tell him what I want is for Stu to understand *psychology*. I want the kid to appreciate the emotional cost of pulling a stunt like he did. Maybe Stu's too immature to understand how trying to "get some" with his girlfriend's best friend right there demeans Chloe; he ought to understand that he's demeaning himself, too. What can honesty and intimacy possibly mean to him if he's willing to make his move in front of somebody else? What can they mean if he wants to involve somebody else without consent?

"What's this 'demeans' bullshit?" Mike fires back. "Who made you Dr. Laura all of a sudden? I'll say it again: Stu is eighteen. Show me an eighteen-year-old boy who wouldn't take a shot at a threesome if the opportunity presented itself, and I'll show you the chip on his shoulder."

Sex should be about exploration and adventure at Stu's age, Mike informs me. I sound like a pearl-clutcher trying to take that discovery away from him. As long as kids are responsible and don't make babies, why not let them enjoy some fun? They've got the rest of their lives for sex to be boring. All Chloe had to do if she wasn't into it was tell Stu no—which, Mike guesses, is what she did. I assure him that Chloe most certainly did tell Stu no. But what if she couldn't? What if she couldn't say no because she was afraid of disappointing him, or getting dumped by him even? How many girls does Mike think grow up living with the regret of not saying no, of wishing they'd had the strength to? Doesn't Stu have a responsibility not to coerce a girl? To respect her vulnerability?

"Good God Almighty, you're exaggerating," Mike says, exasperated. I don't understand how he became the kid's advocate so quickly. "You make it sound like Stu tried to rape your daughter! Did she have to mace him? Pull out the Taser? Look, the kid took a shot, he got shot down,

Kirk Curnutt

story over...." He stops to catch his breath and gather his thoughts. It's hard work for him. "We're not as at odds here as you think, Seahorse. I'm saying boys need to get the kinkier impulses out of their system before they're adults. You want Stu to come out of the womb already haloed in purity. You should know that's not realistic. We all have to learn how to be adults, and that's why Stu needs a father figure like me. He needs somebody to teach him that the time to try to have a threesome is at eighteen. Not when he's twenty-six and with a girl he might marry, and certainly not at thirty-six when he's farmed a couple of babies out of her."

He nods at me as if he's saying the most obvious thing in the world.

"Sowing your oats at thirty-six is when people screw up their lives, not at eighteen."

I blink bitterly as I see Mike remembering what everybody else in Willoughby refuses to forget. I was thirty-six when I committed the Most Infamous Act of Fornication in Elmore County, Alabama.

"Don't look at me like that, Seahorse. I'm not implying that you tried to have a threesome with that Farnam girl!"

# 23

That night I realize I'm in love with Sadie. She drops by Campbell's to play me the demos that she's recorded at Luther's since she won her grant from the Willoughby Family Foundation, and I fall to my knees at the altar of her talent. She can spin a melody that teeters me with a luscious sense of vertigo. Her voice is smoky yet still vulnerable. Mainly I'm amazed by her guitar playing. The combinations of notes she comes up with give me synesthesia. I feel splashes of bittersweet color and drink in the fragrance of melancholy. After we go through all fifteen of her tracks, Sadie is grateful I pick out so many details that I like. We talk about what certain metaphors in the lyrics mean, or how she came up with a rhythm for a particular cut. If I have one gift to give her I guess it's that I'm a good listener. As we drape ourselves in the music, one thing leads to another, and once we're out of songs we're messing around. I lose myself in the curtain of Sadie's hair, kissing her nape and the buttons of her spine. My fingertips go all sorts of weird places—the backs of her earlobes, the valleys between her fingers, the ticklish perimeter of her bellybutton.

We go at it for quite a while, all kinds of ways, but once she orgasms I sense from her that I'm taking too long to seal my own deal. Somehow I have the opposite problem of the last time we rolled the bones like this. Now I can't finish. I wiggle and buckle and damn near throw my back out trying to find the right angle to take me over the cliff, but it's no good. By the time I swing Sadie onto my lap and burrow away, my face in her shoulder blades as she

Kirk Curnutt

leans into the coffee table, I get the distinct impression she's bored. I'm not sure I've ever been with someone who's made less of an effort to hide the fact that she holds on out of pity.

"What are you doing?" I finally ask.

Sadie looks back at me over her shoulder. "What does it look like I'm doing?"

"Honestly? It looks like you're reading." I nod at the book on the coffee table that Sadie's hands are planted next to. She just flipped it over so the back-jacket blurbs are face up. "I can tell you're reading. Your lips move when you do it."

"You don't like my curiosity? Because I'm not sure you can expect me not to wonder what something like this is doing in the den of the ex-girlfriend you just happen to be living with."

She holds up the paperback, as if I don't already know the title. It's called *Intercourse* by Andrea Dworkin, but it's not what it sounds like. It's a serious feminist study, not porn or even erotica. It's the book I went to dig out of my old boxes from grad school when I discovered Stu in my garage.

Sadie bucks her hips, unceremoniously expelling me so she can crawl off my hips and stretch out on the couch, thumbing pages instead of me. Don't ever again question pity sex, I tell myself.

"Ah, this explains everything," Sadie decides. "I was thinking you'd gone soft because you weren't attracted to me anymore. You can't blame me. A girl's going to take disinterest personally."

We must have different definitions of soft. I'm rather

proud of what I'm toting tonight. Sadie's not talking about tumescence, though. She's talking intensity. The last two times we've been together, she tells me, I've seemed timid. Now she knows why. It's Andrea Dworkin's fault.

I sit on the armrest, trying to find a comfortable angle where the Scotch-guarded fabric won't scratch my delicate underside. "I'm just trying to educate myself," I explain. "Don't you want a sensitive man? I can't imagine women find much pleasure in oblivious dudes that grind away like monkeys."

As Sadie points out, there's not much about pleasure in Dworkin. She cracks the book's spine to a passage that's been twice highlighted, first in yellow by me fifteen years ago when I was a graduate student, then again in lime green, just this afternoon.

*There is never a real privacy of the body that can coexist with intercourse: with being entered. The vagina itself is muscled and the muscles have to be pushed apart. The thrusting is persistent invasion. The woman is opened up, split down the center. She is occupied—physically, internally, in her privacy....*

Sadie flips forward a few more pages, finding another one.

*What is entry for her? Entry is the first acceptance in her body that she is generic, not individual; that she is one of a many that is antagonistic to the individual interpretation that she might have of her own worth, purpose, or intention. Entered, she accepts her subservience to his psychological purpose...she finds herself depersonalized into a function and worth less to him than he is worth to himself: because he broke through, pushed in, entered....*

"Damn, Vance, no wonder you've lost your mojo. If I were a guy, this would make my manhood curl up and die, too."

I note her hyperbole by directing her attention to my mojo, which has yet to wilt. I tell her I'm not intimidated; I'm trying to learn. I know Sadie's had to have slept with a guy or two that treated her as a means to an end. If I *was* that guy I don't ever want to be him again. I want to understand from a woman's point of view what sex is all about so that I'm not selfish or disrespectful.

"This whole damn town knows about Ardita Farnam," I tell Sadie, "and I'm tired of it. I don't want to feel like I'm 'getting' sex any more than I want a woman feeling like she's 'giving' it. I'm thirty-seven. I want to know if what I think is real intimacy really is, or if I've been deluding myself."

Sadie tosses the book aside and asks which of my massive seraglio (all five of them) I felt most intimate with. She tells me not to feel obliged to say her just because she happens to be lying naked in front of me. The question is one I can't begin to answer, but she mistakes my hesitation.

"It was Campbell, wasn't it?" she prods. "Don't lie to me."

Why she's so hung up on my best friend is a mystery, but having learned my lesson once, I'm careful not to use the word "jealousy." Sadie recognizes she's gone to that well once too often. She just doesn't understand how Campbell and I can claim to share this great mutual friendship with the history we have. Would she ask Stevie Nicks and Lindsey Buckingham that question? I wonder. Well, actually, she would. But maybe if I share the nitty-gritty of how exactly Campbell and I crossed the Rubicon of intimacy, Sadie will get it. I toss up my hands.

"What's to tell? Haven't you ever had a friend you thought you were beyond sex with, only to end up sleeping with her? A friend that you valued first and foremost because you thought you could control yourself around her?"

"Nope, never. Not a her, not a him. That's the difference between women and men. We can have friends that we never once think of sleeping with. But men, two words into a conversation with a woman and you're wondering if it's going to end in sex. She can be your cashier at Piggly Wiggly, your dental assistant, your–"

"Waitress at Katfish Kountry? Is that where you're headed? If so, touché. The art of being a man is refining your horniness until it has the bouquet of higher inten-tions, and befriending a lesbian is one way of accomplishing that, if only because the odds are so obviously against you."

I tell Sadie how much she would have loved the razzing I took from Campbell's friends when she and I first started hanging out. Brody, Tish, Jill, and their crowd fell all over themselves trying to come up with names for the male counterpart to a "fag hag," to use the impolite term. I was a Dyke Mike, a Lez-Beau, a Strap-Ron. I took a lot of unfunny shit, but I stuck around for a very simple reason: because I didn't think I had a shot with Campbell, I didn't feel obligated to take one. It was a relief, and I congratulated myself for thinking it was a relief to Campbell, too, because here was one guy in the world she could turn to—besides her father, of course—who wasn't going to hit on her. The friendship went to my head. I felt priestly, saintly.

"And you weren't thinking in secret, 'Hey, if I play my cards right, I could land a lesbian?' Because every man wants to believe he can convert a lipstick if he had the chance."

I tell her again that it was more of a turn-on to believe I was above that desire. I was bereft of ill intent. I was an aesthete and ascetic about the relationship. I wanted to exist on the pure vapors of friendship. Sadie keeps pressing me for specifics. She wants to know how Campbell and I tumbled into bed. Were we drunk? Stoned? Was it some kind of dare?

Nothing that exciting, I confess. There was no romancing, no seduction, only a moderate amount of alcohol. One evening eight or so years ago, Campbell was at my place for dinner. She was newly divorced and had just moved back to Willoughby after a half-decade in Nashville with Steve. She rented the house a couple of doors down from me, and we started talking. Campbell needed a set of ears to listen as she talked herself through an identity crisis. She didn't understand why, after spending most of her twenties dating women, she'd married Steve. She thought it was because she wanted a child, and going straight was the quickest way of doing it. She never even told Steve she'd been a lesbian. She knew right away she'd made a mistake, but she stuck with the relationship for Lleyton's sake. Then one day she met another woman and fell hard. The infatuation turned into an affair, which led to all the disasters that accompany those: lies, suspicion, stalking, threats, and lawyers. Campbell knew she had to get out of Nashville when she realized her husband and her girlfriend had more in common with each other than she did with either of them. Both were possessive and controlling, and neither had that internal censor that should stop us from saying angry, abusive things to other people. So she came home and Luther introduced her to me because I was the only other single parent in our neighborhood. We started watching each other's kids when we needed a babysitter, and we became friends. That simple. I was intrigued by her, by the journey she was going through in trying to figure out her sexuality. Campbell liked that I was non-threatening but not milquetoast, either. Plus, I could cook, and I liked to drink wine and gab. One night we were grilling sirloins, and when I asked her to pass the spatula, Campbell just leaned in and kissed me. It was that natural and innocent, that spontaneous, that fun.

"And just so you don't think I'm too pure," I add, "there were moments after that when I was indeed high-fiving myself for 'landing a lesbian.' I would never brag about it to another man for fear it would get back to her or Luther, but I can't deny I heard that boast in my head. Then I would feel bad because I knew I was disrespecting her. Later, when things got complicated, I wished I only had that to feel bad about."

"Aha," Sadie says with a mock gasp. "I know what brought those complications about! All the time you're romping you're thinking, 'This chick is only into me for

Kirk Curnutt

the sex!' and then one day she pops the question: 'What does it mean that we're sleeping together? Where are we going with this? Do you really love me, O Mighty Man-Friend of Lesbians, or am I simply a score to you?' And that freaks you out. All of a sudden Vance Seagrove feels suffocated, imprisoned, deceived even–because you thought that by doing a lesbian you could enjoy the tang without having to dance the emotional tango."

It's painful to know I'm such a cliché. I should get a few originality points, though. My relationship with Campbell wasn't quite as predictable as Sadie makes it sound. Yes, I was thrown for a loop when Campbell started asking if I thought we had a future, but it wasn't because I was scared of commitment. I was a single father. If I were scared of commitment, I'd have dumped Chloe with Deb before Deb ever thought of dumping me. I did have some concerns about Lleyton, but mainly what I couldn't get past was the feeling that I'd failed Campbell. I'd assumed she was sleeping with me to test if she was really gay, which she was, I suppose. "Only I thought of that test strictly in physical terms," I tell Sadie, "nothing emotional. I imagined Campbell asking herself if she could deal with peen the rest of her life."

"Demerits for thinking anatomically," Sadie says in a schoolmarm voice. "You knew better. You were educated. You'd read a book called *Intercourse.*"

"That's my point," I say. "I did know better, and yet something unconscious in me wanted to believe that she wasn't sleeping with me because she craved intimacy, that she wasn't susceptible to the emotional vulnerability of sex. And if it had been a conscious thought, I'd probably have justified it by thinking she was better off with a woman. If her attraction to me was a test, then there was part of me that was content to fail it."

"So you dumped her because in your own mind you weren't worthy of her needs? Wow. That's called a convenient rationalization, Vance." Sadie sits up. "Have you ever told Campbell any of this?"

"Of course not. What would be the point? Besides, I never dumped her. We just stopped spending nights together. The truth would only hurt Campbell, and things between us would never be the same. I'd be nothing more than a second ex-husband."

Sadie disagrees. She thinks Campbell would appreciate hearing it.

"Not because she doesn't intuitively know you were only out to fuck her," Sadie assures me, "but because talking about it would reassure her that she wasn't wrong in thinking you were somebody she could connect with in the first place."

I ask her not to say "only out to fuck." It's not that simple. It wasn't about want. It was about living up to the responsibilities of desire. Sadie stares hard at me, then picks *Intercourse* off the coffee table again.

"Andrea Dworkin isn't about you, is she? She's about Chloe. You're afraid that 'being entered' is teaching your daughter subservience."

I tell her not to talk about Chloe. If she's going there, I need to get dressed. Sadie spreads my book across her chest, wrapping her arms around it.

"You really want to experience the vulnerability that a woman feels during sex? I could show you."

Kirk Curnutt

I gulp, audibly. Sadie asks if I'm scared.

"You're doing exactly what I'm talking about," I tell her. "You're making this about power. I don't want to be the top or the bottom. I want to defy those distinctions. I want to be one. That sounds fruity, but it's honest. I want mutuality."

She shakes her head. "You're naïve then. There's no such thing as sex without power, even when there's mutuality. Maybe you think your lesbian friends lie around tickling each other's tender buttons until they reach some kind of orgasmic convergence, but that's not the way it's done, not even between same-sex couples. Sex is aggression and submission. There's going to be a bottom even if the bottom happens to be on top at that moment. I'll tell you what, though. I'll bow down to your masculinity, just so you don't miss that dominance you don't think you want."

She tosses my Dworkin to the floor and slips to her knees, raising me to my feet. The moist slide of her tongue nearly tumbles me. "You do know," Sadie informs me after several long licks, "that two dudes invented the blowjob, right?"

She's really getting off on this power trip.

"Seriously, head started out as a gay-guy thing. You can see why. It's the one act where it's unclear who's in charge. I mean, here you are, occupying me, only now you're equally vulnerable because of these–"

Sadie clacks her teeth before lightly sinking them into my skin. She asks if I've ever heard of *vagina dentata*. Sure, I say. It's the only Police album I ever liked as a kid. Sadie squeezes me in her fist until I wince. This is no time for comedy, she insists.

"Someday in a higher state of evolution women will grow teeth in their vaginas. That's when sexism will die out. Until it happens, we have the mystery of who gives and who gets with fellatio. Hard to tell, but one thing's clear. We're not talking about this dissolving of roles that's your nirvana. We're not junking the idea that one of us has to be the top–we're just competing to be tops."

This time her nibble is more like a bite. I jump back a little, protectively. She takes me back into her mouth and begins to churn and glide, building up such an intense rhythm that I'm almost distracted enough not to notice the index finger as it comes sliding down my tailbone. The nail tickles my buttocks, tracing circles lower and lower until it's made its determined way...there. Sadie rides the outer ring several times, teasing, before sliding that nail dead center and giving a gentle tap.

"Relax," she whispers. "I don't have belts that cinch this tight."

I take a deep breath and try not to think about the fact that I'm being burrowed. The finger makes its way inside, slowly but intently. The discomfort is so oddly exciting I have to plant a hand to the wall just to stay upright. I beg her to slow down a bit; I shake so badly I'm afraid my new teeth will come loose. Sadie doesn't heed the plea. The finger keeps working upward until it's tapping at the door of my prostate, at which point I whinny like a colt. Then Sadie begins drawing back and forth, rougher and more aggressively, the vertical motion a counterpoint to the horizontal sluice of her mouth. When the frenzy of the dual sensations gets to me, I do something I've never

Kirk Curnutt

done before during fellatio. I put my hands on either side of her head to control the rhythm. Sadie immediately bats them away and gives me another disciplinary twist.

"I didn't know you had that in you," she says with a smirk.

But the only thing I know for sure that's in me is her. To prove she's the top she brings the finger almost out before rushing it back in. My back goes to the wall. I have to grip Campbell's bookcase with one hand and grasp for a nearby sconce with the other. Recognizing my vulnerability, Sadie increases the intensity so the suck and shove blends into one electrical sensation that flashes across my pelvis. I want to push or kick or do anything but stand here, frozen except for my quiver. The pleasure is overwhelming, almost unbearable. I just want the orgasm over so I can sit down and reclaim the inviolability of my body.

"How do you feel?" she asks.

It's the second thing she does after I finish. I would probably feel better if her first wasn't to pull out a glass bubbler and fire up a dope load. I tell her the truth, that I feel like I'll walk bowlegged for a week, but Sadie can't hear me well. She's too busy spraying Febreze around the room.

I don't want to ruin the mood by chewing her out for smoking in somebody else's house. I'm nervous that Campbell will recognize the pot waft, though. She'll freak out about Steve detecting it, and if she says something to Sadie, Sadie will get pissed that I'm pretending I'm Campbell's man this week. Meanwhile, I'll be stuck in the middle, choking on an artificial fog of watermelon, orange, and lemon, and unable to sit comfortably, either. I rise and pull my pants on, suddenly feeling claustrophobic in the study. Sadie picks this moment to tell me she's playing a set at a musicians' showcase in Montgomery tomorrow night. Since it's at a bar, Chloe won't be able to get in, but she's hoping I'll round up Deb, Luther, and Campbell to come hear her debut her new music. I freeze with my jeans halfway up my thighs, uncertain how to tell her that tomorrow is when Campbell and I are supposed to convince Steve she's straight.

"Don't get mad, but I'm already promised tomorrow. To Chloe. I have to take her out to dinner. It's Deb's idea. I have to make sure she doesn't resent me for grounding her. Parenting is complicated, you know."

I don't know why I lie. I justify the fib by telling myself I'll put in a half-hour with Campbell and Steve and then head to the showcase. I can't tell if Sadie buys my phony excuse. She senses the sudden distance between us and puffs harder off her bubbler.

"Should we talk about your hands-on-the-head move? You caught me so off-guard you nearly stomach-pumped me, dude. Domo arigato, Mr. Irrumatio. You must be reading too many of those old leather-bound Philip Roth novels on your bookshelf. You know, in almost every book of Roth's, a chick gets face fucked?"

The comment feels as invasive as how we've both invaded each other tonight.

"Don't talk about those books that way," I snap. "Don't touch those books. Those were my mom's books."

My tone startles Sadie. She gets up, pulls on her yoga pants and T-shirt, starts packing her guitar and notebooks. I fall all over myself apologizing, asking her not to go. I beg her to play for me some more–her songs, anybody's songs–so I can unshoulder the deadweight of my confusion. I just want to listen, I tell her. Not to talk, but to listen.

Sadie obliges and starts noodling, not really playing a song but just trying out snippets of familiar chord changes. After every verse she stops to take a hit off her pipe, making sure the smoke billows, just so Campbell knows she's been in her house.

A knock on the door interrupts us. "Dad, are you in there?"

I hop up, scrambling to Napalm the room with Febreze as I tell Chloe to give me a minute. I'm so busy covering up the pot smell I forget there's a book on the coffee table called *Intercourse.*

"I had a blowout on Highway 231," Chloe says when I yank the door open. She's surprised to see Sadie, though whether my girlfriend's mussed hair or glassy eyes are a bigger giveaway to what we've been up to is anybody's guess. I'm actually more surprised by who's with Chloe: Stu.

"I was just driving along," she says, wet and upset, "not speeding or anything because it's dumping buckets outside, and all of sudden there's this bang. I thought somebody shot a gun at me. That's what it sounded like, a shotgun."

I ask if she's okay. She doesn't look like it. She looks shaken. Chloe tells me the Saturn spun out before it went onto the shoulder, hitting the guard rail only ten yards from the Bibbs-Grave Bridge that crosses the Coosa River.

When she realized how lucky she was not to end up in the water, she called my phone, then Deb's, but nobody answered. Stu was the only one who picked up. I start to ask where her mother is until I remember that Luther and Campbell took Deb to dinner.

"You two have to tell me where you're going to be in case there's an emergency!" Chloe says, both angry and frightened. "I don't know how to change a tire! I've only been driving two weeks!"

I thank Stu for bringing her to Campbell's, then send him home. Chloe and I pile into my car and head to the wreck. It is indeed dumping buckets outside; I can feel my Scion hydroplane as we slide through downtown and approach the bridge. Because I have to grip the wheel tight and focus on the lane line, we go several blocks before I even think to ask Chloe why she was driving in a summer shower. She gives me a line about running out for a drum key to tune her toms, but the explanation sounds rehearsed. I suspect she's been cruising with Stu. And by cruising I mean parking.

We reach the Saturn, which faces oncoming traffic from the shoulder of the southbound lane. I pull in front of the car and click on my brights. The first thing I see is a long gash in the passenger side. The blown tire on the rear driver's side is barely three inches from the blacktop. Ditto for the jack, which has been cranked so high the car looks as if a stray wind could flip it into the gully of wildflowers. "Stu didn't set out a safety triangle or a flare?" I ask.

"What's a safety triangle?"

I tell Chloe we're having a safety lesson if we manage to make it home. Then I tell her to hand me her phone. I

Kirk Curnutt

want to check out her recent calls to figure out what's going on. I don't scroll through the list in front of her, though. I shove her cell in my pocket, pull on my poncho, and slip outside to dig my tools out of the back of the Scion. The rain is sharp as nails on my face. I barely make it to the Saturn before a goatee of water runs off my chin. I want to pluck that imaginary beard with pliers when I see the sticker on the bumper that says DON'T DEFACE MACON PLACE. As I squat down to slip the lug wrench on the first nut the phone rings. It's a number I don't recognize, so I answer it.

"You coming or not?" a voice says. The caller is a man, but too old to be Stu, and way too country to be my dad or Luther. I ask for a name, but the voice refuses. "I was told I'm not to talk to anybody but Chloe Seagrove," the caller insists. "Have her call this number and we'll reschedule."

Between the rain and the traffic zooming by, I don't have time to wonder about the meaning of the message. After a bit of a wrestling match, the lug nuts loosen. I pop the old wheel off and roll it to the Saturn's trunk, where I trade it for the donut. After I let the jack down I jog to the Scion for Chloe's keys. Knowing the spare will make for a wobbly ride, I decide to let her follow me home in the Scion and take the Saturn myself. My pace is quick but not as quick as the scenarios still flashing through my imagination. Chloe was up to something, I know it. The phone call is my proof.

As I squeeze behind the Saturn's wheel, my heel catches an object tossed to the floorboard. Should I be grateful it's not a wrapper that reads I SAID *LIKE* A VIRGIN?

Maybe, maybe not.

It's a half-empty can of Febreze.

# 24

"So now you've pegged Chloe for a pothead *and* a sex fiend?"

This comes from Luther the next morning. I've swung by his recording studio to gently upbraid him for not making sure Deb took her phone to dinner. She can't be a real mom, I intend to lecture him, until she remembers to keep her cell handy at all times in case of emergency. Luther has given me a whole other reason to be irritated. He doesn't think it's a big deal that a can of air freshener was in the Saturn. "Maybe Chloe just appreciates a clean-smelling car," he suggests.

"How many sixteen-year-olds do you know who're bothered by stink?" I ask. "Cheese can be fermenting in Chloe's room and her nose won't wrinkle. The only reason to spritz a car with Summer & Splash is to mask a smell you don't want smelt. And nine out of ten times for a kid that smell is marijuana. Ask Sadie if you don't believe me."

Luther changes the subject by asking if he can catch a ride with me to tonight's songwriters' showcase. He's excited because Sadie has promised to sing his one and only hit, "Riding Freedom's Wheels," which I doubt anybody but its composer has performed since 1966. Campbell clearly hasn't told Luther that she and I are scheduled to bamboozle Steve over dinner. I pass off the same lie I told Sadie last evening, pretending I'm taking Chloe out for a bite.

"If it'll ease your mind," Luther says, motioning me into the studio's control room, "I can at least assure you

Chloe wasn't sniffing Febreze with Stu. He was here last night working on one of his hip-hop do-hickeys. I told him no drinks in the control room, and what do you think I find this morning? A half-empty can of Red Bull sitting on my console."

I point out that Stu had to leave at some point because he brought Chloe home. I've just about convinced myself they were headed to buy pot from the mysterious caller to her phone when she lost control and wrecked. As I rehearse my theory for Luther, I spy the log of files on his console computer screen and tap at a specific title.

"When did Sadie write a song called 'Zoom Zoom Aphrodite'? She's played me every cut she's finished so far and that wasn't one of them. Is this about Storm's garden?"

As Luther explains, the song is Stu's, not Sadie's. He points out when the last version of the file was saved: 10:16 p.m., right about the same time the Saturn went into the guardrail. To him that means the kids couldn't have been together before Stu rescued Chloe from the side of the road. Instead of wondering why Luther is giving Stu an alibi, I reach for the play button. Luther beats me to it. He doesn't like non-musicians touching his equipment. As soon as he clicks on the title, the speakers facing us cackle and boom with a complex hip-hop beat. We have to endure several chants of *yo, hey-ho,* and *that's right, gaaa-hurrrrlll* before the first verse:

*Got my girl in the car,*
*We're gonna zoom, zoom, zoom*
*Got my girl in the back,*

*We're gonna boom, boom, boom*
*Wear out my shocks jammin' low and untidy*
*Stank up my ride as I zoom that Aphrodite*


"Are you shitting me?" I say to Luther. "You let him record this?"

Luther's face goes so white his gray mustache looks blue. He trips all over himself explaining that this is the first he's heard of the song. He let Stu use the studio at night precisely so he wouldn't have to sit through his music.

"Delete it," I say.

"What?"

"I want that crap deleted, erased—whatever the correct term is, I want it gone."

"I can't do that, Vance. Stu would kill me. His mom, too. Iris and Mike Willoughby browbeat me into letting the kid record here. Let me talk to Stu. I'll say the lyrics have to be redone. I'll say the Gold Dust Twinz can't sing this at the battle of the bands. The music's not bad. Stu knows how to lay down a beat."

"Either you delete it, or I will."

I reach across the console and swipe the computer mouse. Luther grabs my wrist, sending the cursor cartwheeling across the screen. Our chairs knock together as we tussle for control. We must look like two kids in bumper cars. I manage to press my shoulder into Luther's chest, giving me enough leverage to highlight Stu's file and pop the delete button. The screen blips; Luther goes limp and groans. "You've just complicated both of our lives," he whimpers.

"Don't worry about it. Stu won't be bothering you."

"What makes you so sure of that?"

I'm out of my chair and the control booth, stomping past Edgar Winter, who canters backward, intimidated by the smell of my anger.

"Because I'm going to kill that little bastard."

At Macon Place I think I've missed him. The south parlor is empty except for a sheet-draped easel and a toolbox brimming with acrylics. Just as I'm about to yank off the sheet, a bathroom door creaks open. Rotten timing. I was looking forward to zooming a boot through Stu's portrait of Chloe as Aphrodite. Instead I meet the kid in the hallway, clapping a palm to the center of his T-shirt and backing him up.

"What are you doing?" Stu says, shocked. "You can't touch me!"

"You have thirty seconds to get off my property. If you don't, I'm calling the police. I don't ever want to see you in this house, my house, or in the garden again. I don't want to ever see you period. You got that? And if I ever hear of you talking again about Chloe like you did in that song, I'll knock your nostrils down your esophagus!"

"You can't kick me out of here! Mike Willoughby gave me his permission! This isn't your garage!"

As Stu tries to take shelter in the bathroom, I remind him that I own fifty-one percent of Macon Place. That means I make the rules. I shove my way past the doorsill, popping him on the breastplate with two fingers. Stu swats at my hand, which smacks into the sink basin. I spot his phone peeking from his pocket and grab for it. I want to see what pictures he stores on it, but Stu is stronger than I expect. He clutches my wrist and bends my hand backwards. I twist sideways, my back slamming against the towel rack. Trying to wiggle free, I yank him into my chest, but our feet tangle. I have just enough time to clutch at the two Ss on the Wussy Pimps logo on his shirt and make sure I'm not the only one going down. I stick out my elbow, thinking a broken arm is better than losing my $3,700 incisors to the toilet bowl. Only I don't make it to the floor. My elbow lands dead center in the stool, splashing blue water everywhere. I might laugh out loud at Stu's soggy do-rag if my own face weren't dripping. With a look of disgust Stu realizes he's strad-dling his girlfriend's father over a shitter, and he jumps to his feet, landing on my ankle for good measure. Despite the throb in both it and my elbow, I have strength enough for one final assault.

"Where's your dad?"

"What?"

"Your dad! Where's your dad right now, Stu?"

He's long gone by the time I can dislodge my arm from the toilet.

Twelve hours later, I sit with Campbell in a cramped sports-bar booth. Across from us is her ex-, a short, soup-can of a guy who looks like he could be an enforcer for the Dixie Mafia. I came tonight entirely prepared for Steve to check me out so intently that his gaze would bring to boil the pitcher of beer I planned to down to lubricate me through this farce. Instead, I'm caught entirely off-guard. Campbell's ex-husband is a nice guy—non-combative, funny, even charming, I dare say. I can't believe Steve wouldn't think his son's mother and I are conning him about being the love of each other's lives, but he doesn't betray a hint of suspicion. He's told us three times now how delighted he is that we found each other.

"It's great to see you happy," he assures Campbell. "Vance, Lleyton has told me about this statue garden of yours. It sounds a lot more interesting than selling cars, which is what I'm stuck doing."

Steve was a golf pro at a course in Nashville, but the luxury resort he worked for went bankrupt. It took him six months to get his current gig at a Ford dealership. The poor guy goes into excruciating detail about the humiliations of unemployment—how depressing it was to be told over and over he was either unqualified or overqualified for jobs, how embarrassed he was to ask his widowed mom to float him loans, how easy it became to lounge around his house all day in his pajamas, skipping shaving, not bothering to brush his teeth, some days not even caring enough to eat.

"At least you didn't have to feel bad about your child support," Campbell says. "You were already used to not paying that."

She's been pecking at Steve all night, and he's been taking it on the chin without striking back. I can't decide if he thinks it's ungentlemanly to defend himself from a woman's anger, or if he's trying to convince me he's the victim in this situation. All I know is I hope that I don't make bystanders as uncomfortable when Deb and I have a conversation in public as Campbell's making me. I squirm in my seat and try to change the tone by describing for Steve how good I think Macon Place could be for our community if Mike Willoughby would only let me open it to the public. Despite the fact that he's a golfer, Steve agrees. He tells me that, before he took a thirty-percent pay cut going from the resort to the car lot, he began attending the ballet, the symphony, and even the opera on a regular basis. "For the culture," he explains, as if I thought he went for the popcorn. At first all that hoity-toity culture was intimidating, Steve admits, because everything he knew about those art forms could fit on top of a tee.

"Then I started studying the background of each work before I went to a performance," he explains. "Like a year ago, when a tour of Poulnec's *Dialogues on the Carmelites* came through Nashville. I see the title, and immediately my mind goes to 'caramel' instead of 'Carmelite.' That's how stupid I am. But then I read the description of what the opera's about, and the story hooked me. It's about these nuns right after the French Revolution who go to the guillotine instead of renouncing their religious beliefs. They're Catholic, so it's a story about faith. I swear, I couldn't have told you when the French Revolution happened when I first read the plot summary. Then I started looking up the history, and the next thing I know, all I can think about is the Reign of Terror and Robespierre, whose own head got lopped off just ten days after the nuns'. I'm telling you, by the time I went to the performance, I knew more of the story behind *Dialogues on the Carmelites* than the opera expert brought in to explain the show to the audience. It made me realize that knowledge isn't that difficult a nut to crack. All you have

Kirk Curnutt

to do is open yourself to learning. That's what I want to do from here on out: I want to learn. The hard part is finding a career that lets you learn and grow. That's why I envy you with your garden, Vance. You're doing it, my man. You're there, you're learning."

The whole time he talks I can feel Campbell next to me wiggle as if she's sitting on a lit match.

"Who are you?" she asks Steve. "When we were married I couldn't get you to open a book. Now you want me to believe you go to operas on the French Revolution? Are you kidding me?"

I excuse myself to the restroom, where a long meditative pee is my only hope of escape. The toilet is no sanctuary, though. I no sooner start to relieve myself than a stranger enters and violates men's room etiquette by bellying up to the urinal next to me. "Christ, that water's cold," he says with a wince. I knew I should've taken a stall. I focus on the greasy tile in front of me, even though in my peripheral vision I can tell the guy's looking straight my way. When I don't respond he asks if I have something against comedy. "Not when it's funny," I mutter into the wall. The stranger is short and built enough like a soup can to pass for Steve's brother. He also sports a pair of those friendly mutton chops where the mustache and sideburns connect in one big stripe of facial hair. The guy looks like a pint-sized version of Lemmy, the bass player from Motörhead.

"Do I know you?" I ask, still not looking.

"No, but I know you, buddy. You're the lucky guy in the booth next to the hot brunette. That woman's gotta be–what?–forty-three, forty-four? That's the best age for women. I'm assuming the lady's with you. If not, be a pal and let a brother know. For a woman that hot to be without a man, that would be a crime against humanity."

I start to tell him that Campbell's a lesbian, if only to stop him from wagging himself so exuberantly as he hoses down the urinal. The stranger doesn't give me a chance to talk. "Yes, sir, lots of beautiful women in this place tonight," he says. "You should see the sandy-haired one that just walked in. Tatts up and down her arms. Got one right on her belly, too. If I don't die of old age before I finish taking this leak I may go introduce myself to her, too."

I freeze at the sink, washing my hands. "A belly tattoo? As in the Egyptian Eye of Horus?" The stranger zips and throws out his palms, a big WTF? expression curling what I can see of his lips under the wooly blanket of his 'stache.

"Horace? Who the fuck is Horace? You college boys, you always got to flaunt your Ph.D.'s, don't you?"

The stranger is out the door before I think to ask how he knows I have a Ph.D.

I take a tentative peek into the bar, but there's no sign of Sadie. I decide I misheard the stranger. Maybe he meant an Iron Maiden tattoo instead of an Eye of Horus. Then I realize I'm the one who mentioned Horus, and I wonder if I didn't hallucinate the whole conversation. As I pass the jukebox I remember the odd call last night on Chloe's phone, and I try to decide whether that eerie voice matches this guy's. I've just about convinced myself that Stu and Chloe's pot dealer is stalking me when, crossing the bar on my way to the booth, I see that Campbell and Steve are no longer talking. They're flat-out bickering. Despite the dim lighting and the crush of a capacity crowd, I can read their lips.

HIM: *I didn't drive three hundred miles to fight. I just want my son.*

HER: *I never said you couldn't see him. All I want is a schedule so I can plan my time and my life. I want structure. That and the money you owe me.*

HIM: *It's always about money with you. Can't I ever have Lleyton without conditions?*

HER: *They're not conditions, you jerk—they're responsibilities.*

I cut a beeline to the bar and order a Sweetwater 420, even though an entire half-pitcher of beer sits unfinished at our table. One sip into the beer, I spot a breaking news notice scrolling at the bottom of the TV behind the bartender.

FEMINIST ROCKER OKSANA DYBEK REPORTEDLY DIES
OF BRAIN INJURY...
"LIFTING BELLY" SINGER, 26, NOT SEEN IN PUBLIC SINCE
JUNE 12 ATTACK IN HERZOSLOVAKIA...
PRESIDENT BRONISLAVIS STYLPTITCH DISMISSES
DEATH RUMORS AS "WESTERN FAIRY TALE"...

I pull out my phone and dial Chloe, but she doesn't pick up. Instead of leaving a message, I go online and search for more information, but there isn't any. Nothing substantive, anyway. At the moment, all that's known for sure is that a single tweet traced to Ekarest, the capital of Herzoslovakia, has ignited a firestorm of grief, outrage, and protest. Lifting Belly supporters are demanding that Stylptitch either release details of Oksana's death or prove that the story is false by freeing her from that medieval prison called The Chimneys. The anti-feminist crowd, meanwhile, reminds everybody about that mysterious picture taken at Stylptitch's palace that purportedly shows Oksana safe and sound, lounging on a chaise longue in a bikini.

"We need to go," I say to Campbell when I rush to our booth. I don't bother sitting down. Steve wants to know if Lleyton is okay, but Herzoslovakia has too many syllables for me to spit out a coherent explanation of what's happening. I throw down a ten-dollar tip for the waitress and motion for Campbell to get up. As I spin toward the exit, I'm greeted by a familiar face in a jarringly unfamiliar haircut. I don't understand why I can't get over somebody growing out a simple pixie cut.

"What are you doing here?" I ask Deb.

"Luther and I were going to Sadie's show, but we got waylaid by Stu's mom. Iris is furious. She's making Stu file charges, Vance. What were you thinking attacking him?"

Steve shoots to his feet, leaning across the table. "Who's Sadie? And who's this Stu? I can't have you around my son if you're attacking people, Vance."

My phone pulses in my palm. Do you know about it? Chloe has texted me. I'm not sure if she's asking about Stu and Iris or Oksana Dybek.

"I–I didn't attack anybody," I sputter. "Iris can't press charges for a scuffle."

"Who is Iris?" Steve wants to know. Deb is grim.

"The police are looking for you. You need to turn yourself in. Brody Dale's on her way to make things as easy as possible."

Steve nearly pounds the table. "Who is Brody Dale? And once more, dammit, who is Sadie?"

As if on cue, I hear, "I'm Sadie," and sure enough, the crowd in the bar seems to part down the middle so she can glide toward us in a crop top and mini-skirt that are almost as red as her face. I'm not sure who's sending me the meaner stink eye, Sadie or the Egyptian Horus glaring from her belly.

"You lied to me, dude. *Again.* You said you were taking Chloe to dinner."

"I wasn't going to miss your show. I was just going to be a little late. I–I've got to get home to Chloe, though, and make sure she's all right. She's going to be upset about this Lifting Belly news–"

Before I can finish, Brody Dale appears behind Sadie, handcuffs in her fist. I tell her there's no need for those. Brody has known me for a decade; she knows that, unlike Stu in the garden, I won't bolt. The deputy apologizes, but rules are rules. The best she can do is to wait until we're outside to order my hands behind my back.

"Who are these people?" Steve demands of Campbell.

"I'm his ex-wife," volunteers Deb.

"I'm his ex-, too." Sadie stares at me so intently I think she'll bring my half-empty pitcher of beer to boil. "I'm his ex-girlfriend."

# 25

For twelve hours in the Elmore County Jail, I share a cell with two drunk drivers, a guy accused of embezzling from his daughter's Girl Scout troop, and a john snared in a truck-stop hooker sweep. Shockingly, none of my roommates are Lifting Belly fans. Since my civil liberties don't guarantee me updates on Oksana Dybek, I have no idea whether Chloe's hero is really dead. By the time Campbell, Deb, and Chloe can figure out how to squeeze $1,500 from my debit card for bail, my feet ache from pacing along the bars, asking to no avail for my phone or at least a newspaper. I can't sit down because I'm torn. On the one hand, I'm nearly frantic not knowing how Chloe is dealing with rumors of Oksana's demise. On the other, I can't stop thinking about the Febreze in the Saturn, the voice on her phone, and that stranger with the friendly mutton chops in the men's room. I know I'll have to confront Chloe about the connection between those things, but I'd rather be reassuring her that she's not growing up in a world where men aren't so afraid of women they stomp feminists' brains to mush.

When I'm finally chauffeured home, Deb and Campbell fill me in on several fronts. There's no need for me to call Sadie to apologize because we're kaput; Steve plans on sticking around for several more days to make sure his kid's not living with a man who beats up teenage boys; and Mike Willoughby's lawyer is filing for a restraining order on Stu's behalf that will bar me from Macon Place. The only thing I say during the ride home is that I need to stop at a drugstore to buy something. I don't answer when Deb asks what it is.

At Campbell's house I find Chloe in the study watching CNN. I slip into the room and take a seat on the couch without saying a lick. She doesn't either. For what feels like an eternity, we wait for the Lifting Belly story to cycle to the top of the newsfeed. When it does we get to read the actual tweet that sparked the rumor (*R.I.P., Oksana, Our Beautiful Fury*) and nothing else. Without any hard facts handy, the anchor is reduced to reading celebrity responses to the report, including two from Liz Phair: *Rise up, HERzoslovakia. Make it OURslovakia.*

Prof. Siddeoms-Wenzel of Belvedere College, the same expert who commented on Lifting Belly when the beating footage leaked two weeks ago, is back. Because the channel's target audience probably doesn't know Patti Smith from a sausage patty, she has to explain what punk rock is, and why it's a politically useful tool for feminist collectives like Lifting Belly or Pussy Riot, one of Oksana's obvious inspirations. Campbell joins us as an earlier performance by the band that didn't end in bloodshed blitzkriegs across the screen.

"I have to ask," Campbell says hesitantly, "why do they take their shirts off when they play?"

As was tradition when Lifting Belly cranked their amps, Oksana and her band in this footage are topless. Their breasts are blurred out, but the multi-colored slogans painted across their collarbones and bellies are legible, written in English: *Amazon Revolution, Death to Patriarchy, End Political Rape.* Chloe explains the tactic as if she's Lifting Belly's press agent.

"They're taking back ownership of their bodies. They

believe that women are only allowed to be visible in society when they're sex objects, so they're exposing themselves on their own terms. Notice that they're not being tarty or erotic in any way. They're angry and aggressive. Seeing those emotions is supposed to mess with your mind because you can't slobber over their beauty. To most people beauty is passive, but anger is action. It was the same way with those Herzoslovakian Furies that Lifting Belly refer to in their anti-Stylptitch song. Those women warriors were some hardcore bitches. The myth says that they sliced off their right breast so they could hold their bows steady when they fired their arrows."

I could live without hearing my daughter say "bitches," but I also have to swallow a smile, afraid it'll come off condescending. I don't undermine Chloe's research by informing her that Greek Amazon legends are built around the same story of the severed breast. Campbell still needs persuading.

"If it's so important for these women to be more than pretty, why are all the band members stone-cold foxes? Oksana was the hottest one, but they're all drool-worthy. Even the bass player is an eight or nine. How often do you see that? I think if Lifting Belly was really radical, they'd have at least one person in the group who was butt-ass ugly."

Chloe tightens her eyes at our host. She knows Campbell isn't debunking her beliefs, just challenging her to articulate them, to see how she deals with the contradictions of the ideas she wants to stand for.

"You're not the first to point out they're all pretty. But

if they weren't, whichever one was less attractive would draw all the attention. She'd be the target for all the conventional ridicule heaped on women who don't fit the beauty standard. With all of them equally gorgeous, you can't escape confronting your expectation that pretty women are expected to be silent objects. Taking off their shirts is their way of punching that expectation in the face."

"Yeah, but don't you do that at the battle of the bands. You find some other way to throw that punch."

This is me. The remark makes me realize why I'm a better listener than debater. I have nothing intelligent to offer the conversation. The video snippet finishes, and the talking head returns, but we can't get past the feeling that the professor's exchange with the anchor is filling up airtime in the absence of new information. After a few minutes Campbell excuses herself to pick up Lleyton, who's spent the morning with Steve. I wait for Chloe to mention the minor fact that her father just got out of jail for wrestling her boyfriend over a toilet, but she doesn't go there.

"I did it for you, you know," I say, finally broaching the subject myself. "It was my way of punching Stu's expectations in the face. Because he shouldn't expect to disrespect you in a song the way that 'Zoom Zoom Aphrodite' crap did."

"He wasn't writing literally about me," Chloe replies, eyes fixed on the TV. "Just like when I wrote 'Daddy's Girl.' I wasn't writing literally about you."

I'm sure she'd like to believe she slit my throat with that remark, but I don't let the blood spurt show. I point out that Stu shouldn't rap about *any* woman the way he does in his ode to "zooming." Chloe points out that I use the wrong tense. I need to say "the way the song *did*" because the song doesn't exist anymore. I deleted it from Luther's computer.

"That's why Ms. Iris is so pissed. Imagine if Stu took a sledgehammer to your Aphrodite statue. It's destruction of property. You'd feel as angry as she and Stu feel."

Her phone blips with a text message. I resist the urge to nab it and see if it's her pot dealer setting up a makeup appointment. Chloe claims the text is from her mom. Deb wants to take her shopping for a new dress. They plan on going out to dinner tonight to the one restaurant in Willoughby, Alabama, that can lay legitimate claim to being upscale, an Italian place called Trattoria Prego. I wonder aloud how Deb can afford a shopping spree and a meal at the most expensive restaurant in the county when she's unemployed. Chloe informs me that my dad gave her $200 because he was so proud of "Daddy's Girl." Treating her mom is how she wants to spend the money. On her way out the door, Chloe throws me a bone.

"Mom says you can come with us to the Trattoria if you want. She thinks it'd be good for the three of us to spend some time together."

I nod noncommittally, but I'm definitely going. No reason Deb should be the only one around here getting a free meal. After Chloe leaves I turn off the news and doze. Campbell's couch is far more hospitable than the metal bench in the jail cell. I could sleep all the way until dinner, but my host doesn't let me. She wakes me up a half-hour later.

"Well," Campbell says, "if one good thing came out of last night, it's that Steve fell for our little act. He's convinced you're all man. He just told me that no guy with enough cojones to beat up his daughter's boyfriend would let himself be emasculated being a beard."

I correct her. A man who poses as a lesbian's significant other is a merkin, not a beard. A beard is a woman who covers for a gay man.

"Don't get mad at me," I tell her, "but Steve wasn't as big of a jerk as I expected. That whole monologue of his about *Dialogues on the Carmelites* last night, that was interesting. Seems to me there's hope for the guy if he's a patron of the arts. It doesn't excuse him petitioning to lower his child support, but he said he wants to learn and grow. If he can care about Catholic nuns condemned to the guillotine, he must have it in him to sympathize with the struggles of single mothers."

My naiveté amuses Campbell. "I wondered about that riff of his, so I did some checking. All that bullshit he was telling us about Poulnec and that opera? Straight off Wikipedia. Steve is snowing us just like we're snowing him. No, wait: he was snowing *you*. He wanted to sucker you into taking his side."

Maybe I am gullible. I have a hard time figuring out how I could fall for what Steve was selling, though, when every word out of my daughter's mouth lately strikes me as a lie.

"There's something I need to show you," I tell Campbell, changing the subject.

I pull a palm-sized packet from under the couch. The sack it's wrapped in is from the drugstore that Campbell and Deb took me to on the way home from the pokey.

"You're showing me a book of matches?"

"It's not matches, genius. It's a five-panel drug-test kit. Each of these little strips checks for something: pot, coke, morphine, meth, and speed. The specimen cup comes separately, though. I'm going to need to borrow a coffee cup, one you don't mind not getting back. What do you think?"

I can see the blood drain from Campbell's face. "I think you're officially insane. You're going to test Chloe for meth and speed? How do you think she'll react to that? And when did drugs come into the conversation? All you've talked about is her having sex."

I return the kit to its hiding place. "I'm her father. It's my job to be nosy. I don't know *that* she's doing drugs. I want to see *if* she is. I'll bet you twenty bucks she has, and with Stu, too."

Campbell looks as if she needs to sit down, but between my gym bag of clothes and her piles of books in the study, there's no space.

"You're going to go *Reefer Madness* on Chloe over a can of Febreze? Even if she lit up all the time, drug tests are no good. Real users hide it. They buy this stuff called Urine Luck—one drop, and they're masked. Besides, I don't believe in drug testing teenagers. It's fascistic."

I want to hear her say that when her kid is sixteen. Campbell just stares at me, appalled.

"You do this," she tells me, "you're pulling a pin on a grenade you can't put back in. Seriously, stop and think this over."

Needless to say, I don't heed Campbell's warning. In my mind the pin was pulled some sixteen years and nine months ago, and everything in between has been a warm-up to this battle of wills that Chloe and I seem destined to wage. Several hours later, Deb, Chloe, and I pile into my Scion and head to Trattoria Prego, which, now that I think about it, sounds a little too much like *pregnant* for my liking. Chloe decides she'll have the oak-roasted rack of lamb and then points Deb to the second most-expensive item on the menu, shrimp and scallops over capellini pasta.

"No, no," Deb protests, embarrassed. "That's forty dollars. That's what I can afford to spend a *week* on food. Did you forget that I'm out of work?"

Chloe reminds us that my dad sent plenty of money for this outing. Deb and I share an uncomfortable look, realizing that we're almost forty and still relying on the generosity of elders. I decide to pick up the bill. What the hell. Another couple hundred dollars on my Visa won't matter. I grit my teeth and invite my ex- to order whatever she wants. I go for a fourteen-ounce strip steak topped with Gorgonzola cheese. And that's not including the appetizer, breads and salads, or the $60 bottle of Chianti I throw in hoping to get rip-snorting drunk.

"Is that the same waitress as the last time we were here?" I ask Chloe after our orders are taken. "You know, the one–"

Chloe rolls her eyes and turns to Deb. "We used to eat here a couple of times a month when Daddy got a paycheck from Mr. Storm. One time when we came he was convinced the waitress was giving him dirty looks.

He was sure she thought we were like—you know... *together*. He's got this delusion that he's too young to have a teenager. He doesn't want to believe that he looks thirty-seven."

"You don't look your age," Deb assures me. "Except for the gray. It's a good thing you have it, too. Otherwise, you'd look twenty-seven."

Chloe doesn't buy it. "Yeah, well, I about hocked up my veal parmesan when he said that. It was *sooo* embarrassing. When Daddy pays the bill, he leaves a message next to the tip: 'She's my daughter, I promise. Please don't call the police.' That's his idea of funny."

"You're talking mighty big for someone who's grounded," I say. Making this point kills the mood, so I change the subject. "Did you like my CD?"

On the way to the restaurant, I played Chloe and Deb Juliana Hatfield's *Hey Babe*, which I hadn't listened to in as least as many years as I hadn't thought about *Exile in Guyville*. "If Liz was my id back then," I explained during the ride, "Juliana was my superego." When Chloe asked what that meant, I fumbled. I couldn't figure out how to explain without starting a fight that when Juliana Hatfield was popular in the early nineties, she generated a lot of publicity claiming she was still a virgin at twenty-six.

"The thing that makes Juliana Hatfield's power pop work," I tell Chloe, "is that the lyrics can get away with being soft and sensitive because the music is so tough and punchy. Here she's singing about some guy ripping her heart out, but she's not wimpy because she's got chops. Whether we like it or not, chops and licks are two things women musicians have to prove they've got. Otherwise people think of them as the guitar player's girlfriend."

Chloe's not interested in talking about Juliana Hatfield or power pop. We're mostly silent until our drinks arrive. After the waitress leaves I lean forward and whisper that she *is* the same one that suspected me of dating a teenager the last time we came here. I say the same thing again when the server brings our appetizers several minutes later. "Next time we come here I'm bringing your birth certificate," I joke, but Chloe doesn't laugh or pretend to hock up the hearty bite she chomps. Her phone rings with a melody that it takes me a whole chorus to recognize: "Fuck and Run." *Wonderful.* The call injects new life into Chloe. She bursts into a smile, looks around the room, then before her mother or I can stop her, she runs off.

For only the third time in fifteen years, Deb and I are alone.

"Is it just me," I ask, "or did she just forget she's grounded?"

As Deb points out, in Chloe's mind the punishment for sneaking out of the house probably pales in comparison to the assault charge her father faces. I clarify that I'm only looking at *misdemeanor* assault, but before Deb can answer an uninvited guest plops into Chloe's chair.

"Looks like we've got a couple of runaways on our hands," chuckles Luke Laughlin, Nina's dad. "The girls ran to the ladies room to talk without us old fogies listening in."

He regrets lumping himself into that category the minute he gets a load of Deb. I introduce the two of them and then watch as Luke struggles to pop his eyeballs back in his head. He's a handsome, fluffy-haired guy in his early forties who's been in the market for a second Mrs. Laughlin since Nina's mom decided she wasn't happy being married to a Baptist choir director. Luck hasn't been on Luke's side, though. The only thing rarer than happily unmarried men in Willoughby are single women—single straight women, that is.

I let my wine sour in my mouth while the two of them make small talk. "Nina's the sister Chloe never got to have," Deb tells Luke. He declines the glass of Chianti she offers, bashfully admitting that his career doesn't allow him to be seen drinking in public.

"I'll have one for you then," I say, quickly pouring my second.

"I'm glad I ran into you, Vance. I planned to call you tomorrow, but it's better that we talk in person. Less chance of a misunderstanding or hard feelings this way. I'm not a sneak, but I was going through Nina's purse this afternoon, and I found a ticket stub. Some woman named Lilith Fair."

Deb expresses surprise that Luke rifles Nina's purse, but our guest ignores her.

"It didn't take long for Nina's mom to crack when I confronted her," he says. "Marci was never a good liar. I suppose if she were, I'd never have gotten suspicious, and I could've saved the three thousand dollars the private detective cost me.... But that's the past. Taking Nina to a concert without my permission was a low blow. I'm sure Nina and Marci convinced you that I'm an old fuddy-duddy who doesn't need to be consulted, but I'm still her dad, and I should have a say in what my kid sees and hears. I wouldn't deny you that right; I respect your parental authority. Have you ever listened to this Lilith Fair, Vance? The language is horrible, shocking. If you think it's okay for Chloe to use such words, that's your business, but I can't allow Nina to, not in good conscience. I'm really sorry. This is nothing against Chloe, but I think it's best if the girls took some time apart. Nina needs reining in."

The Chianti is strong. I'm buzzed. I want to ask if Nina is a horse.

"No problem, Luke." My tongue feels like a river that can't be dammed. "I'm glad you brought it up. I've been meaning to talk to you, too. I have my own worries, so quarantining the girls will ease my mind as well. You won't have to worry about Chloe bringing inappropriate music into your house anymore, and I won't have to inspect Nina's underwear."

Amid the stately décor of Trattoria Prego, the word *underwear* sounds as indecorous as a wet fart. Which is just how three glasses of Chianti had me intending it.

"Excuse me?" says Luke.

"Underwear. I've been finding thongs in Chloe's clothes pile. I'm pretty sure they aren't crawling in there of their own accord. It's obvious that in the girls' friendship Chloe is the artist and Nina the fashionista, so I blame her. I guess it's your business if your daughter wants to sling her ass in a lingerie rope, but my conscience won't allow it. I'm not surprised Nina didn't tell you. What daughter says that her best friend's dad makes her wear a chastity belt when she walks into his house? So you don't think I'm picking on Nina, I make

Chloe wear one, too–all the time."

"Vance," Deb whispers, staring at the tablecloth. I don't know which is likelier, Luke hurling holy water in my face or whacking me upside the head with a hymnal. I certainly don't anticipate the reaction I do provoke. The guy starts crying.

"Make fun of me if you want," he says as he wells up, "but I stand by what I believe in. I don't have much going for me these days, but at least I've got my convictions." He turns to Deb, wiping his tears. "I didn't take it lightly when my wife and I got married. 'For better or for worse,' that's all they told me, and that's all I was prepared for. Nobody said she'd one day wake up and decide, 'Eighteen and out.' That was her explanation: eighteen years was long enough. I'm praying I'll meet a woman who knows what she wants." He stands to deliver his *coup de grâce*. "Just so you know, Vance, I'm praying for Chloe, too."

Luke abandons us to an uncomfortable silence.

"Do you make everybody in this town cry?" Deb asks after a while.

Call me crazy, but I think sobbing was Luke's way of hitting on Deb. When I suggest this, she says she's not in the market for a man. I tell her that's good because according to the last census, Willoughby is home to a whopping three available ones. Up from two as of yesterday, but still, the selection is nothing to brag about. Luke is desperate, Luther's convinced no woman wants him because of his prostatectomy, and as for me....

"Well," I smile at Deb, "I'm sure to you I'm old hat. BTDT, as Chloe likes to say. Been there, done that."

"Really?" She cocks an eyebrow. "So is 'done that' how

you think of me? Wait–don't answer. I can already see the smart remark coming: 'Until last Saturday, Deb, I hadn't thought of you much at all.'"

The imitation is embarrassingly accurate. I feel bad that I sound like such a dick. I feel bad that I could be one. I plant my elbows on the table and remind myself I'm a good listener. I invite Deb to tell me about her life these past fifteen years. It hits me that I don't even know if she's had a serious relationship, or a few of them, since we were divorced. Maybe it's too early for us to have this kind of conversation. Maybe divorced people ought to draw firm boundaries in their dealings. Or maybe I should wait until I'm not sloshed to nudge her into a heart-to-heart. My words come out of my mouth doing pratfalls.

"Surely you've had boyfriends over the years," I slur. "Surely you haven't gone fifteen years without.... you know...."

Deb gives me an uneasy squint. I get the feeling she thinks I'm hitting on her.

"I've had sex since you, yes. Sometimes even actual relationships. Some were good, others weren't. Let's leave it at that, shall we? I'd rather we stick to the subject of Chloe."

There's not much to say after that, so we listen to ourselves slurp wine until our food arrives. I have to dial Chloe's cell and summon her back to the table before her lamb goes cold.

"Hey, Mom, Nina's dad thinks you're hot."

Deb smiles, obligingly. She knows she's being ribbed. She doubts "hot" is a word that's in Luke Laughlin's vocabulary. Chloe slyly admits she's paraphrasing, but she assures her mother that Nina's dad was interested. I start to feel a little queasy. The red wine has made the table wobbly. I keep aiming to cut my steak and hit my potato instead.

"Mr. Luke was asking all kinds of questions about what you plan to do in Willoughby," Chloe informs Deb. "He told me to tell you he might be able to help you find a teaching job."

Deb finishes a bite and then sets her silverware down. "That brings us to a serious subject. Vance, we need to talk about Chloe transferring to Willoughby High in the fall. She really wants to enroll in the new drama track the school's starting this year. It's a great opportunity for her."

A piece of meat goes down my windpipe like a foot. For several seconds I think I'll need the Heimlich maneuver. When the hunk finally inches to my stomach, I realize this school business is the only reason I've been invited tonight. Chloe and her mom have conspired to dope up my glycemic index until I'm too groggy to say no, my own dad financing the plot. I suck a gob of Gorgonzola from between my teeth and tell Chloe to give me her best sales pitch, which she does. Creative arts program. Awesome curriculum. College-level classes on performance studies, theater crafts and design, even the creative process. It sounds almost as appetizing as the next wad of steak I'll choke on.

"So who's Nina's mom seeing these days?" I ask when the spiel's done. "She dating anybody?"

On the ride home, I blast "Nirvana," my favorite song

off Juliana Hatfield's *Hey Babe*. Yes, I admit, the song is about the band, but it's about more than that, too. It's about craving that elusive rock 'n' roll catharsis. The chorus drops a glaring F-bomb that I make no effort to censor. In fact, every time the chorus comes around I crank the volume. Soon the music is so loud that Chloe rolls down the window. "Stop trying to be cool," she chastises me, but I'm so nervous about what I'm about to do I want to lose myself in the whirlpools of distorted guitar. The Trattoria is only ten minutes from our house—or Deb's house now, as it's become—but by the time my Scion climbs the drive my armpits are damp, and my shirt sticks to my back. I park and follow Deb and Chloe inside.

"You better go to Campbell's," Chloe whispers. "Lleyton's dad might be spying."

"Before you go to bed, there's something I need you to do. It won't take but a minute." From my pocket I pull out the specimen cup that I bought this afternoon. Chloe looks to Deb and then back to me, her face coagulating in disbelief.

"Is that what I think it is?" She backs up, a cornered animal. "You're asking me to take a test?"

"Sort of. Well, I'm not really asking. I'm telling." I try to hold the cup steady, but my hands shake. "Just reassure me that I don't have anything to worry about."

"Vance," Deb stammers. "Please. We were having such a good time."

Chloe is choking on her words. "I can't believe... Are you serious? You had that in your pocket all night, at the restaurant even? Why didn't you make me do the test there? You could have humiliated me in public."

"All you have to do is fill it. Put my mind at ease. You pass, we forget this ever happened."

She looks at me with more malevolence than I could ever imagine a sixteen-year-old capable of. Lunging, she grabs the cup and slams the bathroom door. The slam sends such a ripple through the house I expect the seams in the drywall to split. "Don't fill it too full," I say over the sound of her offended trickle. "Get away!" she screams. Something small but hard bounces off the back of the door, near my head. "She threw her shoe at me!" I tell Deb, who buries her face in her hand. The door rips open, and Chloe thrusts the cup my way, its swirling contents lapping the brim. "Stay here," I insist. She slumps to the wall, teeth clenched. I take the test strips from my other pocket and dip them in the cup for the required thirty seconds. Four of the strips come out the way they went in–clean. The fifth is as blue as my mood.

"You see this?" I show Deb. "Your daughter is following in your footsteps. She's an actress. A good one, too–she had me fooled. Here I was feeling like a Nazi for even asking."

Chloe is crying. "Are you happy? What's next, Dad? A pregnancy test? Will that make you quit being weird to me?"

I tell her that she has exactly two seconds to confess when, where, and with whom she's smoked marijuana. Instead, she screams and rushes to her bedroom. I follow until I see her hurl that door shut, too. Why must she be so melodramatic? This is what I want to ask her mother, but the clap of the jamb catches me half-stride and sends me tottering backwards. I'm staring straight into the cup, knowing full well what's about to happen. Why not? My life's full of spills. All I know to do is mop up afterward. Meanwhile, I'm stained in my daughter's urine.

# 26

Like Chloe, I, too, can slam a door–the front door, which smashes so hard into the sill my windows nearly bubble. I can also kick, as my porch sorbet table discovers when it's sent flying over the railing into the viburnum. It's a good thing my Weber Summit Grill is heavy as a tank. Otherwise it might end up in my neighbor's yard.

"You're being ridiculous! Come back and talk to her!"

I ignore Deb and dash instead a hundred yards to where the street twists right toward the Bibbs-Grave Bridge. Crape myrtles and blackgums dribble rain droplets on my head. They should extinguish my fuming, but I only boil more. Not until I cross the Coosa River am I able to think without feeling like a victim of Chinese water torture. As small as Willoughby is, I should be able to hoof to a friend's to cool down, but I'm short on friends these days. There's only one place I can think to go, but I doubt I'll be received warmly.

I head for Sadie's.

I'm barely three hundred feet along the shoulder of Highway 231 when an unfamiliar Mini Cooper pulls over. "Dangerous place for a walk," the driver says as I pass his window. "Need a lift?" His voice sounds familiar, but I can't place him, and he's too swallowed in shadows for me to see his face. When I ask if we've met, the guy giggles. "What? That night in Tijuana wasn't memorable for you?"

I tell him that sarcasm from a stranger is about the last thing I need right now.

"How about getting sideswiped by a stranger? You

need that more? Come on, bud–hop in. I'm not a serial killer, I promise."

I should keep walking, but as drunk as I am, the walk to Sadie's could turn into my Bataan Death March. As I slide into the passenger seat, I see the stranger is built like a soup can. Not until he spits a wad of gravel tearing back onto the blacktop, peeling out of the shadows, do I realize where I know him from. The friendly mutton chops are a dead giveaway. Even so, the guy looks different when he's not standing in front of a urinal wagging himself.

"You were at the bar last night! In the bathroom!"

His mustache coils like a snake as he grins with feigned surprise. He's got the fake thing down pat. "The world's ripe with coincidence, huh? Or maybe not. Willoughby's not that big of a town. I like it, though. Great place for raising kids. You gotta feel safe in a place where Walmart refuses to sell condoms to teenagers. You get a little more art around here, and, wow, this hippie town will be so cosmopolitan. Only one thing I don't get about it. You know what that is?"

"Let me out. I'll walk."

"Settle down, Scaredy Pants. You going to that fancy estate you inherited? Off to buff statues for your grand opening? When is your grand opening? No, wait. I know.... This is a booty call, right? Why else would a grown man walk a two-lane highway at ten o'clock at night?"

When I ask why a grown man is saying *booty call*, the stranger laughs. He tells me I'm funny, then says I'm tough, too. He hopes with my reputation for violence I don't coldcock him. "I'm not your daughter's boyfriend, after all," he adds. I grip the armrest.

"How do you know so much about me?"

"Like I said, this is a small town. Hey, you didn't let me tell you what I don't understand about this place. The teenage girls in this town! I'm used to little girlie culture being about Hello Kitty posters, and those sweatpants that say Juicy and Pink on the butt. A big heart for the dot over an 'i.' Soft, sweet, cute shit, y'know? The girls in this town are buzz saws, though. Loud, brash, in your face. Militant, almost. Everywhere I go in Willoughby, Alabama, I see signs of them. Graffiti, fliers, bumper stickers. Don't Deface Macon Place, one says. This is What a Feminist Looks Like, says another. Then there's F— Mike Willoughby. What kind of parent lets a little girl write F— Mike Willoughby on the wall outside a Piggly Wiggly?"

"Take this right.This is where I'm going. I'll get out here."

The stranger wheels into the lot of a condo community. "Oh, okay. Nice complex. I bet a lot of wiry-looking feminists live here, huh? You sure you're safe? I mean, you need another man for back-up? I'd hate to abandon a guy to a horde of man-haters. Romantic soul like yourself, they'd make mincemeat of you."

"If you know anything about me you know I don't like that sort of talk." I give him the most intimidating stare I can muster, which isn't very intimidating. "Mike Willoughby sent you, didn't he? This is his way of bullying me into selling Macon Place."

As I reach for the door the stranger clutches my kneecap.

"I'm just doing a brother a favor. That's what's wrong

with this world. We men need to stick together, cover for each other." For the first time, his grin is gone. "Some friendly advice. Be wary of women. They can be harmful to your health. Oh, and another thing–you shouldn't hitchhike. You never know what kind of kook might offer you a ride."

I'm barely onto the pavement before the Mini Cooper rips out of the parking lot. A few yards from the security gate outside Sadie's complex, I realize I don't know the entry code. I have to scale the fence, the wrought-iron barbs nearly spearing my groin. I make it over with just a rip in the knee of my khakis and a smutch of grease on my breast. The smutch is okay, I decide. It'll distract attention from the urine splotch beside it.

Sadie answers the door in a goldfish-orange T-shirt. She doesn't look thrilled. She starts to shut the door, but I slide my hand over the deadlatch. She makes sure to give me a good pinch before swinging it back open. I tell her something weird just happened. Two weird things, actually. I know I don't deserve it, but she'd be doing me a tremendous favor if I could come in and just talk them through–

"Hey, whose head is that?"

The answer is obvious. Through the pass-through into Sadie's tiny kitchen I see what looks like a cowl of gray cotton candy. I've only ever seen one person sport that hairdo. Make that two people. Samuel Clemens wore it as well.

"Oh, hello, Vance." Luther waves exuberantly through the portal. "What are you doing out this late?"

I'm distracted by the sharp green of his T-shirt until I

realize he's not wearing pants. His thighs are covered by a modest pair of white boxer shorts, which appear piercingly bright amid the smoky ennui of night. "What's going on here?" I ask.

"We're talking," Sadie insists.

"In underwear? And isn't that–?"

It is. That green T-shirt is mine. I spot the words BRICKS ARE HEAVY as Luther glides into the living room licking the top of a rice cake. I bought that shirt at the L7 concert I attended when I was seventeen, back when I took my one and only stage dive. I left the shirt at Sadie's one of the first nights we ever stayed together.

"I spilled my damn port." Luther's face is more giddy than regretful. "A whole half-bottle right down the chest and into the crotch. Sorry to bare-leg it. This shirt was the only thing in the whole condo I could fit into. Of course, I could've gone for the studded red-leather belt."

I gasp and tell Sadie I can't believe she told him that story. Luther can't stop chuckling over it. Chewing vigorously, he tells Sadie to let me in. Believe it or not, the sight of his spindly legs sticking out from my T-shirt isn't the most startling image of the night. As the door opens I discover somebody else has been invited to this party. Iris sits on the couch, her dreadlocks coiled like Medusa snakes.

"Am I supposed to believe this isn't planned?" Stu's mom asks.

Sadie quickly insists she didn't invite me. Luther assures her he didn't either. Although Iris doesn't look interested in chitchatting, I realize this is my one shot at getting out of a misdemeanor assault charge.

Kirk Curnutt

"Hear me out," I say. "I didn't attack Stu. It was a tussle, and we fell. If I were going to rough up your son, I wouldn't do it in a bathroom. My head almost hit the toilet! I thought I was going to lose teeth for the second time this week."

Believe it or not, the sight of my daughter's boyfriend's mother reclining in my former girlfriend's apartment alongside my lesbian best friend's father doesn't begin to exhaust the oddity of this gathering. On the coffee table beside scissors, a pile of old EPs, and Sadie's notebook of songs is a chafing tray. Piled on it is what looks like a gravelly mound of peat moss, or a moldy heap of okra. A wisp of smoke curls from between Iris's fingers. I sniff at a funny odor.

"Are you guys smoking dope?"

Luther picks a rice crumb from his moustache and studies it. "I've learned so much tonight. They call this stuff Krypie, short for Kryptonite because it's been known to knock Superman out of his boots. I've decided the name is a gross misnomer, though. Far from robbing me of my superpowers, it's convinced me I can leap tall buildings in a single bound."

Not knowing what else to say, I remind Luther that he's in his seventies, a little late in the day to be sparking up. But Luther's not perturbed. He's too busy jabbering.

"It's good you showed up," he says. "We can get everything off our chests. It's not good to harbor resentments. They give you cancer. I should know. I spent so much time resenting people for not supporting my studio and Campbell and even my P-FLAG chapter that I made myself sick. Resentment gave me cancer. Come on, Vance.

You and Iris smoke the peace pipe, and we'll all get well together."

I'm aware suddenly of the contrast between Sadie's place and mine—between the mellow quiet of a night winding down and the slamming doors of a confrontation, between the contemplative talk of friends and the overwrought bickering of parents and teenagers, between the luxury of the unattached life and the grind of instilling discipline. I've never before wondered who I'd be if I weren't a father, but I do now. I could be a vagabond, roaming the road. I could be a prodigal son, squandering a trust fund. I could be a rake, sleeping with anybody I wanted without worrying whether I was a good role model. I could be a free man. As free of obligation as this wisp of smoke that twines along Iris's arm without concern for where it's drifting.

Why do I always have to be the responsible one?

"Fire me up," I say, hopping into Sadie's recliner.

Once in junior high I was assigned to write an essay on the dangers of marijuana. It was in the thick of the battles I waged against my father's second wife, his former secretary, who'd replaced my mother a short four months after Mom died. In my resentment at Janice I devised a scheme by which I would offend my teacher and get suspended from school, somehow proving to my father that this was all his fault. I wrote about why pot was harmful to adults but good for teenagers. "There are three things that it's undignified for people to do after the age of nineteen," my opening sentence declared. "They are 1) using the word *party* as a verb, 2) listening in rapt

Kirk Curnutt

attention to all forty-eight minutes and thirteen seconds of George Michael's *Listen without Prejudice (Vol. 1)*, and 3) smoking dope."

From there I made the case that "M.J." was an initiation experience that taught young people such valuable lessons as laws are stupid, cops are cretins, and only morons grow up. I went out on a note that I was sure would guarantee my status as an *enfant terrible*: "In conclusion, marijuana is okay for kids. To me it's a lot like masturbation. It's fun and it feels good, although it's nothing you want your parents to catch you doing." Rather than excite outrage, my wit earned a middling C+ and a short riposte from the teacher informing me that 1) I wasn't as funny as I thought I was and 2) my pronoun/antecedent agreement needed work.

Predictably, I'd never even smoked pot back then. That wouldn't happen for a half-decade until I was a college freshman, when I tried it once with some older theater types. I never smoked again because it had no effect on me, and I was too Type A for the somnambulistic pace of weed culture.

How funny then that I hold this jay in my fingers like it's the last Fabergé egg on earth. I love the feel of its burn on my fingertips, the aroma in my nostrils, the Cézanne shade of orange that the silky rolling paper flares into when I take a drag.

"Go easy," warns Luther. "I've learned a new catch-phrase tonight: 'Krypie's a creeper.'"

I'd like to explain that while I'm giddy, it's not from the THC. It's the thrill of breaking the rules—my own rules. If nobody else respects the laws of the father, why must I?

As I swallow a toke, Iris squares her bare shoulders. She's wearing her usual backless halter top, her body lithe as a knife. "Your friends really care about you, Seahorse. Why, I don't know, but they've been plying me with Krypie thinking I'll come to my senses about you and Stu and drop the assault charge."

"That's *misdemeanor* assault. A fine, probation, some community service."

"We didn't ask you over for Vance," insists Sadie. She turns to me. "We're just grooving to some tunes. You should hear the EPs Iris's band did back in the day. I'm trying to convince her to dig out her bass and play with me at the battle of the bands. That's why she's here. Luther and I are thinking of forming the first Willoughby, Alabama, supergroup, The New Wussy Pimps."

I need another long drag as I stare down Iris. The longer I hold it in the less myself I feel. So much so that when I open my mouth the voice I hear isn't mine. It belongs to the voice of the guy from the men's room, the Mini Cooper driver. I am a walking, talking set of friendly mutton chops.

"If they're attempting to persuade you, then they're wasting good weed, huh? Because we both know you won't drop the charge. Why should you? This is your chance to extract legal revenge on a man. You haven't been able to do that with your ex-husband, so now you've got a surrogate. I stand by what I've said. What happened between me and your son was nothing but a scuffle and a tussle. Any other father who'd heard Stu's song would have been just as angry. *Angrier* probably."

Luther and Sadie look pained. "That's not quite

Kirk Curnutt

packing the peace pipe," groans Luther. Iris leans forward, her elbows folded over the kneecaps of her capris.

"My son put twenty hours of work into that song. Thanks to you, it's gone in a click."

"If his song was all that great he should've saved a backup copy. The truth is it wasn't great. It was puerile and juvenile. I'll add vile just to complete the rhyme scheme. Worse, it was an insult to Chloe. You know what I'll say in court if you take it that far? I'll say your son hasn't been taught to respect women."

"You don't know what Stu's been taught."

"All I need to know is that he fucks my daughter and then brags about it."

The apartment is so silent I can hear the toilet in Sadie's bedroom gurgle.

"It's time for me to get home," Iris decides, standing up. "Some of us have children to raise. Some of us just are children." She doesn't stop with an insult. She levels a threat. "You don't understand the problems you're creating for yourself, Seahorse. You're dung for."

As the door slams, I'm left wondering two things: Why is Stu's mom suddenly calling me Seahorse? And where have I heard *dung for* recently?

Sadie scratches her elbow. "Well, that didn't go as hoped. We almost had her talked into dropping the charge until you showed up. 'Your son fucks my daughter?' What was that about? Chloe may be your daughter, but you don't own her vagina, dude. If you think you're allowed to be offended because she's had sex, then you need to reread that *Intercourse* book of yours."

Instead of venturing into a discussion of my daughter's vagina, I recount tonight's misadventures. The $200 dinner. Luke hitting on Deb. The drug test. The shoe on the back of the door and the second encounter with the stranger from the urinal. The only part I leave out is the urine spill.

"You should have taped the conversation," Luther says of my bizarre car ride. "Then we could show what a mobster Mike Willoughby really is. Imagine, sending muscle to intimidate you! Storm is rolling in his grave."

Sadie isn't as outraged. "I'm more interested in you and Chloe. Not one hour ago your daughter tests positive for weed, and now you're over here making a wind tunnel out of your mouth inhaling our fatty."

I thank her for pointing out my hypocrisy. Luther taps his index finger to his thumb. I take it as the international symbol for *pass the doochie.*

"All parenting is hypocritical," he says. "We measure our humanity in the gap between 'Don't do as I do' and 'Do as I say.' If we want better for our children, then we have to do them the favor of failing them—that's my thought. It all comes down to how much hypocrisy you can abide. Ask Campbell. She'll tell you I have great tolerance."

"I'm only curious," Sadie counters, "what Vance would tell Chloe if she knew he lit up the same night he busts her for it."

"I know exactly what I'd say," I answer. "I'd say, 'I'm an adult, and I'm allowed to make my own decisions.' Then I'd tell her what I was really feeling: 'Welcome to my life. How do you like disappointment?' Then I'd

Kirk Curnutt

continue with, 'What? I'm supposed to care what *you* think of *me*?' And, after that, I'd add, 'Excuse me, but it has nothing to do with you. It's my life.' From there I'd put in an, 'Oh, fine, hold this against me while you forgive your mother, who's forgiven herself for running out on you.' And then, as a topper, I'd say, 'Payback's a bitch, huh, honey?' *That's* what I'd say to Chloe."

The two of them look as if I intended to burn the armrest. The ash leapt from the jay of its own accord. What does Sadie care about the furniture, anyway? She rents this place furnished.

"While we're on the subject of things that need to be said," I blabber on, "I have a question. Just what's going on here? I mean, am I supposed to believe that this is a hootenanny? We need to be upfront. I came clean about me and Campbell. Tell me about you"–I point to Sadie, then to Luther–"and you. Are you two trying to punish me for being Campbell's friend?"

Sadie tosses her nail polish bottle into her purse, which lies several feet away. "You're an idiot," she says, matter-of-factly. Having finished his rice cake, Luther rises from the couch and returns to the kitchen, where he pours himself a glass from what's left of his port.

"What's to be surprised about? I'm Sadie's producer, remember? Not all of our work takes place in the studio. Sometimes I come over here to listen to new songs, sometimes she comes to my house to play them. I thought it'd be cool if Sadie closed the battle of the bands. These kids need to know what real music sounds like. She didn't get to play the showcase last night because of your...*crisis*. She's going to sing 'Riding Freedom's Wheels.' We were hoping to get Iris to play. You missed Sadie singing my song to Iris. I almost cried—it's been fifty years since anybody's done that oldie moldie."

"It's a great song," Sadie says, though in a strangely unenthusiastic way. Not until Luther opens his mouth again do I discover why she's so hesitant.

"Sadie even wrote a song for me! Nobody's ever done that before. It's called..."

I cut him off with a wild guess: "That Careful Man with Complicated Veins." How did the lyrics that I read the night of the belt incident go? *Sip of port, his lucky star/ Last night he traded his soul for a cigar.* I should've put two and two together. Who else drinks port in this town besides Luther?

His smile fades. "You heard the song before I did?" he asks, sloppy with woe.

"She's *my* girlfriend," I remind him.

"*Ex*-girlfriend," she reminds me. "And I never said the song was about you. Both of you are pitiful. I'm going to bed. Try not to smoke all my weed, dudes."

She leaves Luther and me staring at each other. For all the hostility hanging in the air, he's smiling contentedly. Out of the blue he wonders if I regret breaking my 10 ½ Commandment to date someone so much younger. I tell him the last thing I need tonight is another lecture on relationships.

"I'm not asking for your sake," Luther says. "I'm asking for mine. I need your advice, Vance. I'm not saying it's happening, but if it ever did, I'd want to make sure I was doing it for the right reasons."

"Just because Sadie let you think she wrote a song

about you doesn't mean she's interested. Besides, as I keep reminding you, she's *my* girlfriend."

"And as she keeps reminding you, she's your *ex*-. But don't worry; I'm not interested in Sadie. I'm only wondering if you were attracted to her or to your authority over her. That's a pretty irresistible aphrodisiac for a middle-aged man, isn't it?"

I tell him I've never had any authority over Sadie. Then I tell him I'm not middle-aged. I'm thirty-seven. Luther prattles on as if I'm not even in the room.

"You know Campbell's theory about what women want from a man? A daddy figure. And what do we want? A woman we can control like a daughter. It seems like such an easy trade. With a few years on them, we can claim experience, knowledge, taste, strength, and what do we ask of their youth? All the things we're afraid of losing–beauty, enthusiasm, innocence, eagerness, energy. We're not honest, though. We mislead women."

"You're stoned, Daddy-O. You don't know what you're saying."

"Oh, yes I do. I'm saying we men bring more demands and needs to the table than we bring gifts. That's what Sadie has realized about you. I'm saying that, when push comes to shove, we men are nothing but big babies. I can prove it, too. You want to see?"

He abruptly stands and tugs his boxers down over his hips, revealing a pair of bulky plastic underwear. "I've had to wear these since my prostatectomy. I haven't told anybody–not even Campbell. Don't feel sorry for me, though. It's been an education. Before the operation, my doctor said I might not suffer any impotence. They have ways now of sparing the nerves when they yank out a prostate. I told him to mangle as many nerves as he could get his hands on. 'You'll be doing me a favor,' I said. The incontinence hasn't been a bother, either."

He catches me staring at his spongy crotch.

"It's the absorbent pads. They make me look bigger than I am. You can't imagine how liberating it is not to worry about bodily functions. Think about it, Vance. Not pissing ourselves is the first bit of control we're taught to flex over our lives. Something about mastering the bladder makes us want to impose that same control on the world around us. It becomes our driving motivation in life. Once you lose the power, though, you lose the desire for mastery. Don't you think if you and I gave that son-of-a-bitch Steve a prostatectomy, he'd be a teddy bear? He wouldn't worry about whether Campbell is gay or straight."

I'm tempted to point out that wearing adult diapers hasn't exactly freed Luther of his desire to control others, but something else is on my mind.

"What young woman are you worried you're interested in for the wrong reasons? It's Nina's mom, isn't it? Luke Laughlin was whimpering earlier about hiring a private detective. Oh my God, you and Marci have been having an affair! You're the reason the Laughlins are getting divorced!"

Luther hikes up his boxers and returns to the couch. "That's so like you. Always wanting to see the trees instead of the forest. That's why I'm not sharing my private life with you." His eyes drop to the chafing dish. "How about you roll the next joint? Sadie taught me

Kirk Curnutt

earlier tonight. Let me pass on the wisdom."

What's left to lose? I drop to my knees at the coffee table and take a Krypie chunk between my fingers. Luther spreads out the rolling paper, which is thin with an Oriental design for a watermark. It's made of rice, he explains. No additives. Burns easier, too. When I begin to crumble the clump like brown sugar he hands me the scissors. "Sadie says to trim it, not to hurt it," Luther says. I flush with nervousness, perspiring a little even. Getting high is precision work, I decide. "Not so much," the Chong to my Cheech warns as I pile my prunings. "We're only maintaining." Maintaining? I ask. "Yeah," Luther says, "that's what they call it." I need to learn this lingo in case it's slipped into Chloe's vocabulary. As I lick the paper edge I'm told the trick is to fold more than roll, but not too hard. "It's a fatty," Luther says. "Not origami." My fingers feel thick as kielbasa. By the time I twist the ends, my jay is the shape of a Tootsie Roll. I pass my handiwork to Luther, apologizing for my ineptitude.

"I have a better idea," he decides, removing a glass pipe from a drawer in the coffee table. "Sadie showed it to me earlier, but she put it away when I told her it looked like a cock. She couldn't believe I said that word to her. Neither could I. What weed does to you!"

He grins so broadly his eyes disappear.

"I've never told you this, Vance, but I believe in alternative universes. Somewhere out there you and I live a very different existence. In that blissful realm, we have no worries: Macon Place is a Taj Mahal where artists serve the muses, Mike Willoughby is a derelict drinking Thunderbird on skid row, and your sixteen-year-old is still a virgin."

"I like that. How about in that universe Pink Melon Joy is actually a good band? And Stu plays classical guitar instead of writing rhymes about fucking Aphrodite in a car?"

"Oooh, yeah. And he's never once set foot in the condom aisle at Walmart."

My scowl sobers Luther.

"Of course, you know what else happens in that universe, don't you?" he says.

"Let me think. You don't resent me for having dated your gay daughter?"

"Well, that too, but somewhere out there is a universe where you and Campbell are married. And yes, in it I'm proud to be your father-in-law."

Luther takes a huge hit from the pipe. "You know what else?"

I always heard pot was supposed to bliss a brother out, but Krypie agitates Luther. He no sooner takes several puffs than he's on his feet again, pacing the room.

"You know, Vance, ever since you erased Stu's song, I've been having these dreams–fantasies, really–about me confronting Steve. In every single one, I whip his ass. Mercilessly. I want to thank you for letting me have that dream. It's been great."

He takes another long hit, tosses me the pipe, and then does something wholly unexpected. He stuffs his hands deep in his adult diapers.

"I dream of whipping so many men's asses. I really do. So damn many. You want to know my Top Ten? Well, let's see. There's the cousin who molested my sister from the ages of seven to nine. Fucking Dexter James Winthrop with his greasy duck-ass hairdo. Used to take Caroline in a room and play her Jo Stafford records while he stuck a finger in her and made her touch his dingdong. That's what pedophiles called it in 1956: a *dingdong*. I never knew about the abuse until forty years later when some musician friends of mine started playing 'You Belong to Me' at a party and Caroline had a breakdown. She told me the story, and I swore I would hunt him down. But he was already dead by then. I wish I could go back in time and ram my hand down Dexter James Winthrop's gullet. The dream ends with me yanking his dick up and out his own throat."

"Luther, what are you doing?"

Lost in his anger, Luther begins to paw himself. His hands rumble under the diapers, inching down the edges until I'm seeing more of my best friend's dad than I want to. It's probably ungracious to say my first thought is I don't need to feel so bad about my own little Frito. My second thought is that Luther may very well neuter and castrate himself. With one hand he's squeezing his testicles hard enough to make me want to cross *my* legs. With the other one he snips at his penis with two fingers as if they're scissors. The whole time he babbles.

"Then there's this drummer I used to know, Lou Bishop. He was in a punk band I produced in the early eighties, Sigmund and the Sea Monsters. Oh yeah, Lou was voracious. To him an easy lay was like a Lay's potato chip—he couldn't stop at one. He devoured women by the palmful. Used cocaine to get punk kids in the back of the tour van. 'Give 'em the toot, then you give 'em the root.' That motherfucker actually printed a T-shirt with that slogan on it. It wasn't just the little punk groupies he gobbled up, either. The lead guitarist in Iris's band, Rage McGabriel, she fell for Lou's shit. One night they were coked up and Lou smacked her like a snare drum. I used to say if Rage McGabriel of the Wussy Pimps can get into an abusive relationship, any woman can. So this is your fuck you, Lou!"

Luther punches himself in the groin.

"Jesus!" I hop up and scream. "Stop!"

Luther backs into a corner, pulling at his dick, twisting it between his fingers, flicking it.

"Okay, okay, you don't have time for my whole Top Ten? Let me skip to my No. 1 Enemy among men: Snake Davis. A hairdresser. Let me repeat that: a hairdresser named Snake Davis. In 1969 he's playing quarters with a nineteen-year-old named Lucinda Jessop. Lucinda gets blasted and is sorta half-passed out, so Snake gets on top and helps himself to a fuck. Just helps himself to it. Lucinda is aware of what's happening, but she can't yell or fight back. She has to lie there and take it.

"You know who Lucinda is, Vance? That's Campbell's mom. The most beautiful damn woman I ever wanted to love. Intelligent, hilarious, a kind heart. I married her a few years after she was raped and we had Campbell, but you know what? Ours wasn't a marriage of two. It was a marriage of three because Snake Davis was always there, hovering between us."

Luther is in tears.

Kirk Curnutt

"Sweet Jesus! I used to try to curl up to Lucinda at night so I could kiss her spine and there'd be a damn Wall of China of pillows between us. She could never rest easy in bed with me because she was afraid I would pounce. Because that's what we men do: we pounce. You know what Campbell's mom told me the day I came home to the U-Haul in the driveway? She said, 'I'd rather be alone....' And it's all because of a fucking hairdresser!

"All I want to do, Vance, is to give love and to be loved and every time I try, some Snake Davis has been there first to ruin a woman's sense of security. So this is for you, Snake!"

Luther draws his fist back for a second punch. I dart toward him, one hand gripping his boxing wrist and the other slapping his left palm away from his groin. Suddenly two grown men are playing Pease Porridge Hot around an exposed penis. Luther explodes into a heavy thunderstorm of tears, crying out for Lucinda. His head sinks so hard onto my shoulder I have to stagger back to support his weight. His hands still bat at the space between our bellybuttons, but I can feel the energy of his anger wane as he's drained by his crying.

And then it happens. Luther bear hugs me, but I don't have time to get my own fingers out of the way. Before I know it my hand is a platter, and I'm serving two hardboiled eggs and a wrinkly baby bratwurst.

"Dammit, Luther, dammit! No more Krypie for you, never ever ever. I'm going to lower you down and let you dangle on your own. Try not to take it as rejection. Then I'm going to brew some coffee and sober your ass. Only I need to do one other thing first."

"What's that, Vance?"

"I've got to wash my damn hand."

# 27

I wake up next to Luther, both of us humming "Take Me to the River." I need nearly a whole verse to realize that the melody swims through my brain because my phone is blasting the song. It's one of the prank ringtones Chloe randomly downloads onto my cell. By the time I dig my phone from my khakis the call goes to voicemail. As I fumble to enter my password, Luther's phone begins to blare, launching him onto his feet in search of his pants. When he can't get to them in time Sadie's cell goes off from behind her bedroom door. She rushes into the living room lobbing me her phone.

"I can't find Chloe," Deb splutters in my ear. "She's not at your house. I thought she might have gone to Campbell's to talk to you about last night, but I'm here and Campbell hasn't seen her. Campbell hasn't seen *you*. Where's Chloe? Tell me she's with you, Vance. Tell me."

Within a half-hour our extended family mans every station where Chloe might turn up. Campbell and I head to Macon Place, Luther to his studio, Sadie stays at her place, and Deb crosses back and forth between my yard and Campbell's, staring at the old Saturn parked along the curb, wondering how far her daughter could've dashed without her car. Hours later we've called every friend and acquaintance we can think of, including Brody Dale, who scours downtown Willoughby for us. Nina hasn't heard from Chloe. Neither have Mike's kids, Travis and Zak, aka the Gold Dust Twins. Neither Iris nor Stu answers their phones. "Don't worry," Campbell consoles me after every number I dial and every text message I send. "She'll cool down and come home. Let's be real about this. She hasn't run away." When her optimism begins to feel pushy, I vent my doubt. I'm thinking of two people whose numbers I don't have, two people whose names I don't even know.

I think of the Mini Cooper's driver, the one that I suspect is Mike Willoughby's muscle. Then I think of the mysterious voice on Chloe's phone the night the Saturn went into the guardrail, the voice I assume belongs to Chloe and Stu's pot dealer.

Around lunchtime my suspicions are bolstered, big time. I receive a call and recognize instantly the voice from the other night.

"I need to talk to Chloe Seagrove." The caller and the Lemmy lookalike are definitely different people. Friendly Mutton Chops sounds much more aggressive. "This is the second time Chloe's stood me up," the caller informs me. "I'm not sure I'll agree to a third appointment. My time is money. I've tried to tell her this myself, but she won't pick up her phone."

"Who is this?" I demand.

"I'm not supposed to tell you that. Your daughter gave me explicit instructions not to tell you anything. I have your phone number, Dr. Seagrove, because my aunt belongs to that book club that met at Macon Place a couple of weeks ago. She gave it to me. Just tell your daughter that I need my money by tonight or we're no-go. She'll know what I mean."

He hangs up. Campbell asks who the caller was, and my mind goes to a word that feels like an icepick in my ear: *abortionist.* That's ridiculous, of course. Even if a women's health clinic were anywhere within driving distance, no doctor would call demanding a deposit with such an air of mystery. I take the caller's number and feed it into a reverse look-up search on my laptop. The only information I discover is that the number belongs to a cell phone, no name attached. Frustrated, I slam the lid on my computer. Campbell tells me to step outside and grab a breath of fresh air. When I snap at her, she responds in a sharper, more parental tone, the kind she usually reserves for Lleyton. Chastened, I head to the back porch, pacing until I meander down to the statue garden, where Aphrodite's alabaster form remains faintly yellow a full week after the borax scrub I gave her.

I loiter at the amphitheater stage, my regret over forcing the drug test on Chloe as heavy as the humidity. I realize now that proving she'd smoked pot was a smoke-screen, my way of avoiding the birth control discussion we need to have. I don't know how to have that talk without feeling as if I'm throwing the condom wrapper in Chloe's face. I imagine broaching the subject in different tones of voice, but no matter how sympathetic I try to swing it, in my own ears I end up sounding like Darth Vader. Sunk as deep in my dilemma as I am, it's not hard for someone to slip up beside me. He's so stealth that at first I'm uncertain who he is. He has to grin at me before I recognize him. The stranger looks different again today. More like a Boston butt than a soup can.

"Let me guess," the guy smiles through his mustache. "Feminists got you down?"

I whip out my cell and tell him I'm calling the police.

This is private property. He's harassing me. He and his partner from the anonymous number. They're in this together, I'm convinced.

"Slow down, bud," the guys says. "Talk to your customers like that when you open this art oasis of yours—*if* you ever open it—and you won't last six months. I may not be your ideal clientele, but I can admire the hips and thighs on these statues as well as anybody. Besides, beggars like you can't be choosers. You want to see what a connoisseur of hips and thighs I am? Let me show you."

He pulls an e-tablet from the book bag on his shoulder and begins tapping keys.

"Don't worry, I'm not showing you porn. Well, not the hardcore stuff, anyway. Think of this as PG porn. You ever visited this website?"

The page he shows me is a subfolder on Reddit.com called Gone Wild. It's full of disembodied lips, breasts, and buttocks that are covered by lipstick and tight Ts and jeans, bikinis, or lingerie.

"This is how kids and pervy middle-aged men entertain themselves today. They post their pictures for viewers to comment on. The kids do, I mean. The old men just surf, slobber, and ladle out horny compliments. I know what you're thinking, though. No way that these girls are real, right? They're too professional."

He stops on the blue-tinted image of a blonde in a low-cut halter that reads Sluttony.

"This seventeen-year-old calling herself 'Vanilla'? You're thinking she's really twenty-nine and a mother of four working at some dive called the Sticky Kitty or the Pony Up. You know how I know these babes are real, though? Peel your eyes off the pictures and read the little bios there. You can't fake their vacousness."

Maybe he's right. When asked what she would do with a million dollars, SeXXXyGal, from Altoona, Pennsylvania, reports that she would "spend it." She's apparently related only in cognate and hair color to SexyGurrrl, a U of Arkansas freshman who lists "clubbin'" and "partyin'" as career ambitions. Then there's their distant cousin, SeXXXiBtch, a Michigander whose ambitions include "law school, $$$, and lotsa kids." The most reassuring aspiration? Martiheart20, from "Wouldn't you like to know, Nevada," wants to teach first grade.

The faster the guy flips through the rankings, the less I care to see. It's not the endless spillage of propped flesh that's disconcerting. It's not the teasers of recreational lesbianism that seemed cynically contrived to please the male viewer, or the fake Playboy tattoos dotting the bellies, or the thong strings yanked high enough on the hips that they might as well be suspender straps, or the fact that every girl here has posted at least one picture in which she's flipping the bird to the camera. It's not even the occasional appearance of a Southern woman my age who—as Friendly Mutton Chops points out—feels compelled to brag that she's "still dang hot, too, eh, all you teenage bitches?"

No, what's disturbing is that every third girl on r/Gone Wild (as the subfolder is officially referred to) claims she's sixteen, and half of them list Alabama as home.

"Why am I looking at this?"

"You're a father, aren't you?" the guy shoots back. "You should be aware of websites like this. These girls are your daughter's age. Kids in her generation have never known a time when pornography wasn't part of the mainstream culture. Commodified sex is as natural to their landscape as kudzu and coriander. Hell, in our day you had to rifle your old man's sock drawer, or hope your buddy buried a *Penthouse* in the woods, but for them–Christ Almighty, they have to look away. And what's really scary is that they don't need to have sat through a whole video or downloaded a JPEG to know the poses. For girls coming of age nowadays, the shit's intuitive. Pornography is their Chomskian grammar. It's embedded in them... Hey, Chomskian grammar! Not bad for a guy who's not a Ph.D., huh? These girls, though, they know to lick their fingers while looking up submissively, to bend over chair backs as if offering their hind ends in some primitive baboon ritual, to drop to all fours, close their eyes, and curl their lips as if contracting in orgasm–"

"What's your point?" I interrupt. "I have more important things on my mind."

But the stranger is too fixated to care about my concerns. "Websites like this make you wonder what intimacy means to these kids. It makes you wonder if they feel there's any mystery to their sexuality, or if it bores them. There's a flip side of course. Sometimes concerned guys like us, we have to ask ourselves whether we're really worried about girls who post pictures like these, or whether we're getting off on our prurience. I mean, it's not easy looking at hot bods and not feeling a little itchy. We are men, aren't we? Or maybe I shouldn't presume with you. But this website? Mild, brother, very mild. I can show you another one where you rank chicks' implants."

I tell him to turn his tablet off. I've seen enough. He nods but says one last picture really deserves to be seen. He clicks to a page displaying a close-up of a generously spherical duff. The derriere stands in front of a mirror. At first I'm not sure what catches my attention. Maybe the blue ruffle trim on the stretch-lace boyshorts that barely covers two-thirds of the milky cheeks. Maybe the cursive legend stitched into the waistband (You Are Here). Maybe even the prodigious bulge of the irritated red pimple that pokes out from the bottom curve of the left buttock. Then I realize it's not the behind itself but the mirror, or the two objects reflected in it, rather.

One is a poster of a guitar-clad woman standing over a legend that reads ʀɪᴀʜP zɪL.

The other is a framed Polaroid of a face that's all too familiar, despite the contorted grin and the lidded eyes that, thanks to the strategic placement of the photo, appear to be leering up the thighs of the woman in the poster.

"That's my daughter's room! And *that*"–I point at the Polaroid–"that's *me!*"

The stranger pretends to be shocked. "Really?" He looks back and forth from the picture to me. "You don't think that's your daughter, do you? I mean, I know it's hard to tell without a face. Most fathers can't pick their daughter's ass out of a lineup, now can they?"

"That can't be real! Chloe wouldn't pose like that. She listens to Ani DiFranco! You rigged that picture and planted it! You broke into my house!"

"Slow down on the accusations, bud. You wouldn't want to go into a courtroom jumping to those conclusions, would you? There's such a thing as proof."

He stuffs his tablet back in his bag.

"Maybe you should talk to your daughter. See what she has to say. 'Course, that's easier said than done, isn't it? How do you start a conversation like that? *Dear fruit of my loins, there comes a point in all parents' lives when they discover that their children aren't the people they thought they were. If you don't believe me, go to www-dot....* No, I don't envy you raising a daughter. Not at all."

He pulls a sheet of paper from his computer bag.

"I made you a copy of this picture on a nice color printer. High resolution even. Tell you what, at 300 dpi that pimple looks damn near three dimensional."

As much as I'd like to sock him in the jaw, I'm too flummoxed. The stranger slips away before I can string words together. "Tell Mike Willoughby to leave me alone!" I yell. Only there's no one around to hear except Aphrodite, and even she's so embarrassed by my outburst that she ignores me.

Back in the parlor I find a note from Campbell: *Picking up lunch. It'll be okay, Vance. It will.* I crumple the Post-It and sink onto Storm's Victorian borne, trying to reconcile my best friend's reassurance with the picture from r/Gone Wild balanced on my knee. Maybe it's not so bad after all. Chloe's not flashing the camera, she's not on all fours, and she's not on that implants website–or, at least, I'll assume she's not. If I were smart, I'd tuck the image away, but I'm not smart. I'm still staring at the page when I hear the locks on the front door tumble. "That was fast," I call out, but it's not Campbell who marches into the parlor. It's not Chloe, either. It's Iris, and her eyes go straight to the picture.

"You're downloading porn here?"

"Of course not. This isn't porn." I stuff the print-off in my back pocket. "What are you doing at Macon Place? Didn't we say everything there is to say last night?"

"Chloe is at my house."

The stress and anxiety that I've felt all morning drains away. I'm not ready to tap dance with gratitude quite yet, though. I ask if Iris intentionally ignored my calls, waiting until lunchtime to share her information, just so my suffering wouldn't end too quickly. She insists she had no idea that Chloe was at her place until she ran home for a bite to eat. Stu isn't allowed to have girls over if she's not there, and Iris has been cleaning Mike Willoughby's house since breakfast.

"Don't think I'm happy about this," Iris assures me. "Chloe's upset, and now she has Stu upset as well. Suddenly he wants to drop the complaint against you. He says Chloe will break up with him if the case goes to court. Using your daughter to blackmail your way out of an assault charge, that's a weasel move even for you, Seahorse."

I scoff and ask if Iris honestly thinks I would use my daughter as a pawn. I tell her our kids are already *finito* anyway. I broke them up, and I did it to keep her away from a kid whose judgment I seriously question. I ask Iris if her darling son copped to last Sunday's debacle in the garden. "Your kid, right there in front of Nina, was trying to have sex with Chloe," I inform her. "Thank God Brody Dale caught them before things got out of hand. Otherwise Stu might have raped her—"

The word jumps out of my mouth before I realize what a grenade it is. Iris's face reddens. The bones in her shoulders seem to harden into spears. I keep expecting her to pull one out and gore me straight through.

"You can lecture me and my son about predators when twenty-year-old waitresses don't have to worry about you hitting on them," she fires back. "I don't know what you're trying to pull with this garden story, but Stu couldn't have been here at Macon Place Sunday night. He was with me, at home, listening to my old Wussy Pimps EPs. We were up until two a.m. I'll drop off Chloe after I get off work. Until then, I suggest you quit downloading porn while on this property. Mike Willoughby's gonna *love* hearing about that picture."

I'm less scared of Mike than I am of Chloe. Around dinnertime I sit on the porch steps at Campbell's and wait for Iris's car to pull up. When her Nissan food truck appears it stops in front of my house, several yards shy of me. I watch as Chloe tiptoes through the grass, creeping cautiously as if she expects to get pounced. When she spots me, she doesn't cower. Far from it. For what seems an eternity, we stare at each other across the two house lots separating us, a distance that might as well be a universe. Chloe shrugs and marches past my viburnum, disappearing.

My one consolation?

Unlike other girls on r/Gone Wild, she doesn't flip me the bird.

I retreat to my couch in Campbell's study, resolving to

become a recluse. No more ex-wives, ex-girlfriends, or estranged daughters. Even better, I'll refuse to see anybody. No litigious business partners, mysterious strangers with dubious facial hair, or bitter parents of off-limit teenagers. Not even a bisexual best friend, as Campbell discovers when she pounds on the door wondering if I'm okay. I do pretty well on my pledge, too, at least until the delivery boy from Hungry Howie's appears with the deluxe pizza and cheese sticks I order. If I'm going to become Howard Hughes, I might as well do it Orson Welles style. I gorge on my gluttonous depression, downing the entire order until I'm bloated and narcotized. I stream some Liz Phair and Juliana Hatfield and pretend to read Andrea Dworkin. Mostly I stare at the ceiling.

In the morning, I don't bathe or shave. I sneak out early and trot downtown to Chub and Joe's, where I gobble up a monster pile of cheap biscuits and gravy. By the time I lick my knife clean the waist of my khaki shorts feels like a lasso. Even though a satchel of stomach settles between my hips, I'm tempted to order a side of bacon. Only when the waitress returns from the cash register with my Visa I realize how wise I was not to ratchet my order up past $5.

My card is declined.

"It's three dollars and ninety cents," I note in disbelief.

"Declined is declined, sweetie. And that $3.90 doesn't include the tip. Cash or a different card, please."

Unfortunately, I have neither. Chloe still has my debit card from the afternoon she had to replace her bass-drum pedal, and I rarely carry bills or change anymore. When the waitress refuses to try the Visa again—she's already run it through twice, she claims—we have to call over the manager, and I'm reduced to playing the loyal customer card. Ten years of biscuits and gravy only gets a man so much sympathy. With all the fellow-feeling of a greasy loan shark, the manager lets me have until first thing tomorrow to hustle up four bucks, and that's with him keeping my worthless card as insurance. I stagger outside, where the humidity hits me with a sledge-hammer of panic. I'm in so much debt Visa won't even float me breakfast.

I hoof south on Company Street as fast as a guy can when he's toting a concrete block's worth of gravy in his gut. The mom-and-pop businesses give way to municipal and county buildings, including the courthouse square, the library, the mayor's office. One block short of the Willoughby City Museum and Storm's bronze monument to himself, I scramble into the Elmore County Public Schools superintendent's office to beg for an application.

"For what job?" the secretary has to ask.

"The drama position, the one at Willoughby High. The magnet program. I haven't had a chance to check out the curriculum, but I understand it's very advanced, college level and all. I'd be perfect for that track. My Ph.D. is in theater."

The secretary stops halfway into ripping an appli-cation off a blank pad of forms.

"That position's been filled. Someone was hired earlier this week." She hands me the form anyway. "You can still get your name on-file. We can always use substitute teachers. In fact, most of our full-timers sub for a year before they're hired on."

Kirk Curnutt

I ask who the school system could've possibly hired to teach advanced drama classes. I'm the most qualified guy in this county. As I remind the woman for the second time in less than a minute, I have a Ph.D. in theater. I can't tell what makes the secretary more doubtful, my desperate boasting, my unshaved face and unbathed body, or the biscuit crumbs dotting my chest. She tells me to try the private schools if I need work. I don't admit that I left a job at Willoughby Academy eight years ago. Somehow I doubt she'll believe me when I say I had better opportunities on my horizon back then.

A funny thing about humiliation: it makes you hungry as hell. I nearly eat Campbell out of house and home, munching chips, saltines, and cookies as I wrack my brain wondering how much quick money I might make by selling plasma and hocking my belongings on eBay. Each time I wander from the study, I find Campbell at her kitchen table. "Have you talked to Chloe?" she asks the first time. The second isn't a question. "You really should talk to her." Finally, she issues marching orders. "Talk to Chloe already," she says. One of the few benefits of gorging is that when you cram your mouth full, your ears plug up, too. I shrug, chew, pretend I'm deaf, return to my man cave. Long about dinnertime when I straggle out of hibernation I discover that Campbell has left. The house is empty except for Lleyton, who's in his room playing video games. He informs me his mom is meeting with his dad. "They keep trying to talk," the kid explains, "but they end up fighting." When I ask why he's here instead of at the Motel 6 where Steve's been staying this week,

Lleyton admits he wanted to stay home.

"The hotel is boring. All we do is watch TV. Sometimes I swim, but not a lot, because he has to watch and make sure I don't drown. He'd rather watch TV."

I ask if Lleyton wants to split a pizza. I'm hungry again, but only sort of. The kid gives me a half-hearted okay. We're brothers in ambivalence.

"Awesome," I say without enthusiasm, "but you don't have any cash, do you? I'll pay you back. For the moment I'm stony."

Without taking his eyes off the computer screen, Lleyton pulls open a desk drawer and hands me a twenty-dollar bill. Birthday money, he says. He returns to his game control, which he thumbs with the steady rhythm of a drummer. I'm about to slink off to place the order when Lleyton reveals that the loan isn't interest-free. Only the kid's not charging money. He's going to take his cut out in emotion.

"My dad asks me about you. All the time."

"He does? What does he ask?"

Lleyton shrugs. "You know, like if you yell at me. If you tell me how to act—that kind of stuff. Sometimes I think he's trying to trick me. He'll ask the same questions a couple times an hour. Mom's told me what to say, though. She says that if I don't tell him you're almost my stepdad I'll have to live with him."

I rest against the door. "She shouldn't do that. You shouldn't have to lie to your own dad."

"It's okay. He wouldn't want me to live with him, anyway. We don't talk much. Not like my mom and me. We talk all the time." The screen blips GAME OVER. Lleyton

Kirk Curnutt

tosses the controls to the floor, changing the subject. "What's it like to kiss a girl?" he wants to know.

I need a minute to swallow my surprise before admitting that it's the greatest thing on earth. But only if you do it for the right reasons, I say. If you're greedy and just out for your own fun, it's not so great. If you care about the other person, though, nothing's better.

"Were you greedy with my mom?" Lleyton wants to know.

There aren't minutes enough to swallow that question. I tell him I better order the pizza, but Lleyton has another surprise to spring.

"I tried to kiss Chloe," he confesses.

This is news to me. I tell the kid that Chloe's a little old for him. He's probably better off sticking to sixth graders. Then, out of curiosity, I ask what Chloe did when he tried to land his liplock. Lleyton taps at his breastplate and admits she hit him hard enough to knock the breath out of him. He's afraid Chloe won't babysit him anymore because of it. "She won't talk to me now," he sighs. I get the sense he wants me to do something about it.

"It gets old for girls to constantly get hit on," I say instead. "Sometimes the best thing you can do is be their friend. That's what I've learned from your mom."

I don't press for more details, which means I can't help but imagine them. I picture Lleyton hovering behind Chloe while she tolerates Campbell's TV on one of the innumerable nights I've volunteered her to babysit, the kid buzzing like an agitated mosquito as he works up the nerve to zoom in and nip her on the lips. Or maybe he sidled up to her at the dining-room table while she listened to her MP3 player, catching her by surprise because her beloved music had lulled her into letting her guard down. I even see him ambushing Chloe as she's emerging from the bathroom, leaping into her arms like a toddler upset that his mother stepped from his sight. Pondering these scenarios doesn't make me angry as much as embarrassed for Lleyton and for Chloe both. Because with that pop to the breastplate, Lleyton received his initiation into that aspect of desire that, if you're at all self-aware as a man, you end up sweating over. It's the aspect that says by virtue of the chromosomal quirk of being male you've inherited that right (or is it the obligation?) to be the taker, the one who gets, and that with that right or obligation or whatever it is, you risk rejection, which is about the only thing short of death and intimacy a man really fears. As for Chloe, I'm guessing that the incident was less scary than dreary, a mere confirmation of what three months of dating Stu had already taught her:

*Men take, women are taken. Men get. Women get gotten.*

I feel sorry for both sides in this deterministic game because I have my own humiliating babysitter story. When I was ten, I pulled a Lleyton, and with similar results. Julie Jackoboice was her name. She was fifteen the summer my parents hired her to watch over me. It was a job that Julie seemed to think she was best able to perform by lying on a chaise longue by our pool, reading and cranking Tears for Fears on a boombox. I resented having to have a babysitter at that point, so I holed up in my room and ignored my new warden as much as

Kirk Curnutt

possible, which suited Julie just fine. For the first few weeks she only acknowledged my existence when she called for the peanut butter sandwiches and Pringles she constantly noshed on. Then one day Julie Jackoboice unexpectedly appeared at my door in a lime green romper, a book of my mother's in one hand and a beer of my father's in the other.

"You aren't eighteen," I informed her, nodding at the alcohol.

"The legal age is twenty-one, dipshit. This is your mom's, I take it?"

*Couples* by John Updike was in her hand. Smug little Julie Jackoboice wanted to know whether Mom would get pissed knowing her babysitter thumbed through her books.

"If you get in the inner tube with it and the pages get wet, probably," I said. "But if you stay in the house to look at it, I guess that's okay."

"I'm not talking about taking her books to the pool. I'm asking if she'd get mad because of what's in her books. Don't you know? These are dirty reads. There's lotsa sex in them."

Julie spent the afternoon reading *Couples* in the inner tube, floating with her legs kicking under her and the novel's spine hovering perilously close to the wet lapping. That night after she left and my parents had collapsed into sleep I snuck to my mother's shelf and pored over the pages. They smelled like chlorine. Dotting several of them were fingerprints formed from a combination of perspiration, water, and potato-chip grease. My eyes locked on a sentence: *Mouths...are noble. We send our genitals mating down below like peasants, but when the mouth condescends, mind and body marry. To eat another is sacred.* I followed the trail of prints for a half-hour until I grew afraid I might drift off face down on the book's deckled edges. Before I returned the hardback to its place, I unfolded the dog-ear Julie made on page 529, where the passage about mating genitals appeared. I had no clue what the words said, but I wanted Julie to know I'd been there.

Only she didn't notice. For several nights in a row, I retraced her reading, smoothing out her frequent tabbing. I suspected Julie Jackoboice crinkled page tips by the tens to test my mother, seeing if Mom actually cracked her books open or if they were displayed for show. Meanwhile, my head flooded with mysterious phrases. There was "mixed fur," "mixed liquids," and lastly, "rubescent pudendum," which sounded like an inflammatory condition. The phrases came not just from *Couples* either, but all of Mom's books: Alix Kates Shulman's *Memoirs of an Ex-Prom Queen*, Margaret Atwood's *Surfacing*, and, of course, *Fear of Flying* by Erica Jong. Julie burned through a book a day. Either she was a speed reader or she skimmed for the saucy bits.

Somewhere in the middle of Updike's *A Month of Sundays*, I broke down and decided I couldn't take Julie being oblivious to me. In a chapter with so many big words I thought I would swallow my tongue trying to pronounce them, I left blatant evidence that I'd shadowed her reading. Sure enough, the next day Julie Jackoboice was at my bedroom door, dripping wet in a plaid bikini, holding the novel open at me.

Kirk Curnutt

"Did you do this?" She tapped at something foreign to the page.

I played dumb. "What is that?"

"It's an underline, dipshit. Somebody underlined a sentence. I'm pretty sure it wasn't your mom. I'm pretty sure it was you."

"How's come you think I did that?"

"The underline is in colored pencil." She nodded at my desk, where a set of Dixon Thinex thin leads lay next to an unfinished comic book. The pencils had been my mother's as a child. Julie studied the passage, silently. "You like this, huh? What a freak. You want me to read this to you? Is that what the underlining's all about?"

It was indeed. I did want her to read it to me. I wanted that more than I wanted oxygen, but I couldn't tell Julie Jackoboice that. Apparently my face was far from a blank slate.

"All right." She clapped *Sundays* shut. "Tonight. I'm pulling a double shift so your folks can go to dinner. I'll read it to you, hornball, but you're doing me a favor, hear me?"

I'd have assassinated a president for her. I asked what.

"My boyfriend is coming over. To hang out, maybe watch a movie, maybe swim. You're going to stay in your dungeon while he's here, and you're not going to breathe a word about him, not to Mom, not to Pop."

That night my parents took longer to get out of the house than it would've taken me to plow through Mom's entire library. Exasperated with their endless bath running and clothes ironing and shoe polishing, I marched up and down their hall, practically picketing their bedroom, hoping that by being a pest I would hurry them on. Their door usually stayed shut, but on one pass I noticed it'd come ajar. Through the crack I caught my father waddling out of the shower, naked except for a towel. Pink from steam and a hot-water scalding, he snuck up on Mom at her makeup table. She was also as close to naked as a child cares to see the woman who birthed him. She was wearing nothing but panties. As Dad pulled her into an impromptu embrace the sight of their bare stomachs rubbing so froze me in horror that I couldn't think to dive out of sight or even look away. With a suave grip, no doubt perfected through years of laying shag, Dad grabbed a fistful of Mom's hair, pulled back her head, and sank his ruby mouth around her pale neck. Then he did something stranger still. He stretched his palm across her left breast and squeezed.

There was just one problem with doing that. Mom had no breasts anymore. She'd had a double mastectomy. The radiation had to kill the cancer in the adjoining tissue before she could undergo reconstructive surgery, which is why I saw two incisions zippering her chest. Only the radiation wasn't working. My mother's cancer had metastasized, and the last-ditch scramble to save her was why Julie Jackoboice had been hired to babysit in the first place. (That hair was also a wig.) My dad's dunderheaded attempt at passion reminded me of something I'd denied all summer. My mother was dying.

I'm not sure how I gave away my peeping, but my parents caught me in their doorway. "Get the hell out of here!" my father roared. He clutched at his towel, fearing, I guess, that it would come loose. Later I was spanked for

Kirk Curnutt

making a sarcastic comment about God inventing locks and bolts for a reason. By the time Julie Jackoboice showed up that night, I'd cried enough to refill the pool with tears. Something about the aphrodisiacal mixture of Bubble Yum and the Sunbonnet Sue Avon perfume she wore dried my ducts, however. I was so itchy to put Updike in her hands I felt as if fire ants had chewed through to my insides. After phoning her boyfriend with directions to our address, Julie slumped onto the couch with a cushion of safety between us. She made no effort to mask how dreary a task this would be for her. It didn't matter. Julie cracked open *A Month of Sundays* and began reciting. Updike's bawdy wordplay sparked into an obscene accelerant. All I heard were sounds, polysyllables as tangled as bodies, full of hissing fricatives and heaving plosives. By the time she hit the unfathomable image I'd underlined, my hormones were so heated I was afraid to reach for a dictionary for fear of combusting: *We bent a world of curves above the soaked knot where our roots merged.* What the fuck did that mean? I didn't know. The very possibility of knowing terrified me, and yet that terror was as exciting as the frisk of crushed velvet on my bare soles.

Whatever it meant, the passage reminded me of Dad pulling Mom's head back to kiss her neck, that smooth move foiled only by clutching at an amputated breast. There was no conversation there, no negotiation, no resistance. Despite his blunder, Dad seemed to have Mom so totally in his power that all she could do was moan two words that to this day I can't believe anybody outside of a movie made in 1945 would ever say: "Take me."

*Where was he supposed to take her?* I'd wondered as I spied through their open door. *Out to the ballpark, maybe? ...to her leader? ...home, country roads, to the place she belonged? ...Take me away, Calgon?*

More importantly, if he was taking her somewhere, why wasn't I invited?

Unable to control myself, I reached across the cushion. I sank my pincers into one of the dunes of flesh bulging Julie Jackoboice's T-shirt. I barely had time to consider that the lumpy stitching tickling my palm probably wasn't a nipple before the spine of *A Month of Sundays* cracked me across the nose. As I crashed to the floor, both the pain in my face and the sensation of falling made me realize why my mom had rewarded my dad's move with that hokey Hollywood line. She wanted Dad to take her, so they could both believe, if only for a second, that the cancer wouldn't.

I cried in front of Julie Jackoboice more than I've ever let myself in front of any other woman except my mother. When her boyfriend arrived, he came up with a lie to explain my broken nose. I'd taken a header into Mom's bookcase horsing around the living room. I was such an uncoordinated kid that my parents never doubted the story.

It was several years before I could think of sex without thinking of broken bones. I still can't think of sex without thinking of taking. I'm sure I never matured out of that association because only a few short months after hearing my mother ask to be taken, she was taken from me by breast cancer, and I was doomed to equate sex with death. As that old French phrase for ejaculation *le petite*

Kirk Curnutt

*mort* makes clear, sex and death are the most male of equations. If I ever start to forget that connection, if I ever stop thinking of my lovely mother, I need only conjure up the late, great Julie Jackoboice. Not five years after my mother's passing, Julie lost control of her Miata in a rainstorm, sideswiped a tree, and was launched through her windshield into a cornfield. When I think of Julie, I inevitably daydream about who she'd be today if she'd lived. I do the same with my mother, of course, although picturing her gets harder the older I get. I sometimes think I'll have to give up doing it after my next birthday when, for the first time, I hit an age that she never made it to. The funny thing is what people say when I tell them I was only eleven when Mom died. "That's way too young to have your mother taken from you," they say. I remember Dad tossing out some variation of the same thing when Julie was killed. *Twenty, too young to be taken.* Dirty mind that I have, I always wonder if Julie Jackoboice's boyfriend took her before she was taken.

As for me, I was never a taker. Maybe it's because of that image of my mom and dad in their desperate clinch. Maybe it's because the first time I made love to a woman I also made a baby, and I couldn't help but equate the aggression of sex with the life of innocents who don't ask to be born. Whatever the reason, only twice have I ever been a self-conscious taker. Neither was with Deb; I was too green at twenty. No, it took me until my mid-thirties to work up the nerve to take a woman. The first time was when I bent Campbell over her own bookcase after a Rotary Club ball, drunk after too many Seagram's 7s and too many choruses of Morris Day and the Times' "Jungle

Love." The second was with Ardita Farnam, and the entire population of Willoughby, Alabama, can tell you how well that went.

I remember the exact moment I knew that I would take Ardita. It was in the minutes leading up to our first kiss. I can picture it easily because my choreography came straight from my father's fancy footsteps of seduction, or at least the limited amount of his repertoire that I'd spied in that overheated hour before Julie Jackoboice socked me. I'd eaten at Katfish Kountry dozens of times. In Willoughby, Alabama, once you tire of Chub and Joe's, and you can't afford the Trattoria Prego more than twice a year, you're pretty much stuck with the place. Ardita frequently waited on me, but thinking of her sexually was as ridiculous as pooting in the dessert line or walking out on my bill. I can't even honestly say I was attracted to her. She was too scrawny, too girly for me, I suppose, and definitely too close to Chloe's age. I doubt we would've even struck up a conversation that fatal night if she hadn't asked me what I did for a living. I humbly (humbly!) mentioned I was Storm Willoughby's majordomo. Storm himself was dying at the time. I had no clue that his will made me responsible for saving Macon Place, for keeping it from becoming a memory as well. At the time I was dealing with the knowledge that I was on the verge of losing him, just as I had my mother. When Storm went, so would the security of my future. Someone else was being taken from me, but here was Ardita, making herself available, readying herself for the taking.

If I were worthy of that thing called manhood, I'd have

sat her down and taught her all the wily ways men snooker women into measuring their self-worth in increments of attention and cash. Instead, I had to teach her by experience and lose my own self-respect in the process. Three hours and seven coffee refills after finishing my dinner, as I recited the legends behind Aphrodite and other statues, she abruptly told me to meet her outside for her break. That's when it hit me: *This is going to happen. I am going to make this happen.* Because the setting for this first kiss was the rear exit of a greasy restaurant, the nimbus of want enshrouding us wasn't the tingle of an invigorating shower like Dad had enjoyed but the all-together-less-romantic smell of a dumpster reeking of fried fish and broccoli offal. Ignoring the odor as best I could, I grabbed a handful of hair just as I'd seen my father do, and I bent Ardita's head back so I could sink my incisors into her neck. (It's a move I doubt I'll ever do again without worrying whether my dental implants will come loose.) I suppose I expected Ardita to say exactly what my mother had, but the girl's post-adolescent brain hadn't been fed on the junky diet of melodrama that my mother grew up consuming.

"Are we really going to?" That was the response I got.

So what if it wasn't quite as succinct or as poetic as *Take me?* What if it didn't ring with the same beguiling mystery of paradox that had been haunting me since my mother expressed the desire to be dominated in the form of a command: *Take me.* I wanted Ardita to mean the same thing, and so I took her that night in my car after she clocked out. Then I took her the next night, again in my car, only this time under the Bibbs-Grave Bridge on the banks of the Coosa River, and again a few nights later, and so on and so forth for the better part of a month. I took what I could get.

Only I discovered immediately that I'm not what you might call a guilt-free getter. First, there was the grueling ritual of coming home afterward and seeing Chloe. I honestly wish I'd died before disappointing the person whose approval means the most to me. Then there was Ardita herself. No sooner had I taken her than I recognized the plea inherent in that interrogative of hers. The reason she couldn't say "Take me" was because she had no reason to trust me the way my mother could trust my father, and so what she actually meant by "Are we really going to?" was "You won't hurt me, will you?" Poor kid. She didn't understand that by only wanting to take her I had already hurt her. She was too inexperienced to appreciate how my annoyance at her need to talk, my irritation at her need for support and reassurance in the moments we weren't locking legs, was doing her dirty. Nor could she foresee how her eventual request that we tryst somewhere other than in my Saturn, where we were always fretting about seatbelts in our spine and kicking the gearshift out of neutral, was going to humiliate her.

"We could go to Macon Place," she suggested. "I bet that old guy sleeps hard. He'd never know."

The idea horrified me. Macon Place was too intimate, too connected to me. Didn't she understand that this was just sex? I couldn't say that, so I went for the next best thing. I put the onus on her. If she really wanted to do it someplace else, I said, we should do it in her parents' Alabama room.

Kirk Curnutt

Why there? It was simple. I couldn't stand her father, even though my introduction to the guy wouldn't happen until he unexpectedly flicked on the light of said Alabama room to discover me taking his daughter. Even before that awkward moment, I hated Mr. Farnam for no other reason than he was all Ardita could talk about when I wasn't taking her. Complained about, actually. In her vernacular, he was a real *dilweed*. He was on her back constantly to go to college when she only wanted a couple of post-high-school years to chill and party. He threatened to charge her rent and a cut of the utilities if she didn't get a plan for her future. He even berated her about how a girl who graduates in the top half of her class at Willoughby High is capable of more than refilling a crusty all-you-can-eat buffet bar that's one egg-white away from starting a salmonella outbreak.

Oh, and when she wasn't home, Ardita groused, her dad would snoop through her room.

Like I said, poor kid. She didn't realize that in airing her resentment she was providing me a perfect nemesis. Not that I pitted myself against Daddy for his little darling's sake. Not by a chivalrous long shot. This was a *mano-a-mano* thing. For someone who's never had the pleasure, getting caught *in flagrante delicto* might seem the worst embarrassment possible. Getting caught by your lover's father takes it to a whole other level. Only I'm not sure I was embarrassed.

When the light blasted on and the pall descended over Mr. Farnam, there was the appalling part of me that wanted to jump up, punch my fist in the air, and sing, *Na na na na–na na na na–hey hey hey.... Say good-bye!*

Because in taking his daughter I was privy to a part of her that Mr. Farnam would never know, a side of her that he could never possess or control. The evidence was right there for his trembling eyes to descend upon. It was unceremoniously put on display as Ardita jumped off her knees to screech out of the room, leaving my ejected self out in the open, bobbing like a divining rod drawn to water. Was I slyly taunting the bastard or merely in my own state of shock when I hopped up and began spewing apologies with my pants still at my ankles? I'd like to think the latter, but I have my doubts. I can't believe I would've left myself exposed if at some deep Alpha-Dog level I wasn't trying to cow Mr. Farnam into bowing at the altar of my prowess. I'm pretty sure that's how he interpreted it, too. Otherwise, he wouldn't have said what he did. "Put that thing away!" he screamed. "Put it away, dammit, so I can beat you shitless!"

That's how I know Stu didn't leave that condom wrapper in Chloe's room by mistake. It was that *mano-a-mano* impulse that made him do it. Even if he wasn't aware of that aggression, even if he wasn't consciously flexing it, the belligerence was there. The wrapper was his way of wagging himself in my face, as surely as I was guilty of wagging mine in Mr. Farnam's.

So what's a dad to do? Stick to boys. As the cliché goes, they're easier to raise. For three days, working hard to convince myself I don't miss Chloe, I become the father that little Lleyton's never had. He shows me how to slaughter legions on his Xbox playing *Assassin's Creed*, and together we read *The Dark Knight, Spawn, Punisher*

Kirk Curnutt

and other gory selections from his comic-book collection. Campbell nearly keels over when she walks in on us beating the hell out of her furniture as we reenact SmackDown moves downloaded from WWE podcasts. "I'm being overtaken by the He-Man Woman Haters Club!" she despairs. That's before I pull out my best dad trick and turn Lleyton on to good music. No alluringly blunt, disarmingly aggressive indie/punk chicks, though. We're talking open-shirt, tight-jean, groin-gripping dude rock. *Cock rock.* Good-bye, Liz Phair–hello, Led Zep. Sayonara, Juliana Hatfield–crank it up, AC/DC. For those about to rock, we salute. "Big Balls" injects Lleyton with such a dose of testosterone he decides he wants to play the drums. Go for it, I smile. You can be the male Keith Moon.

The funny thing about being estranged from your own child, meanwhile, is how quickly you grow accustomed to her absence. It's as if I never ate a meal with Chloe, never took her to a single concert, never hugged or comforted her or dabbed a tear. In what little I see of her, she's a blur, dashing down the driveway to hop in the Saturn before I can corner her, which I make no effort to do. I watch her come and go with the same disinterest I feel for passing traffic. Even her name becomes an empty word. I can say it without a pang of loss. When Campbell begs me to go home and reconcile, I send her packing with the same reply. "The last thing Chloe said to me was, 'Leave me alone!'"

So I am.

So there.

Then, a half-week after my daughter and I break off diplomatic relations, I awake one morning to discover that my father is now Henry Kissinger intent on brokering détente. Miles Seagrove pulls a chair to the couch where I'm sprawled and snoring. Opening my eyes, the first two things that I see are the hairy black holes of his nostrils.

"My phone's been ringing off the hook this week," Dad says. "All about you and this long swan dive into the empty pool you insist on taking. One day it's Campbell calling to say you've gotten teeth knocked out and need implants. The next it's Deb telling me you and Stu have gotten into it and you've been arrested. Then it's Sadie claiming you're being stalked by some mystery man in a Mini Cooper who's bullying you to sell your half of Macon Place. Then it's Sadie again, upset because she's found out you've spent $200 on a fancy dinner but you won't pay her the $140 you owe her for tickets to some concert, and now she's late on her car payment. Son, you're not an adult if your father has to cover your girlfriend's car payment. That's not even mentioning Chloe—"

I sit up. "Chloe called you? About me?"

"Several times. Let's see, first it was about you refusing to get a lawyer to make sure you get a little something out of Macon Place after years of working there. Then it was about you and Stu getting into it. Then it was about you spending money you don't have on drug tests. That's where I lost the thread of the story. Do I need to tell you things can't go on this way? Your attitude, your finances—somebody's got to set you straight. You've got a daughter to raise."

Kirk Curnutt

I'm already tired of this lecture. I tell Dad I don't appreciate him riding to the rescue like he's the parental cavalry.

"You've never once said you support what I want to do with Macon Place," I whine. "I'm sure you think I don't have $4 handy because I've blown out my credit cards on coke and hookers. The truth is I've sunk every dime I've got into that estate trying to do something for the community that I believe in. A little support would be nice, a few encouraging words instead of shooting me down. I certainly wouldn't expect you to be an investor. You've got to save your money for all those women on the Internet."

Dad doesn't blink. He reaches into his pocket and hands me a folded slip of paper. It's a check. For $14,000.

"The government has raised the annual maximum a parent can give a child," he says. "Used to be $10,000, now it's fourteen. This should help smooth things out until you find a job."

I ask if he waited until I stuck my foot in my mouth to make his donation. Then I tell him I don't want his money. I remind him I've been on my own since I was twenty years old. His reaction isn't encouraging. He chuckles.

"All right," I growl. "Never mind the damn money. You're wrong about the daughter part. Chloe has Deb now. She doesn't need me. I've decided to let Deb have my house."

"And you plan to live here at Campbell's? Hmmm. You might want to ask her if that invitation's open. She's pretty upset. I don't blame her." He flips open a nearby pizza box with the toe of his sandal. What little is left inside looks as if it was ravaged by a coyote. "And you really intend to abandon Chloe because after sixteen years you suddenly have to share her? It doesn't work like that, Vance. Fatherhood isn't a toy you get to sulk away from when you don't get your way. Now, as soon as you clean this room, you're going over to your house, and you're sorting things out with my granddaughter."

I tell Dad he can't speak to me like this. I'm not sixteen. He agrees. I'm only acting like I am, he says.

"What do you think Chloe has been up to for three days?" he asks. "You probably imagine her running around with Deb, shopping together, getting a pedicure, delighting in not having to deal with you. But that's not the case. Ask her mother if you don't believe me. Chloe's all balled up, a bundle of nerves. She's convinced you're mad at her."

"She's right. I am mad. Furious even. She's made a lot of bad choices lately."

"Then you understand why she's mad at you. Your choices haven't exactly been unimpeachable these past two weeks."

He poses a hypothetical: what if he gave me the opportunity to sit down with Janice, my former step-mother? It'd be my chance to air all my resentments, once and for all. I could tell Janice how hurt I was that she married Dad only four months after my mother died, how she stifled me with all her household rules, how annoyed I still am that she refuses to believe that Beth Tulbert and I didn't have sex in her Grand Prix. Would I do it?

Kirk Curnutt

I don't have to ponder the invite. I have no interest in talking to Janice.

"You're right," agrees Dad. "What would be the point? The conversation would be twenty years too late. And that's why you're going to talk to Chloe pronto. I don't want you two to be twenty years down the road resigned to what you didn't resolve today when you had the chance."

I tell him he suckered me on that question. Dad pats my shoulder, then does something extremely weird. He brushes his hand through my hair, smiling and wincing, as if he's trying to find in me a little boy he once knew.

"You're so obtuse," he says. "Who do you think called me back to Willoughby to light this fire under you? Your daughter's waiting on your porch. Like I said, you can go as soon as you clean this room. And as soon as you listen to this song I brought for you. It's by Dick Haymes, naturally."

# 28

I don't walk over to my house right away. I figure I
ought to shower and shave and appear presentable
instead of looking as if I've spent three days rolling in
pizza sauce. When I do cross Campbell's lawn, I discover
I'm not the only one worried about appearances. My little
punkette has dressed for battle. Chloe wears combat
boots, burgundy lipstick, and a raccoon's worth of
eyeliner, hair in those funky, top-of-the-head ponytails
again, looking very much as she did the day that the
women's book club visited Macon Place. On closer
approach I see that on her T-shirt is the cover of Sonic
Youth's 1990 record, *Goo*, which featured an artist's
rendering of a famous paparazzi photo of two hipsters in
sunglasses on their way to testify in a notorious British
serial killer case. If I remember right, the words alongside
the drawing say something like, "Within a week we killed
my parents and hit the road." Well-played, Chloe. I give
bonus points, too, because I've never seen that shirt
around our house. I'm almost positive it's Stu's.

"What's happened to us?"

This is a question you pose to a spouse or a lover, not
a child, and it catches Chloe off-guard. After three days of
steeling herself against my tyranny, she's come prepared
to fight for her right to...what? Smoke weed? Stay out late?
Get laid? I drop onto the step next to her.

"I want it to be like it was when you were seven or
eight," I say. "We did everything together then. We used
to go to concerts. Remember when Cowboy Mouth
played Montgomery? We were right at the stage. I had

to spend the whole show making sure you didn't get crowd surfed. Putting you in the middle of a mob like that wasn't my smartest move, but I didn't care. It made me feel cool–a cool dad. I miss that. I haven't felt cool in a while."

She's not interested in my nostalgia. Or my self-pity. "You always make it about you," she grunts.

"No," I counter, "I've always made it about *us*. I thought if I did we'd never have these problems." I tell Chloe it's killing me that we're not close anymore. I wish I could express the affection I feel. I wish we were so close I could show my love the way it seemed natural to do when she was a child. To remind her how exactly I did that, I take her face in my hands and kiss her. On the lips. She's repulsed.

After several seconds of not knowing what to say, Chloe tells me I'm never to do that again.

"Why?" I ask. "Is it gross? Pervy? Why does it have to be? It's innocent. All it is is love, pure love. No taint of the unseemly, nothing taboo. It should be your security, honey. You can kiss your mother and sleep in the same bed with her and there's no whisper of anything wrong. It should be that way with me, too, but your mom has something on me I can't overcome: she's a woman. I know how it is with girls–you feel safer with other women. Not so preyed upon. But you should be able to feel that safe with men, too. That's where I went wrong. I withdrew when I should have been giving you the reassurance you need to feel that men will need your love and friendship more than sex."

"Oh, God, there it is." She shakes her head. "Can

anything ever be about more than that subject for you? This isn't about sex—not for me. It's about you not believing anything I say. It's about you being so convinced that every word out of my mouth is a lie that you'd rather I not say or do anything at all so you can control me. I'm tired of being controlled. That drug test—then breaking up the band—it's like I can't do anything without you threatening to take it away."

I cut her off, telling her she's got to know I can't let her play the battle of the bands. There have to be consequences. She smoked pot, and pot has consequences.

"I don't want to be in Pink Melon Joy anymore," Chloe snaps. "We won't ever be any good. The band's become one more thing I'm tired of dealing with. You can add Macon Place to that list, too. It's all work. First I have to browbeat Stu and Nina into practicing and then I have to browbeat you into even thinking about bringing people to the garden. I shouldn't have to tell you not to spend all of our money on some place you can't make a living from. I'm just glad Mom's here now so I've got somewhere to go when we lose everything."

I don't understand what she thinks we're on the verge of losing. I have enough in the bank to get us to September, I assure her. Maybe even October if we're lucky. Chloe's eyes widen in fear.

"That's two months away!" she says, nearly shouting. "Get a job already! Don't you see how crazy this family has become? You're supposed to be telling me that, not the other way around. I mean, what is it with that place? Mr. Willoughby is dead. Let it go! Move on!"

I point out the irony of her telling me to move on. Not

Kirk Curnutt

a week ago she was the one insisting she couldn't give up on Stu because she didn't want to be like me, Mr. Short Term. "Maybe that's why I can't let Macon Place go," I confess. "There are only two things in my life I haven't let slip through my fingers, but they were the two things I valued most: you and Macon Place."

"It's statues! *Statues!* Are they more important than, like, me going to college?"

I tell her she doesn't need to worry about college. I would never fail her on something that important. "Macon Place may be a bunch of alabaster bodies," I say, "but they're important to me for what they represent. Do you know what that is? It's their timelessness. Nothing in that garden has changed in the decade we've been in Willoughby. Every time I step into Storm's garden I can see you at five years old running down the walkway to play next to Aphrodite. I like it there because I can relive that moment or any other from our past over and over. I've lost so much already—my mom, your mom, now Sadie in all likelihood. Some days I feel like I've lost you. I can't take losing anything else."

She doesn't answer. The conversation has hit a dead end. I pick at the skin of my palm.

"Do you know when I feel like I've most lost you? It's when I'm being lied to. I know you've lied to me, bald-faced, and it breaks my heart. Am I that hard to be honest with? You're way more honest with your mom than with me, Chloe."

"We used to be close because we had something other than sex to talk about. There was music and softball and whatever I was into, but now all you can focus on is what you're afraid I'm doing." For the first time she takes her eyes off the walkway pavers and stares me down. "You're afraid of what I might do because you know what you've done. Everybody knows you're no saint when it comes to the sex stuff. How stupid do you think I am?"

Now it's my turn to stare at the pavers.

"You obviously know about Ardita Farnam. I'm sorry that you do. Maybe someday I can explain it to you, but you're sixteen, and right now it wouldn't be appropriate. When you are old enough, and if you want to hear me out, I promise I'll be honest. It's only been the past few days that I've been able to do that with myself about Ardita."

Chloe rests her chin on her knees, nervously twisting the knot of a boot lace.

"Okay, since you want honesty, I'll tell you something I lied about. You can't get mad, though. It's not fair to ask me not to lie and then go crazy if you don't like what you hear."

I swallow hard and wonder if I really do want to know what she's about to reveal.

"Stu wasn't lying about that night in the garden," admits Chloe. "I was. He wasn't there. It was Zak that the police chased. He was the one trying to have sex. And with Nina, not me. She probably would have been willing, right there in front of me, if Brody Dale hadn't shown up."

"Wh–why would you lie about that? Were you trying to flaunt something? You had to know what you were guaranteeing. You had to know you wouldn't be allowed to see Stu after I heard that story!"

She shrugs. "Maybe that's what I wanted. I don't know. I was just tired of fighting with you and Stu both. I've been so frustrated that I want somebody to decide what's going to happen, once and for all, so I don't have to. But it all blew up, Daddy. *You* blew it up. Why did you have to pick a fight with Stu? That just made everything more real. You got his mom involved. Why couldn't you just break us up and then leave it alone? That's what any other parent would've done!"

I put my arm around her. "See! This is great—we're talking! I wish you could've talked that night. Because I would've said what I'm saying right now. If you have doubts about Stu, then that's a sign he's not right for you. A boyfriend is never worth the worry, that's what I'd have told you. Your mom would've said the same thing, and I wouldn't have gotten mad even though she would've been talking about me. You shouldn't feel that you have to have a boyfriend, Chloe. I don't want you growing up feeling like you need a man to feel like you're somebody."

Her eyeliner begins to streak. The toughness is draining out of her.

"You know that even if Stu turns out to have been a mistake, there are other mistakes that I *could've* made, but that I didn't? You believe me, right?"

What I believe, I want to tell her, is that I suddenly understand why she has to lie to me about sex, and about why I can't confront her over the condom wrapper, not ever. The person she has to lie to right now is herself. She has to tell herself if she wants to break up with Stu that losing her virginity wasn't a big deal, that maybe it didn't really even happen, that she won't be able to find the strength to walk away from her doubts if some external authority–someone she's afraid she might disappoint–is demanding that she cough up truths.

"Whatever mistakes you might've made, you can learn from them. They only count against you if you make them a second time, or maybe the third. For all the mistakes I've made in life, I learned from the biggies. Trust me. I made sure they didn't happen again."

My consolation doesn't soothe her. In fact, it has the opposite effect of what I intended. Chloe bursts out crying. Frantically, I beg her to tell me what was wrong with what I said.

"It's that word! I hate that word so much! The way you use it all the time, the way Mom uses it.... It doesn't do anything but remind me–" She has to stop to gulp away her tears. "I mean, *dammit dammit dammit*...don't you think I know I was a mistake?"

"Wh–what are you talking about? What mistake?"

"It's been obvious my whole life! If it's not people telling me Mom ran off because she couldn't handle her mistakes, then it's Mom herself feeling like she has to tell me that she regrets every single day what she did and breaking down wanting my forgiveness. I've *been* forgiving her for eight years now. I don't want to anymore! And you.... Every time you brag about how you kept me, how you didn't leave like she did–'I met my responsibility,' you always say, like that's all I am to you...*a responsibility!* Can't you make it less obvious that you two didn't want me?"

She sobs into my shoulder. "We didn't plan you," I stammer. "How could we? We were kids. We weren't much older than you are now. But not planning you isn't the same as not wanting you."

This doesn't calm her. I scramble, not knowing what else I can say.

"Okay, listen," I decide finally. "I shouldn't tell you this, but I want you to understand just how young I was, and how much I've had to grow up. When your mom got pregnant, I'd never even.... I mean, I was a.... Well, I was green. You get my point. It was my first time! That's funny, huh? It always seemed a little humiliating, as if it was some kind of cosmic joke on me. But that's the selfish way of looking at it. Now I see things differently. I'm proud you happened that way. Don't get me wrong; I'm not going to print it on a T-shirt and parade it around town, but it seems like you were meant to happen unexpectedly. I–I shouldn't have bragged about not abandoning you. I'm sorry. It's been my way of saying I need you, not that you should be grateful. Don't you see? You're all I have. What do I have to brag about except being your dad?"

I stroke her hair for several minutes as she cries. "I want you to know something." The words are easier than I thought they would be. Words are always easy when you genuinely mean them. "I'm glad your mom has come back. Honest. I want her here, for you. Let's find her, and we can do something together, the three of us. I'll be nice to her, I promise."

I lead Chloe inside to the living room, where Deb is folding a load of laundry. She immediately begins wiping her daughter's tears, leaving me to wonder why I didn't think of that. Flummoxed, I sink along the wall, uncertain what emotion I feel more. Relief, regret, worry–they flush over me equally. I hear Chloe speak of her family in a voice that's neither angry nor sad but merely vulnerable. I am humbled wondering how much hurt I may have caused over the last sixteen years by patting my back for being a good dad.

# V

# Anarchy in the

# Patriarchy

BAND ON THE RUN:
PUNK PROVOCATEURS ESCAPE TO FREEDOM
WITHOUT MISSING A BEAT


PARIS (AP) — A quartet of punk-rock musicians whose beating by a repressive Eastern European regime went viral described on Thursday how they made a daring jailbreak and escaped with the help of funds raised secretly by Western rock 'n' roll stars.

Visibly battered, members of the feminist collective known as Lifting Belly made their first public appearance after being rescued in a daring commando raid—possibly by an all-female paramilitary force—from a notorious state prison in the group's native Herzoslovakia.

Speaking for the group, singer-songwriter Oksana Dybek, 26, said the secret fundraising effort was crucial in freeing the band from captivity.

"Security at The Chimneys is known to be lax," said Ms. Dybek, referring to the nickname of the prison in the Herzoslovakian capital of Ekarest. "Our manager knew she could procure forces that would liberate us if she could only raise the right amount of cash. We're lucky that so many stars in America support Lifting Belly's fight for freedom."

Ms. Dybek's head was still bandaged from the injury she sustained on June 12 when state police under the direction of Herzoslovakian president Bronislavis Stylptitch violently interrupted a protest staged by the band in the capital's main public square. Footage from the assault sparked international condemnation of Stylptitch, who last January dissolved the country's parliament and instituted a new constitution declaring himself chief of state for life.


Kirk Curnutt

"I was in a coma for five days," Ms. Dybek said in a press conference held at Lavoir Moderne Parisien, a popular theater in the 18th arrondissement that has agreed to host and house the band. "I am able to speak now, but only haltingly. I can play two chords on my guitar, but punk rock requires three, so until I can form a D in my second fret Lifting Belly cannot perform live."

Ms. Dybek added that she was unaware of rumors she had died in captivity until she arrived in Paris. On June 20 a hoax tweet prompted a wave of online mourning when it hinted Ms. Dybek had succumbed to her injuries. Ms. Dybek claims the rumor was started by Mr. Stylptitch's administration. Although the president's spokesman denies such claims, Internet sleuths traced the tweet to a Herzoslovakian teenager whose father works as a custodian at The Chimneys.

"Stylptitch is a master of propaganda," Ms. Dybek said. "He made a calculated wager that the controversy over my supposed 'death' would pass quickly online. Once it did, I and the other members of Lifting Belly would disappear into the prison system forever under different names. It happens all the time to women in Herzoslovakia. That was the fate we were facing if we weren't rescued."

Ms. Dybek also said that President Stylptitch's propaganda bureau had manufactured rumors that Lifting Belly was a prank and that she herself was in the ruler's employ. Only days before erroneous reports of her death, the Eastern European gossip magazine *Pupok* (*Bellybutton* in English) published a photograph that supposedly proved Ms. Dybek was a guest at Mr. Stylptitch's palace, not a prisoner at The Chimneys. The photograph was discredited when Internet sleuths proved the image was an altered version of a 1962 paparazzi photograph of actress Sophia Loren taken from afar at the Royal Palace in Naples, Italy.

"You would think the propaganda machine could find a more obscure picture to doctor," Ms. Dybek added.

The majority of the press conference was devoted to questions about the mysterious raid that spirited Lifting Belly out of detention. A woman identifying herself as the band's manager, Angele Mory, 42, said that she raised more than $100,000 in American dollars to finance the escape.

Ms. Mory declined to identify the name of the paramilitary force that entered the prison on Thursday night. She would neither confirm nor deny reports from Ekarest that the heavily armed group was composed entirely of women. She also declined to answer any questions suggesting the rescuers modeled themselves upon the Herzoslovakian myth of The Furies, an all-female band of medieval warriors who, according to legend, deposed King Nicholas IV in 1445, instituting one hundred years of matriarchal rule.

"The Furies is legend," Ms. Mory insisted. "But the struggles of Herzoslovakian women are real. They are the struggles of all the world's women."

The group's manager did assert several times that the raid occurred without injuries either to the unidentified guerillas or to the prison staff. Ms. Mory suggested that the lack of resistance to the commandos reflects a lack of popular support for Mr. Stylptitch.

"The president cannot sustain the power structure," Ms. Mory said. "Stylptitch could only dissolve the parliament with the backing of the military, but now he is losing the support of the generals and colonels. We believe democracy will

Kirk Curnutt

return to Herzoslovakia by the winter holidays."

According to Ms. Dybek, the guerillas transported her and her bandmates from The Chimneys to a waiting black van, which then rendezvoused with Ms. Mory outside Ekarest. After a two-hour car ride to a waiting boat, the women were ferried across Lake Stempka to the Gulf of Finland. From there they rode a chartered plane to Helsinki before boarding an Air France flight to Paris.

Neither Ms. Dybek nor Ms. Mory would identify the names of American rock 'n' roll stars who contributed money to Lifting Belly's escape. Internet rumors have linked the fundraising operation to singer-songwriter Liz Phair, whose 1993 double album *Exile in Guyville* is widely regarded as an indie-rock classic. Reached at her home in California, Ms. Phair declined to confirm she marshalled fellow musicians to support Ms. Mory's daring plan.

"I'm pro-women, pro-freedom, and pro-music," Ms. Phair said. "I'm happy to know Lifting Belly is alive and ready to rock as soon as Oksana fully recovers. I'll be the first in line to download their new album."

According to Ms. Mory, several record companies are wooing Lifting Belly. In addition to music, a major speaking tour is planned for early next year, with stops in New York, New Orleans, Los Angeles, and the state that drew laughter from journalists when Ms. Dybek identified it as her favorite in the United States:

"Alabama," she told reporters.

# 29

At dawn on Saturday I head to Macon Place to set up for the battle of the bands, but I'm not the first to arrive at the garden. When I pull up to Storm's back gate, I'm greeted by a large white van with a computer monitor and deck of electronic doodads visible through its open door. When I jog to the amphitheater I discover two trailers parked on either side of the stage. Rising from the roof of each is an LED screen, 8' x 13' if they're an inch. Workmen wander the proscenium arch, stringing cable and setting up cameras. I feel as if I've stumbled onto the set of a Madonna concert, not a humble showcase for teenage musicians with some of the dumbest band names I've ever heard: Riffbait, the Saint Valentine's Day Manicure, Atticus and the Finches, Scott Got a Sponge Bath, and, of course, the Gold Dust Twinz.

"You must be Chloe's dad," a man with a clipboard says. He shakes my hand but doesn't shake me out of my shock, mainly because I recognize his voice. It's the mystery man from the cell phone, the one I thought for sure was Stu and Chloe's pot dealer.

"I'm Ricky Koester from Central Alabama Sound and Video," the guy informs me. "Sorry I was so cryptic when we spoke, but your daughter was very insistent. Mum was the word."

"Chloe hired you?"

"She sure did. She's a tough negotiator, too. Worked me down to the last extension cord and power strip. Just so you know, we've got a pair of SMD LEDs up and running for you today, 16:9 ratio and 6,400 pixels with a sixty-frame-per-second refresh rate. We've got two Sony HVR-HD1000U cameras piping into an Image-PRO II switcher. I'll be editing live in the van. We'll take the live stream to the YouTube channel your daughter set up for today through Flash Media Live Encoder software on a dedicated laptop. We'll be streaming through a 5Mbps hard-wire connection, so you won't have any worries about the upload crashing."

My head swims from all the names and numbers. There's only one figure I care about.

"This has got to be expensive. How much is this costing?"

The man smiles as if telling a two-year-old not to be scared of the dark. "That's something I'm still sworn to secrecy about. We're getting a lot of free advertising from this gig, so I was able to cut Chloe a good deal, trust me. I have to admit, I was skeptical about working with a sixteen-year-old, but your daughter did her research. She knew exactly what she wanted for this event."

As Koester returns to his setup, I don't ask the other question boxing my brain: Central Alabama Sound and Video doesn't happen to employ a short guy with friendly mutton chops, does it? Say, a guy with a habit of showing up unexpectedly at the oddest of times?

Watching the technicians, I'm left wondering what I envisioned for today. It certainly wasn't on the scale that Chloe is aiming for. Over the next three hours I watch another crew of workmen arrive and set up exhibition tents between the amphitheater and Storm's house. Two food trucks park at opposing ends of the garden and fill the air in between them with the enticing aroma of barbecue and gyros. People stream in with cartloads of their pottery and paintings, setting up arts and crafts booths. Even a clown strolls by with a sign advertising face painting for kids. I recognize many of these folks. They're locals, eager to let Mike Willoughby know they support my hopes for Macon Place. Commanding several booths are women from the book club that met here earlier this month, among them Miss Kathy, the president who's also our go-to taxidermist. As I try not to notice the displays of stuffed squirrels and deer heads she sets up, I spot a bevy of Campbell's friends—Tish and Jill from the P-FLAG banquet, among them—sporting green T-shirts with the word VOLUNTEER on the back. Other faces I see belong to total strangers. I wonder how they even heard of the garden, much less little old Willoughby, Alabama. I suddenly feel puny and insignificant. My imagination could fit into a thimble and still have elbow room.

I look around for my daughter, but I can't find her. The only person I see who's more than a passing acquaintance is Luther. He's setting up the backline of band amplifiers with a crew of volunteers, preparing to make sure the mix on his PA system is sharp and clear. When I hop onto the stage he shoots me the same look gardeners give stink bugs when they find them foraging their tomatoes. I ask if he's seen Chloe, and he motions toward Storm's mansion, saying something about her getting into character. I head to the house, checking the kitchen and parlor. They're deserted, though. I go out the front door and step down the wraparound porch to the circular drive, where I run into somebody I'd prefer not to deal with: the ersatz business partner who's suing me.

The only good thing is that Mike's not having the greatest of moments either. He's at the open hatch of his Ford Explorer, which is cluttered with clubs and dirty Polos, arguing with his wife, Terri. It's somehow appropriate that the backdrop for their blowout is a bank of newly installed port-a-potties.

"Like trying to reason with a brick wall," Mike grouses when his spouse stalks off to the footpath that connects the driveway with the statue garden. "A pregnant woman in a crowd in 100-degree heat is insane! I told her she needs to go home, but she wants to see Zak and Travis rap with Stu.... I'm glad I ran into you before the show, though, Seahorse. I've got something I want you to do for me. Come here."

I make the mistake of heeding. When I step to his Explorer, Mike reaches into a brown bag and hands me a specimen cup. My second mistake is to ask what the cup is for.

"What do you think it's for, dumbass? It's for drug testing. I've heard a rumor that doesn't make me happy. Go fill it for me so I can know what I need to know. I can't be associating with a drug abuser."

I ask if he's kidding. He asks if he looks as if he's kidding.

"Iris is behind this, isn't she?" I say, furious. "I wondered why you were suddenly so generous about Stu. 'Let him paint in the parlor, Seahorse!' 'Let him rap in the battle of the bands!' 'Give him a break, Seahorse—he doesn't have a dad!' You've been using Iris to dig up dirt on me! Wasn't it low enough to sic that fuzz-faced stalker on me? Now you have to conspire with my daughter's boyfriend's mom?"

Mike throws up his palms to protest his innocence, tipping the cup. If it were full, he would douse his own chest. "Stalker? What stalker? Has anybody ever told you that you're paranoid? Can I help it if Iris happens to mention you and weed in the same passing sentence? You're the one that got high in front of her two days after you beat her kid up!"

My excuse seems flimsy even to me: I was stressed. Why bother offering it when Mike won't bother to listen?

"We can do this now, or we can do it in court," he tells me, holding the cup out to me. "Your choice. Make sure you're not being selfish, though. Maybe you're willing to risk the embarrassment of dope smoking going on your public record, but you've got a daughter to think about. How is Chloe going to feel knowing her dad's a pothead?"

I'm so angry waves of heat rise off my shoulders and spine. I tell Mike to shut up and write out the transfer of deed. I'm done, finished. He wins, Macon Place is his. "I'll take the $750,000," I growl. "Buy me out of Macon Place, but not a single word out of your stupid mouth about Chloe. You don't deserve to say my daughter's name. Whatever wrong I've done, I've been a good dad."

Mike's eyes tighten. "$750,000? Who said $750,000? That figure went off the table long ago, my friend. God, you've got balls. Do you know how much it has cost me for you to come to your senses? You can't refuse to take a lawsuit seriously and then expect me to pick up the tab!" He reaches into the pocket of his golf shorts, handing me a slip of paper. "My top offer."

When I open the slip I have to count the zeros twice

to make sure I'm not overlooking one.

"$75,000? That's ten cents on the dollar for my half!"

Mike taps the figure. "It's this," he says, as he pushes the cup at me again with his other hand, "or piss."

Just to be a bastard he says it over, but oddly, I'm not offended. I'm too distracted by a gaudily framed certificate of appreciation buried in his soiled shirts. When I lean in to read the citation, INTEGRITY is the first word my eyes land on.

"Is this new?" I ask, picking the frame from his laundry pile. Mike tells me the commendation just arrived the other day. It's from the PGTAA, the Professional Golf Teachers' Association of America, awarded for a sportsmanship program Mike's company developed for kids.

"Golf ethics?" I'm jolted by a memory. "Hey, do you remember a few weeks ago, when you and I and Luther played Rivervesper? I brought Campbell's son, Lleyton."

"How can I forget? I wanted to kill that kid."

"He's a good golfer, though. He only lost to you by a stroke, right?"

We lock gazes. "Something like that," Mike admits, coolly.

"You know, Lleyton told me the craziest thing on the way home. He said he won that game, that he *would've* won it if you hadn't moved your ball. You kicked it onto the green to make your putt. *Some days are diamonds, and some are dung.* Isn't that what you told him?"

The color drains from Mike's cheeks. "You're going to blackmail me, motherfucker?"

Well, why the hell not? I wonder. Turnabout is fair

play. I tell Mike to think of how messed up Zak and Travis will be knowing the main male role model in their lives is a cheat. Think of the baby Terri's carrying. Imagine the shame she'll feel knowing that the Professional Golf Teachers' Association of America revoked her daddy's certificate of honor. I expect these threats to melt Mike to a puddle, but instead he does the unthinkable. The bastard calls my bluff.

"You do what you have to," he says sternly, "and we'll see who comes out on top."

As an exclamation point he slams the Explorer's hatch shut. If I didn't jerk my hands out of the cargo bay I might lose more than bargaining leverage. I might lose fingers.

As Mike marches into his daddy's mansion, intent on making sure it's locked up so nobody uses the bathrooms, I follow the footpath back to the garden. There must be a hundred exhibitors and volunteers wandering around by now. I go up to a half-dozen different ones and ask how they heard about today. One woman who's driven from east Georgia shows me a flier she pulled off a crochet crafts website. DON'T DEFACE MACON PLACE, it says. A BENEFIT TO SAVE ALABAMA'S ONLY GREEK STATUE GARDEN. Of course, Chloe is listed as the contact.

On my way back to the amphitheater, I hear my name called. When I twist to look up the hill toward the house, I see Nina's dad, Luke Laughlin, running at me. He looks frantic and desperate, crazed enough that I expect him to tackle me. He asks if I've seen his daughter.

"Nina says she doesn't want anything to do with me!" Luke huffs bitterly into my face. He's out of breath. "And

Marci is telling her she doesn't have to! This is crazy, Vance, crazy! That girl needs her father more than ever!"

When I ask what he's talking about, Luke admits that when Nina wasn't looking this morning he snuck onto her laptop and accessed all her social media accounts: her Facebook mailbox, her Tumblr page, which she publishes under a pseudonym, her SnapChat account, along with five or six names of apps I don't even recognize. "They have this thing now," Luke says, almost trembling, "this thing called Thought Catalog. Nina has published four articles on it under a pen name, 'Barbie Dahl.' You get it, Vance? My daughter is online calling herself some combination of a Barbie doll and the guy who wrote Willy Wonka! One of these articles—I can't believe I'm telling you this—is called 'The 10 Best Places to Have Sex When You Both Live with Your Parents.' She's bragging about the fact she and that little peckerhead Zak did it in Mike Willoughby's bed! One of the other articles is about how she lost her virginity. It happened two years ago, Vance. Two years! She was only fifteen then!"

I take Luke by the shoulders and try to calm him down. "It's okay," I say. "Our daughters are growing up. This is natural. Chloe's had sex, too. I know it for a fact." I tell Luke that sex is going to happen, that he and I have to make sure our kids, whether they're girls or boys, are smart about the choices they make. *Smart and informed.*

"On Monday," I tell Luke, "I'm putting Chloe on birth control. Come to the gynecologist with us—you and Nina both, I mean, not just you. We'll get the girls protection, together. It'll be better for them to go with a friend, and they'll see that we're good dads because we respect their sexuality. We don't have to be scared of them becoming women. We can do this, Luke. We can handle this like real men should."

Luke steps back, horrified. He looks as if I just vomited in his mouth. "That's the worst idea I've ever heard! The only place I'll be Monday is at my lawyer's! I'm taking this information to him, and I'm getting custody of Nina! And I'm calling you and Chloe as witnesses. If you have anything to confess to me, Vance Seagrove, you better do it right now, before you're sworn in and on record!"

I have a sudden fear that Mike has told Luke about me smoking weed. But that lapse in judgment isn't what sparks his anger. He accuses me of having an affair with Marci. I try to talk sense into him, saying I have a girlfriend–*had* one, anyway–and that I don't need to hit on my daughter's best friend's mom. That's when Luke leans in and guts me like a deer.

"I know all about you. This whole town knows what a dirtbag you are. You and that waitress from Katfish Kountry, that Ardita Farnam girl. And now Marci goes and lets Nina get a job at that hellhole? I'll depose everybody at that restaurant if that's what it takes to save my daughter from predators like you!"

He stomps off, his head twisting so far right and left as he cranes to find Nina I expect to hear his neck snap. I don't have much time to think about Luke's accusation, though. My phone pings with a text message from Campbell. She says to meet her, Deb, and my dad down at the gate. We have a problem.

When I reach the back entry to Macon Place, I see the wrought-iron gate that I opened when I arrived this morning has been swung shut. Brody Dale stands in front of it, facing out and blocking the button that opens it.

"Chloe waited until this morning to tell us," Campbell says, looking distressed. "But she, Stu, and Nina sold two thousand tickets for today."

I'm convinced she must be as generous with her decimal point as Mike was stingy with his. I was counting on drawing two *hundred* kids, plus some random parents.

"We need more security," adds Deb. "Brody has three or four off-duty friends coming over, but that won't be enough to control this crowd. We can't leave Brody out there much longer by herself. The gates are supposed to open in fifteen minutes, but the kids want in right now."

I hear the crowd chant from the other side of the garden wall: *Open the gate! Open the gate!* With his phone at his ear, Dad tells me he's calling Montgomery for reinforcements. There must be off-duty cops down in the capital willing to rush up here at the last minute for time-and-a-half pay. I peek through the gate at the throng rippling past Brody's shoulders. I ask Deb and Campbell how much Chloe charged for those two thousand tickets. Ten bucks a pop, I'm told. That means we're looking at pulling in twenty grand, minus expenses for the emergency security. I could almost enjoy the windfall except for one more thing I hadn't counted on.

"We're going to need to move some of the statues before we let the kids in. I roped them all off yesterday with stanchions we had in the garage from earlier garden parties Storm threw, but it wouldn't take but one stumbling kid to knock the whole collection over like dominos."

I call Luther and tell him to round me up some muscle. Then I jog up to the garage for our John Deere Gator. In my head I draw up a list of the most valuable of the statues, thinking we have just enough time to haul five or six to safety in the back of the utility vehicle, two per trip, before we have to open. Because the statue that had the most sentimental value for Storm is the Aphrodite of Knidos, we start with her. I'm not happy to see that Stu is one of my movers. The cuffs of his jeans are so floppy I can picture him tripping over them while hoisting Praxiteles's masterpiece. We manage to wiggle Aphrodite off her base and waddle her next to the Gator's 4' x 4' cargo box when one of the team breaks our concentration.

"Look!" the volunteer yells, pointing. A teenager is straddling the brick top of the garden wall, throwing up his arms in victory before slithering down the rough surface and landing in a hedge. "Don't worry," the kid says as he passes the table where Campbell, Deb, and Dad stand preparing to take tickets and stamp hands. "I paid on the Internet!" To prove it, he tosses a stub at them. Before I can even think to light out after him, gatecrashers pour over the wall like water bubbling out of a saucepot.

"We can't run the Gator to the garage with this many kids bum-rushing us," I say. "We'll end up mowing one down. The best we can do is get to the stage and put Aphrodite in the wings. Then we can rope her off."

My crew manages to raise Aphrodite into the back of the Gator. After tying her down, I drive slowly to the side of the amphitheater, honking to clear a path the entire way. By the time we position her onstage, it's clear she's the only statue we'll have time to move. Macon Place is swarming with too many teenagers, all of them streaming to the stage to stake a spot. It feels as if every kid on earth under the age of eighteen is here. There's only one I know of that I'm not seeing.

I work my way back down to the ticket table and ask Deb if she knows where her daughter is. She says the same thing Luther told me: Chloe's somewhere inside Storm's house, "getting into character." Before I can point out what a potential public safety hazard our entrepreneurial sixteen-year-old has created, a man comes up and claps his arms around Deb's shoulders. I recognize him. His name is Grady Turnipseed. I spotted him earlier setting up a booth of the ceramic figurines he sculpts in his spare time. The figurines aren't the only thing Grady is known for. He also happens to be the principal at Willoughby High School.

"Here's our newest faculty member!" Grady says, giving my ex-wife a big bear hug. "We've got so many kids wanting to sign up for the theater track we may go ahead and start school back up in July!"

"You got that job?" I blurt. Deb is embarrassed. She knows I had to work hard not to say *my job*.

"I was going to tell you, Vance. After the concert. Or tomorrow, maybe, or Monday. Sometime, anyway."

Grady releases Deb before taking hold of her hand and patting it. "We're so excited to have Chloe, too," he makes a point to add. He seems awful touchy feely for a high-school principal. "She has so much talent. Chloe and Deb both do!"

When I admit my confusion, Deb informs me that she enrolled our daughter at Willoughby High yesterday.

Apparently that's also news she planned to break after the concert, or tomorrow maybe, or Monday. Angry, I stomp away, Deb calling after me. I head back to the stage, patrolling for contraband booze and pot. I have to resist the temptation to boss around some teenagers so I can feel in control of my life.

Dad texts me at ten a.m. promptly to say Brody has opened the gate. The crowd swells again, but our audience is peaceful and orderly. The kids are even using the trash and recycling bins I positioned at various points. I begin to feel better about today when law enforcement arrives and the off-duty cops appear bored and blasé, as if they can't believe we thought we even needed them. Onstage, Luther and some of the youth-group kids he mentors, Stu among them, do a quick soundcheck, rolling through some easy blues. Then Ricky Koester tests his LED screens, throwing up crowd shots that get the kids hooting and hollering. I worm my way stage right and make sure the stanchions I placed around Aphrodite haven't been knocked out of place. As I slip back into the crowd, a female body rushes into my arms, kissing me with enough tongue to scrape the plaque off of my teeth.

"Five o'clock," Campbell whispers in my ear, stroking my nape. It's not an invitation to rekindle our affair with some happy-hour nookie. She's directing me to a figure staring at us from Miss Kathy's taxidermy booth. It's Steve, her ex-husband. When I ask why he's crashing a teenage battle of the bands, Campbell's answer is obvious. "He's checking up on me," she whispers. "It's never going to stop!"

Kirk Curnutt

I tell her it'll stop when she makes it stop. "Steve's here because he knows we're bullshitting him. He's going to stick around until he proves it. You've got to come clean—for your sake and Lleyton's. This charade is messing your son up. It's messing you up. You're telling Lleyton that if we don't pull this act off he's going to have to live with Steve. If I threatened Chloe with Deb like that you'd call me to the carpet."

I'm not sure what shocks Campbell more: that after years of relying on her advice I'm giving it for once, or that my advice actually possesses a modicum of sense. Before she can answer, I spot a different sweat-stained figure traipsing through the crowd, throwing his head left and right like a man expecting a mugging. And for good reason, too. He's carrying a cashbox under his arm.

"It's no use," Dad gulps after Campbell and I race to find out why he's abandoned the ticket table. Perspiration rolls down his face. "Deb and I were doing the best we could moving the line through the gate, but the natives got restless. The kids who didn't climb the wall just started barreling through the gate. I was lucky to get away without getting trampled. Your battle of the bands is the new Woodstock, Vance. From here on out, this concert's free."

I escort Dad to Storm's house, where we lock the cashbox in the safe in my former employer's closet. We make it back to the amphitheater just in time for Luther to kick off the music with a short list of rules. The kids boo him. "Maybe you'd rather hear these rules from one of your own," Luther responds, his feelings visibly hurt. "Okay, well, then, here's the reason we're all here today.

Here's your host, Chloe Seagrove!" The audience lets out a roar and thunderstorm of applause as Chloe steps out from behind the flats and baffles lining the back of the stage. She looks as cocky and wiry as rock 'n' roll should in leather shorts and combat boots, her bob streaked with blond highlights. THIS IS WHAT A FEMINIST LOOKS LIKE, her T-shirt reads. As the applause dies down, someone in the crowd wolf-whistles. Laughter bursts through the rows of kids, threatening to tip the balance of power. "Lookin' good!" some twerp yells. I'm seized by a sudden panic that we're in store for the same heckling as at the Liz Phair concert. Chloe is undeterred, however. She leans into the microphone and says, "Come up here and say that!" in a voice as tough as beef shank. Girls in the audience cheer and throw their arms above their heads.

"Before the music starts," Chloe says, "I want to introduce you to someone I've gotten to know a little bit. Someone who's everything that, to me, music should be about. There's a word called 'empowerment' that gets thrown around a lot. Sometimes it's applied to people who haven't really earned it. But let me tell you, this person has. This person is pure punk rock."

One of Ricky Koester's crew steps forward long enough to hand Chloe an iPad with a long cord dangling from its tail. As Chloe pokes at the keyboard the LED screens on either side of the stage go to fuzz before dissolving into the strangely familiar face of a young woman.

"Hello, my American friends," the woman says, beaming in via a Skype session. Her English is choppy from her heavy accent, but her voice is taut and determined. I think the resolution on the screen looks terrible until I realize the dark patches on her face are bruises, not shadows. "This is Oksana Dybek from Lifting Belly. I wish I could be with you today. You are going to have fun. I don't want to hold up the program by talking too much. I only wish to say that in music there is great freedom and great rebellion, but there also needs to be great care and concern for others."

I look around the crowd for an explanation. Deb is a few yards away, standing in a patch of shade with Dad. Prepared to learn I was again left out of the decision making, I ask if she knew Chloe had arranged this guest appearance. Deb shakes her head, clearly as surprised as I am.

"I knew," a voice says. It's Sadie, stepping up to my shoulder. She looks pretty rock 'n' roll, too, in a leather vest that doesn't cover the Eye of Horus tattoo around her bellybutton. "So did Luther. We were sworn to secrecy. Chloe wanted to show you and Deb what she's capable of. She needs you especially to know that she's not a fuck-up, Vance."

"I never thought she was," I stutter.

Onscreen, Oksana finishes talking about her band's imprisonment, and how they hope to be ambassadors for freedom when she's well enough to play guitar again. "I wish I could be in *Ahlah-bahma*," the punk rocker says, "because I would like to sit in with my new friend, Chloe. I hear she is a good drummer. Until Lifting Belly comes to the United States, I want you to do me a favor. I want you to look to the nearest person you don't know and hug them. Tell them, 'Everything will be all right.' Then look to the second-nearest person you don't know and do the same."

It's a hokey gesture, but it works. It works as well as I remember it working years ago at the Cowboy Mouth concert that Chloe learned it from. I throw both thumbs in the air and hoot my approval at the stage. The move seems as much of a gift of bonhomie to me as to the crowd that laps it up.

Topping a surprise appearance by a famous punk freedom fighter like Oksana Dybek would be difficult for any concert. It's especially hard for a battle of the bands held in the hinterlands of Willoughby, Alabama, though I'm not sure what level of rock 'n' roll catharsis I thought we could pull off today—the reality is our line-up is terrible. As in, by the third band I'm ready to go hang out at Miss Kathy's booth and play with the stuffed squirrels and chipmunks. The performances aren't tedious because the musicians are bad. For the most part, these kids are impressive, especially considering they're teenagers. It's just that they're not that original or inter-esting. And the reason for that becomes glaringly obvious as we lumber through the order of appearances. From snotty punk to pointless virtuoso Van Halen noodling to heavy metal that you'd have to be a Visigoth to get into, the competition is an unending parade of testosterone-fueled attitude. "There's not a single girl in any of these bands," Campbell notes as the fourth group takes the stage. "You should've let Pink Melon Joy on the bill, Vance. Some estrogen would be a nice leveling influence. All these boys are doing is the musical equivalent of lighting their own farts."

I can't disagree, but I point out that the kids don't seem

to mind the flatulence. Every few songs I have to rush to the front of the sawhorses and put the kibosh on moshing outbreaks. In the meantime, I scan the audience for contraband. By the time the last act rolls around, I've collected a six-pack of Pabst Blue Ribbon, two bongs, and three baggies of weed. I make sure to give the pot to Brody Dale for safekeeping, just in case Mike Willoughby decides to pat me down.

Finally, we make it to the last act signed up to compete. "And now for something a little different," announces Chloe. "Something with a little rhythm... maybe. Put your hands together for the Gold Dust Twinz!"

Stu, Zak, and Travis strut to the proscenium to a funkier beat than anything we've heard today, their shirts off so their fake gold chains sparkle against the pimply backdrops of their hairless chests. For three songs that sound exactly alike, they bob, weave, shout *hey yo*, and grab their crotches—all of which, of course, is a prologue to their showstopper, "Zoom Zoom Aphrodite." Stu no sooner begins burping the verse about backseat *boomin'* than he locks eyes with me. He keeps them locked even while gyrating through the Twinz's complicated choreography, which includes hip thrusts, pantomimed fanny swats, and what appears to be simulated sex with a statue. Aphrodite looks as if she'd like to break her hand out of her *pudica gesture* pose and smack him upside the head.

Once the Gold Dust Twinz finish, Chloe announces that a special guest will perform while Luther consults the online survey manager that kids call up on their phones to cast their vote for the winner. Sadie strolls from behind the bank of PA speakers, greeted by a predictable torrent of wolf whistles. "Why does she have an electric guitar?" I ask, but there's nobody around but Dad to answer. Campbell has slipped down to the sawhorses to huddle with Deb. "I was going to sing some of my songs," Sadie informs the crowd. "I'm proud of them because it took me a long time to figure out what I had to say as a writer. Then I heard a song that I wish I could've written at sixteen. Honestly, I wish I'd written it at twenty-three. It's such a good song I thought you'd like to hear it...."

As she speaks, Stu lugs a familiar set of drums center stage. *No, no, no,* I sputter. *Pink Melon Joy is not playing!* But nobody's around to listen. Dad has joined Campbell and Deb at the barricade. Chloe plops her stool behind the bass drum, Nina next to her rattling maracas and a tambourine. The real surprise is Iris, who's reliving her own punk career by strapping on a bass. "We are a Willoughby, Alabama, supergroup!" Chloe shouts into her mic. "And we believe in the Gospel According to...*Punk!* We are The New Wussy Pimps! A-one! A-two! A-one-two-three-four!"

Chloe bashes her kit so hard the vibrations seem to shoot kids into the air like bursting kernels of popcorn. From what I can decipher of the lyrics, the band is playing "Daddy's Girl," whose chorus rattles with fury and verve. "I'm bringing anarchy, anarchy!" yells Chloe. "To the patriarchy! Anarchy, anarchy! To the patriarchy!"

The New Wussy Pimps are ragged and under-rehearsed, but Chloe sells her song with such intensity I can't help but want to pump my fist. There's no hint of the self-doubt that ruined her performance at the P-FLAG banquet. With her hair flung across her eyes and her arm muscles hardening into rocks as she bounces and bobs to the thud of her kick pedal, she looks absolutely liberated. She's so confident in the crucible of her aggression that neither a boyfriend nor a father's confusing expectations of what a girl her age should be—baby vamp or virgin punk—can touch her right now. The sight of that confidence is enough to seduce me into mouthing the chorus. Even though the volume is piercing enough to crucify, I elbow my way to the sawhorses to join the rest of my daughter's fan club. Campbell and Deb dance together, while Dad does his patented deckwalker step. I, meanwhile, play some wicked air drums.

As I bash an imaginary cymbal, a face in my peripheral vision catches my attention. I lock gazes with our latest gatecrasher, who nods and points at Chloe approvingly. As he gives me a thumbs up, I recognize him. Despite the gesture, his friendly mutton chops don't look so friendly.

The stalker weaves my way. I scoot sideways to a spot of shade where Mike and Terri Willoughby cluster with several other parents. "You still want to claim you didn't hire him?" I growl at Mike as I stab a thumb over my shoulder. Before Mike can answer, I circle to the backside of the stage, where I duck behind a mountain of amps, drums, and guitars.

"We only know two songs," I hear Chloe's voice boom from the PA, "so this is our other one!"

The stalker swings around the corner. I wait for him to pass before I hop out and tackle him by the hips. "I'm here to help a brother!" the guy yells as we go down. I put him in a neckhold. He wiggles, trying to roll on top, but I hold tight until we're basically spooning. I can feel Chloe's beat rumbling the ground. It thumps behind a sweet lilt of a tune, the rhythm tightening with each downbeat as it burns its way to the chorus. *Whatever happened to a boyfriend?* Chloe is singing. *The kind of guy who tries to win you over?*

Tennis shoes drop off the back of the stage; somebody squats over us in disbelief. "You're beating somebody else up?" asks Stu, wide-eyed. "Help me!" I scream. Before Stu can, the stalker lands an elbow chop to my neck. As I writhe, the stranger leaps up and rolls himself onto the stage. Stu pulls me to my feet, and I give chase. The stalker dips between the backdrop of flats and baffles as the band hits the first chorus. I realize the New Wussy Pimps are playing Liz Phair's signature song, "Fuck and Run." I'm four beats away from hearing my daughter rain F-bombs down on two thousand people.

I stagger between the backdrops, dizzy and disoriented. All I can see are the backs of the band and the sea of dancing teenage faces out front. The stalker sidles along the left side of the stage. Our eyes meet, and he breaks for the lip, prepared to jump. I bowl myself into the backs of his legs. I would deck him if something didn't break his fall. It's the Aphrodite of Knidos. As the stranger crashes into the statue's hips, she wobbles, and I leap to catch her before she can spill. Time seems to stop, and I remember the one and only time I ever climbed a concert barricade to stage dive. 1992, a place called the Visage in Orlando. I was so scared I froze in place. I might never have jumped if L7's lead singer hadn't launched a Doc

Marten into my buttock. I remember how awkward and graceless I felt, more like spilling than flying. It's the way I feel now. I catch Aphrodite by her egg-stained waist, but I have no footing. As we go over the stage edge, Luther is directly under us, waving his arms frantically, trying to catch the statue. It's too late. Aphrodite and I crash onto the ground, and she explodes into shards. A squeal flashes from the crowd as its front rows collapse on top of us. I try to claw out of the swarm, but the weight of the entire audience is on my shoulders.

Teenagers clamber over me like ants on sugar.

# 30

As it turns out, Mike wasn't lying when he claimed he knew nothing about my stalker. Friendly Mutton Chops was never in his employ. In the minutes after the New Wussy Pimps finish battering "Fuck and Run" into submission and the crowd pulls back so I can separate myself from Aphrodite–as I strip off my shirt to reveal a crazy quilt of nicks and slices in my chest–the stranger cops to being a private detective hired by none other than Campbell's ex-husband, Steve.

"To prove she's still queer," as he politely puts it.

Mike's first reaction is to again accuse me of paranoia. I'd like to clock him and the stalker both, but Mike tromps away offended and my lookalike Lemmy is the only one displaying any common sense right now. He makes sure the bleeding isn't serious, and he calls for alcohol and swabs to doctor my wounds.

"You won't sue me, will you?" the guy begs as Chloe and Campbell run to the nearest drugstore for a first-aid kit. I almost laugh. He sounds exactly like OVERGROWN ADOLESCENT ME I and II at the Liz Phair concert, the guys who cost me my front teeth. Maybe if I were more litigious I might not be broke.

"Nobody was supposed to get hurt, nothing broken," the stalker assures me. "Usually when I turn a screw on somebody, they don't fight back. All you had to do was admit that you were shamming the ex-husband, and my job was done."

"And posting my daughter's picture on Reddit.com was your way of cracking me?"

Kirk Curnutt

The man throws up his palms at this accusation. "I don't mess with the Internet," he insists. "I've got a real job. I wouldn't have known about that picture if not for the lesbian's son. He told his old man about overhearing one of your daughter's friends on her phone, some girl named Nina. The dad told me to download it for leverage. You think the old guy over there is okay? He seems a little dazed."

A yard or two away, Luther rests against a magnolia trunk, holding the spot where Aphrodite shrapnel glanced his temple. Deb is at his side, dabbing a blood trickle with a napkin.

"What I want," I tell Friendly Mutton Chops, "is for you to tell Steve to be a man. Tell him to pay his child support and quit worrying about Campbell. She's a good mother. Whether she dates a woman or a man is none of his business. Tell him I better never hear of him threatening to bring the gay thing up in court."

"I hear you, Jack. I don't like deadbeats either. I only came to the garden today to find the cheapskate. He bounced a $1,500 check on me. Stiffing a brother isn't smart business. He knows it, too. The minute he saw me he skedaddled. I'll find him, though. I've got his address. If I were you, I would *show* him instead of *tell* him what you'll do if he bothers the lesbian again. If you know what I mean."

As tempted as I am, I can't hire the stalker to threaten Steve. Dad appears with a fistful of Don't Deface Macon Place T-shirts to stanch my bleeding. Friendly Mutton Chops explains how to clean the cuts and leaves. I spot Stu packing equipment on the amphitheater stage and call him over. He asks if I'm okay. I ask to borrow his cell, telling him mine was cracked when Aphrodite and I took our header into the crowd. It's a lie. When Stu hands me his cell, I scroll through his pics until I find the derriere shot uploaded to r/Gone Wild. "When did you take this?" I demand. The kid blubbers excuses without admitting anything, his voice vinegar in my cuts. I drop the phone on the ground and crack it with a single stomp of my heel.

"Tomorrow I'll buy you a new phone. As soon as I can find one without a camera."

Stu floats off in a cloud of shock. "You think that was a good idea?" Dad asks. I pick up Aphrodite's severed head, which has survived relatively intact except for her nose. It lies a foot from Luther.

"I can't leave her like this. She meant so much to Storm. We won't be able to patch her up even; there are too many pieces. She was more fragile than I thought."

Dad offers to pay for a new statue, but I tell him there's no point. "I couldn't have made a go of Macon Place, anyway," I admit. "I wasn't doing it for the right reasons. I honestly did think this place would make a great arts center, but what I really wanted was to freeze a moment of time so I didn't have to let a part of Chloe and me go. Teaching wasn't such a bad life. I suppose I can go back to it. If they'll hire somebody who's been arrested for assault."

"Misdemeanor assault," Dad corrects me.

A soft drizzle breaks. The crowd begins to disperse. The exhibitors pack up their arts and crafts as kids make a beeline for the exit. Deb, Dad, and I help Luther to the front porch of Storm's house. Campbell and Chloe return

Kirk Curnutt

with disinfectant and bandages. I let them tend to Luther and stipple my own chest with band-aids. When I finish I tell everyone to head home. I'm going to stay and clean up the garden. I need to collect Aphrodite's alabaster remains, maybe have a funeral.

"I'll go with you," Chloe decides, hopping up. "I've got to talk to Stu."

As we circle around Macon Place, I tell my daughter how impressed I am with all of today's surprises. Selling two thousand tickets, hiring Ricky Koester's crew to livestream the battle of the bands, but mainly landing that cameo from Oksana Dybek.

"How did you manage that?" I ask. "At this point, I wouldn't be surprised if you were one of those mercenary Furies in Herzoslovakia who broke Lifting Belly out of prison."

Chloe shrugs, modestly. "It wasn't that hard. I have Liz Phair's email, remember. When I saw how active she was online demanding that Bronislavis Stylptitch release Oksana and the band, I asked Liz if she could put me in touch with their manager. I sent a link to the website I made for Lifting Belly. The band liked it and the THIS IS WHAT A FEMINIST LOOKS LIKE stickers and T-shirts I printed up. I asked Oksana if she would Skype into the concert, and she said yes. The whole plan came together without a hitch—at least until Aphrodite got broken."

I'd like to thank her for her syntax. She's kind not to say, "Until *you* broke the Aphrodite statue, Daddy." As we walk along I slip two fingers into my back pocket. Behind my wallet is the download from r/Gone Wild. I've been toting the derriere picture all day, knowing this is a conversation that Chloe and I must have. The thought of pulling the image out now burns worse than my scraped chest, though. I let Chloe go backstage where Stu is still packing up Luther's equipment. I stay out front and begin piling pieces of Aphrodite into the cargo box of my Gator. I'm not sure there's any point to salvaging them. I hold a severed chunk of pelvis in my hands, thumbing the spot on the tailbone where, according to legend, a young man left a mark that so saddened him he committed suicide.

"Have you seen Mike? All he's done all day is tell me to go home, and now when I want to, I can't find him anywhere. I've got his keys."

It's Terri Willoughby, wife of the man suing me and mother to two-thirds of the Gold Dust Twinz. Her forehead is glazed with sweat and she's wobbly as she stands with her legs akimbo patting her protruding stomach. I think Mike had a point when he said a woman in her final trimester doesn't need to be wandering around in one-hundred degree heat and humidity. I tell Terri the last I saw of Mike he was diving out of the way of Aphrodite shards like the rest of our audience. As I speak I'm distracted by the sight of Chloe leading Stu by the hand up to the house. Terri doesn't notice my wandering eyes. She's too busy cussing out her husband. I offer to ride her up to the house in the Gator, but she decides to aim her cussing at me.

"You should never have let Chloe sing that horrible song," Terri tells me. "I can't imagine any parent being proud of a daughter dropping F-bombs in public, much less screaming them into a live microphone. That went out onto the Internet, too! You have to lay down a firm line, Vance. Your problem is that you're more worried about her liking you than respecting your authority. I'm no fan of Stu's music, but I told Travis and Zak they could perform today as long as there was no profanity. Chloe is too sweet to use that sort of language. She's a girl. Somebody needs to teach her what it means to be a lady. It certainly won't be that horrible Iris woman or that tattooed Sadie creature. I'm so relieved Chloe's mother has moved to town."

I tune out after about the fourth word, too preoccupied by that handholding between Chloe and Stu. I don't like the look of it. I excuse myself to follow my daughter and her boyfriend, telling Terri that I'm happy to take Mike's keys so she can head home in her own car. By the time I jog to Storm's house, the kids are nowhere in sight. I follow the footpath all the way to the driveway, where I stumble upon a couple locked in an embrace. Only it's not Chloe and Stu. It's Luther and Deb. I gape for twenty seconds before they notice me.

"This is the younger woman you asked my advice about?" I ask Luther. "I thought you had the hots for Marci Laughlin. This is my ex-wife!"

Luther looks pained, though I'm not sure it's because of me. A bandage the size of a wallet is taped to his crown, and dried blood is matted in his white hair. "And you!" I say to Deb. "This is who you've been meeting for coffee? I've slept with his daughter!" I throw up my hands and stumble off, but Deb doesn't let me get too far. She catches me in the shade of the house. She tells me she's worried Luther has a concussion. She thinks she ought to take him to the emergency room.

"We're just friends," Deb explains. "That's all you need to know. He's a sincere man, and I'm almost forty. It's nice for a woman to have a man who can be a friend."

I ask if Chloe knows.

"She's been pushing Luther on me since I got to Willoughby. Chloe wants me to be happy. She wants you to be happy, too."

I don't know what to say. Deb does. She's not finished.

"Campbell and Sadie told me about the condom wrapper. I should've heard that from *you*, Vance, not from them. I can't believe Chloe didn't tell me herself she's had sex. You were right. She's going to hide things from me. It's devastating. Tomorrow we're sitting her down and getting her on birth control. She's younger than we were, for God's sake."

"Tomorrow may be too late."

I don't know why I say this. Something about the confident way I saw Chloe lead Stu from the amphitheater. *Lose the gum, champ* is all I can think. I leave Deb to run a circle around the house. Nothing. I scamper up the steps and through the front door. The parlor, the kitchen, the ballroom–they're all deserted. I scramble upstairs and throw open bedroom doors. Again, nothing. At least not until I reach Storm's old bedroom, the very room he died in. The one Ardita Farnam wanted to tryst in, for that matter. The knob won't budge. I press my ear to the door and hear rustling sheets, low moans of pleasure. Surely not. I fumble for my keys, only to realize there's no keyhole. The lock is on the inside. *Lose the gum, champ*. Frantic, I ram my shoulder against the heavy wooden door. In the second it takes for the latch to break, I realize again I'm reliving that brutal karma of fatherhood. I've been reincarnated as Mr. Farnam as he flicked on the light in his Alabama room. As the door swings open and I stumble inside, I'm confronted by the same thing he was: two blurred, tangled shapes that refuse to come into focus for the simple reason I can't believe what I'm seeing—a dab of black hair, the arch of a back, jutting hips, the sideways smile of buttocks, a pair of hairy male legs poking from under the squish of feminine flesh. A woman's face robbed of privacy, hardening into embarrassment.

"Chloe?" I gulp. As a squeal splits the air.

"Get out of here!" Mike Willoughby screams. He leaps up so fast that Iris falls backwards off his lap onto the floor. I can't budge. Mike's exposed penis bobs accusingly at me. Is that a challenge to some sort of duel? Only Mike is reaching for something. It's not a pillow or his pants; it's a golf cleat. He pegs me with it, square between the eyes.

I spill backwards into the hall and stumble downstairs, not stopping until I'm outside and on the porch. I stoop in pain when I touch the tender triangle between my brows—first teeth, then cuts, now bruises. I won't live to see forty. As I stand up, I'm confronted by a sight only slightly less bewildering than Mike and Iris. Stu sits on the bottom step, eyes rimmed with tears.

"You got what you wanted," he sniffs upon seeing me.

"You think I *wanted* to catch your mom screwing the guy who's bankrupting me?"

Thankfully, Stu doesn't give me the time to ask this.

"Chloe dumped me!" he yells without pause. "And you

don't have to look so happy, Dr. Sea-G. It hurts, you know. It fucking hurts bad."

I sit down next to Stu, looking over my shoulder every few words, wondering how to whisk him away from Mike and Iris and spare his innocence.

"I–I owe you an apology, Stu. Blaming you for that night in the garden wasn't fair. I should've checked things out before accusing you of disrespecting Chloe. I know it's not easy right now, but give it a few weeks, and you'll see breaking up is the best thing for you and Chloe both. Seriously. Being platonic friends with a woman is great. That's all I've wanted all along for you and Chloe. To be friends. You will, too. You'll be just like me and Campbell. You'll be best friends."

My clichés aren't what Stu wants to hear. He plasters his palms to his face and sobs. I don't know what else to do but throw an arm around his shoulder and let him cry into mine.

"I want her to understand how I feel! That's why I was painting her. She wouldn't break up with me if she saw how I pictured her! I love her, Dr. Sea-G. I really love Chloe!"

I don't answer. I just hold him, silently, until Mike races onto the porch, his face flushed with a look that says, "You told him?" I press my finger to my lips to shush him. Mike groans and paces nervously until Iris appears. When she sees Stu crying, she races down the steps and pulls him out of my arms. "Oh my God, no!" she yells. "It's not true. Whatever he told you it's not true, baby!" I attempt a getaway, but Mike cuts me off before I can reach my Scion farther down the drive.

"You've got to understand," he gasps. "It's not serious. It never was. That's why we were ending it. We'd both agreed that this was the absolute last time."

"Don't talk to me. I don't want to hear it. I don't want to know."

Mike grabs my arm. "You can't tell Terri. Please, this would kill her. I know you and I've had our problems, but she's innocent in all this. You can hate me, but surely you don't hate her."

I'm incredulous. "You think I would tell your wife about this? To get you back?"

"No, of course you wouldn't. You're a good guy, Seahorse. You wouldn't intentionally hurt anybody. Everybody in town knows that. Mistakes happen, right? That's what this was, for Iris and me both. We got carried away. You know how it happens–you've been there. You knew it was wrong, too, but you still did it. Listen, listen: That $75,000? I wasn't serious. You deserve market value for your half of Macon Place. Christ, you took care of my dad and his garden for years!"

"So now you want to buy my silence?"

"Don't call it that. I'm just trying to give you what you deserve. And you'd be giving me a chance to make it up to Terri without hurting her. Come on. Don't do it for me–do it for my wife. Do it for Stu, for Christ's sake. You of all people know how this could hurt a kid. Nobody needs that."

I scoff. "The crazy thing is that I thought you genuinely cared about Stu! I took you seriously when you said he needed a father figure. He does–and instead he got you! You don't care about his music or painting. You let him have the parlor and play the battle of the bands to nail his mom, that's all. And you know what else? Even if Terri never finds out, it won't be the same between you two. You'll be living a lie from here on. And not just you, but her, Zak and Travis, and a baby that hasn't even been born yet!"

"I–I've been a shit, a selfish shit, I know. What excuse do I have? I hate myself. I don't want to anymore. I want to be different, really. Maybe this needed to happen for me to know how badly I need to change. I–I'll go see a counselor. How's that? I'll go see that same one you did. You're always saying you learned from your mistake. Why can't I? I'll figure out why this happened and make sure it never happens again. Let me make things up to you–to you and Chloe–and that can be my first step. The first step on my road to recovery."

I'd like to tell Mike that the road to recovery doesn't let you walk off your mistakes; it just reminds you of the regrets you have to shoulder. I can't figure out what I can say to him without sounding morally superior, however, and that's not a claim I can make with a straight face. I want badly just to walk away, to never look back on Macon Place or my years of working for Storm Willoughby, but something keeps me from doing that: Chloe. And I'm still broke. My Visa is still maxed out. I haven't even paid off my four-dollar breakfast bill at Chub and Joe's yet. I have no job, no prospects even, just responsibilities, and supporting my daughter is my first one. What other choice do I have? I'm as stuck as when Mike pulled out that specimen cup.

"Just give Macon Place a chance, a fair chance," I say.

Kirk Curnutt

"You saw today what's possible. There is an audience for the garden and the amphitheater. The community wants it. But you're right, we need to do this professionally. I'll commission a feasibility study and put together a Board of Advisors. Then we'll work on fundraising. I'm not asking for my old salary, either. Just to show you I don't intend to live off the Willoughby tit forever, I'll go back to teaching until I can make the garden viable–*if* I can."

Mike bobs his head, eager to strike any terms I name. I'm not satisfied, though. I still feel dirty. I grope for something to raise me above the swamp of complicity, something that'll let me believe I'm capable of better.

"There's something else I need."

"Anything," Mike greedily concedes. "You name it. Anything you want."

"I said 'need,' not 'want.' There's a difference."

"You're right–you're absolutely right. What do you need?"

"If we do fail, if we end up selling Macon Place because we can't make the grounds self-supporting, I need Storm's statues. Every last one. I need them in ways you will never understand, Mike."

# 31

Funny how you can wake up rich with everything you could want and still feel pretty poor. Three Sundays into summer, three weeks and a day after finding a condom wrapper in my daughter's bedroom, I watch yet another rainstorm beat a drumroll on my blue roof. The eaves choke on runoff; the yard bubbles with pummeled grass and mud. Many more showers like this and Willoughby, Alabama, will wash away.

I rise at dawn and fill the pot of my Krups coffeemaker and down two quick cups—no milk, no sugar, just the burn needed to work up the courage to tiptoe to Chloe's room. All I wanted after my encounter with Mike was to talk with her—not about Stu or Reddit.com's Gone Wild folder or condoms, but about music and bands, the fun stuff that used to fill our days. She and Deb were MIA the whole evening, however. By the time they returned from Luther's, it was nearly midnight, and I could tell Chloe was tired. Now, standing over her bed, I find my daughter sleeping hard as she spoons with her mother, the two of them connected by the umbilical cord of a shared pair of earphones. It's a stab to the heart to realize I'm but one of many demands on her time now. I wonder if she'll feel pressured to prioritize those obligations, and what number I'll end up among them relative to Deb. I'm going to have to compete for time with my ex-wife, I know. Hoping I can do it selflessly and with some grace, I tickle Chloe's big toe until she wakes.

"Come with me. And bring Liz Phair."

Out in the hall I discover the earphones belong to a

Kirk Curnutt

new iPhone. I ask if it was a gift from her grandpa.

"No, Mom gave it to me. You aren't mad, are you?"

"Please don't ask me that anymore. I don't want to feel like you think I'm angry all the time. I'm a cool dad. As long as you can stream music on that thing, I'm fine with it."

We go to the porch. As I open the screen door, I knock over a bulky object propped against the sill.

"It's Stu's painting," Chloe realizes, glumly picking up the 30" x 22" burlap-wrapped canvas. "He must've called me a million times last night about it. He said I need to see how he'd pictured me before I can tell him that we're over for good."

I ask Chloe how she knows the breakup is for good. She shrugs.

"It was what you said the other day. If I have to list reasons to stay with him, well, that's too much work. I guess when it's right I won't doubt it. Isn't that how it works?"

I lie and say yes. There's never a doubt when it's real love. Why disillusion Chloe? She's only sixteen. The twine on the canvas is knotted too tightly to untie, so she has to run inside for scissors. As she snips the string and tears away at the burlap, I close my eyes, not eager to see my daughter turned into an *objet d'art*. My resolve doesn't last long. Chloe lets out a gasp that makes me gape. The reality is more shocking than I'd imagined. The painting is an exact copy of William-Adolphe Bouguereau's *The Birth of Venus*, the work that Chloe described during the test tour of the garden that ended with Lleyton face down in the dirt. Unlike the more famous depictions of the goddess of love by Praxiteles and Botticelli, Bouguereau's is one of the rare images of Aphrodite that doesn't employ the *pudica gesture*. The painting is good, too. I mean, really, really good. Stu could be a forger, except for one detail.

"She has your face," I point out, tapping at Aphrodite's chin.

Make that two details. Chloe gestures to one of the two male figures in the tableau. Both are actually centaurs, not men. One has a thick beard, while the other is clean-shaven and blowing into a conch.

"This guy has your face," Chloe says, tracing the features of the former.

She leans the painting against the porch wall. I can tell she's irritated. She'll have to decide whether to give it back or, if she keeps it out of kindness, what obscure closet to chuck it in.

"So no regrets?" I ask. "No mistakes you wish you'd avoided?"

Chloe tucks a strand of bob behind her ear and makes an indifferent face. "I told you I broke up with him, Daddy. That's all you need to know."

I smile. We're back to "Daddy" finally. Why ruin a good thing? I sit Chloe in my rocker and ask her to play me her favorite Liz Phair. She and her mother fell asleep sharing her playlist. The least she can do is share it with me, too. Chloe rolls her eyes at the request. I settle into the other rocker and slip in an earpiece. Reluctantly, Chloe pushes play, and my Sunday silence shatters under a barrage of distorted guitars and cracking drums. This is post-*Exile in Guyville* Liz Phair; poppier, not as heavy as "Fuck and Run." Some fans like it, some fans don't. I fall into the first category, I decide. However loud, the music is soothing.

Kirk Curnutt

When the first song ends I ask Chloe why it's her favorite. She says something about it sounding "summery" and leaves it at that. I have her play me another track, and then a third. I make her explain what the lyrics mean, and then I give her my interpretation. With each question and answer she's a little less grudging. The song I like best is one called "Friend of Mine." It's a ballad about–what else?–how men aren't the greatest caretakers of emotion. The lyrics are less angry than sad, a lament for lost friendship between the sexes. I tell Chloe how much I like the sense of soldiering on in Liz's voice. "I can empathize," I assure her before admitting that both Stu and I are probably guilty of the same sins as the man the song addresses. I suppose it's my way of inviting Chloe to ask whether Sadie and I will patch things up, or whether we're over for good like her and her boyfriend.

"There's another version of this song you should hear," Chloe says, thumbing her keypad. "A cover. It's only a couple of years old. You'll love it because it's by Juliana Hatfield."

Juliana's version isn't all that different from Liz's original, but there's something deeply comforting about hearing the voice of a woman whose music I love singing a song by another female songwriter I adore.

"Have I ever told you about the summer *Exile in Guyville* came out?" I ask Chloe. "I listened to it and Juliana Hatfield's *Hey Babe* nonstop. If Liz was my id, Juliana was my superego."

"You've told me that plenty, Daddy. I still don't know what it means."

I close my eyes and grip my armrest, lost in the

emotion of "Friend of Mine."

"It means the right side of my brain is talking to the left side. It means the song makes me feel whole."

"That's good." She gives me a tolerant smile. "Can I go back to bed now?"

"In a little bit. First we need to talk." I pull out the earbuds and power down her iPhone. "We're going to talk later with your mom, too, but right now this one's between you and me. She doesn't have to know about it. We need this conversation, for each other as much as for ourselves."

I reach into my robe pocket and hand her a folded sheet of paper. Chloe opens it, surprised to discover a laser-jet print of a pair of buttocks, only two-thirds of which are covered by lacy boyshorts. I ask Chloe to explain the picture to me. Her eyebrows arc.

"I think it's pretty self-explanatory."

I tell her to look in the background, pointing out that the picture was taken in our house. In her bedroom. I point to the Liz Phair poster in the background and the Polaroid of my face under it. Chloe asks where the picture came from. I tell her not to play dumb.

"I know all about Gone Wild on Reddit.com," I say.

Her eyes leap from the image to me and then back. "You think *I* would put this in a web folder called *that?* You think this is *me?*" She rattles the paper at me. "My butt doesn't look like this! Mine's not this bi—"

Her confusion hardens. She jumps to her feet and disappears inside, returning a moment later in a pair of sweats, my keys poking from her fist. I ask where she's going as she rushes into the rain. I tell her we're not done talking, but apparently we are. Chloe leaps in my Scion and roars off.

For a good hour I try to calm myself by repeating the Liz Phair playlist. Eyes closed, I listen to "Friend of Mine" alone three times straight, twice by Liz and once by Juliana. I could probably fall asleep if I weren't aware that my toes are wet. I assume it's the rain splashing through the balusters, but when I open my eyes, I discover that the storm hasn't blown onto the porch. Instead, it's a dog—an albino Chihuahua—and he's licking my feet.

"Whatever you do, don't pet him." Campbell stands on my top step, a leash wrapped around her wrist, water cascading off the back of her umbrella. "Edgar's a snapper. Chihuahuas are touchy little bastards."

I turn the music off, almost afraid to move. "You'll be proud of me. I just started The Talk with Chloe. We haven't finished, but it was a start."

Campbell doesn't seem to hear me. She's too busy looking at the Volkswagen in my driveway.

"What's Sadie's car doing here? You two aren't back together, are you?"

Not hardly. I tell Campbell that Sadie dropped by last night so we could talk.

"We talked like we've never talked," I admit. "It was really nice. Nothing serious—mostly about her songs, where art and beauty and creativity come from. That kind of stuff. I've learned a lot from Sadie. I don't have much to offer in return, though. I wasn't the best boyfriend she's ever had."

"You can't be too terrible if she stayed the night."

"We drank too much wine, that's all. Sadie didn't want to drive, so I let her have my bed, and I crashed on the couch. Not that I wasn't hoping she would ask me to stay with her, but she didn't. I don't think Sadie trusts me."

"I wouldn't trust you either," Campbell says in a way that makes me chuckle. I suppose that's why it's good for men to have a woman for a best friend. Somebody needs to call us on our bullshit. Without warning Campbell changes the subject, asking what I did to Iris at Macon Place yesterday.

"She must've called me five times last night saying she needed to speak with you. You wouldn't answer your phone. If there was ever a call that was in your interest to take, Vance, that one was it. I couldn't believe it when she told me Stu was going to drop the complaint against you. You must've dug up some real dirt on her."

For a second I consider telling Campbell about stumbling in on Mike and Iris. It would almost be a relief to set the story circulating and let somebody who's a more deserving dickhead be known for committing the Most Infamous Act of Fornication in Elmore County, Alabama. But I can't do it. I think about how embarrassed Chloe is knowing about Ardita Farnam, and I remember Stu crying on my shoulder. Why make a kid hurt more?

"I discovered she smokes weed." I smile at Campbell. "I told Iris if she didn't drop the charge, I'd tell Mike. She knows he'd never hire her to clean his house again, and she needs the money. I had her over a barrel. Not very noble of me, I admit, but hey—survival of the fittest."

"How did you find out she's into weed?"

I smile even more broadly. "I smoked it with her."

Campbell's brows scrunch under her bangs. "You're fibbing to me! I can tell because your eyes twitch when you're being evasive. Why would you want me to believe you're into pot? Are you still trying to be cool? Oh, well. If it's any consolation, there's at least one other fib you don't have to worry about making you twitchy. I told Steve the truth about us. The whole truth. You don't have to worry about testifying if we go to court."

"Really? You told him you're gay for good?"

"You sound like my dad. No, I didn't say that. Even after all that's happened, I don't feel that I need to define myself. There's only one category I'm willing to put myself into. I'm a good mother to my son."

I assure Campbell that she is indeed. Then I mention another good mother I'm fortunate to know.

"Deb needs to hear that from me, too. I know that now. She and Chloe both.... Hey, speaking of Deb, do you know about her and your dad? Looks like they're headed for a hookup. She claims it's just a friendship, but we both know how that works."

Campbell smiles as she gives Edgar a yank. He keeps trying to lick the balusters, but she pulls him toward my feet. "They haven't said anything outright, but I've had my suspicions. I hope they do get together. They deserve it. They've had as rough a haul as anybody."

"Sure, but you know what this means for us, don't you? Their ending up together is the end of you and me. We can never get back together now. You'll be Chloe's stepsister. I could never sleep with my daughter's stepsister!"

Campbell laughs, but it looks like a grimace. "You still

have a lot to learn, Vance. I do, too, I suppose. Just don't let your mouth outgrow your ears. You've got the best set of ears I've ever poured my secrets into, male or female."

She tugs Edgar back to the sidewalk and heads home. I listen to the rain again for a while. As my eyes settle on Sadie's car, I start to feel melancholy and lonely. I go inside, but before I can hike the stairs to my bedroom, I catch a prowler in my living room. It's my dad. He stands at the shelf of my mother's leather-bound books, sliding one out from the row of embossed spines.

"You never told me that you snuck the box these were stored in from the attic," he says, clearly embarrassed that I walked in on him.

"Those books have been sitting right there for a decade, Dad. You could have recognized the titles at any time."

He agrees with a nod, telling me that Chloe was the one who finally let him know the collection was Mom's. All this time Dad assumed they were my books from graduate school. As he talks I notice something funny. As long as I've displayed the books, I've kept them in alphabetical order by author. I know the list so well I can recite the fifteen names and titles without effort. Only as I eyeball the spines I realize there are sixteen of them.

"You're not pulling one off the shelf. You're adding one, aren't you?"

Miles Seagrove smiles bashfully and passes me the volume. It's Mary Renault's *The Praise Singer*. I've never heard of it.

"I was going to sneak it in and see how long it took *you* to notice it here," Dad admits. "The title itself isn't important. This just happens to be one book your mother and I read together. We did that sometimes, although not as often as I would've liked. I always seemed to have too much going on at work to concentrate on novels. Look inside. You'll see why this one was special."

I flip through the pages. Several are underlined and annotated in different colored inks, sometimes with little notes and comments, but more often with abbreviations and question marks.

"Your mother was telling me what was important, what to look out for. She liked to write down questions that she wanted us to answer together. I didn't do it as often as she did; I wasn't as careful of a reader. But we did talk about things she underlined and highlighted. After she passed, I fished this one out of the box when Janice made me haul your mom's books to the attic. I've kept *The Praise Singer* in a drawer in my nightstand for thirty years. I just enjoyed having it handy when I wanted to remember your mother. When Chloe told me you had her other books bound, I decided I would get this one done in the same color and style for your collection. I've had the book long enough. You should have a chance to enjoy it. Maybe you'll learn something about your mother and me reading the notes we wrote back and forth."

I sit on the armrest of my couch, overwhelmed as I thumb again through the pages, slower this time so I can drink in my mother's handwriting. Dad laughs when I ask how he became so good at setting me up to discover what a jackass my resentments make of me. I almost start to cry thinking of this book sitting in his nightstand for thirty years. Finally, Dad takes Mary Renault from my hands and shelves her, telling me that I have the rest of my life to explore the annotations. Right now he plans to run to the grocery and buy eggs, sausage, and biscuits and gravy for breakfast. "I want to cook for everybody," he says with gusto, instructing me to invite Luther and Campbell over. He's so excited I expect him to ask me to call Mike Willoughby, too. Dad peeks out the window at the Volkswagen behind the battered hull of my Saturn.

"I hope Sadie will stay, too," he says, practically glowing with hope.

I promise to talk her into it. As Dad heads off to get dressed, I make my way to my bedroom upstairs, where I slide onto the mattress behind Sadie, dousing her shoulders in kisses.

"Be a good boy," she drowsily warns me.

"Let's get married. I want to–tomorrow. I don't want to lose you. For real. There's nothing we couldn't work out if we tried. I could help you with your music. I'll be your manager. Chloe can run your fan club."

Sadie asks if I've been smoking her weed again. I'm in too serious of a mood to laugh.

"I need something permanent in my life. I thought Chloe was that something, but she's sixteen, and soon enough she'll have her own road to go. I–I know the things I've done wrong, but I can learn. I can change. All you have to do is tell me what you need, and I'll give it to you. Please."

The longer Sadie waits to answer, the heavier my chest feels.

"I'm twenty-three," she eventually says. "I don't need a man. Having one is nice, yes, but it can also get in the way. I don't want to spend my time training you how to treat me. There are too many creative things I could be doing, and, honestly, they're more rewarding. I don't mean that harshly. I care about you and Chloe, but if we got back together I'd be doing exactly what you dreaded she'd do with Stu. I'd only be staying with you for fear of being alone. You wouldn't want Chloe to be with a man because he needs her help. You shouldn't want that of me, either."

I push back against the mattress, the silence excruciating. When I can't take it I wrap my arms around Sadie, and we lie together, even though it's painfully clear we're not together.

"Maybe you could tattoo my name somewhere. It doesn't have to be anywhere visible. I'll take a heel, a vertebrae, even a buttock—just something to let me believe I'm not a regret."

She laughs, softly. "You got a song out of me, remember? 'That Careful Man with Complicated Veins.' That's what I have to give, but you've never listened to it, not all the way through."

I tell her I thought she wrote that one for her own dad. Luther still thinks she wrote it about him.

"I wrote it for you all," she says. "You're all fathers. I never told you the inspiration for that song, did I? It came from a conversation with Chloe. She was talking about how she didn't feel like you two could talk anymore. She couldn't explain why; all she could say was, 'I'm too complicated for him, and he's too careful.' You know what she was talking about, right? She's too complicated because she's got this thing now—her sexuality—and you're too careful because you don't trust your own."

I wince, haunted, as always, by the specter of Ardita Farnam. I ask Sadie if she has a copy of her song handy. She points to her purse. I hop up and find her iPod. We share the earphones, but even with only one ear I recognize Sadie is right. She's got too much to offer to settle for me. The song is soft, plaintive, but most of all intimate. Indeed. There's a deeper intimacy between Sadie's voice and the gentle melody than any words of mine could manage. There's only one discordant note, two-thirds of the way through. It's a single squeal.

"What was that?"

Sadie points to the window. "It sounded like a tire squeal. From outside."

I hop up and rush to the window, where I see my Scion parked crookedly behind Sadie's Volkswagen. The driver's door is open, and Chloe is stooped in the grass, sopping wet. The red ink on her shirt that spells HELLHOLE KITTY runs to her stomach, resembling a gunshot. As she rushes to the porch, I realize those are tears, not raindrops, splattering her cheeks.

"Where are you going?" Sadie calls out, but I don't answer. I rush downstairs and hit the porch to find Chloe kicking holes in Stu's Aphrodite painting. The frame comes apart, and she rips away a long swatch of canvas, hurling it into the yard. Then she runs past me without a word, though the look of death in her eye is telling enough. The screen door slams at my back before I can ask what's wrong. A whole minute passes before I think to follow her to her bedroom.

She's stretched out on her floor, her head pillowed in

an unfolded mound of laundry. Deb is tumbling from the bed to reach her. "Baby, what's the matter?" Chloe doesn't answer, so I stretch out next to her. She buries her face in my shoulder. Her sobs jolt my body like electrical surges. "You're soaked," Deb says. "Why? What happened? Come on, tell us. You can tell us anything."

Chloe's head lifts a little, but her voice is so soft neither Deb nor I understand. We have to ask her to repeat what she's said. The second time we get it, loud and clear.

"He cheated."

"What are you talking about?"

"Dad," she yells, exasperated. Her face is a red mess. "Stu cheated on me."

"What? He couldn't have–yesterday he was crying all over me over you."

Deb is more logical. "Maybe there's been a mistake. Sometimes you can misinterpret things, especially when emotion's involv–"

"How do you misinterpret that news when you're told it point blank?"

"Stu admitted he cheated?" I ask.

"No, he never would have. It was Nina. She told me. That picture you showed me is of her! He took it, right after they did it. Posting it to that website was his joke on me. Nina wanted him to take it down."

"What picture is she talking about?" Deb demands. "What website?"

Chloe doesn't answer the question.

"Nina said what happened has been bothering her so much she'd decided to confess it to me," she says instead, shivering. "But she didn't, of course, not until I confronted her. She kept saying she's sorry, as if that made it okay. I mean, in one breath she tells me she did my boyfriend and in the very next she wants me to forgive her. What is that all about?"

"When—when did this happen?" I ask.

"At my birthday party, here in *my* room. In my room! I never thought—I mean, I don't even remember them being out of sight together. I was in the living room the whole time." Chloe explodes in a new fit of tears. "She said she's been waiting three weeks for me to confront her. She thought for sure I knew. He left the condom wrapper in my trash. He wanted her to come over and get it when I wasn't looking."

I feel nailed to the floor.

"I made Nina take me to his house," continues Chloe. "I had to hear the truth from him. I scared Ms. Iris banging on their door. And you want to know what he says—his explanation? *It just happened.* That's all he can say. How does doing somebody *just happen?*"

I hold my breath, Deb and I staring at each other.

"It's so not true. It *didn't* just happen. It happened because she would and I wouldn't. That's all he ever talks about—sex. It's all he ever thinks about. I told him no all the time. He knew what he was doing. It was his revenge. He was getting me back because I wouldn't—"

"It's okay," Deb says again, stroking her hair. "It'll be okay."

I lie still, pinned to the ground by Chloe and Deb's weight. I try to rock Chloe to calm her, but she's not a baby anymore, and a sway's no longer enough to soothe. I feel her wet clothes soak through my own. The bleeding

Kirk Curnutt

ink on her T-shirt stains my chest. Her breath grows hot on my neck, and I feel her tears pool at my throat. Why doesn't Deb say something? We need to be encouraging, but our clichés fail us. We need to tell our daughter she'll feel better with time, that she won't ever hurt worse than what she does now. We must assure her with a straight face that the pain is only overwhelming because it's so new to her, and that it's only new because it's a part of growing up that will fade away as she matures and her life settles and steadies. I want her to know that there's no betrayal in adulthood, that in the mature world things don't *just* happen and nobody makes excuses for their actions, that we don't treat each other callously. These are the things parents are obliged to tell their children, but they're stones in my throat. Chloe could take one look at the grownups around her–at Steve and Mike and Iris, but most of all at me–and know how untrue those words are.

As we lie here, Deb wiping Chloe's tears with her thumbs, I recall the story about the Aphrodite statue that Storm Willoughby told me my first day at Macon Place. Why he was so infatuated with her? Maybe it was because Aphrodite is known by many nicknames that personified qualities Storm and I coveted. As Chloe has taught me, she is *Ambologera*, the Postponer of Old Age, *Peitho* or Persuasion, *Epistrophia*, the Heart-Twister, even *Charidotes*, the Joy-Giver. Or maybe Storm decided I should learn her myths and legends because Chloe was with us, and he was reminded of how Aphrodite had been born from the divine foam of her father's genitals, which his son had severed at the request of his mother, who was tired of her husband's infidelities. My best guess is that

Storm's reasons were academic. The Aphrodite of Knidos is the most influential female form in Western art, after all, and it's because of the *pudica gesture*, the hand that draws your eye to the spot it covers as certainly as it shields it. As Storm always claimed, sculptors and painters have tried to decide the meaning of that stance by copying the expression Praxiteles gave her face. Eyes staring straight ahead, lips vaguely parted, Aphrodite is neither modest nor embarrassed. She looks confident, self-assured, a little haughty even.

"What no one can figure out," Storm told me that day, "is whether this is the natural look of a woman when she's by herself, out of men's eyes, or whether it's what a man imagines her to look like. It's a hard question to answer. Maybe it's easier to talk about the difference between the naked and nude. The first implies a state of innocence and naïveté, but the second carries with it the shock of the erotic. It makes us aware of our sexuality and all its mix of emotions, from desire, to shame and pleasure, to regret. You don't believe there's a difference? Then you should hear what happened at the temple where Aphrodite was worshipped."

Then he told the story.

"The Roman writer Lucian traveled with two friends to Knidos to view the statue. A lot of Romans did that at the time—that's how alluring Aphrodite was. She was a tourist attraction. Her beauty brought tears to their eyes and made them quiver with lust. One of Lucian's friends kissed her on the lips, which wasn't uncommon. Lucian himself was more reserved. He walked circles around Aphrodite, thinking through the riddle of her beauty. But then he noticed a spot on her tailbone. At first he thought it was a defect in the marble, which excited him. He liked the idea that there could be a flaw, even a small one, in such an impressive work of art. 'Fate tends to thwart that which would otherwise reach perfection,' he said with delight. But then the attending priestess intervened to explain that the spot wasn't a fault of the medium, but of the audience. This was a human mark, deposited there by a young man so infatuated with Aphrodite's image that he lost all sense and made love to the statue. He no sooner finished than he was despondent. He'd soiled her. Ashamed, he fled the temple and hurled himself off a cliff into the Gulf of Hisaronu."

I'm not sure why this memory now haunts me. I can't even say what it means, other than it reminds me that there's no love, no art that human fallibility can't stain.

Then, the longer my ex-wife and I hold our crying daughter, the more I'm aware of a strange sensation on the right side of my ribcage. It's not really a discomfort so much as a distraction. The more I focus on it, the heavier it begins to seem. I lift my back to leverage my chest against it, but the pressure's too great. My breath goes shallow as my lung cramps. When I finally figure out its source I wonder if it won't outright crush me until I'm nothing but the width of a dime.

It's the weight of Chloe's breasts, two fists raised in self-defense, threatening to snap my sternum.

## ACKNOWLEDGMENTS

Many thanks to the many friends who talked me off the ledge of abandoning this project over the years it took to reach this final stage. First and foremost, huge gratitude goes to the wonderful folks at River City Publishing, especially Dr. Al Newman and his wife, Mrs. Carolyn Newman, RCP's publisher, who kindly decided this story was worth the paper it would be printed on. Fran Missildine Norris embodies exactly the sort of gracious, inspiring editor/collaborator/sounding board that every writer should wish to work with. In so many ways I could never have dreamed up this book's plot without the essential friendship of April Hager Jones, RCP's invaluable publicist. She made the novel happen in more ways than one. Jack Durham did a fantastic job with the cover. He captured the novel so well I swear I see myself in Bouguereau's *The Birth of Venus*. Special thanks to Marlin Barton for guidance and advice and to Martha-Claire Jones for teaching me the correct way to open a Sweetwater 420. Dana Coester allowed me to adapt her poem, "That Careful Man with Complicated Veins," from a life long ago into Sadie's song lyrics. Kendal Weaver lent his Associated Press expertise to editing the Lifting Belly subplot into a reasonable facsimile of a wire story. And thanks to Sarah Kalsey who kindly helped proof. Rosemary James and the Pirates' Alley Faulkner Society do God's work with the William Faulkner/William Wisdom Creative Writing Awards. An earlier version of this book was a finalist for the Society's unpublished novel award.

Finally, to my family, who gave me the space to dream and the time to type: you rock.